FOR THE LOVE OF RUBY

She backed up, thinking that she shouldn't be here with him, shouldn't be having the desires she was having.

Will came toward her. And then he was kissing her, and she was kissing him. Heart pounding and blood shimmering. She kissed his mouth and his neck, tasted his salty skin and inhaled the heady scent of him, felt his warm, silky hair and his full, strong muscles. He kissed her eyes and her neck and as far down on her breasts as the neckline of her dress would allow, and she wished for so much more.

He drew back, and she lifted her head to look into his intense, stormy eyes. She wrapped her arms around herself and choked back tears.

"Oh, Will, I don't want to come between you and your daddy and Lonnie."

"I know."

He didn't know what else to say to that. He didn't want to hurt his father or brother either.

But he wanted Ruby Dee.

THE
LOVES
OF
RUBY
DEE

CURTISS ANN MATLOCK

AVON BOOKS  NEW YORK

THE LOVES OF RUBY DEE is an original publication of Avon Books. This work has never before appeared in book form. This work is a novel. Any similarity to actual persons or events is purely coincidental.

AVON BOOKS
A division of
The Hearst Corporation
1350 Avenue of the Americas
New York, New York 10019

Copyright © 1996 by Curtiss Ann Matlock
Inside cover author photo by Glamour Shots
Published by arrangement with the author
Library of Congress Catalog Card Number: 95-94728
ISBN: 0-380-78106-9

First Avon Books Printing: February 1996

AVON TRADEMARK REG. U.S. PAT. OFF. AND IN OTHER COUNTRIES, MARCA REGISTRADA, HECHO EN U.S.A.

Printed in the U.S.A.

RA 10 9 8 7 6 5 4 3 2 1

☙ AUTHOR'S NOTE

The stories I write spring from my strong beliefs: in the beauty and endurance of the land and of those who work the land, in horses and pickup trucks and classic cars, in hot southern women and hard men in boots and blue jeans, and in the hope that tomorrow is going to be a better day. I like to mix in a little mischief—maybe a lot of mischief—and add a touch of country blues, such as found in the songs of Mary Chapin Carpenter, Kathy Mattea, John Berry, Don Williams, and Patty Loveless (my favorite singers), to name a few.

If you like all those things, you might enjoy this book. If you don't enjoy this book, find one you can. A good book lets us escape our lives, and gives us heart to live them, too.

I wish to thank Phillip Butler and Machelle Courtney for their advice on ranching operations; any mistakes are totally mine. I thank Bob Hooker for always knowing people to help me with my research, and Mark Whitman for his expertise on horses, and for keeping me riding. Thanks to all at Computers Plus, who keep me going and have the patience of Job with me.

My sincere gratitude to my editor, Carrie Feron, for her faith in me, and to my agent, Ethan Ellenberg, not only for his faith, but for his easy laughter. Thank you, Johnny Quarles, for introducing me to Ethan.

To the booksellers who have recommended my books over the years, and to the many readers who have taken time to write that you've enjoyed my stories: thank you, thank you!

And to friends and dear hearts—Genell Dellin, Dixie Browning, Mary Williams, Robin Kaigh and Leslie Wainger—thanks for your support.

Curtiss Ann Matlock
Cogar, Oklahoma

THE
LOVES
OF
RUBY
DEE

1

THE AFTERNOON RUBY DEE came to them was one of those hot summer days peculiar to the high plains, when heat shimmers up off the land and blurs a man's vision, so that he might mistake what he sees at first glance. That he was mistaken was Will's first thought when he saw coming down the dirt road what looked like a convertible tugging along an aluminum camper, going as if hellbent to outrun the rooster tail of Oklahoma red dust billowing up behind.

Will thought he'd either had too much sun or that being bucked off the horse had addled his vision.

They were out in the blazing sun, at the training pen, working on the wild stud horse Will had caught over in New Mexico. Lonnie and the old man were giving instruction, but it was Will on the horse, taking his life in his hands. That was the way it always was: his brother and his dad throwing out opinions and Will doing all the real work.

The old man sat in his fraying green-and-white lawn chair, leaning forward on his cane and calling

1

gruffly through the rails. "Don't give him time to think, boy—kick him and hold on."

The old man had always figured, get on a horse and show him who was boss right off. Force was his way. He got aggravated to distraction every time he watched Will work with a horse. Will didn't know why the old man insisted on coming around and watching. His watching aggravated Will to distraction.

Lonnie sat humpbacked on the top rail. He had his straw Resistol pushed back a fraction, dark hair falling on his forehead, and a pinch of Skoal in his bottom lip. He watched the horse real sharp and couldn't resist humming low. Lonnie was one for slipping his opinions in unnoticed, and he especially didn't want to be noticed contradicting the old man, but he couldn't help adding his two cents' worth— in this case the humming meant to soothe the animal. Lonnie's way was to sweet-talk—animals or humans.

Will's way generally fell somewhere in the middle. He worked patiently and firmly, aiming to teach new behavior, not simply to overpower instincts. He'd been working with this horse—a stocky blue-black roan mustang with a lot of quarter blood—for two weeks. He'd had a saddle on him a number of times, but this was the first day he had been on the roan's back. This animal was totally different from some hand-raised colt, which was why Will was so fascinated with him. With this horse, Will had to keep his wits sharp.

"Okay, now, buddy, we got to take a step." Speaking in a low, rhythmic voice, he lifted the soft cotton reins and moved his legs to give the horse the feel. Then he clicked to him and pressed his legs into his belly, gently. He was pleased with how quiet the stud was, him being wild and all.

The roan took two nervous steps, and the next instant he reared, pawing air. Will leaned forward; the horse came down, ducked his head and went to sunfishing. Will was thrown in the dirt on about the third curve.

The first word he heard, when he could hear, was the old man saying that he ought to have learned how to stay on a horse by now. Lonnie was laughing fit to be tied.

Will hauled himself up off the ground. He supposed his first lesson was that the ground was a lot harder at forty-two than it had been at thirty-two. There was a ringing in his ears, and his right shoulder felt like it could rub his left. He looked around for his hat and felt pretty foolish. He could hardly believe he had been thrown. He hadn't been thrown from a horse in a long time—years.

The horse stood across the pen, watching him. Will paused to catch his breath. Sweat burned his eyes. The old man groused that he'd better get at it.

About that time, Lonnie said, "Wooeee . . . will you look at that?"

He was staring off toward the road, and his expression was enough to make Will climb up beside him, throw a leg over the rail and look, too. And that's when he saw what certainly was a strange apparition in their part of the country.

Will shifted his hat lower over his eyes and peered harder, but the sight didn't change. It was definitely a convertible flying across that dusty dirt road, and when it turned up their drive, he could see it wasn't anything new, but a classic '60s Ford Galaxie, pale yellow, gleaming in the sun. The Airstream camper behind it was at least as old but not in nearly such good shape. Though the door was tied shut, it flopped with every bounce of the trailer.

Lonnie let out a faint whistle. "You suppose that's the housekeeper you hired us, Will?"

Will said, "I ain't hired anyone yet."

He jumped to the ground. Lonnie came after him, and the old man struggled up from his chair.

The three of them stood there and watched the outfit come clanging up the drive like a passel of pans in the wind. When it came to a stop at the side of the house, the dust finally caught up and engulfed the car and trailer, obscuring them. When that dust cloud settled, the woman was out of the car and standing there, in a dress that flowed down over a willowy, womanly body and caught in the breeze near her ankles. The rockabilly tones of Elvis floated from the car, singing "Return to Sender."

Will felt like someone had hit him upside the head.

"Well, now." Lonnie gave a grin of real pleasure. "I believe I'll just go make the lady welcome."

He strode toward the woman, spitting out his Skoal and straightening his hat as he went.

Beside Will, the old man gave a snort. He leaned over, spit a brown stream of tobacco, then looked at Will with pale eyes cold and hard as January ice.

"I told you I don't want a woman in my house, and I sure as hell don't want no floozy in my house. You send her back to wherever you found her, boy."

Will was forty-two, but his daddy was still calling him boy. And saying it like Will was just another hired hand.

Will clenched the fist frozen at his side, while the old man turned and, leaning heavily on his cane, stepped away. His bad leg buckled, and Will reached out to grab his arm, but the old man jerked away and headed on his own steam up the graveled path toward his workshop. More than likely he had a bottle hidden in there, and if there was anything more Will did not need, it was to have the old man get soused and start in.

He looked back at the woman, the convertible and the trailer. She was leaning over into the car, stretching. Graceful moves, as if she flowed over the car. Will saw that she wore western boots, deep red ones. Elvis quit singing. The woman straightened and smiled at Lonnie, greeting him.

Will hadn't expected this at all. When he had spoken to her on the telephone, he had imagined someone a lot like Maggie Parsons, who had recommended the gal and set up the whole thing. Maggie Parsons was head nurse at the county health department, and was a solid hundred and sixty pounds of practical no-nonsense.

With a heavy sigh, he went to catch the blue roan and tie him where the rails gave a bit of shade. He peered through the rails, getting another look at the gal. He looked down at himself and tried to knock some more dust off.

As Will walked over to join them, Lonnie was making up to her as sweetly as a boy hoping for warm cookies, and she was smiling. Then she caught sight of Will. She watched him come.

He noticed her hat was well used, not one of those silly things only for show. Then he saw the flashy earrings fluttering and swaying from her ears, just like the hem of her dress, which the wind molded against the curves and indentations of her body. She was a smallish woman, not over five four, and slender. She had full, rounded breasts, though.

The surprise came all over Will again. And he thought: *We're needing rain, but we sure don't need a tornado.*

"This is my brother, Will," Lonnie said. "I guess you two spoke on the phone. Will, this is Miss Ruby Dee D'Angelo, in the flesh."

The gal stuck out her hand. The bunch of bracelets on her wrist jingled, and her bright rosy fingernails flashed. "It's nice to meet you in person, Mr. Starr."

Will managed to take her hand and shake it and say a polite hello. Her grip was firm, but her hand soft and smooth. She had a husky voice for a woman, as he had heard over the telephone, but in person it had a distinctive, sultry tone. Her smile was more like just a hint of one, but there was a warmth about her face. Her skin was like fine porcelain, and her eyes were dark. Dark as strong, steaming coffee.

For a long moment he gazed into those eyes, and by heaven, she looked back. He took note of her, and she took note of him.

Then Will looked away and shifted his stance to ease himself. She hadn't looked away. He could still feel her eyes on him, and he felt mighty disconcerted. He felt like something had been put over on him, though he wasn't certain what it was. He looked over at her car and trailer.

"There wasn't any need for you to go to all the trouble of bringing your stuff up here right off, Miss D'Angelo," he said.

"Oh, it wasn't any trouble," she said, a trace of amusement in her low, husky voice. "It's the easiest thing in the world to bring my trailer. I don't have to do any packin' then." She added in a practical tone, "It saves goin' back for it, and you did say you were needin' someone right away."

Will had said that, as best he could recall. The night he had spoken to her, he had been under the influence of another big fight with the old man, another cold ham sandwich and another six-pack of Red Dog.

The trailer had definitely seen better days. Along with the brown stains edging the windows, dents—looked like from hail—covered it. In contrast, the Ford convertible looked almost showroom-new. A Galaxie with sweeping lines, a sexy machine—as sexy as the gal, Will thought, his gaze lighting on her for a second before moving on to the dusty tires. There was nothing new about the tires. The front one was nearly bald.

There was a little dog, a black and white collie mutt, front feet up on the driver's door of the car, wagging its tail. Will recalled then that she had told him she had a dog. He had told her that would be fine. That had certainly been the Red Dog talking.

"I'm sorry I was late," she was saying. "I had a flat tire and I got lost a couple of times. Oh, the map you sent was perfectly clear. But you know, things don't always look in real life like they do on a map. I'm not very good with them, I'm afraid."

"They're skimpy on state signs when you get out this way, too," Lonnie put in. He always could make conversation.

"I'm sorry about your flat tire," Will said, feeling something was needed on his part.

"Oh, I did just fine. I keep Fix-a-Flat in the trunk. It works real well."

She put a hand on the car and leaned on it. Her rosy fingernails were stark against the pale yellow.

She had a way of moving that drew a man's eye. That drew his eye and made the rest of him want to follow right along.

Lonnie walked around the front of the car, admiring it. "I'll say this is some pretty cool machine you're drivin', gal."

Lonnie's calling her "gal" sent irritation crawling all over Will.

"Thank you," she said, pleased as punch. "I got it directly from the man who bought it new. It was garage-kept, and it has the original engine and only sixty-five thousand miles. I enjoy it, but I sure should have put the top up before comin' down y'all's road. The top's kinda broken, and it isn't too easy to get up. I have to get out and pound this thingamajig." She pointed to the thingamajig and fiddled with it.

Lonnie jumped right in, saying he would be glad to look at it for her. Will thought that looking at it was about all Lonnie would manage to do. Ask Lonnie for a screwdriver, and you had to describe it to him.

Will broke in. "Miss D'Angelo's had a long drive, Lonnie. I imagine she could do with a cold drink. We can go inside, out of the heat, and discuss things."

Her dark, coffee eyes swung around to him. She regarded him steadily. "Yes. That would be nice."

With Lonnie leading, they went inside through the back door. When he realized he was staring at the girl's swaying hips, Will averted his eyes downward. His gaze landed on the dog that went along at her heels.

In the kitchen she looked around, frankly curious. She went to the counter top and ran a hand over it.

Suddenly Will saw the kitchen as she saw it. A big, drab room, yellowing with age and neglect. The curtains were long gone, the walls and cabinets once white, and now dirty ivory from cooking grease and smoke, the gray linoleum wearing through in places. The only so-called wall decorations were the big, plain clock and the "Western Horseman" calendar. The green vinyl chair seats supplied the only color, and they were patched with silvery duct tape. The old man had spilled coffee grounds and left his coffee and spit cups on the table.

Will thought of her car and all the stuff piled in it, and he looked at her dress. Color, all of it, vibrant and warm.

"Will, do you wanta beer?" Lonnie was bending into the refrigerator.

"Dr. Pepper," Will said quickly. He cast a questioning eye at the gal. "We have some Mountain Dew, if you'd rather have it."

"I like Dr. Pepper just fine." Her face was solemn as a judge's, her brown eyes looking straight at his.

Will said, "Lonnie will get our drinks," and gestured toward the alcove on his right and stepped aside. "My office is through here." Lonnie was coming from the refrigerator, three cans in hand. "Put those Dr. Peppers in glasses, Lonnie. With ice," Will said, and turned to follow the girl through the small alcove and the open door. He pushed the door closed behind him.

The office had been made by enclosing the side porch some fifteen years ago, when the old man had dumped the management of the ranch into Will's lap. That was the same year the IRS had come after them because the old man's record system had consisted of scraps of paper, half of them torn from napkins, tucked into a small envelope. These days Will managed with the help of a computer. Lonnie served as his top hand, when he wasn't off playing the rodeos and the girls. But Hardy Starr still owned the Starr Ranch, and he never let anyone forget it. For their work, Will and Lonnie got a salary, just like the other hands.

The only thing that kept the office from being as drab as the kitchen was the books and magazines that crammed it. This was Will's domain. Sometimes the old man came in and wanted to see the accounts, acting like he knew what he was looking at, and once in awhile Lonnie poked his head in for a chat, or to bum a ten, but mostly Will was in here alone. He liked it that way. Here he kept a couple of his antique bridles and bits, and he had pictures scattered around, shots of the ranch's top bulls and Will's best horses, with their ribbons and trophies. None of them were more recent than five years ago, though. He had seemed to lose interest in all of these things over the past few years. These days, sometimes he had trouble calling up enough interest in anything just to get out of bed.

Miss D'Angelo glanced around the room, then slowly brought her hand to the crown of her hat. The fabric of her dress stretched tight over her breasts for an instant. Will saw beads of moisture on her pale skin, where it dipped between her breasts. She slipped off the hat and raked her fingers through her hair. It was wavy, and it fell from her fingers like dark honey rippling in sunshine. She let her hand drop as if it were heavy. All of her movements were like that, slow and heavy and languid.

Will wondered how she would be in bed. Then he snatched off his own hat and tossed it to the desk.

It gave up a little puff of dust. He, too, raked his hands through his hair. It was soaked with sweat, and so was his shirt. Sweat, around the gal, seemed in poor taste.

"Ah . . . if you'll excuse me, I'll go wash up. Just sit down, if you'd like. Lonnie'll have the drinks in a minute."

He went back through the door and pulled it closed behind him. It had not been this awkward when he'd hired the four other housekeepers, he thought. Of course, none of those housekeepers had been like this gal.

Each of the previous housekeepers had been on the far side of fifty and quite substantial in frame, and one of them had been a man. One of them, the second one, had been almost a man, and Will had had high hopes for her. She had been a solid chunk of a commander in Big Smith overalls. She hadn't been much for cleaning, but she could flat-out cook, and she'd matched Hardy curse for curse and chew for chew. The old man had been sufficiently impressed by her size not to threaten her physically. But one afternoon he had found a girlie calendar from somewhere and waved it in her face. He had actually chased her with it out across the yard, no mean trick for a man with a cane.

Ruby Dee D'Angelo, Will thought, was more like the girl on the girlie calendar than a housekeeper.

"Did you know we don't have any matchin' glasses in this house?" Lonnie said. He had two glasses on the counter, filling them with soft drink while he sipped beer foam from a third.

Will stripped out of his shirt, threw it on top of the washer and stepped to the sink, then stuck his hands and arms under the faucet flow. Lonnie poked at an ice cube in one of the glasses.

"I hope you washed your hands," Will told him.

"I washed my hands. I'm not a heathen. No matter that I live like one half the time, with nothin' but jelly glasses to drink out of. It seems like people who have two pickup trucks worth thirty grand plus apiece in the garage and are sellin' some bulls for ten grand apiece could at least afford matching glasses."

"What we don't have is time and inclination," Will said. "Shit! We don't have soap, either." He pumped the silly little plastic bottle furiously, but all it did was spit at him. "Squirt me some of that dish soap, Lon."

"Well, when the gal goes for groceries, you tell her to get some glasses, too," Lonnie said, squirting the green liquid into Will's palm. "It's embarrassin' having to use jelly glasses when people come by."

"Yeah . . . and how often do people come by?"

People weren't given to visiting the Starrs. Once in awhile a couple of Lonnie's buddies would show up, but they always hung around out at the arena. Will couldn't be called a socializer, and if the old man had anything at all to say to anyone, it wasn't good.

Will worked up suds, and the water ran dark. He stuck his head down and rinsed his face, threw water on the back of his neck. Lonnie handed him the towel, and he dried his face vigorously.

"Miss D'Angelo isn't gonna have time to do any shoppin'. She isn't stayin'."

Will said it straight, going on the supposition that the sooner dealt with, the sooner done with. When he looked up, his brother was staring at him.

"You're not even gonna give her a try, are you? You get one look at her, and you make up your mind to that." Lonnie shook his head angrily. "I told you that you should have gone down and interviewed her yourself in Okie City. It makes damn little sense to bring her all the way up here for nothin'. That isn't a nice thing to do at all," he added righteously, which was pretty silly. Lonnie threw around righteousness the way some people did their socks, using it when it suited him.

"She came up here on provision, and she's been well paid for her time and trouble," was Will's answer as he finished drying his hands and arms. "Besides, I interviewed the four before her, and none of them turned out to be what we hoped when they got on the job. I didn't have time to go chasin' down to Oklahoma City on a fool's errand. There's a ranch to run, and the old man to see to."

"Meanin' I can't do either, right?" Lonnie said, peeved.

"No. Mostly what it is, is that you don't *want* to do either."

That truth sat there a loud second.

"You just don't like to leave this ranch anymore, is what it is," Lonnie said, pointing at Will. "You've gotten to be like an old woman that won't let go."

They stared at each other, the barbs they had slung echoing in the angry silence that followed.

"I guess we're both doin' the best we can," Will said flatly, and turned on his heel.

He went to the back porch, where the shirts he'd brought home from the laundry still hung from the ceiling hook. He tore off the plastic wrapping and jerked a shirt off the hanger, then slipped into it. The damn cuff was ragged. He rolled it up.

Lonnie leaned against the counter, sipping his beer. "The old man has run off four housekeepers in the past five months." His gaze said he held Will to account for it.

Will said, "He run off three. I ran off the last one." The last one had been the male housekeeper, the great idea that had turned bad. The man had liked to sleep half the day and smoke smelly cigars the other half, and when Will had caught him stealing from the kitchen money to play poker with old buddies who suddenly started dropping by, he had sent him on his way.

Lonnie sighed heavily. "Look, Will, if you're upset by the way I was playin' with the gal, you got the wrong idea. I'm just like that with women. It doesn't mean anything, and you ought to know that by now. Let her stay until the old man runs her off, so we can at least get one or two good meals. It wouldn't hurt to come in here and see a face prettier than yours, either, and I don't think I need to feel ashamed of that."

Will shook his head as he buttoned his shirt. "I know, Lon. I'm damn tired of cold food and dirty laundry and tryin' to keep the old man from killing himself, just as much as you are. But look at her. She's ... " He gestured toward the office, unable to find words for what he wanted to say. "It's a cinch the old man would chew her up and spit her out in all of five seconds, Lon."

That familiar stubborn look came over his brother's face. "Maybe she looks tender, but that sure is a refreshing change from those you've been gettin' in here. She's a woman who happens to look and act like one."

Will clamped his mouth shut at that.

"Aw, Will, face it. Nobody you get in here is gonna change the facts. The old man is mean as a junkyard dog, and always has been. Mama left because of it. And now he's eighty-five, has diabetes and is off the beam from his stroke. He ain't likely to get better, and he'll have us all sick and crazy before he's through. If it wasn't for him, we wouldn't have to live this way. He keeps the hands run off and us tied here, same as if we had a rope around our necks."

"Mama left because she got a boyfriend," Will said, jerking up his zipper and fastening his belt. "And I hadn't noticed you keepin' yourself from going off to your rodeos and women. When did that happen?"

Lonnie said, "I'm here now, and it sure ain't because I couldn't be off workin' somewhere else." He poked his finger at Will. "I work this ranch, same as you. I've given half my life to it, and I'm damn tired of being treated like nothin' but a no-account hand that the old man can't even stomach lookin' at. I've had it, Will."

Looking at Lonnie's flushed and furious face, Will swallowed and clenched and unclenched his hands. He wanted to take off right then, head out and never look back. But Lonnie was his brother and the old man was his dad, and somehow Will had to keep them all together. That had been his responsibility for twenty-five years, to keep them together. God, he was damned tired of the load.

He breathed deeply and said, "Aw, Lon, the old man—"

Suddenly he saw the girl. She stepped out from the entry to the office and stood gazing at him with her big brown eyes.

Embarrassment washed over him. He and Lonnie hadn't been yelling, but Will wondered how much she had heard. Her dark eyes went from him to Lonnie and came back to rest on him. They were totally unreadable.

"Could I use y'all's bathroom?"

It was Lonnie who jumped to show her, with the dog at her heels, the way. And as she followed his brother through the archway to the dining room, Will gazed at the girl and thought how there had not been a pretty young woman in this house since the day his mother had left, twenty-five years ago.

There never had been a dog.

≈ 2

RUBY DEE REGRETTED having to interrupt the brothers' conversation, it being neither polite nor prudent to interrupt an argument. But she had been about to ask for the bathroom before Will Starr had raced off and left her in his office, and now she was about to pee her pants.

Lonnie Starr was just as sweet as he could be, showing her through the dining room and into the hallway to the bathroom. He was a man at ease with women. The other one, Will Starr, was not.

She had not needed to hear what Will Starr said in the kitchen to know that he did not want her here—and with her ear pressed to the door, she had heard almost every word. She had known it, though, from the first sight of him walking across to greet her. Disapproval had been all over him like a wash of paint.

Oh, he was attracted to her. She had seen that, too. Felt it in a vibration, as well as caught it in a glimmer of his blue eyes, before he'd hidden it. Ruby Dee was good at reading people. And men always seemed attracted to her. A lot of them seemed to disapprove

17

of her, too. Miss Edna had always said Ruby Dee frightened men, said that they were put off by the way she met their gazes with her own and didn't pretend to not know what was going on. Ruby Dee just didn't know how else she was supposed to be. She was who she was, and didn't see any need to hide it.

"Well," she said in a shaky whisper, and then she began to cry.

Sally nudged her knee with a cold nose, offering consolation—and seeking it, too. Border collies were possessed of a nervous disposition, and when Ruby Dee got shook up, Sally did, too, no doubt recalling when she had been lost at the 7-Eleven and the dog catcher was trying to get her.

Ruby Dee flushed the toilet and turned on the water in the sink, then sank down onto the side of the tub—and boy, that tub needed scrubbing—and cried into the dingy hand towel, the only one that had been hanging on the towel rod. Judging from the towel and the tub, the water was hard, and they needed to add baking soda to their wash water.

That was what tears were to Ruby Dee—wash water, as good at cleansing hurts from the spirit as a bath was for dirt from the body. It was Ruby Dee's opinion that crying was a necessity for good health too much neglected by people. Most people were ashamed of crying, as if it were a weakness, but to Ruby Dee there was no more shame to be found in crying than there was in taking a shower or a tea-spoonful of cod liver oil. All three things were healing to a body.

Healing was Ruby Dee's calling. She was by license a practical nurse, but she considered herself a healer, which in her estimation stood a lot higher than a nurse or a doctor. Nurses and doctors could be trained, as far as it went, but a healer was one who had received a special talent directly from God. Indeed, Miss Edna had said that Ruby Dee was next to God in bringing living things back from the brink of death and comforting those who were slipping over. Her exceptional abilities in this direction kept her almost constantly employed in private home care.

"Oh, Miss Edna," Ruby Dee whispered into the dingy towel. "What am I gonna do now? I've driven all this way, and he disapproves of me, and I'm so tired." Ruby Dee sank into her melancholy like a pebble tossed into cream gravy.

The next instant Ruby Dee heard Miss Edna's familiar *"Straighten up!"*

Miss Edna had been one of those to disdain crying, and "straighten up" had been a favored command. Mostly she'd said it while she watched the *Nightly News* with Tom Brokaw. "People just need to straighten up," she'd say. "You tell them to straighten up, Tom."

Ruby Dee thought she should have told people to cry more. "If you had done more cryin', you would have lived longer, Miss Edna," she mumbled in aggravation.

The frequent death of her patients was, of course, the major problem with Ruby Dee's occupation. Her patients were predominantly elderly or people who'd been sent home because medical science could do very little for them. Ruby Dee could only bring these patients back from the brink of death so many times before they finally slipped over and left her. This was very hard on her spirit, and led to a lot of crying. She had been crying every day for a month, because of Miss Edna's finally having slipped over and left her. Ruby Dee had done everything she knew how to do, and still Miss Edna had died.

Sniffing, she fished in her pocket and brought out a lace-edged hanky bearing the carefully embroidered initials EMS. Edna Marie Summerill. Miss Edna had given Ruby Dee all the lovely handkerchiefs she owned. "Someone who cries as much as you do should always have a hanky," Miss Edna had said.

Folding the hanky so that she wouldn't soil the embroidered initials, as Miss Edna had taught her, Ruby Dee blew her nose, hard.

Sensing a return to calmness, Sally moved away and went to make a place to lie on some towels in the corner.

"Sally, don't be sniffin' those towels. Come here; you can lay on this rug. That's a good girl."

Ruby Dee didn't know how long those towels had been lying piled in the corner, but she knew that, left too long in a place that wasn't too clean anyway, towels could draw centipedes, and she certainly didn't want Sally dislodging one and possibly getting bitten. Ruby Dee had been terrified of centipedes ever since the age of five, when she had been bitten by one.

It had been the day after her daddy had gone off and left her with Big Grandma. Her daddy had gone off and left her a lot, the final place being Big Grandma's house, where she was to reside in the closed-in front porch with the rotted floor.

Ruby Dee had been digging through her meager clothes piled in the corner of the porch-bedroom, when she came away with not only a T-shirt in hand, but the biggest, meanest, cinnamon-crusted monster momentarily attached.

Unfortunately, Big Grandma, not at all happy to have had a child dumped upon her, was also totally against crying, and Ruby Dee was crying up a storm. Big Grandma had slapped Ruby Dee silly, saying, "Stop cryin', or I'll give you somethin' to cry about!"

That attitude never had made a lot of sense to Ruby Dee. She had come to learn early, though, not to expect human beings to make sense. Humans were perhaps the only beings in the good Lord's universe that on a regular basis did not make sense. This belief freed Ruby Dee, as a member of the human race, from the constant need to make sense or explain herself. It also led her to a great degree of tolerance for and even acceptance of her fellow man. As she saw it, if people would accept each other as they were, everyone would be a lot happier, and then, of course, healthier. It really was that simple . . . and that impossible.

Her eyes fell on her boots, and she automatically dusted them, using the now thoroughly damp dingy towel. Her boots were brand-new Noconas. She had bought them with the money Will Starr had sent her for traveling expenses, which was hers to keep whether or not she took the job. Will Starr had struck her as being a mite stuffy, but he wasn't a cheap man.

By all rights, she should have spent the money he sent her on new tires, but instead she had bought five cans of Fix-a-Flat and these boots, nourishing her spirit.

Undoubtedly Will Starr would have disapproved.

Will Starr was the older one by a good chunk of years, and she wondered at this, because the brothers certainly looked enough alike to have come from the same pod, so to speak. They were good looking men, as far as that went, both with solid, square faces, shiny mahogany hair and light eyes. Lonnie Starr was lighter, though, in spirit and appearance. Will Starr struck Ruby Dee as being as stormy as his steel-colored eyes.

Suddenly she remembered all the water she had been running to cover the sound of her crying. With a stab of guilt at being wasteful of a precious natural resource, she rinsed her face, shut the water off tight, then patted herself dry with the dingy towel. It was really wet now, so she spread it neatly on the towel rod.

Well.

She stared at herself in the mirror and took her fingers to her hair. She had nice wavy hair and it hardly ever needed anything done to it. Her features were on the plain side, but her complexion was that of peaches and cream, so she didn't bother with makeup, except lipstick. She brought a tube from her pocket and carefully put it on. Heated Sunset. There, she felt stronger.

Idly she opened the medicine cabinet. It, too, was not very clean. Certainly it was a man's cabinet, one man, she would guess, probably the eldest Starr, because there was an old-fashioned shaving-cream cup and brush on the shelf. She liked him for that, for the cup and brush conserved, but the plastic disposable shavers made her subtract a point or two. There was a bottle of Old Spice aftershave, which looked as old as the shaving-cream cup and was all sticky around the top. The shelves were caked with who knew what-all. This cabinet was not at all sanitary. Ruby Dee took the dingy hand towel again and wiped the shelves as best she could.

She looked around the room. It smelled musty. It was lime green, a popular color of the forties and fifties, and she guessed that not one thing had been done to it since then, except to install a new shower curtain, which was black. And caked with soap and hard-water deposits. Vinegar would handle that.

From what she had briefly seen, there was no sign of a woman anywhere, and the whole house was ugly. There were hardly any pictures on the walls, and all the furniture was at least thirty years old and had been bought with no taste in the first place. It was dreary and sad, and no doubt an indication of the state of the people living in it.

She could help them, she thought, if Will Starr would allow it. Or if she could get herself together enough to do it.

Moving to the window, she pulled back the curtain. Dust flew, and made her sneeze. She blew her nose again with Miss Edna's hanky, then clutched it and gazed out the window at the rolling grassland stretching down to a line of trees, all of them leaning toward the north. Bent that way from the constant south winds. Past that thin line of trees, the land rolled into more grass, browned now by the harsh sun. No other houses, not even electric lines. Just land and sky, far as the eye could see. It was peaceful.

Putting her hand into her left pocket this time, Ruby Dee brought out a piece of paper folded into a small square. It was pressed and crumpled from where she had tucked it inside her bra for at least a week, but doing that had proved to be uncomfortable. Her sweat had made the paper stick to her skin.

Carefully, she unfolded it—half a sheet of cheap, thin copy paper, on which were pasted cut-out pictures. One was a small newsprint photo of a white clapboard house, from a real estate ad, with the description of it as a cozy country cottage on five acres. Next to that was a cut-out of two little children in striped overalls, holding hands. Below that was a Dodge pickup truck, the image of Sally, taken from a snapshot, and a single, fancy, hand-tooled boot. Squeezed into a bottom corner was the image of a man in jeans and shirt. Where the man's face should have been was blank.

She gazed at the paper for a long time. Then she refolded it and tucked it back into her pocket. Laying her forehead against the window, she whispered, "Miss Edna, are you there? What am I gonna do now?"

She sensed Miss Edna again. *"Don't pout, Ruby Dee. It does nothing but cause wrinkles."* Miss Edna had always been a stickler about her complexion, which had been youthful, even at her death, at seventy-three.

"That is so easy for you to say. You are up there with God and St. Peter and your Sherman and your Henry and a host of angels. I'm down here alone, just like I always have been, thirty years old and with my eggs drying up, living in a tin can, and my closest friend is a dead person."

"Cast your cares upon the Lord, for he cares for you."

"He took you and left me alone," Ruby Dee said sharply.

Miss Edna left on that note.

Ruby Dee knew people would think she was crazy for talking to Miss Edna, but the fact was, talking to

Miss Edna kept Ruby Dee from going crazy just then. She could tell Miss Edna things she would never have told anyone else, and she saw no reason to stop just because Miss Edna was dead.

3

WHILE THE GAL was in the bathroom, Lonnie again took up the matter of keeping her. From the minute he had laid eyes on Ruby Dee D'Angelo, he had been taken with the idea of having her around the house. He wanted her there something fierce.

Lonnie knew actualization of his desire was slim to none, because even if Will let her stay, the old man would keep them all in an uproar, but a part of him just wouldn't let go of the idea. And if nothing else, he figured he could at least harass Will, because as he saw it, Will and the old man were dealing him an injustice that wasn't necessary at all.

"So are you gonna go in and get the chicken dinners from Reeves's tonight?" he asked, following Will into the office and throwing himself down in the old leather chair. He wanted Will to think about what they would be having to do.

Will raked a hand through his hair. "I don't know," he said irritably as he began to dig through papers on his desk.

"If you hired Ruby Dee D'Angelo, you wouldn't

have to go get chicken dinners ... or anything else."

Will ignored him. He picked up a paper, looked at it and threw it aside, frowning.

"What is it?" Lonnie asked, getting up and reaching for the paper.

Will said, "She just won't work out, Lonnie. There's no sense in gettin' everybody in a ruckus by tryin' to make it work."

Lonnie had a sense that Will might want to try the gal after all. Will seemed to be arguing with himself. Lonnie read the paper. It was the gal's résumé. "This looks pretty impressive to me."

"The references the other four gave were good, too," Will said, a certain defensiveness in his voice.

"Well, maybe this gal's are true," Lonnie replied, pressing him. "And if you don't hire her, what are we gonna do?"

"We keep lookin', that's what we do."

Lonnie didn't like the sound of the decisiveness returning to Will's voice.

"Keep lookin'? Where and for how long? It's a cinch we ain't gonna find anyone within three counties, and the rest of the state is beginnin' to look bleak. Damn, Will. It's time you quit lettin' the old man call the shots on this tune. You're foolin' yourself, thinking you can find just the right person to suit him, because there isn't such a person on this earth."

"What do you want me to do, Lonnie? Tell him he has no control over his own place?"

Lonnie breathed deeply. "It may be time to think about puttin' the old man in a home." The minute he'd said it, he knew he shouldn't have. He had been thinking it for a long time, though.

Will drew himself up and said in a voice as hard and flat as sandstone: "I don't guess I will."

Then he turned and strode to the kitchen.

Lonnie followed. He had more to say, though he wasn't quite certain what it was.

Will reached for his Dr. Pepper and went to peer into the dining room, looking toward the hall. Then he turned around, a perplexed look on his face. "The water's runnin' full blast in the bathroom."

Lonnie went over beside him. Sure enough, the water was running. He turned back toward the kitchen. "Maybe she's takin' a shower."

"She would do that, do you think?"

Lonnie had to laugh. "I was only jokin'. She's just doin' whatever it is women do in the bathroom, and whatever it is, it takes them a long time."

It was funny, when Lonnie thought about it, but he had a lot more knowledge about females than Will did. The trouble with Will was that he lived by a rigid set of rules, and those rules kept him from sampling the joys of women. Will seemed to set himself above all that. To Lonnie's mind, Will's only interests were the land and horses and cattle, and if a woman was to walk up to him buck naked, he probably wouldn't see her.

"You know, big brother," Lonnie said now, "it would do you good to have that gal around here—and in more ways than just for housekeeping and tending the old man. It would show you what you're missin' in this world. Since you and Georgia called it quits, you've shut yourself away here with the old man for so long that you've forgotten what a woman's touch is like. You get more like the old man every day, big brother."

Will swung his head around. "If you know so

much, Lonnie, why don't you just get yourself off to one of your girl friends and let them put you up for awhile in the manner you'd like to live."

Will's tone sliced into Lonnie. He gritted his teeth and then scooped his hat off the table, pointing it at Will.

"It's truth I'm not the brain you are, but I'm here to tell you that I know enough to know that you're so damn afraid somethin' you do or say is goin' to give the old man another stroke that you're turnin' yourself inside out. You don't even know who you are anymore, and neither does anyone else, and the old man is playin' his ailments up for all their worth."

It was so rare a thing for Lonnie to speak with raw passion that he startled himself, shut his mouth and breathed deeply through his nose. The next instant, he finished his speech. "And all your pussyfootin' around him ain't gonna make one bit of difference, because someday that old man is gonna have another stroke . . . or die from all the drinkin' he does, or from the junk he eats, because he's too stubborn to listen to anyone."

Will's eyes could have started a fire. He said, "*That* old man is your father."

"Huh! He gave up bein' a father to me a long time ago."

Lonnie's words rang in the air as he and Will glared at each other. But he wasn't sorry. No, sir.

But he was some frightened for having revealed so much of himself. Setting his hat on his head, he retreated into indifference. "You do what you want about the gal. I'll do what you suggested and go somewhere I can get a friendly breakfast each morning. I'll be out of here tomorrow."

Without meeting Will's eyes, he ducked out the door, resisting the urge to slam it, though he let the porch's screen door bang behind him.

Running was what he was doing. He felt as if he couldn't get away from the house fast enough.

He glanced at the old man's shop as he passed. The door was closed but the windows open, and he could hear the whir of the big steel fan. The old guy wouldn't break down and buy an air-conditioner. He was so tight with a penny that he squeaked when he walked.

Walking along the edge of the graveled drive, Lonnie headed for his pickup, parked beside the horse barn. He had to push to walk, since the edge was sandy the way the whole drive used to be when he was a kid. So many times he had come racing up it, churning up sand. He could still hear himself calling, "Wait for me, Will!"

"Well, come on, squirt, we gotta get those calves fed."

"My legs ain't as long as yours," Lonnie would grumble.

"They will be someday . . . someday you'll be bigger than me."

Back then Lonnie hadn't seen how that could happen at all. But he was taller than his brother now by half a foot, and his inseam measured thirty-six, where Will's was just thirty-four.

Pausing underneath the locust tree, he dug the tin of Skoal out of his back pocket and tucked a pinch in his lip. He had been dipping since he was fifteen, the year he had passed Will in height and had started running off with friends for the high times and the gals in towns and at rodeos. Will used to dip back then, too, but he'd had a fit about Lonnie's starting, and he had even punched old Wildcat Burns for giving Lonnie the dip.

Lonnie thought of what he had said to Will about the old man not being his father. That was truth— not pretty, maybe, but truth.

There had been a time, dim in his memory, when the old man had set him on his first horse, and had taken him out and bought him his first pair of boots. But the old man had been fifty-five by the time Lonnie was born. He had had little patience for a wet-nosed kid. It had been Will who Lonnie had trailed after. Will who had taught him to tie his shoes and button his shirt. Will who had picked him up and held him, after their mama had slung him in the dust and driven off with that mineral-rights buyer from Amarillo.

After that, when Lonnie would cry at night, Will would take him into his bed. "Come on, Lon. You don't need her . . . you got me, now, don't ya? You'll always have me."

Lonnie had made Will swear never to go away, and Will never had.

When the leaving did happen, it was always Lonnie doing it. When he just couldn't stand the old man's meanness or the coldness of the house, he would take off. Sometimes for a week, sometimes for several months. But he always came back.

Without fail, when Lonnie would turn and come up the drive, his heart would lift. For some really stupid reason, he would have convinced himself that the old man would be glad to see him and that being home would ease the ache inside him. But each time, within five minutes he would discover that the old man was as obnoxious as ever and the house cold and empty as ever.

Still, Will was always there.

That's what was eating at Lonnie now. He thought it true what he had said to Will, that his brother was growing too much like the old man. Will was withdrawing, going away, just like their mama, and even the old man.

Lonnie didn't want that to happen to Will. He didn't want that to happen to himself. He didn't want to lose Will.

But he couldn't ever have explained that to anyone. Just thinking it all embarrassed him.

☙ 4

WHEN Ruby Dee came back into the kitchen, Will Starr handed her the glass of Dr. Pepper. The glass was dripping sweat. He quickly apologized, grabbed a towel and wiped it for her. His hands were dark and rough—the strong, banged-up hands of a man who worked hard for a living and then came inside and scrubbed raw to get clean, making his hands drier and rougher still.

He braced himself against the counter, looked at her and said, "Look, Miss D'Angelo, there's some things we have to get straight."

She piped up, saying, "I'm not what you expected, am I, Mr. Starr?"

That gave him a start, causing his blue eyes to widen for an instant. And then he breathed deeply. "No, ma'am, you're not quite what I expected." His eyes rested on hers; then they skittered down her body. Quickly, before he realized what he was doing, and shyly, too. Ruby Dee felt something touch her as he did that, something of surprise and pleasure.

He wiped his hand on the taut thigh of his jeans. She noticed his eyes had taken on more of a blue color from his shirt. He was a quietly handsome man, probably too quiet, too plain to turn a woman's head, until a woman caught sight of his eyes. His eyes would arrest any woman, or man.

They were striking, seeming to burn out of his deeply tanned, craggy face like two beams of light. And his was a strong face. The face of a man, not a boy.

His hair and mustache were a rich brown. His mustache leaned toward red, but he had no noticeable gray in either his mustache or in his hair. That was a bit uncommon for a man who had to be over thirty-five. She gauged his age by the fine lines around his eyes and by the way he filled out his clothes with the thick muscles a man got only when he came into his prime. And Lordy, the man had muscles—his shoulders were wide and thick.

Will Starr wasn't as handsome as his brother, she thought, but she liked the look of him better. She had a thing about older men. Miss Edna said it was because she had never had a father.

She was looking at his wide shoulders when he said, "Look, I owe you an apology. I didn't fully read your résumé. Had I read it as carefully as I should have and seen that you were only thirty, I could have saved both of us a lot of time and you a lot of trouble. But I did specify when we spoke on the phone that the job was on speculation. Either one of us was free to change our mind after we met."

Will remembered that he had stressed that. He didn't think he needed to feel bad that she had up and taken it upon herself to bring everything she owned with her.

"Oh," she said. Her right eyebrow rose, and she gave him a look, a look that jangled him, and he didn't like that. "So you want someone older, more experienced. . . . Maybe someone with a wart on her nose would qualify."

So then Will felt foolish, and highly irritated. Straightening, he set his glass on the counter and gave her a look of his own.

"Ma'am, I just don't think this is a job for a young and pretty woman such as yourself. You'll be the only woman in this household. As you saw on the drive out, there's no one livin' right next door. The closest female neighbor is three miles down this road, and she's eleven years old. You'd have this house to take care of, as well as seeing to my father, and he's a downright crotchety old man. Many days you'll be stuck here with him from dawn to dusk, or even for several days at a time, when I have business away. If you run out of milk, you have a ten-mile drive one way to get some. For a full grocery store, you'll have to drive about forty miles, and there certainly aren't any big shopping malls like you have down in Oklahoma City.

"If you're anticipatin' meeting some of those cowboys like you see in the movies, you're gonna be disappointed. This isn't one of those big Texas spreads, and the only time I have a lot of help around here is for a few days in the spring and fall. From now until then I have one full-time hand, and he's nearly twice your age and married."

And then he added, "There is my brother, of course, and you might as well know he likes the ladies, which is another reason I think it just wouldn't work out to take you on."

There it was. He never had been much of a diplomat. He had said what he had to say, and as nicely as he could, and he searched her face, wondering if he had hurt her feelings.

Then he realized she didn't look hurt at all. She looked like she was fixing to jerk him up and set him straight.

In that slow way she had of moving, she propped a hand on her hip, took a stance that showed what she had to give, and, with her eyes bright as two drops of hot crude oil on a plate, she said slowly and precisely, "Mr. Starr, if it was cowboys I wanted, I could've had my pick down in Oklahoma City."

With her eyes holding his, Ruby Dee let Will Starr take that in.

"Yes, ma'am, I imagine that's so."

"Oh, yes, sir, that is so. I feel about men pretty much the same way I do about television—something I can live without. It's okay for a bit of entertainment, but mostly I prefer a radio—heard but not seen."

He didn't say anything to that, just kept looking at her. He was flushed, and she sensed he was embarrassed, as well he should be.

"Well," Ruby Dee said, and let that sit for a few seconds, while she gathered steam. "Bein' isolated and stuck with a grouchy old man—you explained that when we spoke on the phone, Mr. Starr. I understood fully what I would be dealin' with. I came out here as a professional. Now, perhaps I don't appear to be what you were expectin', but I can tell you a few facts that aren't in that résumé."

She leaned forward, holding his eyes with hers. "If it's experience you're wantin', I have it. I have been an LPN for six years, but I've been a healer for all of my life, startin' with holdin' my daddy's head and keepin' him from drownin' in his own vomit when I was just three years old. At the age of five I was takin' care of my crazy great-grandma—just her and me livin' together. I did such a good job of it that for four years no one knew my great-grandma had gone to live back in 1936 most of the time. We didn't get caught, until one day a developer came, wantin' to buy her land, and insisted on talking to her. For some reason she thought he was her dead husband, and before I realized what she was about, she'd shot him. She missed anything important, and got him in the leg.

"They took her away to the nursing home, and I went on to take care of myself and other kids who no one else wanted to look out for. Since I was fifteen I have been makin' a living by carin' for people in one way or another, and all of those years before and since add up to hard experience, because when you're young, you tend to get the jobs that no mature adult will take on. I have been talked to worse than you can imagine. I've been spit on and punched and scratched. Once a lady with a real hot temper took a butcher knife to me, and another time a seventy-year-old man, who wasn't near as feeble as he pretended, tried to rape me. I find it hard to believe your father could be much worse, Mr. Starr. Do you think he could be?"

It suddenly occurred to Ruby Dee that perhaps the elder Mr. Starr was worse. She couldn't imagine how anyone could be, but she needed to know.

Will Starr's eyebrows went up, and he swallowed. "My father wouldn't try to rape you."

Ruby Dee felt some reassured. Will Starr appeared to be pondering, so she went on with whatever else came to mind.

"You are concerned that I won't stand up under the isolation out here. Well, right now that isolation is exactly why I've come. That, and the fact that your father is not bedridden and at death's door. I'm really tired of old people dying on me."

Will Starr sort of started at that.

"As I see it on your side, Mr. Starr, you all need me. You've already gone through four housekeepers, and the way Maggie Parsons tells it, you aren't gonna find another one anytime soon. It seems to me the worst that can happen to either of us is that you'll fire me or I'll quit. So I'm still willin' to give it a go, if you are."

Finished, she waited. She really had gone on; she could do that—get carried away and go on. It was no wonder Will Starr was staring at her.

His gray-blue eyes had gone steely as little ball bearings. She wondered what was working behind them. It was disconcerting the way he was looking at her. His eyes drifted down and back up her body, assessing her. His look was as strong as if he'd run a hand over her, checking and searching and weighing her flesh. It made her squirm inside, causing her to feel absurdly shy, annoyed.

Then he asked, "Can you make apple pie?"

Ruby Dee was surprised, but she answered quickly enough. "Yes. We are what we eat, and the body more readily accepts the nourishment of food that is tasty. I can make an apple pie to crawl fifty miles for, and one with little sugar, too, that your daddy can eat. I also make buttermilk biscuits that won a state-fair ribbon once. I don't make them often, though, because of their high fat content."

His sharp, ball-bearing eyes bore into hers. "All right, Miss D'Angelo, we'll give it a try."

He stuck out his hand, and after a moment's hesitation, she shook it. His shake was strong, his hand moist, his steely eyes like blue flame.

Will Starr explained that Ruby Dee would have complete charge of the house, but the most important thing was to see to his father.

"His medicines and an instruction sheet from the doctor are in this cabinet." He pointed. "Dad takes pills to thin his blood, and some for his arthritis—for the swelling of his joints—and he has pain medication for that, too. I've been settin' his pills out for him, but I'm not certain he always takes them. He simply refuses sometimes. He says that he feels fine, so he doesn't need to take anything." His expression and tone stated clearly that he found this idea of his father's somewhere near lunacy.

Ruby Dee felt called on to defend the older man. "When you think about it, it is his body. He feels good, so why take medicine? He's probably tired of taking pills. You don't have to agree with it, but surely you can understand it."

"Oh, I understand my father, all right, Miss D'Angelo. He doesn't take the medicine because he thinks all the rules that apply to the rest of us don't apply to him."

His voice was sharp and tired at the same time, and Ruby Dee felt she had been told.

He led the way through the house at a rapid pace. The soles of their boots echoed on the wood floor, and Sally's toenails went pitter-patter. Except for a worn rose-patterned rug beneath the dining room table, the floors were bare, and in need of polishing.

Through the downstairs hallway he pointed out his father's room. With a quick glance, Ruby Dee saw a massive, dark old bedstead with a messy, unmade bed, a jumbled nightstand and a dingy window shade crookedly pulled halfway down.

"Where is your daddy?"

He gestured. "He's in his shop—out back."

"He can get around pretty good, then?"

"His knees are stiff—the right one's almost locked in place—but he can get anywhere he wants to go. He still drives a pickup truck, mostly just around here, because he doesn't have a license anymore. It's automatic, and we've had it fixed with hand brakes, so it's easier for him. We got him a wheelchair back last winter, but he just uses it to roll things around in his shop."

"What does he do in his shop?"

"Leatherwork—halters, saddles, things like that."

He paused at the stairs for Ruby Dee to go up ahead of him. She noticed, too, that he stepped back—he seemed to keep at least three or four feet from her, as if he didn't like breathing anyone else's air.

The room that was to be hers was at the top of the stairs. Like the rest of the house, it was ugly, but not without hope—the hope being a south-facing window that looked out over the backyard, barns and pastures. She could see out to the east and west a little, too—red sandstone buttes and rolling grassland.

She would have to share the upstairs bathroom. "We're not really set up for live-in help," Will Starr said. "But one shelf in the bathroom closet will be yours."

Ruby Dee caught a glimpse of a big, claw-footed tub, and then Will Starr was already heading back downstairs, saying, "You won't be expected to do anything with mine and Lonnie's rooms. We can keep them."

She imagined the men would rather not have her poking around their rooms. She could understand that, but she offered to change their bed sheets.

"Well, that's fine, if you want," he said. "But you don't need to do any more."

Actually, his tone said: everything else is off limits.

Back downstairs again, he paused in the kitchen. "Is there anything special that you need?" He was really cool now.

"Well, I'd like to have a nice place to park my trailer. It's not convenient to use permanent—it needs electric and water and sewer hookup, you know—but I'd like to be able to go to it on my days off."

He said, "The east side of the tractor barn ought to do. There's a cottonwood there for shade." He paused. "Will you be startin' right away, or would you want a night to get yourself settled?"

"I'm here, so I might as well start."

He nodded. "I'll leave you to look around on your own. And I'll send someone up to help you bring your things in." He stepped into his office and came back with his hat. Holding it in his hand, he said, "If I were you, I wouldn't go to a lot of trouble bringin' in just everything."

His steely blue eyes were straight on hers for a

brief moment. And then he was out the door, closing it softly behind him.

Well, Ruby Dee thought, as she watched his wide shoulders disappear from sight.

❧ 5

SWEAT WAS TICKLING the back of Will's neck when he got out of the house. And the house was air-conditioned.

It seemed like the gal raised the temperature of a room the instant she entered it, bringing her swinging earrings and throaty voice and way of walking that was like an evening wave rolling up on the beach in the middle of summer.

Will had the feeling that he'd just set off going ninety miles an hour down a dead-end road. Even though a man knew what was going to happen at the end, he still didn't stop, or even let up. It was just something he had to do. He was of the same mind as Lonnie: he wanted Ruby Dee D'Angelo in the house. And he sure wanted a few decent meals and the old man looked after, he thought angrily.

He strode across the backyard and headed up toward the horse barn. He slowed a bit when he passed the old man's shop. The door was closed, and no sound came from inside, but Will knew his father was in there. He couldn't have been anywhere else, because his old Chevy pickup sat parked only a few feet away.

Will kept on going. He had to consider everything for a few minutes, before he faced the old man.

He fully intended to find Wildcat and tell him to go help Miss D'Angelo move in. Then he remembered it was Sunday, and Wildcat Burns was in Harney with Charlene Legget, the widow he had married last year. Wildcat and Charlene were no doubt watching old movies on the VCR. Charlene's having a VCR and knowing how to work it were the main reasons Wildcat had finally, at the age of fifty-two, given up being a bachelor and living in the small cottage there on the ranch.

That left Lonnie to help Miss D'Angelo, and Will didn't like that at all. It wouldn't be too much of an exaggeration to say that if you gave Lonnie ten minutes with a woman, he'd at least have her kicking off her shoes and anticipating more. In Lonnie's defense, he couldn't seem to help himself. He was as addicted to loving women as some men were to alcohol. And most women were like hothouse flower buds when they saw him, swelling up and spreading open.

Lonnie was at his horse trailer, a fancy, three-horse slant-loader, with tack room and sleeping quarters. He had paid for the rig from his winnings on the rodeo circuit a few years back. He was best as a calf roper, but he could compete in every event. He'd been to the finals in Las Vegas four times and had won a champion buckle twice. Yes, he was good at riding in the rodeo, but in Will's opinion what Lonnie was best at was the rodeo life, which kept him moving from one place to another, and one woman to another.

He already had the trailer hooked to his big white dually pickup. He was stowing things in the sleeping quarters, pitching things in; Lonnie never had been too neat. In order for him to use the bed, he'd have to find it first.

Ignoring Will, he went about his business. Lonnie always did that after an argument, acting like he was alone in the world. It irritated Will considerably.

"You're not wastin' any time," Will said.

"You were the one who told me to go."

Will didn't want to get further into an argument, so he let that pass. He said, "If you got a minute, you could go on down and help Miss D'Angelo haul her things into the house."

He'd meant to get a jump out of Lonnie, and he did. Lonnie stopped, and his head came swiveling around. "You mean she's stayin'?"

"She's hired on," Will said. "I doubt we can really call it stayin'."

He and Lonnie looked at each other.

Will said, "What about you—are you stayin'?" He figured Lonnie would, yet he had a niggling doubt, enough to make him hold his breath.

Lonnie averted his eyes to the rope in his hands. "Yeah . . . guess I might. At least long enough to get a breakfast or two." Then a grin split his face.

He gave Will a shove, and Will shoved him back. Lonnie sobered. "What's the old man got to say?"

"I haven't told him yet. Maybe you'd like to do it."

Lonnie just shot him a look. "I'd better not keep the lady waitin'. We don't want her to change her mind before we get a good meal." He slammed the trailer door and strode away.

Watching him, Will felt a strange envy . . . of Lonnie's youth, of his easy nature, of the time he was going to spend with the gal. Uncomfortable with the feeling, he turned from it.

He patted his pockets, by habit looking for a cigarette. He'd wanted one badly back at the house, but the one left in his dirty shirt had been all broken up and damp.

Will didn't keep any cigarettes in the house, tempting and within easy reach. He kept a couple of packs in his pickup truck, and each morning he put the four cigarettes he allowed himself for the day into his shirt pocket.

He went to his pickup, shook four from a pack, tucked one between his lips and stuck the rest in his shirt pocket. He figured he deserved an extra ration.

Squinting, Will gazed out at the land. It rolled away in all directions, rising in flat planes of grass and dipping into small canyons of rocks and trees. Then there was the wide blue sky, which was an equal part of the land; it nurtured the land, and the land nurtured it. The grass was ripening and burning up underneath the sun, and the pond down beneath the cottonwoods was drying now, too, all normal for midsummer in that part of the country.

He thought how this land had once supported buffalo and the Comanche, and how the old man had worked it longer than Will had been alive.

The old man.

Will had never deliberately and openly gone against the old man's wishes. Anytime in the past when he had needed to accomplish something that his father disagreed with, Will had either been able to figure out how to get the old man to accept it, to the point where he even took credit for the idea, or he'd managed to get it done on the sly, so that the old man never found out. That wasn't exactly honorable, Will thought, but neither was he deliberately contradicting the old man.

It did not seem right to deliberately contradict the old man, who was not only his father but owner of this ranch, with eighty-five years of living under his belt, and as such deserving of a certain amount of respect.

But this time there seemed no way Will could work the old man around to agreeing to Miss D'Angelo. And there certainly was no way of hiding her.

The memory of finding the old man in his shop, draped across his stitching bench, played across Will's mind. The man he had thought too tough ever to die had suffered a stroke. Small and with little noticeable effects, what that stroke had amounted to was an announcement that the old man was reaching his twilight, and no one on God's green earth could put a stop to it.

The old man was clinging to the reins, but the horse was out from under him and racing away. The smart thing would be to let go of those reins and let that ornery horse go on, but the old man was a lot more stubborn than he was smart, always had been.

Refusing to admit he needed help, he took his medicine twice or not at all, and he lied about it, too. Though his eyesight was failing, he continued to drive the rutted roads and trails—no amount of finagling on Will's part had been able to put a stop to it—and he took his rifle out when he drove around the ranch. He'd shot one of Joe Allen's herd dogs, mistaking it for a coyote.

He ate greasy eggs and burnt ham that he cooked himself when Will couldn't get to doing it, and twice he had almost set the kitchen on fire because he'd forgotten to turn off the stove. He insisted on eating Snickers bars and Twinkie cakes and drinking whiskey, too, even though doing so made his blood sugar rise high enough to ring bells. Once he fell in the tub and had to stay there half the day, before Will came to find him. Worse, lately there were times when the old man got confused, forgetting exactly where and who he was.

It scared the living daylights out of Will to think his daddy might be losing his mind.

Will threw the remainder of his cigarette onto the ground and stepped on it. Reluctantly, he started off toward the shop. His stomach twisted as tightly as a knotted rope as he imagined the old man's reaction when he was told the woman was staying.

Oh, geez, Will hoped the old man didn't keel over dead.

As he approached the shop, Will saw Lonnie and Miss D'Angelo messing around at her car again—Lonnie with his hat pushed back and giving the gal his most charming smile. One thing was certain, Will thought, things were definitely going to change a bit around here. The thought was fuel to the smoldering fire inside him.

He knocked on the door, only because he thought it polite, not because he expected the old man to answer. The old man never answered a knock.

"Dad?"

Turning the cracked black enamel knob, Will opened the door and stepped inside. He blinked, his eyes adjusting. Light sliced across the room from the west window, illuminating sparkling dust dancing in the stuffy air. The heavy, familiar scents of dried-out lumber, tanned hides and oil enveloped him.

The shop, which had been salvaged from a two-room shack, was lined with saddles in various stages of dilapidation, leather hides and strips, old stirrups and the wood of broken saddle trees. Will had always wondered why the old man kept broken trees. But he'd never asked.

A workbench stretched across the rear of the shop, illuminated by a rusty fluorescent light fixture suspended by nylon cord. Tools were set neatly in niches on the wall behind it. A number of them were well over a hundred years old, having belonged to Will's great-grandfather, who had been a saddle-maker of some repute down in Texas.

Will's gaze first touched the amber pint bottle of whiskey on the workbench, and his stomach got one notch tighter. Then he looked at his dad, who leaned heavily on his cane over at the west window.

The old man turned his head slowly and sent Will a glare that would have felled a man not familiar with it.

Hardy Starr had prominent, high cheekbones, a big beak of a nose and eyes that glittered like diamond arrow points from behind gold wire glasses. He'd been a powerful man, stocky, and he was some still, though shrunken by the years and horse wrecks. He still had a thick head of silver hair. His hair was reassuring to Will, since it was a good indication that he himself wasn't likely to go bald either.

Will wasn't thinking that right now, though. He was thinking of just what he could say to bring his dad around to acceptance. He could say how tired he was of eating burnt toast and cold sandwiches and never having clean underwear, all practical points.

But when the old man hit him with that glare, he ended up saying, "I hired the woman."

The old man went up like a flare. "Well, I ain't havin' it," he said flatly and as firmly as setting his words in stone.

Will took hold of himself and tried to back up and sound reasonable. "Dad . . . don't condemn this woman by what she looks like. She's highly qualified and experienced, and she was taught by Maggie Parsons. Give her a chance. She says she can make a real good apple pie." With a sinking feeling, he knew nothing he could say would make a difference.

The old man limped forward, smacking his cane hard on the wooden floor.

"I don't care if she's the queen of Sheba," he said.

"The queen of Sheba" was an expression Will had heard from the old man all his life. It grated on his nerves.

The old man jutted his face at Will. "I put up with them others you paraded through here, but by God, I ain't puttin' up with this one—or any other ones you bring in, either. We're callin' a halt to this whole biz-ness. It's *my* house and *my* ranch, and I still say what goes on here!"

With the old man's words, the fraying rope inside Will burned clean through.

"Yeah," he said, "it's *your* house and *your* ranch. You sure as hell never let anyone forget that—never mind that I've lived here and worked side by side with you for forty-two years. Never mind that it's me"—he jabbed his chest and flung his hand in the direction of the house—"that's fixed windows and wiring and reroofed that damn house . . . me that's built this whole place into what it is after you just about lost it! And after all that, if you can't consider me an equal owner, I imagine I can just hit the road and go find myself someplace that's my own."

The words, so long held inside, came bursting out, hot and hard.

The old man's face turned red as watermelon flesh. Even before Will finished, he was yelling, "Just go ahead! B'God, I don't need you here runnin' my life. No! There won't come a day when I need anyone here tellin' me how to live! I don't need any of ya. . . . Go on, get!"

The old man came at him in a fury. "You get on . . . just like yer mama did . . . just like that no-'count brother of yers always does. Run on outta here! I don't need any of ya!"

And then the old man swung his cane.

Will saw it coming but was so stunned that all he could do was make a half turn. The blow caught him on the shoulder, with enough force to knock him off balance and into the wall and utility hooks hanging on it. His cheek felt a sharp pain. He saw the cane go up in the air, and all he knew then was that he had to get hold of it.

"Dad! Dad, stop it!"

He caught the cane in midair. For several seconds he and the old man struggled for control of the knobby stick. Will jerked hard. The cane came free in his hand, and the old man stumbled backward, flailing his arms. One hand clawed at the corner of the glass-fronted cabinet, but then his veined hand slipped away, and he spun over to the wall.

There came a loud crack, and the old man went

down with a plop and a sharp cry of pain.

Will, gasping for breath, stood there staring in horror and thinking that he just might have killed his own father.

✍ 6

LONNIE STARR LIFTED Miss Edna's urn out of the front seat of the Galaxie. "The sun's got this thing hot—what is it?" he asked, turning it in his hand.

"Miss Edna's urn," Ruby Dee told him as she reached for the cardboard box containing her most precious possessions.

"You mean 'urn,' as in a dead person's ashes?"

She supposed he would be surprised. A lot of people would be.

"Uh-huh. Please don't drop it. Can you hold this bag, too?"

"You carry a dead person's ashes around with you?" He looked from the urn to her.

Putting a hand on her hip, she said, "I don't take it to the grocery store with me, if that's what you mean. I had it in the car with me to keep safe for the trip." She tilted the small box, showing him. "I like to keep all my precious things with me—Miss Edna's Bible, my favorite pictures . . . my nursing license. My Webster's dictionary isn't really valuable, but I can't do without it. I'd rather keep these things

53

in the car with me, because the camper could come unhooked and turn over or go into a ditch or something, and all my stuff would fly out. Clothes and linens and dishes can be replaced, but these things can't."

Lonnie Starr looked at the box and then at her. "Didn't you ever think that you could wreck the car and all this stuff would get lost that way?"

"I did once. Since I couldn't do anything about it, I didn't think of it anymore."

Lonnie Starr chuckled at that as he peered into the box. He asked who Miss Edna was, but before Ruby Dee could answer, the sound of shouts drew their attention. They each looked in the direction of the voices, which appeared to come from an old white-gray shack up behind the house. The place looked like it could once have been part of a house—it had the long, skinny windows of an old house, and several of the glass panes showed their age, with air bubbles and ripples—but had long ago been relegated to a storage shed. The actual words were indistinct, but Ruby Dee thought she recognized one of the voices as being Will Starr's, and boy, did he sound mad as could be.

"The chips have hit the fan," Lonnie said. Nonchalantly, he lifted the bag she had indicated, as if whatever the shouting was about didn't concern him . . . or as if he wasn't going to let it concern him.

She didn't think it polite to ask, but she certainly wondered what was going on, in the little shack as well as with Lonnie Starr. His merry hazel eyes had turned dark, rather like a dull mud puddle, even though his face remained as pleasant as ever.

"We'd better get your Miss Edna out of the sun," he said and turned for the house.

But he hadn't taken two steps when Will Starr hollered at them. In the doorway of the old shack, he motioned with his arm. It was obvious he meant come on the double.

Lonnie Starr murmured a curse and dropped the bag and Miss Edna back on the car seat and strode off toward his brother. Ruby Dee set her box of precious things beside the urn before running after him.

Will Starr and his daddy had argued and come to blows. Will Starr had a nasty puncture wound on his cheekbone, just below his eye. It would need stitches. He wiped the blood away with his sleeve, but succeeded only in smearing it.

His daddy, a stocky man with a shock of white hair, sat across the room, on the floor, his foot having gone through a rotten floorboard. Both men were white as starch, and as stiff, too, and the aura of hostility was thick as smoke from an oil fire.

Will Starr took his daddy beneath the arm on one side, and Lonnie grasped him on the other, and they got the older man up and out of the hole. The elder Starr immediately commanded his sons: "Leave be," and shook them off as he would flies. The next instant he promptly about fell over, because the ankle that had gone through the floor gave way. Will Starr caught him. His daddy said he was fine and blamed his almost falling on Lonnie Starr letting go so quickly.

"Gimme my cane."

But even with his cane, he couldn't manage more than two shuffled steps. He couldn't put weight on the foot that had gone through the floor, and he was awfully shaky, besides. His white face was now gray, with a red nose.

Will Starr said, "Dad, you've hurt that ankle.

Don't try to use it. Let's get you over to the door, where you can sit in the fresh air."

To which his daddy said, "Ever'thing on me's hurt, and fresh air ain't fixed it yet."

Lonnie Starr didn't say anything. He stepped through the door ahead of them, shoved his hands in his pockets and propped a boot and his back against the shack.

Will Starr got an old chair from the corner, set it just outside the doorway and helped his daddy into it. The older man braced himself hard on the arms of the chair, and Ruby Dee saw that his fingernails were long and unkempt, with blue showing underneath their yellowish color, and he was shaking like a leaf in a high wind. His blood-sugar level was no doubt soaring like a kite.

As he relaxed, he emitted a rush of breath. Ruby Dee was close enough to him to catch the hint of whiskey on it. Whiskey was poison for anyone with diabetes, not to mention an eighty-five year old man. Of course, it had been Ruby Dee's observation that most anything a person enjoyed was poison to a body after about fifty years of age.

"Well, Mr. Starr, we'd best take a look at that ankle," she said, crouching on the ground in front of him and reaching for the foot that had gone through the floor.

The man's hand came flying, as if to swat her, and she ducked. She had quick reflexes—had to, in her work.

"All of ya'all get away from me." The old man glared at her and then looked up at Will Starr. "Haven't you done enough? Leave me be." His tone was sharp as a knife blade.

Will Starr said tiredly, "We're gonna have to get

you to the hospital, Dad. Lon, go bring the truck over."

"I ain't goin' to no hospital," the elder Starr said.

"Of course not," Ruby Dee said, which caused Will Starr to frown at her, and his daddy to eye her. At least she had gotten their attention.

She was still crouched there, in front of the elder Mr. Starr. She met his gaze but kept her expression casual as could be, saying, "We need to see if your ankle is broken. Then you might want to go to the hospital, although I wouldn't advise touchin' anything there. It's been proven that a hospital is a very germy place. I might be able to tell if it's broken— your ankle—and I really need to look at it, because I can't just leave you here. You see, I'm a nurse, which means I am duty-bound to help hurt people. If word got out that I just left you—a patient in need—and didn't try to do what I could, well, they just might take away my license. And then what would I do? I have bills to pay. Besides, if we don't get this boot off your foot real quick, your foot or ankle might swell and the boot would have to be cut off, and you don't want to ruin a good pair of boots. Well, these are pretty old, but they just get good then, don't they? Nothin' better than boots at least ten years old, I always say. It takes that long to get them to fit a body's feet like a glove."

The whole time she was talking, Ruby Dee was removing his boot. The old man gave a little "Oh!" and the boot was in her hand. He wasn't wearing any socks. Quickly Ruby Dee felt for damage. His foot was puffy and warm, but she had expected that, what with his diabetes, and no socks, besides.

Almost spitting bullets, the old man jerked his foot

away. "I ain't a-goin' to the hospital. You boys get me in the house."

He reached for his boot, but Ruby Dee snatched it right out from under his grasp and straightened, saying, "You might as well just go on in and wait it out. Either it'll get better, or you'll be cryin' for somebody to take you to the hospital, probably in the middle of the night." She looked at Will Starr. "Y'all go on inside. I'll get my things and be there directly."

Will Starr looked like she had slapped him upside the head, but she paid him no attention. Pivoting, and carrying the old man's boot with her, she strode away toward her trailer.

Will stared after her. She strode firmly, her lean legs outlined by her dress, the hem fluttering with each step. He wondered if she was really that callous, or if she simply knew that the old man's condition wasn't serious enough to warrant a trip to the hospital. And he wondered, too, at her gall in directing him.

The old man said, "She took my durn boot," and that brought Will back to the situation.

"Let's get you inside, Dad. Lonnie, take his other side."

"Well, I ain't a-goin' to the hospital," the old man said, as if unaware no one was arguing with him. "You boys get me in the house. Ouch! Dang it, Lonnie, you ain't haulin' a sack of feed grain. There's nerves in that arm. I could'a managed to walk some, if I had my boot. You make sure you get my boot back, Will. That dadburn woman's a thief."

What Will would have said in that minute, had anyone asked, was that only one of Hardy Starr had ever been made. Here the old man had come close to cracking open the head of his own firstborn son and to crippling himself even more than he already was, and to a possible second stroke or a heart attack, but what concerned him most was the loss of a boot that looked as if it had been dragged behind a horse for a hundred miles. The old man always had stood guard over his possessions and been tighter than a pig's ass when it came to spending money.

By the time Will and Lonnie got the old man into his room and set down on his bed, he was breathing hard and not saying a word, never a good sign with him. He looked wrung out.

"You okay, Dad?" Will asked, feeling concerned.

"No, I ain't okay, but I don't see that talkin' about it does any good. Now, hush up and get my other boot off. Lonnie, fix them pillows so I can lean back. And get me somethin' to prop this dang foot on."

Will figured the old man wasn't going to keel over dead any minute—his meanness wouldn't allow him to. He'd just die straight up.

They got him settled back against pillows, with his injured ankle resting on a rolled-up cotton blanket. Will suggested getting him out of his clothes, but his daddy said he hadn't gotten out of his clothes in the middle of the day at home in his life, and he wasn't about to start now. "Such is for hospital folks."

Then he wanted his cane, even though he wasn't going anywhere, and Lonnie, intent on disappearing, quickly said he would go get it. Will was left at the foot of the bed, staring at the old man's shock of silver hair and remembering how that hair had swirled as the old man came at him with the cane. He felt sick.

Tenderly he fingered the cut on his cheekbone, felt

the dried blood and the swelling flesh. No doubt it didn't look good, but the old man hadn't shown any concern about it. Not one word; not so much as a glance. The sick feeling turned to anger. An anger that frightened him and made him a stranger to himself.

Then Miss D'Angelo came sweeping through the door, with her fluttering earrings and swaying walk, bearing a tray in her hands. "I brought one of your pain pills, Mr. Starr, and an ice pack. It'll help bring down that swellin'. I have some tomato juice, too. You seem like a tomato juice man."

The old man lifted his arm and pointed at the door. "Well, now, young lady, you can just get your wigglin' bottom right back out of this house. You've caused enough trouble. This is still my place, and I say what stays or goes, and you're goin'—you and your fancy bitch dog. Get on outta here!"

The last came out a roar that pushed the gal back a step.

The words echoed inside Will's brain. They were equivalent to the firing of a gun, sending the racing horses of fury up and out of him.

Gripping the turned footboard of the dark old bed, Will leaned forward and locked eyes with his father. "Yes, sir, this is *your* place. By God, you sure do own it, but right now you can't run it. Right now you can't get out of that bed, so whether you like it or not, *I'm in charge.*" He poked his chest with his finger and then pointed at the old man. "And I've got two choices for you: you can let this woman take care of you, or you can go into a nursing home and be taken care of there. It don't matter to me one iota which one you choose, either, but I damn sure know I'm not gonna be nursing you. And I'll tell you something more—once you get out of that bed and on your feet again, you can just see to the runnin' of every damn part of this place, and *I'll be out of here*."

Shoving himself away from the bed and the old man, he turned on the gal, saying, "You said you could handle him, Miss D'Angelo, so you just go ahead and have at it!"

Will stalked away from them and past Lonnie lurking in the hallway, the way he wished he could stalk away from his whole damn life.

As the echo of Will Starr's boots died on the wooden floor, Ruby Dee wished heartily that she hadn't witnessed what she had.

Her gaze met that of Lonnie Starr, who hesitated in the shadowy hallway, a pained expression on his face. Then she looked at the elderly Mr. Starr. The man's white hair stood on end. His expression was cold and hard; the bitterness emanating from him was strong enough for Ruby Dee to taste it.

It scared her a little. She had the distinct impression that if he could have gotten his hands around her neck, he would have strangled the life out of her. And he appeared strong.

"I'll just leave this for you," she said, her voice breaking as tears threatened.

It seemed a little foolish to think he would actually choke her, but she stayed out of his reach as she found a place for the juice and the pill on the cluttered nightstand, then quickly dropped the blue ice pack on the bed near his hand.

He sat stony-faced. A man clinging to his pride . . . and his misery. Her heart cracked open and poured out. She wanted badly to say something to ease him, but no doubt he would most appreciate being left alone. She had witnessed his humiliation by his son; now he would sooner die than speak with her.

As she passed through the door, the ice pack whizzed near her head and smashed into the doorframe to her right, at eye level. It fell to the floor with a thud.

Ruby Dee whirled, fire leaping to her tongue. But when she saw the elderly man's hand raise the glass of tomato juice, she grabbed the door. Just as she brought it closed, the glass crashed against it on the other side.

For a moment, trembling, Ruby Dee stood with her hand on the doorknob. Sally was cowering against the wall and gazing questioningly up at her. When she turned, she found Lonnie Starr standing in the dining room entry, his expression much the same as Sally's.

"Should I get back to bringing your things in?" he asked, raising an eyebrow and looking hopeful.

Ruby Dee thought about that, while he continued to look at her and wait.

Then she breathed deeply and said, "Yes. And start with the things in my refrigerator, so I can begin makin' supper."

There was nothing better than a good meal to soothe ragged tempers.

7

LONNIE HAD NEVER been bothered much by a woman's tears. Tears were simply a part of a woman, and he loved everything about women. Generally he was confronted by a woman's tears when he was leaving her, and he had learned how to handle that. He was so comforting that he always left a woman smiling through her tears.

But Lonnie had never seen a woman tune up and cry at a news blurb on the television, which was what Ruby Dee D'Angelo did. All she needed to hear was the announcement made at the commercial break during *Wheel of Fortune*—"Three people are known killed when a tornado touched down in a trailer park south of Wichita, Kansas"—and she had tears coming down her cheeks.

"Oh, my . . . oh, my." With a dish and a towel in hand, she sank down in the chair across the table from Lonnie. They had been watching the little television on the kitchen table. Mostly Lonnie had been watching Ruby Dee.

She wiped her cheeks. "I'm sorry . . . but I was in a tornado once. Have you ever been?"

"No. I've seen more than one but haven't ever been in any."

"Well, I was, when I was ten. Me and five other kids huddled in a room. The adults were in the closet, but there wasn't room for us kids, so they left us in that room. The tornado took the whole house— it wasn't very big—all except that room. When the tornado got done, we were still in a huddle, with the floor under us and no walls, and the closet blown to bits, too." She shut her mouth, got up and went to the sink.

Lonnie wondered whether the adults in the closet had lived, whether they had been her parents, and if they had been, how they had left her out in the room. But he didn't think she wanted to talk about it, and he really didn't, either. He'd had enough disturbance for one day. When the news was about to come on, he changed the channel to the *Andy Griffith Show*, which was on a channel without any news at all.

Lonnie was unsettled as it was, being caught between his natural aversion to contention and his natural attraction to females. Ruby Dee fascinated him.

She wore a June Cleaver apron and a brightly printed silk scarf wrapped in a turban around her head, saying it kept hair out of the food and cooking smoke out of her hair. None of it matched—the turban, the apron, the dress or the boots—but on her it all seemed to go together. She was the most exotic sight Lonnie had ever seen.

"Your daddy may be too angry to talk to me, but he's not too angry to eat my food," she said, coming into the kitchen with the old man's empty supper tray. Her little dog was right at her heels. It wasn't ever far from her.

"You did threaten him," Lonnie reminded her, although he was surprised the threat had worked. He figured that the old man had simply been more overcome by the good food than by the threat.

"Oh, he wasn't bothered by that. He knows he's got to eat if he's gonna stay out of a home—and if he's gonna drink that whiskey he's got hidden under his pillow."

"He's drinkin'?" That fact and the casual way she mentioned it threw Lonnie into confusion. "Shouldn't we get it away from him?"

She looked at him for a second, her eyes dark and quiet, and shook her head. "I don't think he has much left in that bottle, anyway." She bent over to load the dishwasher. "He's been drinking for many years, you know . . . and you can understand it when you see how stiff he is. He probably aches all the time."

She put a hand on her hip. "Besides, he's not a child or a fool. We are to care for him, but we are not to keep him. God does that."

Lonnie thought about that. Whether the old man was a fool or not was open to question, as was just how much God kept him. What wasn't open for question was Lonnie going in there and taking the bottle away from the old man—he wasn't going to do it.

"Do you think your brother would really put him in a home?" Ruby Dee asked, leaning back against the counter. She held a cherry tomato to her mouth and sucked on it.

"I don't know." Lonnie didn't want to talk about it. He didn't think he should tell her that he thought the old man ought to go into a home. He watched her eat another cherry tomato and wondered if she knew how sexy she looked doing it.

Then she said, "You better go see if he needs to go to the bathroom now. I add whole wheat flour to my cornbread, which gives it twice as much fiber, and I doubt he's used to that. And he sure needs to get washed and changed."

Lonnie was startled at the suggestion. He didn't like having anything at all to do with the old man, most especially anything that had to do with touching him. He didn't like the idea at all. Stuff like that was what Will did, and sitting here entertaining and admiring a woman was what Lonnie did.

But Ruby Dee fixed him with a look. "You have to. He needs help, and he won't let me touch him."

Lonnie was confused by her manner. He had not expected her to press him in any way. He didn't like being ordered but he didn't want any arguing, either. He'd had all the arguing he could stand. He stood, stretching. "I think I ought to go check on Will first." Maybe he could get Will to come in to see to the old man.

Lonnie stepped out the back door. The breeze had died, leaving the air still and warm and filled with heavy scents. The sun was setting in a ball of fire, late, the way it did on a summer night, and cast a golden glow over the house, barns and horses behind the weathered fences . . . and over Will, atop the ornery blue roan in the training pen.

He'd been there since he had stalked out of the house that afternoon. Now he was trotting the horse in circles. As Lonnie neared the pen, he saw the horse was lathered and Will's shirt and hat were soaked with sweat. But if either of them was tiring, it wasn't apparent. The stud's tail was still high and swishing, his ears were still back, and Will's muscles were still taut.

Lonnie climbed up on the rails, straddling the top one. He saw the cut on his brother's cheek was real swollen. Will didn't look at him, just kept the horse moving.

"Ruby Dee made a great supper—fried chicken and corn bread and beans. Apple pie, too."

Will stopped the stud, tugged on the hackamore reins and backed him up a step. "I smelled it. Where'd she get the chicken?"

"From her own refrigerator, in her camper. She's using a lot of her own groceries. Said she has to use 'em, or they'd spoil, you know."

Will pulled a cigarette from his pocket. It was bent, but he stuck it between his lips anyway. Will smoked those cigarettes bent half the time. "Did the old man eat?" he asked.

"She told him she was going to stuff it down his throat if he didn't. I don't know if it was that, or if it was just such dang good food, but the old man ate." Lonnie debated with himself, and then said, "She says he's drinkin' from a bottle hidden under his pillow."

Will looked at him a minute, then lit his smoke. Lonnie waited for him to comment about the old man's bottle, but he didn't.

Lonnie said, "She saved you a plate."

Will lifted the reins. "I'll be in later."

That irritated Lonnie. "What about the old man?"

Will bumped the horse's side and moved him at a slow walk. "I hired the gal to take care of him. And you're in there to give her a hand if she needs it, aren't you?"

"Yeah . . . I can give her a hand." The way Lonnie saw it, he'd been doing his part, and now Will ought to quit sulking and get in there and do his. "You gonna stay out here all night?"

"Might," Will said.

He bumped the roan faster. The horse humped his back and fought the hold Will had on his head. Then he managed to rear up. While he was up, Will stepped neatly out of the saddle to the ground, holding the reins and pulling that roan right over backward. It wasn't so good on a saddle, but such a maneuver did put a horse in his place. The trick for the man was to be able to step out of the saddle before he got the horse on top of him. Will did it better than most.

The horse scrambled to his feet and shied in a circle, but Will jumped back into the saddle, and they went at it again.

Men got themselves killed on stubborn horses like this one. Lonnie didn't know why Will was even messing with him. There were six other horses up at the horse barn that could use training, true quarter horses bred right there on the ranch and worth real money.

Lonnie said, "If you're gonna work all night, you'd better turn on the light out here. You're liable to have that horse fall back on you and squash you right to hell."

"I don't imagine light will keep that from happenin'," Will said in that distant manner that made Lonnie want to fly over and grab him by the throat.

He wanted to yell at Will that he didn't need him, but he knew that would betray how he really felt, and he wasn't about to do that. He clamped his jaw shut tight as Will's, climbed down off the fence and strode back to the house.

It all made Lonnie mad and more unsettled than ever. He wondered if Will was really going to leave, like he'd told the old man. Lonnie couldn't imagine that. But Will had never before threatened to leave. Never. And he sure was acting different than he ever had.

Lonnie wondered what he would do if Will did leave the ranch.

He came back into the kitchen. "Will said he'd be in later."

Ruby Dee nodded but didn't look at him. She was wiping the coffee maker.

"I guess I'll go check on the old man." He hoped she would tell him not to bother, but she just asked him if he wanted her to heat him up a cup of coffee before she poured it out. She didn't smile. She wasn't one for smiling a lot, but her voice had a warm, gentle sound.

"No . . . thanks just the same."

Lonnie went through the darkened house toward the old man's room, thinking how he had always made it a point to stay away from the old man. Helping him into the house that day was the first time he had touched the old man since he'd been a boy.

Suddenly he recalled the day his mother left. He had been five. That day he had come into the kitchen and found the old man crying, with Will patting his shoulder. For a moment, Lonnie had thought maybe the old man was having some sort of attack, because he wasn't making a sound, but his big chest was shaking. Oh, the old man had been big to Lonnie back then. Formidable. Why, Lonnie had once seen him take on a bull and knock the animal to the ground with one smack of a club. Now he sat, leaning heavily on the table, great, soundless sobs shaking his body.

Then the old man had wrapped an arm around Will and pulled Lonnie to him, too. Lonnie had started bawling. Will had started saying how they didn't need their mama anyway, and he patted Lonnie. Lonnie hadn't even been thinking of their mama; he'd been scared to death by the old man.

When he peeked into the bedroom, he thought at first that his dad was asleep. But then the old man raised his head and said, "I ain't dead yet, so you can quit flyin' over me like a lazy buzzard."

"I came in here to see if you needed or wanted anything," Lonnie said hotly. He might not have answered so smartly, but the old man was stove up in the bed, and Lonnie was a safe distance away.

"Aw . . . you ain't never cared what I might need or want. What—you tryin' to impress the hussy?"

"I sure didn't come in here because I wanted to. She sent me to see if you might need to get up and go to the bathroom. And there's no call to go insultin' her. She's not done anything but be good to you."

"Uhh! I'll tell you a few things, boy. . . ." He leaned forward. "I ain't noticed you havin' truck with no woman that ain't a hussy, and I can say whatever I want in my own house . . . and when the time comes that I need you or anybody else to get me to the bathroom, I'll blow my brains out."

Lonnie swallowed and made a fist. The old man looked at him with pure hatred, eyes glittering like he'd gone mad. A chill swept through Lonnie, because he knew the old man meant exactly what he said.

Then the old man, who hadn't wanted anything, said, "Before you go on back to your sparkin', get me your crutches we keep handy in the closet underneath the stairs."

"They'll be too tall for you," Lonnie said, bringing the crutches. He adjusted them the best he could.

Next the old man had him shift the roll underneath his hurt ankle and open the window.

"The air conditioning is on," Lonnie said and immediately wished he hadn't.

The old man barked that he didn't care one iota, he wanted the window open. "And go get me that pee bottle I got in the hospital the last time I was there."

Lonnie found the plastic bottle in the bathroom closet, brought it back and thrust it at him. "Is that all?"

"Get on back to that woman."

Back in the kitchen, Lonnie strode over to the back door. "He won't take any help," he said. He reached up and got the shotgun that hung above the door. It was the only gun left in the house. He grabbed the box of shells kept atop the refrigerator, took the shotgun and shells onto the back porch and stuck them in the cupboard behind an assortment of seldom-used household things. The old man would have to do some looking to find them.

Good God, Lonnie fervently hoped Will came back in soon.

Ruby Dee cast him a thoughtful look, but she didn't question him. He sure was glad, because he didn't want to think about any of it.

She had taken the turban off her head, and her

hair tumbled against her pale skin. Lonnie liked pale-skinned women.

She had the old man's stock of medicines in front of her on the table. She was reading the typed pages of instructions from the doctors and writing in a spiral notebook.

That wasn't exactly what Lonnie had hoped would happen; he'd been hoping she would talk with him. Instead she asked him questions about the old man.

"How long has he been taking this blood pressure medicine?"

"For a few years now. Is D'Angelo your maiden name?"

Her eyes lit on his for a second. "Yes." She looked at the vials. "The date on this arthritis prescription is only two months old. Has he been taking it as long as his blood pressure medicine?"

Lonnie couldn't say. He couldn't tell her much about the old man's health, because he had never paid much attention to it. He did tell her the old man had had his stroke back in February.

"Me and Will came back from checking the cows—they were calvin' then. Will found the old man passed out. He seemed okay after a few days, but the doctors said he'd had a stroke."

"Has he seemed confused once in a while since then?"

Lonnie shrugged. "He's old."

"He's eighty-five, but he's not so old." Her brown eyes rested on him, and Lonnie wondered what she meant, but he didn't want to ask and look stupid. Old was old, wasn't it? Eighty-five was old . . . the old man was old . . . what was she thinking?

"Your résumé says you're thirty," he said. "You don't hardly look it."

"I didn't lie."

"Oh, I didn't think you did. I didn't mean it like that. You just seem awfully young to be doin' this kind of work—takin' care of old people."

She kind of smiled and shot him a glance, but she didn't say anything to that.

He wanted to kiss her, but he imagined she would take offense. He sure didn't want to run her off.

Abruptly she closed her notebook and rose to put away the medicine. "It's time for me to take a bath and get to bed. I'm an early-to-bed person." She picked up the notebook and headed out of the room, but then she turned. "If there isn't anything else you need," she added, a questioning look on her face.

Lonnie could have told her about a lot of things he needed—erotic pictures flashed across his mind. And he thought that she could read his mind.

He shook his head and said no, he was fine. And then he watched her leave, with the dog trailing after her.

With a confusing disappointment settling heavily on him, he got a bottle of beer from the refrigerator. On his way up to his room, he glanced in at the old man, who had fallen asleep—or else was pretending to be. In his room, in the dark, he tugged off his boots, stretched out on the bed, propped against his pillow and leisurely drank his beer. He could look right through his doorway and across the dark hall to the bathroom door. Light shone through the crack beneath it, and he could hear the splashing of water as Ruby Dee D'Angelo dribbled it over her body—a bath, not a shower.

He imagined her in the tub, her auburn hair curling around her pale face. Her skin milky white all over. His groin warmed pleasurably, and he elaborated on the mental images. He waited to see her when she came out of the bathroom, and fantasized about her appearing in nothing but a towel.

But he fell asleep before she came out.

When Hardy opened his eyes, he saw Jooney standing in the doorway. "Jooney?" Good Lord, he was glad to see her! His leg was hurting near to killing him, and she would make it better. Then Jooney came forward, and with keen disappointment he saw it wasn't Jooney, but that hussy gal.

"It's me, Mr. Starr—Ruby Dee."

"I can see that! You caught me half-asleep." It could happen to anyone, coming out of a dream, but everybody thought he was losing his mind. Everybody was stupid.

He'd been dreaming about Jooney. And as he righted his glasses it startled him to realize how much like Jooney the hussy gal looked. He had noticed it before but passed it off. Now he looked more closely.

Jooney's hair had been that same reddish color, though longer. It had fallen in waves all the way down her back. The gal's eyes were very much the same, though, dark like coffee beans, and her skin was pale as buttermilk. And, by God, she was wearing a gown like Jooney would wear—a white gown that covered her from her neck to her toes, which were bare and peeking out beneath the bottom stretch of lace. He could see the dark shadows of her breasts through the fabric.

Jooney's laugh came to him. She would laugh and tease him when he'd gone to feeling her breasts.

He blinked. It irritated him, that this girl could look so much like Jooney. Jooney had been special.

"What do you want?" he demanded.

"I heard you moanin' and talking. Is your ankle hurtin', Mr. Starr?"

"Aw, everythin' on me hurts. I'm eighty-five."

His leg, that blamed bum knee and that blamed ankle, ached like the dickens. That was why he was dreaming so silly, about Jooney. Dreaming of the accident that had ruined his leg forever, back that time he and Jooney had been riding the river, and that crazy horse had gone down with him and broke his leg. Jooney had splinted the leg right there. He'd bitten the tip of his tongue off in order to keep from crying in front of her. In his dream, though, he'd been calling for Jooney to come help him, and he'd heard her calling back, but she hadn't come.

The gal disappeared, and Hardy was just about to reach for the bottle of whiskey behind his pillow, when she returned with her arms full.

"You can't have any more of your pain pills, but I brought you some aspirin." She took what she had in her arms and put it on the chair, then brought him three aspirin and a glass of water. "If you'll let me, I can make your ankle and that bad knee feel better."

He stared at his foot, refusing to invite her to do anything at all, wanting Jooney and to be young again.

The gal turned to leave.

"Wait a minute. . . . I thought you was gonna do somethin' to my leg."

"Do you want me to?"

He wasn't about to say he did.

He said, "Isn't fixin' me what you're bein' paid to

do?'' He figured he had her with that one.

She looked at him for a minute, then reached for her things and went around the bed to sit near his hurt ankle. She moved his leg over to her, and he told her to be careful. She rolled up his pants leg. His ankle was quite a sight, all swollen like a melon, but then, his feet and ankles sometimes swelled these days—Mother Nature's tricks to make his life hell, as he saw it.

The gal poured something from the bottle into her palm, and then rubbed it gently on his ankle.

"What in the hell is that?" It was oily and thick as snot.

"Castor oil, and I'd appreciate it if you didn't swear."

Hardy started. That was what Jooney had said to him. She had made him watch his mouth and had read the Bible to him, too. He stared at the gal's hands, small, young hands. A chill came over him. He studied the gal, the curve of her cheek and the wisps of hair that curled to her shoulders. Thoughts of Jooney came so strong that he felt off-kilter, as if he were lost somewhere in time.

"It's an old remedy," she said, keeping her eyes on what she was doing. "Your mama might have used it. Lots of people discount it now, but in ancient times castor bean plant was called the Palm of Christ, because it was believed to have healing properties."

"We used it to get rid of moles and warts," Hardy said. Jooney had used it to take warts off his hand, and it had worked. "There ain't no warts on my ankle."

"It will soak in and help the sprain." She glanced up at him. "Who was Jooney?"

"She was a gal I knew a long time back," he answered, not knowing why he should. So he added, "And it ain't none of yer bizness, is it?"

The gal looked at him, her eyes all warm and liquid. Her eyes were so much like Jooney's. It unnerved him, and what was worse, he thought he might cry.

He said, "Now, are you 'bout through?"

She said she would do his knee, too, if he wanted. He told her to suit herself. She did his knee, rubbing that oily stuff on it and binding it up with an ace bandage. He jumped when her hand first touched him. He felt embarrassed about her touching his bare skin like that, but the ache began to ease with her massaging. He thought of telling her to stop but couldn't get the words out of his mouth. So he settled for pretending to fall asleep, hiding himself with his eyes closed. She said something to him, but he didn't answer. A few minutes later, he felt the bed move as she got up, heard her gathering her things to leave. There wasn't anything wrong with his hearing, not like with his eyesight. He heard her bare feet patter across the floor and head up the stairs.

He was left there thinking about Jooney. And he didn't have enough whiskey to drown the thoughts. He wondered if he could think himself dead and set out to give it a try.

Ruby Dee knew good and well that Hardy Starr was awake. His trick wasn't anything new to anybody. Ruby Dee herself had employed it when she didn't want to face up to something.

Sally was waiting in the hallway. She got up and followed Ruby Dee up the stairs, hopped up on the bed, made a circle and lay down. Ruby Dee wiped

her hands with a cloth and replaced her bottle of
castor oil into her medical box. Confident that Hardy
Starr would sleep more comfortably now, she closed
her door.

The room was already a lot prettier, more welcoming as a place of her own. It hadn't taken much to
make it so. Ruby Dee's own pillows with lace-edged
cases were on the bed—four of them. Ruby Dee
could hardly sleep with fewer than four feather pillows. She had run an oiled rag over the dresser and
placed Miss Edna's urn and Bible and the framed
photographs of her mother and father there, along
with her small jewel box and the Webster's
dictionary that Miss Edna had bought for her. It had
a zippered genuine leather covering. Atop the
dictionary was the paper of pasted cut-outs, which
she'd unfolded and straightened as best she could.

The room was lit with a warm, coral glow, because she had draped a red printed scarf over the
bedside lamp. Ever since reading that lighting tip in
a woman's magazine, Ruby Dee had followed it.

Once, however, a scarf she had draped over a
lamp had caught on fire. Ruby Dee had thrown a
glass of ice tea on it, which dampened the fire but
caused the light bulb to explode. For a week she had
found glass splinters and sticky spots from the sugar
in the tea all over the lamp base, the table, the wall
and the floor. Not wanting to repeat that disaster,
she had never again tossed a scarf over a small lamp.
This particular lamp being enormous, with plenty of
space between the shade and the bulb, she considered it safe.

The room was a little stuffy, so she opened the
window. It was stiff, and she had to tug hard, but
then it suddenly flew upward quickly, startling her.

The fragrant summer air came through the screen, and Ruby Dee breathed deeply. Cicadas were kicking up a ruckus in the trees and bushes, and birds were calling, too—a chuck-will's-widow far out in the trees, she guessed. The sky was bright with diamond stars. The moon was a half curve and bright. It was amazing that only half a moon could light so much—it lit the leaves of the big elm in the backyard, the roofs of all the buildings, the white pipe fencing, even the wooden fencing.

She saw a figure then, out in the small pen, way over to the side. It was so far over that she could see it well only with her head just about resting on the screen.

It was Will Starr, and he was still on that horse. He was just sitting there on it, in the middle of the pen. Bathed in the moonlight, both of them, man and horse, looked like ghosts. The horse's tail swished once, twice. The animal blew through his nose, and the sound came all the way up to her.

Will Starr's hat came up slightly. After a moment, Ruby Dee realized he was looking at the house. Ruby Dee had the feeling that he looked at her window. Looked right at her.

She went very still. He couldn't clearly see her, not in the muted glow of the lamp, but she believed that he was looking at her, just as she was looking at him. Ruby Dee knew this clear and strong in that moment, when she continued to look at him and remember his intense blue-gray eyes, and the way he had looked at her that afternoon.

Then she pulled back inside the room. Leaving the window open, she slipped into bed and turned out the lamp. After she got settled, she could still hear the night sounds coming through the window, among them the thudding of the horse's hooves way out in the pen.

She wondered if Will Starr was going to stay out there all night.

Will sat the horse, quiet now, worn out. Up above, the stars twinkled like glitter and a bright half moon was on the rise. Over at the house the light was on above the kitchen sink. Lonnie's window was dark. There had been a faint glow from the gal's room, but it was dark now, too. The old man's window was on the opposite side of the house, and Will couldn't see it.

Will had told Lonnie that he might stay out in the pen all night just to get Lonnie's goat, and because he had been gripped by the rare euphoria of recklessness. Recklessness had been his refuge. He had wanted to run clear away from the ranch and the old man and Lonnie, but he hadn't been able to, so he'd run off into recklessness, and damn, it had felt good.

But when a man has lived a life of responsibility for forty-two years, it's hard for recklessness to get much of a foothold. At around midnight the recklessness faded, leaving him high and dry.

He started to feel bad about the way he had talked to the old man, and to worry about him, too. Maybe the old man needed something, and Lonnie wasn't any good at seeing to it. Will believed the gal should be good at seeing to it, but he didn't know for sure. He also worried that the old man might have another stroke. He wanted to go up to the house to check everything out—and to have the meal Lonnie had talked of, and take a shower.

But he didn't want to step back into any of it. He

felt like he just couldn't take anymore, and he was afraid that by now the gal would have had her fill of the old man, and if he went up to the house, she would be ready to leave.

He pulled the saddle off the roan and set it on the ground, then threw the saddle blanket over the fence rail to dry. The scent of sweat and dust was familiar, even comforting. Gingerly, his legs stiff, he crouched beside the saddle to have his last cigarette. The colt didn't move off but stretched his neck and sniffed the cigarette. Will broke off the tip end and gave the tobacco to the horse.

What he'd said to the old man played through his mind. He'd told him he would send him to a home, but that had been anger talking. Still, no matter how much he didn't want to do it, if Miss D'Angelo didn't work out, he knew he'd probably have to, because he just couldn't take care of him.

He'd also said he would be leaving.

That stood out in his mind. He'd been thinking about leaving for some time now ... for years, he guessed, but these last months, the prospect had been tugging at him. He'd even checked out places to buy and lease.

It tore him apart to think about leaving this place; made his throat get all tight so he could hardly swallow. But the fact remained that he didn't want to go on with the ranch the way he had been. No, he couldn't continue like this.

The desire for something all his own burned inside him. He wanted a home of his own, and a family, too, as farfetched as that was beginning to seem. He was forty-two and not married, and the one woman he'd thought he might marry had married someone else. The years were ticking away. If he didn't get something of his own now, he'd soon be too old.

He raised his eyes to the gal's window. He wondered if she was asleep. Wondered if she slept in a gown, or in the nude. Wondered if she was very experienced with sex. She'd pretty well said she didn't want anything to do with a man.

The sexual thoughts he kept having about her rather startled him. He hadn't had such thoughts in a long time.

With a deep sigh, Will slid to the ground, propped his back against the saddle and stretched out a leg. Feelings he didn't understand—didn't care to understand, by damn—twisted like a cyclone inside him.

But the sand was cool now and quite comfortable. In the distance he heard coyotes calling, and the sounds of critters filled the air. The country could be a noisy place, but it all lulled him to sleep.

☙ 8

FROM A HABIT of long standing, Ruby Dee awoke
before dawn. She got up and hurried to wash
and dress and go downstairs. Activity gave her
mind something to think about, instead of how lonesome she was. And she wanted to prove to Will Starr
that she was good at what she did. She wanted to
make him glad he had hired her.

Then she might just quit on him, she thought
righteously and laughing to herself, sweetly feeling
God laughing with her, too.

"Come on, Sally . . . you need to go outside."

Casting her a mildly reproachful look, the dog
slowly rose and followed.

The men's bedroom doors were open. She
couldn't tell in the dimness if they were in their
rooms, and she resisted the impulse to peer into Will
Starr's bedroom. She certainly didn't want him to
see her doing that.

All was quiet, except for Hardy Starr's robust
snoring—he was most definitely in his room. By just
the glow from the light above the kitchen sink, Ruby
Dee and Sally made their way through the house.

Ruby Dee let Sally out into the fresh morning, turned on the coffee maker and then switched off the light, so she could look out the window. The eastern horizon was just turning rosy, the dark of night lifted enough to allow her to see the buildings and outlines of fences. Stars were still visible in the clear sky.

"Good mornin', Miss Edna. . . . Where are you?" she whispered.

"Watchin' the sun come up. There's a good view from up here."

"I guess I'm happy for you," Ruby Dee murmured, not feeling happy at all.

Talking to Miss Edna didn't seem to help much this morning. She hugged herself, rubbing her arms hard.

Ruby Dee guessed she would have this scared, lonesome feeling for all of her life. One of the times her daddy had gone off and left her had been at dawn. At the Tulsa bus station. Her daddy had driven there when it was still dark, and he had sat her in a row of chairs, while he went to find a friend. But he hadn't come back. She had only been four, but she could still remember sitting there, her feet dangling, seeing the sun come peeking through the windows, while a pinched-faced lady hollered at her for crying. A policeman took her down to the police station, and that was where her daddy had come to get her. He'd forgotten her, and only remembered her when he was halfway to Ponca City. To this day, Ruby Dee couldn't go into a bus station.

Miss Edna had always found humor in this story, because she said it showed how strong Ruby Dee was to have survived the adversities of her youth.

Miss Edna could find something good in a person drowning in mud.

A movement caught Ruby Dee's eye—Sally running into the horse-training pen. She was wagging her tail in greeting at someone.

Why, it was Will Starr . . . straightening and dusting himself off. Ruby Dee stared, shifting herself around to accept the idea that he had actually been out there all night. His anger had been that deep.

Sally received a touch and then she was off, running across the pen and out of it. Will Starr banged his hat against his thigh. He moved as if he were stiff as a board, which of course he would be, having foolishly stayed out there all night. Ruby Dee turned from the window, stood with her hands braced on the counter.

Well.

In quick motion, she got two mugs and filled them with coffee, added a bit of honey to her own and then, on a second thought, put some in Will Starr's cup. A man who had slept on the hard ground all night would surely need a little sweetening. Carrying the two mugs, she headed out the back door.

The cicadas in the bushes and trees were loud, calling up another hot summer day. They stopped their racket when the screen door slammed. The morning air was fresh and cool on her face as Ruby Dee strode across the sloping lawn and gravel drive. Will Starr's head came around, and then slowly his whole body followed. His gaze straight upon her, he walked to meet her at the fence rails. If he was surprised, he had covered it by the time she reached him and could clearly see his face.

He looked like a fighting rooster who had lost and been abandoned alongside the road. His hair stuck up, and his cheeks were shadowed by a beard and dirt. The wound high on his cheek was an angry purple and swollen like a goose egg. Though his eyes seemed sunk deeply into their sockets, they were sharp, luminous pinpoints.

"Good mornin'," she said and stuck his cup through the fence rail.

"'Mornin'." His voice came low and gravelly.

He hooked his hat on a fence post and reached to take the cup. Then he lifted it to his lips and took a deep swallow, while Ruby Dee watched in wonder, because the coffee was steaming hot.

She said, "I hope you like it with honey," which was really a silly thing to say, because if he could drink coffee that hot, he wasn't going to be bothered by a little sweetening. Tough, she thought. He was tough.

"Fine."

He drank again, and she watched, thinking that he couldn't possibly taste the coffee at all. It could as well have been swamp water she gave him.

Then his steely eyes focused on her, settled on her like a light beam. "You wouldn't happen to have a cigarette on you, would you?"

She shook her head. "I don't smoke."

He eyed her and said tiredly, "No, I didn't imagine that you did." Raking a hand through his hair, he leaned against the fence rail and turned to look at the horse.

Holding her coffee carefully, Ruby Dee climbed up on the bottom rail, in order to lean upon the top one. "It is amazin' that days so hot can start out so cool."

Will Starr gave a little grunt.

Ruby Dee sipped her coffee, and her gaze fell on

his saddle, which lay in the sand. "That doesn't look like such a comfortable bed."

He said flatly, "May've been hard, but it was peaceful."

Their eyes met, and then his shifted away. She looked for a moment at his tousled dark hair. Thick hair. Warm and lush-looking. Her hands had the urge to reach out and touch it, pull his head to her and run her cheek over its softness.

Well, goodness! Silliness could sure take hold of a person. Firmly, she turned her eyes in the direction he did—to the horse. The animal appeared as battered and worn as the man. Tough, too.

She said, "I suppose you've been told that horse isn't very pretty."

"He's a wild mustang," he said, as if that explained it all.

"He has a chest on him . . . and he has good, strong legs." She was trying to look at the horse in a positive light.

"He'll go the distance and have some left over."

"Only if he has good feet." She looked down, to see him looking up at her.

"What would a city girl know about horses' feet?"

"I never said I was a city girl."

He stared at her, and she stared at him. Something sparked between them, quickly, flying away yet leaving the feeling lingering.

She said, "I've lived off and on in the city, but I happen to have been born right over alongside Highway 283." She gestured with her cup. "I was a bit of a surprise, comin' a month early. Daddy was on his way to a rodeo at Cheyenne. I came so quick, there wasn't time to get to the hospital. . . . Mama and Daddy wouldn't have had the money, anyway."

She sipped her coffee and gazed off at the land. "My daddy was a bronc rider, and we went to a lot of small country rodeos. I was on a horse before I could walk, and I spent a lot of my childhood at country homes with farm animals—horses, cows, goats."

She looked at him again. "One reason I took the job when Maggie Parsons called me was that I wanted to see where I was born. I didn't know the exact place, of course, but I just looked at all the highway to the south of town and got a feel for how it would have been. It's really pretty out this way, isn't it?"

"There's some that think it's just barren."

"It isn't barren, it's"—she thought and then spoke with satisfaction—"spacious. You can see the sky so clear. It's like there's more of heaven, and there's nothing to crowd out a person's prayers."

Will looked at her. She was dead earnest and gazing up at the sky. Will looked upward too. He had never been quite certain there was a heaven, mostly because if he had been, he would have had to be certain about hell, and he didn't like the idea of that. He had committed too many sins to like the idea. He mostly didn't think about it, because then he had to think about what would happen when he died, and the way he saw it, he was struggling enough just to live.

He looked back at the gal. She leaned on the rail, sipping her coffee out of the mug she held with both hands. Fingers long and slender, bright rose fingernails. Earrings, small silver feathers, dangled from her ears. She had on a dress this morning, too, like the one from the day before, made of a light, flowery fabric that flowed and fluttered over her body, and those red boots. He didn't think he had ever seen a woman wearing a dress like that and climbing up on a fence rail. Of course, he couldn't say he had seen everything in this world.

Her gaze came swinging down to him. "Have you ever heard of my daddy—Jaime D'Angelo? He used to ride both saddle and bareback broncs and did pretty well."

Will knew the type of man her daddy would have been—the kind who was addicted to the rodeo, who never could leave it, and just went further and further down. He'd seen lots of men like that; Lonnie might have been one, had he not had the ranch to fall back on.

Will shook his head. "I only did some high school rodeo. Lonnie might know of him, though. He's the rodeo rider and winner."

She gave a little shrug, and a heavy, sad look came over her face as she took a drink of coffee. "It was a silly question anyway. It was twenty years ago, when Daddy was doin' well in the rodeo. I just asked you about him on an off-chance. You know how odd coincidences can happen."

Will felt very awkward. She had told him some personal stuff and now she was sad, so sad she was near to crying, he saw, slipping a furtive glance at her. The prospect of any sort of crying unnerved him. It made him feel as he would if a bull came after him in the middle of a pasture.

He downed the rest of the coffee, and then he thought to tell her how good it was. "I appreciate the coffee, Miss D'Angelo. I don't think I've tasted better."

It relieved him to see pleasure come into her eyes. Every emotion the gal had came right out her eyes, and she was fairly bursting with emotion.

"Don't you think you should call me Ruby Dee?
I mean, if you go on callin' me Miss D'Angelo, I'm
gonna have to keep callin' you Mr. Starr, and there
are three of you Mr. Starrs. That's gonna get awfully
confusing. Maybe I could call you Mr. Will."

He gazed at her, studying her eyes. She sure
sounded like she was staying.

"You can call me Will, no Mr. needed."

"Well, please call me Ruby Dee, not just Ruby.
Ruby Dee is my name."

Will rubbed at his mustache, feeling both relief
and a strange apprehension. He wished he could
conjure up some wild recklessness to lose himself in
again, but apparently he had sapped that well dry
the night before.

"How did the old man do last night?" he asked,
reaching for his hat and brushing sand from it.

"He ate well, and that helped get his body back
on even keel—helped him tolerate that whiskey he
was sippin'. He had some pain, but he finally let me
rub a tonic on his ankle and that bad knee of his and
bind them up. He was snoring his head off when I
came down this mornin'."

Will was surprised that the old man had let her
do anything. He didn't like to be touched. "You still
think his ankle is just sprained?"

"I believe so, although I could just as well be
wrong. But even if it is a fracture or a torn ligament,
racin' right down to the doctor and puttin' up with
all they'd do to him can wait. Let him have a few
days to rest up, eat well and settle down."

Will slowly put on his hat. "That all makes good
sense to me, ma'am, but I'd advise you not to hold
your breath, waitin' for my father to settle down."

Their gazes held again for brief seconds . . . her eyes so dark and steaming and staring right back at him. Then he gestured at the horse—"I need to put him to pasture"—and started walking off.

She called after him, "Your daddy might not need to see a doctor, but you do. You need to have that cut stitched. I can do it, if you'd rather not drive in to the doctor, but I don't have anything to numb it."

He stopped, gingerly fingering the wound. The tenderest touch made him wince, but he said, "Thanks just the same, but I'll just clean it and leave it be."

She frowned. "It's gonna scar."

"I never did make a livin' with my face."

She gazed at him for a moment with those dark eyes. Then she climbed down from the fence, a flash of bare leg showing clear to her thigh.

"I'll be fryin' up that bit of ham I saw in your refrigerator and makin' biscuits and eggs." She scooped his empty coffee mug off the fence rail, turned and headed back up the slope and across the drive. Her stride was long and free; her hair and the hem of her dress swung easy. The collie came running up to her, and she bent to pet it, before swinging on in that breezy manner.

Will, his body stiff as a corpse, crossed the pen and let the horse out into the adjoining, high-fenced pasture. The horse loped away, head high, mane and tail flowing. Will stood there a moment, watching. The roan, so scruffy and poor-looking a moment before, had become a grand sight, with all his muscles moving in powerful rhythm. That was because a horse was designed to run, Will thought, giving brief consideration to what man was designed to do. He couldn't come up with anything in particular.

He gazed out at the pastures and the land rolling away. The sun hadn't shone yet, but the sky was bright yellow to the east. Days started so beautifully, he thought, but ended up just hot and sweaty. That was his life, one hot and sweaty day coming after another. The thought made him depressed.

He looked up at the house and thought he saw Ruby Dee D'Angelo's shadow at the window.

He shut the gate, turned back and hauled his saddle out of the pen and rested it atop the hitching rail. He headed to the house by way of his pickup, where he took four cigarettes, stuck them in his shirt pocket and stood there to smoke one. His movements were easier now, and he suddenly anticipated a good breakfast. He wasn't going to speak to the old man before he had it, either, because he didn't want his enjoyment of breakfast spoiled.

He was crossing the gravel driveway when Wildcat Burns's faded blue pickup came rattling up the drive. Will's stomach tightened. If he had had a gun, he would have shot at Wildcat and sent him right back down the drive.

"Mornin', boss." Wildcat unfolded himself out of his truck. "Got visitors?" He nodded his head in the direction of the convertible and camper, which Lonnie had pulled up near the tractor barn.

"Sort of," Will said and left it at that.

Wildcat hurried to catch up to him. "You look like you already got throwed this mornin'. The sun ain't even full up." He frowned, apparently giving great thought to these two facts.

"No, it ain't," Will said. "Why are you here so early?"

"Oh, Charlene stayed up all night watchin' some romantic movies, and she got to pesterin' me this mornin'." He had the nerve to look forlorn about it. "I just wadn't up to anything like she saw in those movies. She got put out with me, and wouldn't make any coffee. I figured I might as well come out here and have coffee with y'all."

Will had always wondered if Wildcat made up these stories about Charlene's abundant sexual desires. But the stories had to be believed, simply because Wildcat was incapable of making up lies of any sort. And whenever Charlene was with Wildcat, she had a kind of hot gleam in her eye and kept putting her pudgy hands all over him. It was amazing. Charlene was hitting fifty, was plain and round as a paper plate, and Wildcat was ahead of fifty, lean and leathery as mule hide.

What happened to your face?" Wildcat asked.

"I ran into a wall," Will said and then clamped his mouth shut. He saw no good in conversing with Wildcat at this point.

Wildcat didn't need others to make conversation. He gave his opinion that the wound was nasty and recommended putting Bag Balm on it.

The warm aroma of coffee came out of the house even before they'd reached it, and when Will entered the porch, he found the back door open. Ruby Dee D'Angelo stood at the kitchen counter, humming and swishing her slim backside to a country tune he recognized but couldn't place. Hearing footsteps, she swung around. She had wrapped a red scarf over her hair and put on a bright yellow checked apron. Those feather earrings dangled from her ears. Will figured it safe to say that she was not a sight he had ever imagined seeing in his kitchen.

Then Wildcat's breath whooshed at his shoulder.

Will stepped forward and pulled off his hat. "Miss

D'Angelo . . . Ruby Dee, this is Wildcat Burns. He's our top hand. Wildcat, this is Miss D'Angelo, our new housekeeper."

She bestowed her fleeting, warm-as-sunshine smile upon them both and stuck her hand out to Wildcat, then jerked it back. "I'm sorry, my hands are all full of biscuits," she said, her voice vibrating with husky laughter.

Wildcat's eyes were just about bugging out. He bobbed his head at her and said something about his hands being too rough for shaking. He did think to snatch his hat from his head.

Will tossed his hat on a chair and went straight for the coffee. He caught a sweet scent as he passed Ruby Dee. A woman scent.

He poured two mugs of coffee and gave one to Wildcat, saying, "You can go on and get started feedin' the stock."

Being dense as a fence post, Wildcat said, "I ain't had no breakfast yet. . . . I'd sure like a couple biscuits, if you're gonna have enough, ma'am."

She said there would be plenty, and Wildcat slid himself into a chair at the table. After a minute, the little television on the table drew his attention. He reached over and turned it on, tuning in the early morning farm and ranch report. They were giving the weather. Wildcat was an avid weather-news watcher.

With a deep sigh, Will leaned his backside against the counter and sipped his coffee. The woman made the best coffee he had ever tasted. He looked at the coffee maker, wondering if it was the same one he used every morning. It was, and that seemed awfully strange. There was a woman in the kitchen, and it seemed everything had changed.

His gaze reached her and stopped. He watched her arranging the plump biscuit dough in two oiled iron skillets. He watched the way her flour-coated fingers moved, lightly and nimbly. He wondered what their touch would feel like.

She opened the oven door, bent to slip the skillets inside. Will found himself looking at her neatly curved bottom, covered by the thin fabric of her dress . . . and maybe panties, but he wouldn't bet on it. He had the urge to reach out and cup her bottom.

He averted his gaze, and saw the little dog looking up at him with an accusing eye, just like it knew what Will had been thinking.

"You sure you won't let me tend to that cut now?" Ruby Dee asked, startling him. She was rinsing her hands. "It's tryin' to get infected."

"It's not so bad. . . . I've had worse." The idea of her getting close enough to touch him made him a little panicky. He set his empty cup on the counter. "I'm gonna get a shower. I'll take two of those eggs, hard-cooked, when I come back."

He strode through the house. He didn't so much as look in the old man's room but took the stairs two at a time.

At the top, he chanced to glance into Ruby Dee's room, and that glance caused him to stop. He felt like a peeping tom, but he peered in anyway. Then he stepped inside and looked around.

A nightgown hung over the footboard of the bed . . . white, with lace at the bottom. Pillows were piled at the head of the bed, covered with cases of lilac and pink, with lace edges. A red-fringed scarf was thrown over the shade of the bedside lamp, and scarves hung from either side of the window shade. They didn't match. On the dresser top were squeezed a portable radio, a couple of books, some framed photographs, and a gray-and-gold vase of some kind. An odd-looking thing.

He moved closer and peered at the photographs—one of a man and woman, looked like it was on their wedding day; another smaller one of an old lady with a gardenia pinned on her dress.

Then there was a piece of paper lying on the books, pasted up with a bunch of cut-out magazine pictures, not cut in squares but right around the outline of the figures.

His eyes roamed the room and returned to this paper, and he thought: in just a few hours, the woman had infused the room. It was jarring. He wasn't certain he liked it. It made him wonder who she was, what she was about. What could happen to all of them, with her there?

He wanted her there, powerfully. He liked the way she made him feel . . . potent feelings that reminded him that he was a man, and made to mate with a woman . . . feelings he'd begun to believe had died. She fascinated him and she scared him, the same as a meteor landing in the pasture would.

Turning from the room and the confusion tugging at him, Will strode down the landing to Lonnie's room. His bedroom door was open, but he was still asleep on the bed, burrowed face down and still fully dressed. Lonnie hated mornings; if he had his way, he wouldn't get out of bed until noon.

"Get up, Lon." Will nudged the bed. Lonnie opened his eyes and blinked groggily. "Get up, Lon. . . . There's a woman in the kitchen."

That brought Lonnie straight up and grinning.

Will turned and went on into the bathroom, shucking his shirt as he walked. The first thing he noticed was the pink bottle of lotion on the shelf beside the sink. He stared at that, and then he was looking at his reflection in the mirror.

He peered closer, touched his fingertips to the wound just below his eye. Damn! Touching it set it to throbbing. It was an ugly thing, all swollen, purple and scabbed over, and he darn near had a black eye.

He saw something else unsettling in that mirror, too.

Will stared at himself. The man looking back at him was a man he didn't recognize at all. And so was the man he was seeing inside. *He didn't know who he was at all.*

Then he was only seeing Lonnie's foolish face, as his brother came bursting in and demanding to use the sink to shave before going downstairs. Lonnie didn't realize how close he came to Will drowning him.

As Will came down the stairs, he considered how he could slip past the old man's room without being seen. There wasn't any way, of course. He had never been a man who slipped around on tiptoe, and he wasn't about to start. And he might as well speak to the old man, because he was going to have to do it sooner or later. He would rather it be later, after he'd had a good breakfast. The smell of it coming from the kitchen had his stomach ready. He hoped the old man would still be asleep; he slept later and later these days.

That hope was squashed when the old man called to him. There wasn't anything else to do but go in and see him.

"I got somethin' to say to you, and I want to do

it standin'," the old man said, struggling to get himself up on Lonnie's crutches.

Will didn't want to, but he helped the old man straighten up. It hurt him that his dad was such a pitiful sight . . . tobacco stains on his shirt, pants leg rolled up, showing his bandaged joints and white leg. There was stale whiskey on his breath.

Then the two looked at each other. Will wondered if the old man would say he was sorry about the cut on Will's cheek.

He looked at it for a second, but what he said was, "We'll do it your way. I'll have the gal here, 'cause I don't have no choice. The only old-folks home I'm ever goin' to is the Starr plot over in White Rose cemetery. I always figured you knew that."

Will, pressed on by anger, replied, "And I always figured you knew that I wasn't after takin' this place from you. I don't want anything but what's my due." That wasn't really the way it was, but he didn't think he could explain it all to the old man. He didn't *want* to explain.

"You get a damn good salary, and the Starr to run. That would be enough for 'most any man."

"I guess I'm not just any man," Will said, clenching his fists. "I'm a rancher, same as you."

Maybe a part of Will expected the old man to say that this place was Will's, too. That he had earned his share of it and that the old man was proud to be partners with him.

The old man said, "You still aimin' to leave here?"

"Yes, sir," Will answered. "And I figure half the stock that come out of Big Bubba as mine, since I bought that bull with my own money. Do you have a problem with that?"

The old man jutted his chin. "I don't guess it would matter one way or the other if I did."

Will wanted him to have a problem with it. He wanted to go at it with the old man, because he wanted a different ending to this tune. Frustration had him by the throat. It was damned unsettling to realize he was thinking of socking the old man, who wasn't only his father but a stove-up old coot.

Clamping his jaw shut and keeping his hands at his side, Will strode from the room.

He'd said it now, straight out, he thought. He was leaving. There wasn't any taking it back.

And now his whole breakfast had been ruined.

"Let's go," Will said, striding into the kitchen. "We got a lot to do today."

Wildcat and Lonnie looked up in surprise. Lonnie had sense enough to keep quiet and get on his feet. But Wildcat said, "I ain't finished my eggs yet."

"Bring them along then," Will said. He stopped beside the table—Ruby Dee D'Angelo had set a full table, complete with napkins and a pitcher of orange juice—and grabbed two biscuits, broke them open and stuffed a bit of ham inside each. He held the biscuits in one hand, jammed his hat on his head with the other and then grabbed hold of Wildcat and urged him out the door.

Ruby Dee D'Angelo stood in the middle of the kitchen, steaming coffee pot in hand. The last thing Will looked at was her coffee-brown eyes. He felt them on him as he went out the door.

He was sweating again.

9

WHEN THE MEN drove off for the day, Ruby Dee was in the backyard, feeding the birds the remaining biscuits. Actually, she crumbled them and threw the pieces on the ground, while the birds, watching from the power line and the trees, waited for her to finish. Ruby Dee had been hoping to feed the chickens, but the Starrs didn't have any chickens. They had a big, wild barn cat that terrified Sally. There were a few horses in pens, and some cattle, too, in a fenced pasture to the west. Ruby Dee thought she would take time soon to go and look at them.

The Starrs and their hand, Wildcat, were squeezed together on the seat of a big old flatbed pickup, with Will Starr behind the wheel. They had a stock trailer hooked behind, carrying three saddle horses. They were on their way to sort cattle, so Will Starr had told her. It sounded like something done to laundry to Ruby Dee. He stopped and told her not to expect them back before supper time.

"If there's an emergency with Dad, call the mobile phone number," he said, and then drove off.

Lonnie waved gaily. "Can't wait for supper, Ruby Dee!" he called. Lonnie Starr had few shy pockets. The way he said her name was funny, too, making it sound like the ringing of a bell.

Will Starr, on the other hand, wasn't comfortable calling her by her given name. He made it sound like a skip over a ravine. And when he looked at her, it was mostly in a shadowed way. His disapproval was gone, though.

There was a lot to Will Starr, she thought, but it was buried in deep pockets inside him. Lord only knew what was going to happen if all the seams on those pockets burst at once. They were splitting some now.

Ruby Dee called Sally, so the dog wouldn't chase the birds from the crumbs, and went back inside the kitchen. She stood there a minute, gathering the strength to deal with Hardy Starr. He desperately needed to get in a better mood. His thoughts were poisoning him, as much as anything. He needed cleansing inside and out, and a bath would certainly be a step in that direction. The man had spent all night in the clothes he had been wearing the day before. That was not healthy for mind nor body.

When she went to get his breakfast tray, she said, "Would you like me to give you a shave, Mr. Starr?"

It had been her experience that nothing made a man feel better than having someone give him a shave. And nothing led to rapport with her men patients like giving them a shave. Shaving broke the ice, because it was such a personal thing. Once started, Ruby Dee suspected there wasn't a man alive she couldn't seduce with a shave.

Hardy Starr looked startled, as if she had proposed something indecent. "I don't care if you was the queen of Sheba, I wouldn't want you to give me a shave! What I want is for you to get out of here and leave me alone. And take that good-for-nothin' mutt with you."

He spit tobacco into his spit cup and then glared— a look that was enough to melt the flowers right off Ruby Dee's dress. Sally slunk backward. Ruby Dee got hurt and stubborn.

Hand on her hip, she approached him. "How about we get you bathed, Mr. Starr. I think you'd feel a lot better."

That suggestion went over as well as the one about giving him a shave.

"You or no woman is gonna be bathin' me," he said.

"I'm a nurse, Mr. Starr. I've bathed lots of men."

"Then you ought to be content with that," he told her smartly. "Go away and leave me be. I might be dead by nightfall, anyway."

Ruby Dee didn't want to hear him talking about dying. It so upset her that she said very foolishly, "If you plan on dyin', you'd certainly better get bathed and be prepared for laying out."

They went at this sparring for a full five minutes, but in the end, he agreed to Ruby Dee's putting the two-step kitchen stool in the bathtub, with soap and towels at hand, which would enable him to bathe himself. When she went to help him get the bandages off his knee and ankle, he slapped her hands away. Then he hobbled into the bathroom on his crutches and slammed the door shut in her face.

She hadn't really been going to go into the bathroom with him. She had just wanted him to think so, in order to keep him stirred up. It was better for him to be stirred up than languishing in thoughts of death.

She busied herself with changing his bed linens and dusting and straightening his room, getting rid of the spit cup and bringing a fresh one. She didn't know who had invented chewing tobacco, but in her estimation that person had not made it into heaven. In the Bible one read about all kinds of people drinking, but one did not read about the filthy habit of tobacco.

Beneath the bed, she found a bunch of candy wrappers and empty Skoal cans. These she threw away. The whiskey bottle beneath his pillow was empty, but she put it back. He would know she'd found it, but he would also know she didn't pilfer things that didn't belong to her. Every now and again, she would tiptoe to the bathroom door and listen for the sound of water splashing, which told her he was still alive and functioning.

After nearly forty-five minutes, Hardy Starr came hobbling out of the bathroom. He was still all bristle-faced, but he had combed his hair and he had on a clean shirt and overalls. Ruby Dee viewed him with satisfaction.

"You'd be real handsome, Mr. Starr, if you'd let me give you a shave." She cast him a tempting look.

"Leave me be," he told her. He wouldn't even let her massage and wrap his ankle and knee back up. And he didn't want anything to eat or drink, either. "Are you deaf?" he yelled. "What I want is for you to go away!"

Well. The bath had not made the transformation she had hoped for Mr. Starr.

She left him, as he wished. There were times when being alone was the best medicine. Right at that minute she would just as soon have been alone, too.

Gazing out the kitchen window, she saw the wind snatch fine sand from the rock bluffs that rose to the east, past the fenced pastures. The red dust puffed up, then disappeared to parts unknown. These men and their contention could wear her away like the wind did that sandstone, she thought. Right then she felt it wouldn't take much for that to happen. She sensed herself as not much more than a crumbling lump of clay.

Turning her attention to the house, which couldn't grouch at her, she went at it in the fashion of a preacher with a mission to win souls at a revival—relentlessly, with purpose and gusto. Ruby Dee considered cleaning nursing business. If the world was cleaner, there would be a lot less sickness. And cleaning the house was something worthwhile to throw herself into, so she wouldn't have to think about herself so much.

She cleaned the dishes and kitchen counters until they shone, and then she went at the bathrooms in the same way. She dusted and mopped the rest of the house, which didn't take a whole lot of time, since she didn't do the living room or the men's bedrooms. There was no helping the dingy walls or the pitiful furnishings, but what she did do made a definite improvement. She left the doors to the living room slid back. The room really was ugly, but the light that came through its windows was bright and cheery, and improved the feel of the entire downstairs.

A couple of times, recalling the charm of Miss Edna's home, Ruby Dee suddenly started crying, but she didn't stop cleaning. Cleaning and crying seemed to Ruby Dee to go right together.

Several times she stopped and checked on Hardy Starr. He was either dozing or just sitting there, staring. After checking on him the third time, she got a knife and went outside to cut some flowers. The only ones were the brown-eyed Susans that grew along the fence rows. She cut their tough stems, brought them in and put them in water in an old quart Mason jar and carried them into Hardy Starr's room.

He spoke to her then. "They won't last but an hour."

"Then you'd better enjoy them fast," she said.

She fixed sandwiches, canned pineapple and iced tea for lunch. She had half of a Vidalia onion, which she was saving to flavor the supper meal. After arguing with herself, she cut off a thick slice and put it on Hardy Starr's plate. Onions were good for purifying the blood, and heaven knew Hardy Starr could use that. Besides, older men just seemed to love raw onions.

She carried Hardy Starr's lunch in to him, received not a word for her effort, and ate hers with Sally out on the back step. It was quiet, the cicadas having stopped by this time, the birds taking shade. The roof overhang provided Ruby Dee with shade, but the heat swirled around her. She thought it delicious to sip ice tea in the heat.

Ruby Dee's thoughts went to the farm she had wanted just about ever since she could remember. Not really a working farm—she could earn her living as a healer—but a small farmhouse and some land on which to live. A place like Big Grandma's farm.

Big Grandma had been stern and impatient and as unlike a child like Ruby Dee as a big old woman could be. She was one of those who believed in using the rod, in this case a tree switch on Ruby Dee's legs. Still, they had found something in common, which was that they both loved the farm. Oh, Ruby Dee had loved the animals and the barn and the grass that tickled her nose. She loved the peace of the farm. She had been happier there than anywhere, except with Miss Edna, of course.

Ruby Dee looked out across the backyard at the barns and the fenced pastures. She thought about how she wanted a nice barn and pasture, great places for children to play. And how she wanted a couple of boys or a boy and a girl. She would dress them in Oshkosh overalls. She would play with them and never use tree switches on their legs. There would be haystacks to jump in, and a swing made of rope hung from a barn rafter.

These dreams were what her paper of cut-out pictures were about. The things she wanted. It had been Miss Edna's idea a month before she passed on; she'd called it Ruby Dee's dream paper.

"I worry about what you'll do after I'm gone, Ruby Dee," she'd said, not fretfully but in that fact-of-the-matter way she had. "You don't half have a plan. You don't know what you want half the time."

"I know what I don't want. It's about the same."

But Miss Edna shook her head. "You have to be specific about what you want to get it. You have to *see* it clearly."

So to please Miss Edna, Ruby Dee had found pictures of the things she thought she wanted and pasted them on the paper. She had actually gone and toured the house advertised by the real estate company and had looked into buying it, but she didn't have the down payment the bank insisted upon. She had always paid cash for anything she bought, which left her without a credit history. Banks were big on credit history and very small on self-employed practical nurses.

Getting into the spirit of the thing, she had cut out the drawing of a boot from *Western Style* magazine. She wanted a pair of Blutcher handmade boots—a lot of the country-western singers had those.

And she'd put the picture of the man on the paper to please Miss Edna. Ruby Dee wasn't certain she wanted a man, but she knew having one would be the best way to get children.

When it came to romantic relationships, Ruby Dee did not have a good track record at all. Men generally liked her, but usually they didn't want to marry her. The couple of men who had wanted to marry her, Ruby Dee hadn't wanted.

Ruby Dee had been very sensible about men all of her life. Because of her helter-skelter existence, often placed in foster homes that were less than they were supposed to be, she'd grown up fast in the sexual department. Very early on she had learned what a prize her sexuality was—so many boys, and men, too, were after it that she knew it was valuable. She made up her mind to keep it untouched until just the right man came along with whom to share it.

She was twenty-seven before she lost her virginity to Beauford Vandiver. He was the first, the only, man she had ever loved. They were to be married.

"Beauford Vandiver was a nefarious scoundrel. You should have known that from his name," Miss Edna said, still aggravated from the other side.

"How can I follow you when you use big words like that?" Ruby Dee asked. "And with that reasoning, who would trust Santa Claus?"

Beauford had been one of the prettiest men Ruby

Dee had ever seen, and just as sweet as he could be. He liked to be waited on and spoiled, and he sure liked sex, but in those ways Ruby Dee found him no different from most any man she had ever known. And she liked to wait on Beauford, she liked to spoil him and she liked to have sex with him.

But they did not get married. *"Your guardian angel saved you,"* Miss Edna said.

A day before their first wedding date, Beauford broke out with the measles. On their second wedding date, it snowed and Beauford got trapped at his office. A month later Beauford told her he needed more time to think about marriage and that he was taking a job his architectural firm had offered him, building a hotel down in Acapulco. Ruby Dee saw his picture in the society pages, his arm around the daughter of the president of the firm.

Ruby Dee didn't know if she could ever love another man. She still liked men. She just couldn't seem to stop liking them. But she was no longer certain she wanted to risk getting involved with one. That just hurt too much.

Perhaps she could simply contract with one to give her a child. It seemed a viable alternative. That or artificial insemination. She wondered if Will Starr would be willing to give her a child. She knew she and Will Starr would have no problem having sex . . . not at all. But some men were touchy about being used that way.

She was rubbing the sweating glass over her neck where her dress scooped low and mulling over the possibility of adopting a foreign child, when a red Suburban drove up. A woman got out. Ruby Dee rose. She felt a foolish annoyance. She had enjoyed sitting in the quiet and dreaming her dreams, and this stranger had come butting in, forcing the return of reality. There were few things Ruby Dee hated more than reality.

Sally started across the yard, wagging a tail in greeting, but Ruby Dee called her back.

The woman stared over the hood of the Suburban. "Is Will around?"

Her voice was forceful as she came around the car. She had blond hair—frosted, for sure—styled poofy, was older than Ruby Dee by some years—maybe in her late thirties—and was very pretty. She wore a starched turquoise shirt, with a fancy silver brooch at the neck, creased Rockies jeans and shiny boots. She stopped and put a hand to her hip—her left hand, which had a ring on it with a diamond the size of Mt. Everest.

"He's gone out to sort cattle," Ruby Dee said.

"Oh." The woman stared at Ruby Dee. Ruby Dee stared back. "Who are you?"

"I'm Ruby Dee D'Angelo. Who are you?"

The woman regarded her a moment. "Georgia Reeves. Are you the housekeeper Will sent for?" she asked. She had a perfectly made-up face, her lipstick a cinnamon shade. Ruby Dee wished she had freshened her own lipstick; it was all gone now after eating her lunch.

"I'm the nurse, come to take care of his daddy. Would you like to speak to Mr. Starr?" she said, just thinking of it. "He's inside in bed. He hurt his ankle yesterday."

The woman grinned wryly and shook her head. "Nooo . . . I don't need to be seein' Hardy Starr." Pivoting on the ball of her boot, she strode back around the car. The big diamond on her hand caught the light. "Tell Will I came by," she said, not both-

ering with a "please." She jerked open the car door
and slammed it shut behind her. With quick turns,
she headed the Suburban away in a cloud of dust.

Ruby Dee wondered who the woman had been. A
married woman, but she had been jealous of Ruby
Dee. She had acted a little possessive, to Ruby Dee's
mind. A little uppity. Of course, Miss Edna had always said Ruby Dee had an overactive imagination.

"I don't think I would like her much," Ruby Dee
told Miss Edna.

"Mind your manners, Ruby Dee," Miss Edna
scolded, giving instruction, as always.

Ruby Dee went back inside and put fresh sheets
on Lonnie's and Will's beds. Will's bed looked so
comfortable when she finished that she lay right
down on it and fell asleep for nearly an hour. When
she awoke, she smoothed it over perfectly, so he
wouldn't be able to tell she had slept there. It embarrassed her to think she had done that. Sometimes
she was pretty silly.

Back down in the kitchen, she made lemonade.
While she was doing it, Will Starr called to make
certain everything was okay. She told him about
Georgia Reeves stopping by, so she wouldn't forget
later. She didn't want him thinking she couldn't be
trusted with a message, and she didn't want that
Georgia Reeves thinking she deliberately hadn't told
him. She realized that many people would consider
her silly for thinking that about Georgia Reeves, but
most people didn't have as good an understanding
of women as Ruby Dee did.

She took two glasses of the lemonade and a plate
of crackers spread with peanut butter into Hardy
Starr's bedroom. He was reclining on his pillows,
staring out the window.

"I made lemonade, Mr. Starr . . . from real lemons."

He looked at her, then back out the window.

Ruby Dee set his glass and the plate of peanut butter crackers on his bedside table; then she pulled the ladderback chair from against the wall and sat beside his bed. She sipped her lemonade, and then ate one of the crackers. She considered what to do about Hardy Starr. He was really beginning to worry her.

Seeing the remote control for the television, she picked it up and aimed it at the TV. "Does this work?" The television came on with a crackle—the *Donahue Show.* "Isn't television a miracle? We can see other people arguing all the way from New York City. If you want my opinion, one of the things wrong with the world today is TV talk shows. Glorifies people at their worst."

Hardy Starr didn't say anything. It was really annoying, the way he sat there, annoying and worrisome.

She had seen many people like this, giving up on living. Her job was to snatch them back from the clutches of futility, but she felt herself failing with him. That scared the daylights out of her. She sure didn't want another old person dying on her.

"Mr. Starr, I know you don't want me here, but somebody has to be, and frankly, I'm a lot better at this than either of your sons. They can ranch, and I can take care of people. You play your cards right, and you'll be glad to have me here." She gave him a saucy, sexy look and winked.

His pale eyes regarded her for three long seconds. "I ain't wanted anythin' from a woman in twenty-five years, and I sure don't now that I'm an old man, so you can just take yer wiles right on out that door." He gazed at her as if she were disgusting.

Tears welled in Ruby Dee's eyes. She rose and carefully put the chair back against the wall. Then she stepped beside the bed and leaned over, braced her arm on the mattress edge and jutted her face toward Hardy Starr.

"You may be old, Mr. Starr, but you are still alive. You still have your mind and your mobility, such as it is. There are millions of people in this world who can't say the same. And yes, you are old, but that doesn't mean you're no-account. All those years made you tough—that's why you're still alive. It takes tough people to handle being old. And what's more, at eighty-five or a hundred and eighty-five, you're still a *man*. I think you've forgotten that, and I've just been tryin' to remind you!"

Shaking with emotion, she left him. In the kitchen, she hugged Sally and railed at God for giving her a job she just wasn't up to. She had lost her talent, she thought. She had lost her gift, and she didn't much care, either. Here she was thirty years old, and what did she have to show for it? Broken romances, a lot of dead old people, and a barren womb.

She wanted to sit there and cry, but she felt herself sinking into such a pit of despair that it scared her. What would happen if Will Starr came in and found her on the floor, crying?

She got up and made supper, because she couldn't think of another thing to do, and if she didn't do something, she was likely to go crazy.

When she searched the refrigerator, she was disappointed to find that she had been wrong about another plain yellow onion's being in there. All she had was two slices of the Vidalia left, and half of the slice she had given Hardy Starr, because he hadn't eaten all of it. Someone leaving half of a sweet Vidalia was so sad.

Hardy picked up the television remote, clicked off the television and threw the remote on the floor. He thought the gal might hear it and come running back in, but she didn't. Went to show just how much attention she paid a patient, he thought.

He listened carefully, and he thought he heard her crying. Women . . . they worked at a man with their tears! Then he heard her moving around, heard the kitchen radio come on. The gal was annoying with that radio. Made him think of Lila and her running around. Lila had been crazy for honky-tonk music.

All the previous night and all that day, Hardy had been trying his best to think himself dead, and that he had not succeeded made him mad. He most generally had always done what he set out to do. The few things he had failed at were lulus, though—saving Jooney, satisfying Lila.

He supposed he would have to consider the horse that had ruined his leg pretty much of a failure, too, since he'd thought he had the bugger well broke. He had not done well in raising Lonnie, but then, that hadn't been something he had really set out to do, either.

He lay there and listened to the gal's movements in the back of the house.

"You're still a man." Her words echoed in his mind. She had meant them. The passion he had seen in her eyes had surprised him.

He reflected on the statement. He wasn't so certain as to the truth of it. Hell, he was eighty-five years old. What could be expected of him at this age?

He tried to go back to thinking himself dead. Though he had not succeeded, he wasn't ready to give up.

The sun was far to the west when they got the last cows and calves separated and headed into an adjoining pasture. Lonnie leaned on his saddle horn and wiped sweat from his eyes with his sleeve that was soaked and dirty, too. He really hated to be dirty.

He heard Will give off a curse and saw him spur his horse into action. Too late, though. Will yelled and pointed. A cow and its calf had gotten separated, and now the calf was racing along the fence. The dang thing squeezed through, and then it and the mama were loping away. There was never any understanding why the stupid critters did these things. About six cows decided to turn around then, and Lonnie had to help Wildcat get them. A handful of cows could sure wreak havoc. And there wasn't anything more difficult than trying to herd one damn straying cow with her calf. Lonnie was for leaving her.

"We still got 'em . . . what in the hell difference does it make which side of the fence they're eatin' on?" he said.

"I guess the difference between havin' eight hundred dollars or goin' hungry," Will answered, real smart-like.

Lonnie gazed at him, keeping his jaw tight.

Will was separating the cattle because he was cutting out what was his. He hadn't said it, but Lonnie knew that was what was going on.

Lonnie knew that Will was counting and separating the herd because he was still planning on leaving. He was a little amazed at Will staying angry this long. Will had a pretty good temper, one as hot as the blue flame on a gas jet. But generally, Will managed to keep a cool head even when that gas jet was burning inside him. Him staying so hot-headed for this long was highly unusual.

A dozen times that day, Lonnie had wanted to talk to Will about it, but he hadn't been able to bring himself to broach the subject. He was afraid of what Will would say. Better to let sleeping dogs lie was his opinion.

He hoped, counted on it all blowing over. These situations generally did blow over once people calmed down. Of course there was no getting around that Will didn't seem to be calming down. That did not bode well at all. Still, Lonnie kept hoping for the best.

"We need rain," Will said after they had loaded the lathered horses into the trailer.

Lonnie looked around. He wondered what made Will say that; everything looked the same to him as it had a month ago, as it would a month from now. Still, Will was the rancher. He could smell rain or a dry spell a month away. To Lonnie, the land was just something that helped him have horses, but he didn't need it.

He had the sudden, vague but startling thought that Will went with the land. Neither this land nor Lonnie's life would have been the same without Will. He didn't understand these thoughts . . . didn't want to understand them.

All three men crammed back inside the pickup, not bothering to turn on the air conditioning, and headed home. Wildcat started telling them what was on television that night. It was his and Charlene's favorite night for situation comedies. Wildcat couldn't recall the year he turned forty, but he knew the names of all the actors and which years their television shows had run since the beginning of television. That fact was interesting, but his telling them all was boring as hell.

The minute they turned into the drive, Lonnie looked anxiously for Ruby Dee's car. He was relieved to see it still there beside the barn. He turned his gaze to the house in anticipation. He wasn't certain which he looked forward to most: the food or seeing Ruby Dee. He just couldn't get over there being a woman like Ruby Dee in the house. To his mind it was a phenomenon befitting deliberate enjoyment.

They got the horses out of the trailer, rubbed down and put away. After that, Will sent Wildcat on home.

"I sure appreciate it," Wildcat said. "Charlene gets real put out if I'm late on Monday nights."

As Wildcat drove off, Lonnie rolled his sleeves up, and Will lit a cigarette.

Lonnie said, "My stomach thinks my throat's been cut. I could eat a five-pound steak, with potatoes."

"We got stock to feed first," Will said, shaking out his match.

"It won't hurt none of them to wait while we get a bite to eat. We got light for another three hours."

But Will said, "I don't want to have to be comin' back out to take care of it. You get the stock in the west pasture. I'll take care of the horses."

Will's tone got under Lonnie's skin. "Will, did it ever occur to you that I'm not some hired hand?"

Will looked at him a second. "Suit yourself. I'll handle it." He strode away to the barn.

Frustrated as all get-out, Lonnie fed the livestock, just as Will had told him to do. He thought about how, all his life, he had been doing whatever Will told him. He didn't see how it would hurt Will any to *ask* him to do something.

Lonnie never had been one to stay mad for long, however, and by the time they had finished the chores and were on their way to the house, his good humor had returned. When he stepped into the kitchen, he figured he had stepped into heaven.

The room smelled of spicy meat, and Ruby Dee was as flushed as a ripe peach. Turning from the stove, she said, "I hope y'all like chicken fajitas."

Lonnie threw his hat aside and reached for her. "Ruby Dee, I could kiss you!"

He would have, too, but he caught a warning look in her eye. A sternness that surprised and embarrassed him. But his pride wouldn't let him release her, so he settled for dancing her around the kitchen, as if that had been his intent all along.

✺ 10

"I DON'T SEE why your daddy couldn't sit in here, too," Ruby Dee said. "He's not sick; he only has a hurt ankle. I'll go ask him to join us."

She strode out of the kitchen, while Will stared after her, and got an overall sinking feeling.

"Aw, geez," Lonnie said, casting Will a glance that said it was all Will's fault, while he froze midway to his seat and appeared to be ready to make a run for it.

Will considered turning and walking right back out the door. Walk out and keep on going to Texas and on to old Mexico, maybe to the beach. He knew he was thinking crazy, but it helped in that minute.

Ruby Dee came back alone, a little red in the face. "He doesn't want to."

With immense relief, Will sank into his chair. He wanted a meal in peace, and he wasn't going to apologize for that. He felt it showed a lot about the state of his life that he was focusing on this meal as a starved man did on a chicken bone.

"Your daddy has eaten today, and he hasn't complained at all about his ankle," Ruby Dee said, as she brought the rest of the dishes to the table. She lowered herself to the edge of her chair, then sat with her back straight, her hands clenching a dishcloth. "But he is brooding somethin' awful."

"He's always broodin'," Lonnie said in a comforting tone. "That's normal for him ... wouldn't you say, Will?"

Will said, "Is the swelling down on his ankle? Can he use it?"

"I'm not certain. He wouldn't let me look at it after his bath, wouldn't let me bind it up. He hasn't used it that I've seen. Other than one trip to the bathroom—and he almost fell on those crutches—he's just stayed in that bed. Won't talk, doesn't read or watch television, or anything."

A look of such despair flitted over her features that Will became concerned—for the old man, and for Ruby Dee, too. He felt he should do something, but he had no idea what.

Then she frowned thoughtfully and said, "He's awfully tolerant of pain, but I think we would know if he was hurting a lot. And he hasn't been deadenin' his pain with whiskey, because his bottle is empty."

"Maybe we should take him to the doctor tomorrow and get him checked out," Will said, not wanting to do that at all.

"I guess that would at least get him out of broodin' and into pure-D mad," Ruby Dee said. "Can he read?"

The question sort of surprised Will. He was reaching for the tortillas. "Not too well," he admitted.

"I was beginning to think that. A lot of very unhappy people can't read very well." Her brown eyes met his, and then her gaze shifted away. "I couldn't read very well for a long time. It makes a person feel stupid, and so many people think you are, but you aren't. Reading just comes easier for some people than for others. I learned to help myself by working crossword puzzles."

Will said, "Dad had to drop out of school before the third grade," and reached out to take the lid off the dish of tortillas. He chanced to look across and saw, to his profound amazement, that Lonnie had his head bowed. Ruby Dee did, too. For a couple of uncertain seconds, Will's hand held the lid hovering over the tortillas. Then he set it back on the dish as quietly as he could and waited, his head partially bowed, watching the other two. He hadn't asked a blessing since Sunday suppers at his aunt Roe's.

When Ruby Dee's head came up, Lonnie's followed, as if on cue. Will again reached for the tortillas, and this time he almost dropped the lid when Ruby Dee shot up out of her chair and went to the counter. He saw after a few seconds that she was making the old man's supper tray. He thought that he should offer to take the tray in to the old man, but he didn't.

She took it into him, and when she came back, she didn't tell them how he was doing. Will wasn't about to ask, and Lonnie was too intent on Ruby Dee even to think about the old man. He was at his most charming, tossing out witty remarks and smiles like fall leaves.

"I'll tell you, Ruby Dee," he said, "if you have been married, you give me the name of the fool man who let a great cook like you get away. I'm sure I could sell him a Red River bridge." Lonnie was a master at getting information without really seeming to ask questions.

She shook her head, an amused grin on her lips

and lighting her dark eyes. "I haven't been married."

Lonnie's eyebrows went up. "No? Huh." He winked. "You may not get away from here, with cookin' like this." He bit into his juicy fajita and kept his twinkling eyes on Ruby Dee.

Most women her age had been married at least once, Will thought, wondering about her. She had said she could have any cowboy she wanted in Oklahoma City . . . but she hadn't wanted any. Maybe she was a lesbian. Then he figured he hadn't ever been married, and he got really tired of people speculating about him. Of course, no one wondered about his sexual persuasion, since he and Georgia had carried on an affair all those years.

Lonnie said, "How did you learn to cook like this? Can we offer your mother a great big thank you?"

"My mama died when I was two. I just seem to have a natural talent for cooking. It is a healing talent."

"Oh, I'm sorry. Is your mama the lady in that urn?"

Will saw Lonnie point his fork upward, and the black-and-brass vase Will had seen on Ruby Dee's dresser came to mind. He didn't think they could be talking about a dead person's urn, no.

Then Ruby Dee said, "Oh, no, that's Miss Edna. She was my last patient. Well, really she was my dear friend. We lived together for the past four years, and she was like the mama I never had. But Miss Edna couldn't cook at all."

So there was an urn filled with a dead person's ashes on her dresser. Will was surprised, but only mildly. It was hard to be surprised by anything after forty-two years of living with the old man.

Lonnie said, "Oh. I grew up without a mama, too. She ran off when I was five, but I don't recall her being around much before that anyway."

Will disliked Lonnie talking about their mother that way. It was one thing for Lonnie to make those sorts of comments to Will, and another for him to spread the family's dirty laundry around to other people. Will had socked him once for talking like that in front of a bunch of guys, and Lonnie cast him a nervous glance now, before chattering on.

"You know, after all those years of fixin' for ourselves, it seems like Will and I would be better at it than we are. Neither one of us can cook worth beans. I did take home-ec one semester in school," he said with a grin. "I learned to make peanut butter cookies, but what was more important, I learned which girls would make peanut butter cookies for me."

Will took exception to the comment that he couldn't cook. Maybe he was no chef, but he could cook quite passably. He made great over-easy eggs and real good hamburgers.

He didn't see the need to inject any of this into the conversation, though. He was dog-tired after spending the night outside and then working all day, and he had no inclination to converse at all. Pulling inside himself was as close as he could get to going off to Mexico.

A couple of times Will's eyes happened to meet Ruby Dee's. He noticed her looking at the wound on his cheek. He could feel it had swollen. He imagined he did look a fright.

Lonnie was now on the subject of brothers and sisters. Ruby Dee said she had been an only child, as far as she knew.

"But I don't guess anyone can really be certain of that, can they?" she said pointedly.

Lonnie agreed and added, "I've sometimes wondered about my mom and if she had more children, ones we never knew about. Haven't you, Will?"

Will said, "Not particularly. Hand me that salsa."

"Will likes his food hot, in case you hadn't noticed, Ruby Dee."

What Will noticed was that Lonnie hadn't mentioned the children he might have fathered.

Lonnie went on to the subject of his favorite foods. His list included just about anything with sugar in it. Ruby Dee's list showed a definite preference for Mexican food, and when Lonnie commented on this, they learned that Ruby Dee's daddy had been Mexican.

"He was from Texas, not Mexico," she clarified. "Still, to my mama's family, he was Mexican, and that was it. They never did get over it."

For a second, it seemed Lonnie was at a loss for words, but then he came out with, "That happens."

Will didn't think that was really saying anything at all, but it did seem to allow Lonnie to go smoothly on to less personal matters, such as Ruby Dee's liking for the rodeo and where she had gotten her dog.

When Ruby Dee refilled Will's coffee cup, he thanked her, then watched her breasts as she straightened. He met her gaze, and he knew she'd noticed him looking. He felt his face grow red.

He said, "You don't have to wait on us. . . . We didn't hire you to be a maid." That was the most he had said since sitting down at the table.

She shrugged, the gesture sensual, and a small, slow smile touched her lips, while her gaze lingered on his. Then her eyes shifted to his wounded cheek.

She didn't say anything, though, just turned back toward the counter.

Will's gaze touched on her swaying earring and moved downward, following the graceful sweep of her back. When his eyes came around to Lonnie, he found his brother watching him.

The next instant Lonnie jumped up and offered to help Ruby Dee with the dishes. Will sat there for a minute, watching them, as Lonnie teased and flirted. Lonnie started to put his arm around Ruby Dee's shoulders, but his arm stopped in midair, and then he scratched his head, as if that was what he'd been going to do all along.

Will finished his coffee, then slowly stretched his legs and rose. He guessed there wasn't any more putting off going to speak to the old man. He didn't expect much to come of it, but he felt ready. He got a cup from the cabinet, filled it with coffee, and, without saying a word, took it in to the old man.

The old man was in bed, just as he had been that morning, except the bed was now made and his clothes were clean. He was rumpled, though, and his hair stood on end worse than usual. Looking at him, a sense of helplessness swept Will. The old man appeared to be withering away.

Will said, "I brought you a cup of coffee, Dad."

The old man looked at him but didn't move.

Will drew a deep breath and stepped over to set the coffee mug on the nightstand.

Then he drew the chair from the wall, eased his dirty jeans and sat. His joints creaked. He and the old man looked at each other.

"How are you feelin', Dad?"

The old man said, "Leave me be. I'm dyin', and

pretty soon you can have this place, just like you want."

"Aww, geez, Dad. What are you tryin' to do—punish me? For what? Because I want somebody in here to take care of you? Because I'm tired of being treated like some kid hand?" He pushed to his feet, raking a hand through his hair. "Why is it like this between you and me? Huh? I come in here and ask a nice, civil question, and you gotta dig at me."

He stopped then, his words getting all jammed up in his throat. The old man just looked at him. Baiting him, Will thought.

Will said, "I'm glad to see you feel strong enough to irritate me," and walked out.

In the hallway, he patted his pockets for a cigarette, which he didn't have, of course. He continued on through the kitchen, past Lonnie and Ruby Dee, standing side by side, who turned to look at him. Letting the screen door slam behind him, he stalked out into the dwindling light of evening.

Impatiently, he tugged his shirt from inside his jeans and let it fall loose. His body had cooled, but his shirt was stiff from dried sweat, and he itched.

At his pickup, he got two cigarettes, lit one and walked down to the high-fenced pasture to see the mustang. The little border collie appeared and walked along beside him, which came as a surprise. The only time he had ever spoken to the dog had been that morning, and he'd done nothing more than pass a hand over its head. He guessed dogs were a lot different than people. It didn't take much to impress a dog.

The roan colt stood in the middle of the pasture and eyed Will. Will leaned against the fence and enjoyed his smoke. The little collie sat at his foot, and together all three of them watched the red sun disappear and lights come on in the windows of the house. Will could see Ruby Dee and Lonnie pass in front of the window above the sink. Once it looked like they were dancing again.

Will resented Lonnie highly during those minutes. And he resented Ruby Dee, too. Both of them having a good time, no matter that Will was dog tired and the old man was set on dying.

He resented Lonnie and resented being the older brother and the son of a woman who'd run off and the son of a obnoxious old man. He resented the hard-rock place he found himself in, wanting to leave and yet feeling his insides tearing at the thought of doing it.

As Will saw it, he was in his middle years and had very little to show for his living. All the guys he had grown up with had families and places of their own. Keith Clarke had four children by a second wife and a big spread with his brother and was selling bull semen for twelve thousand a pop. Red Markham had married Kathy, and they were teaching school and raising three boys, doing Little League and scouts and all that stuff. Jon Leedy was building houses down in Amarillo, was on wife number four and had about seven kids, which made him pretty messed-up, but at least he had something to show for the past twenty-plus years.

Looking out across the fenced pastures and the lengthening shadows, Will thought how he might have been married and had kids out there now, playing in the evening, if he could have gotten past the old man.

Will couldn't say he had ever been in love, but he'd been close with Georgia. He guessed one of his big problems was that he couldn't forget what had happened to his dad when his mom had walked out.

He'd been in the hallway that morning, had heard the final words that passed between his parents.

The old man had said, "Don't go, Lila. . . . I love you."

And his mother, in a tired, sad voice, answered, "Love don't water roses, Hardy. I'm witherin', and I just can't stand bein' dry no more."

Will knew very well that his mother was speaking of their bed being dry. Hearing that cut a pain through him the same as a double-bladed knife would.

Will tossed his cigarette butt into the dirt and rubbed his eyes. They were tired after the day in the bright, hot sun.

He thought then how his life wasn't the old man's fault, any more than his eyes burning was the sun's fault. Every man made his own life as a result of his decisions. Will didn't like sunglasses sliding down his nose, so he wouldn't wear them. And it had been his own decision all along to be a stand-in dad for Lonnie and to stay and try to help the old man. It had been his own decision all along to cling to a place he'd always felt was his by right and virtue of his work. His decision, for a thousand and one reasons, to stay on at this dead-end place and to take what the old man gave.

Knowing it was all his own fault did not improve his mood at all.

It was fully dark now. A faint sound came to him—the squeaking of the back screen door. Ruby Dee's husky voice called out, "Will?" She said it only once.

"Yeah?" he hollered back, feeling a strange anticipation. Ruby Dee wanted him for something.

"Georgia Reeves is on the phone."

His anticipation faded. "Okay . . . comin'."

He strode toward the house. Halfway there, he realized the little collie was walking along beside him. A tiny spark of pleasure sliced through him, but when he opened the back door and the dog raced inside ahead of him, he realized the only reason the dog had come along was to get inside.

Ruby Dee was alone in the kitchen, bent over, writing something at the table. The radio on the counter played low—a country tune.

She looked over at him.

"I'll get it in my office. Could you hang this one up?" Will pointed to the wall phone.

She nodded, and he went on through the alcove, closing the door behind him. He switched on the green-shaded desk lamp, plopped down into the cushioned oak chair and paused to catch his breath. He wondered about Georgia coming by and calling.

The last time Will had been with Georgia, she had yelled at him, "You only come around here when you've had a fight with your daddy. I'm tired of you using me for a comfort station."

He could have pointed out that she used him just as much, for home and car repairs and an occasional horny night. By the time he had thought of that, though, he was already outside and trying to find his boots in the dark yard, where she had pitched them. He'd cooled off a lot by the time he found them, and throwing her words back in her face had come to seem more trouble than it was worth.

Two weeks later Georgia had married Frank Reeves and become the proud mistress of a brand-new double-wide manufactured home with a huge redwood deck, and co-owner of the thriving Reeves's Quick Stop in Harney.

When Will picked up the phone, he would be speaking to a married Georgia, and he didn't know if he was up to that just then. The day had been tough enough. But that wasn't Georgia's fault, and he saw no call to be rude. And he guessed he wanted to talk to her.

He said hello, and Georgia's voice came back at him across the line: "Hello, stranger." She could have a sexy voice, when she wanted. He squeezed his eyes closed, memories racing through his mind. Georgia said, "I came by today. . . . Did that girl tell you?"

"Yes, she did. I'm sorry I missed you." That wasn't exactly the truth. He had enough of his own problems right that minute and didn't care to add Georgia to them. Still, he felt called upon to be polite.

He regretted saying it, though, when Georgia said, "Are you, Will? I always had the feelin' you never missed me one bit. That you'd just as soon be out there with your cattle and horses."

Now, that was a lie. "I missed you, Georgia, lots of times. And I told you that, too."

"You came to my weddin', and you didn't say a word, didn't even stay to kiss the bride."

Will wondered right then how this subject had gotten started. He and Georgia were arguing, and they weren't even together anymore—and she was married, by damn!

"You married a fine man, Georgia, and the day you did, I didn't see any reason to cause talk that could come back to haunt you and Frank later."

The line hummed for a few seconds before she

said, "You know I would have married you, Will, if you had ever been willin' to move off from your daddy."

It was an old song between them. He didn't like the way she was making him feel guilty. He didn't have anything to feel guilty for.

She said, "We were always good friends." There was hope in her voice.

"Yes, we were," Will said, and regrets washed over him like big ocean waves.

"I'm sorry I didn't wait for you . . . but I didn't see any future in just waitin', Will."

He closed his eyes again. "There wasn't, Georgia. And that's my regret."

He thought she might be crying. "Well, I just want you to know that just because I'm married to Frank doesn't mean we can't be friends, Will. I really want you to know that."

"I'll always be your friend, Georgia."

Again the line hummed. "Come 'round to see me sometime, Will. Come for a visit, not just to get a Moonpie at the store."

Will didn't have to say anything to that, because she hung up.

He replaced the receiver and sat thinking about Georgia, wondering where Frank was that night. Likely hauling cattle up to Kansas. Frank was a trucker who hauled cattle. Will wasn't certain why he did, because Frank was a wealthy man. That was why Georgia had finally married him. She had told Will she was tired of scratching day to day, while she got more lines on her face.

Georgia didn't have to worry about her looks; she was a handsome woman. But she was forty years old this year, and she hadn't taken that well.

Will felt disappointed, for himself and for her. She would have been a good wife. She liked the country and knew about cattle. Georgia had been married once, and she knew the realities of a marriage. That was her word—"reality."

"Marriage gets boring, that's the reality of it. I don't expect fireworks anymore, Will. You don't run around on me, and I won't run around on you, and we'll do okay."

Will knew there was no such thing as fireworks, that it was a myth, but Georgia saying it like she did made him depressed. He downright hit bottom when he thought of Georgia calling him up, when she was a newly married woman.

Shoving himself to his feet, he went out to the kitchen. He was hoping Ruby Dee was still there, sort of holding his breath, until he saw her still at the table, the little dog lying at her feet.

Will felt strange, self-conscious. He cast her a nod and went to the refrigerator. There was no more beer. He glanced over and saw the light burning on the coffee maker, the pot about half full. He poured himself a cup, then thought to ask Ruby Dee if she wanted one.

"No, thank you. I'm about ready for bed." She stretched her arms high above her head, causing the fabric of her dress to bunch and lift her breasts.

Will felt himself grow warm. He leaned against the counter and sipped his coffee. He tried to think of something to say, but he didn't think asking her why she had never been married would be considered casual conversation.

He said, "You've had one full day. Ready to quit yet?" And he guessed that wasn't casual conversation, either.

But she sort of grinned and shook her head. "Not yet. Maybe tomorrow."

Again they were quiet. After a moment, he remarked how good her coffee was, and she said she put a little baking soda in the grounds.

"It helps sometimes, when the water is hard."

"We have a water softener," Will said. "It broke last month, though, and I just haven't seen to it. I'll take care of it tomorrow." Then he added, "But my coffee never did taste this good, even with the softened water."

After another minute of silence, Ruby Dee rose. "I guess I'll go on upstairs. I like to get to bed early."

Disappointment stabbed Will; he felt aggravated that he couldn't be more glib, so she might have stayed and talked with him. He wished her good night and stood there, watched her slow, swaying walk and listened to her quiet footsteps recede.

Pouring himself the last of the coffee, he turned off the machine and went back to his office. He sat stiffly, downed several big swallows of coffee, then flipped open his address book, found the number for Ambrose Bell and dialed.

The ring came five times before Ambrose answered in his slow, craggy drawl. "You got Bell here."

Will exchanged pleasantries and heard about Ambrose's latest heart problems, and then he said, "I went by the old James place today, Am. Do you still want to sell it and the quarter section with it?"

"Why, yes, I do. You thinkin' to add it to the Starr?"

"I'd like to talk to you about buyin' it," Will said, not truly answering the question. He wasn't ready for people to know his business yet. "I'd like to see about leasing some range land from you, too. How about if we meet sometime in the next couple of days?"

11

SITTING IN THE ugly old overstuffed chair, Ruby Dee tugged off her boots. For half a minute she admired them. She removed her socks and wiggled her toes. The wood floor felt deliciously cool to her bare feet when she stood to remove the rest of her clothes and slip into a cotton robe. She hung up her dress, then gathered her panties and bra, along with the clothes she had earlier tossed on the chair, when she had showered and changed before supper, and put them in the laundry bag hanging in the closet. Ruby Dee had a habit of orderliness.

A light rap sounded on the door. She hesitated a minute, knowing it was Lonnie. Then she turned the glass knob and pulled the door open.

Lonnie was bare from the waist up and rubbing a towel over his thick, dark hair. Ruby Dee, of course, was used to bare bodies, but bare, healthy bodies in this form—hard-muscled and tanned—were rare for her, especially only a couple of feet from her nose. His body also came with a heady scent of masculine cologne.

She looked up and found his eyes observing

her intimately, while his expression remained innocent. Oh, Lonnie Starr had a way about him, and Ruby Dee couldn't help but return his grin.

He said, "Boy, nothin' like a shower to bring a body back to life." He flicked the towel over his hard-muscled shoulder and leaned against the doorjamb. "It's a clear night. Why don't we sit out on the front porch? The lights out back won't bother us there, and we can really see the stars." His eyes regarded her intently.

Ruby Dee shook her head. "I don't think so, Lonnie. I'm goin' to bed with a book."

"A book?" He arched his eyebrow and cast her a teasing grin. "Now, you can't really rather go to bed with a book than look at the stars." He said the word "stars" as if it had a double meaning.

Ruby Dee gazed at him and felt a familiar sweet stirring in her belly. A woman would have to be dead not to be stirred by Lonnie Starr and his hazel eyes.

"Come on, Ruby Dee. . . ." he cajoled, saying her name like the soft ringing of a bell. "The stars are a sight out here, like nowhere else on earth."

She wanted to. Badly. She wanted to see the stars and flirt with him and touch him, too, God forgive her; it was all His fault anyway.

Ruby Dee stepped backward and cast him an amused grin. "I appreciate your offer, Lonnie, but I'm an early-to-bed person." Gripping the knob, she slowly began to close the door.

He searched her eyes. His easy grin faded, and his eyes darkened. "That's right . . . you said that. Good night." He flashed her a small grin, and then turned away.

Ruby Dee shut the door and leaned back against

it. Pressed against it and breathed deeply.

Well.

She heard his door close with a hard click. She felt the cotton fabric of her robe lying against her thighs, and she saw again his hazel eyes.

Tears blurred her vision as she thought of the confusion and hurt that had crossed his face.

Pushing from the door, she moved across the room and put an Elvis tape in her little stereo. Her gaze fell on Miss Edna's urn, and she took it up and held it close.

Miss Edna would put her warm hand on Ruby Dee's head and say, "Child, this, too, will pass," and Ruby Dee would always feel better.

But the urn was cold and hard, and brought so little comfort.

"You know, if it wasn't for you decidin' to die," she said to the urn, setting it back on the dresser, "I wouldn't be here, havin' to make these kinds of decisions."

For a moment her gaze lit on her dream paper. She had the thought that she surely could get Lonnie to father her children and not even know what he was doing. Perhaps the thought was a little naughty, but it was the truth.

But she heard Miss Edna saying, *"Build the nest, first, Ruby Dee, then have the chicks."*

Turning her thoughts from nonsense, she hauled out her tiny portable typewriter and dictionary, got herself settled on the bed and set to work transcribing her notes on Hardy Starr. The rosy glow from the scarf-covered lamp made the print easier to read. When her back began to hurt, she took the pillow Sally laid her head on and tucked it with the others behind her back.

Sally did not appreciate the removal of the pillow and cast Ruby Dee an accusing look.

A short time later Ruby Dee heard Lonnie Starr's boot steps coming down the hall. She heard him hesitate at her door, then was relieved to hear him go on down the stairs.

She lay back against her pillows. "Miss Edna, I just don't know how life can get so empty and so full at the same time."

Will stared at the green screen, transferring the information to the computer from his scribbled notes for that day. He intended to have all the ranch records up-to-date when he left. He didn't want to feel any guilt about leaving. He ignored the voice that told him not feeling guilt would be impossible.

He heard Lonnie's footsteps approaching through the kitchen and sat back in the oak chair, expecting him to come to the office. But the footsteps passed, and Lonnie went out the back door. The screen door banged. Half a minute later pickup lights illuminated the black night.

Will rose and stepped to the window. Lonnie's truck came shooting down the hill from the barn, and the tires slung gravel as they hit the drive and headed for the road. Lonnie appeared to be a little peeved. Most of the time Lonnie drove fast, though.

No doubt he was headed into Harney to have a couple of beers at Reeves's Quick Stop, play a bit of pool and flirt with the women. He had been seeing Georgia's sister, Crystal, occasionally that summer, and Will really didn't like that. Crystal was way too young and had no sense where Lonnie was concerned.

Will turned off the computer and the office lights.

Suddenly, he felt oddly lost . . . as if he should be doing something. For the better part of two days he had been running on high, and now he'd dropped to a pit. Wanting a cigarette, he considered going out to his truck, but this time the strategy of keeping them out there won out. Will was tired and wanted a shower more than he wanted to walk all the way to his pickup.

The old man was snoring when Will passed his room. Will stopped and looked in. The old man, still on top of his covers and fully dressed, had turned on his side.

At the top of the stairs, Will saw the crack of light at the bottom of Ruby Dee's door. He could faintly hear music . . . and what sounded like the clicking of a typewriter, which was curious.

For a couple of seconds, he paused there, thinking about knocking on her door and asking her if she needed anything. He felt sure he would luck out and get to see her in her nightgown, which was a really juvenile hope.

Checking his foolish impulse, he walked on to the bathroom.

While he was showering, having forgotten about his wound, he proceeded to scrub his face. The touch caused his wound to hurt so bad tears came to his eyes. Out of the shower, he studied it in the mirror, then applied ointment from a tube in the medicine cabinet, too tired to fool with it further.

Wearing boxer shorts, he stretched atop the spread on his bed, stared at the patterns the moonlight made on his wall and smoked a hand-rolled cigarette. He had come across the makings in his underwear drawer. He'd long forgotten about it and the tobacco was stale, but it was better than nothing.

His door was pushed closed enough for privacy but not fully shut, because he hated to be closed into a room. Made him feel like he couldn't breathe. He listened to his clock ticking, the old man snoring, and the faint music coming from Ruby Dee's room. A couple of times he heard the squeak of her bed-springs, so he figured she was in the bed.

She apparently had a fondness for Elvis. Will's taste ran to the Eagles, Bob Seger and southern jazz. Mostly he liked silence.

Watching the spirals of smoke rise silvery in the moonlight, he mentally counted the number of strides down the landing from his room to Ruby Dee's. Four long strides would probably do it, maybe five.

She was there, not more than five strides away, just on the other side of the door. A couple of times, Will thought he could even catch her scent.

Late like it was, Georgia Reeves, who ran the place now for her husband, turned out the lights except for one over the cash register and two at the grill and tables. The only light near the pool tables came from the lamps hanging above them, illuminating soft green tops, leaving everything else in shadow. Lonnie leaned over a table, took aim with the smooth cue and, with one play, sank his last two balls into separate corner pockets.

"Aww, shit . . ." Cletus Unsell moaned.

Straightening, Lonnie grabbed his long-necked beer with one hand and dropped his cue stick in the rack with the other. "Pay up, Cletus."

Cletus counted out the bills and handed them over. "Give me a chance to get even?"

Lonnie shook his head. He was bored with the

game. He sauntered over to the booths, where several guys were sitting, killing time until Georgia closed up. Georgia sat on a stool at the cash register, counting money.

Reeves's Quick Stop was the hub of little Harney. It was on the southeast corner of a crossroads. On the northeast corner was Pruitt's full-service Texaco, on the northwest corner the post office and the Style Shop, which did men and women's hair, and the Dairy Freeze, and on the southwest corner the Harney Lumber, Feed, and Hardware. Spreading out from the business square were a few houses and mobile homes.

Reeves's was open in the summer from 6:00 A.M. until midnight, and, like a thousand other such places that dotted the rural areas of the state, it was a combination gas station, grocery, cafe, and general hang-out.

A year ago Frank Reeves had put in three pool tables. They had doubled his profits and broken up at least one marriage, when Polly Spivey was given the ultimatum to chose pool or her husband. Polly went off to Las Vegas to play professional billiards. She had even been in a tournament on ESPN, dressed in a black sequined gown and doing trick shots.

Lonnie felt restless, like he had jumping beans in his pants. He stood and talked for a while with Roman Torres and Royce Hall.

Behind them, Crystal Hewitt was cleaning the grill and fountain. Royce tried to talk her into making him a hamburger, but she wouldn't. She didn't so much as spare him a glance, but she sent several looks and smiles Lonnie's way.

He had known Crystal since she was a plain,

skinny kid. She had gone off for a year of college and had returned to work for the summer in the store for her sister, Georgia. She wasn't so plain anymore, and she wasn't skinny. Lonnie had dated her a couple of times, and had also run into her at a club down in Elk City once or twice. He knew she liked him. What he liked about her was the way she looked at him, like he was really something.

When she started to get the trash bags out of their containers, Lonnie hurried to help carry the bags outside. He heaved the two he carried into the Dumpster, then took the other two from Crystal and tossed them in.

"Thanks, Lon."

"Sure." They stood there, looking at each other, teasing each other. "You might give me a reward."

"Oh, I might."

She looked at him for another few seconds. He and Crystal had made out before, which consisted of hot kisses and her letting him feel her with her clothes on. He wondered what she would feel like under those clothes.

Then she stepped forward, lifted her face and gave him a quick kiss. Lonnie grabbed her hand and tugged her over to his pickup truck, around to the driver's side, where they couldn't be seen from the store.

"Now, Lonnie . . . I got work to do." Crystal laughed breathlessly, and didn't stop him when he pulled her into his arms.

"You been lookin' at me all night," he said, warming her with his eyes and rocking his pelvis against hers.

Her gaze fell to his mouth, and she said, "Well, considerin' what else there was to look at, I don't think that's much." He heard the desire vibrate in her voice, and she played her fingers at the back of his neck. "Georgia says you got a girl out at your place who claims to be the nurse for your daddy."

"She is."

"Georgia says she didn't look like any nurse."

"I didn't know they looked a particular way."

He did not want to talk about Ruby Dee. He pressed Crystal against him and kissed her, first quickly, then more thoroughly. He licked her lips and felt her shudder.

She drew back and gazed up at him, her eyes heavy with desire. "Everybody says you play with all the girls," she whispered in a ragged voice.

"Do they? Do you always listen to what everybody says?"

"Oh, Lordy, Georgia'll have my hair," she said as her mouth eagerly sought his.

Lonnie hadn't expected this. He had just been teasing, looking for a little flirting and maybe a feel. A diversion.

But Crystal came at him hot and wild, and the kiss boiled his blood. He sank into it, letting the heat melt away the restlessness that gripped him. Letting it melt away the wanting and the loneliness that gnawed at him when Ruby Dee had refused him.

Lungs burning, he broke away, gasping for breath. Gazing downward, he saw Crystal's breasts heaving.

She said, "Lon, I got to get back," and pushed away, but he grabbed her, kissed her again and shoved his fingers between her legs.

"Lon . . ." she protested, but she only struggled about half a second, and then she was pushing against his fingers.

That surprised Lonnie, but he got past it.

He felt her muscles throb right through her denim jeans. He was doing some throbbing of his own. Painful, delicious throbbing. He kissed her, and she moaned deep in her throat and shoved hard against him. She was suddenly wet and hot between her legs.

Lonnie pretty much lost it, having the wild idea to haul her up into the seat of his pickup.

"Crystal! You and Lonnie quit foolin' around out there, and you get in here."

Georgia's voice was like a bucket of ice water. Georgia's voice had that quality even when she was talking normal.

Crystal broke away with a moan of disgust. "I'll be there in a minute!" she called, and gave a little stamp of her foot. Her woeful eyes came up to Lonnie's, and she reached for him. "I'm sorry, Lon."

He gave her a crooked grin and kissed her softly.

"Crystal." Georgia came out from the doorway, coming toward the dumpster.

"I said I'm comin'."

Crystal paused to look back at Lonnie. In the dim, silvery light from the store, he saw her eyes, heavy with desire, her lips bruised from his kisses. He silently cursed Georgia.

Crystal said, "You can call me sometime."

"I will."

He opened the door of his truck and hopped up into the seat. He had not been with a woman for a number of months and was frustrated as hell. But deep inside he felt as if he had just escaped something. There was a light in Crystal's eye that made him cautious.

As he slowly turned the pickup and headed

around the store, Georgia came striding out the front door and flagged him down. He lowered his window.

"Look, Lonnie, I don't want you fooling around with my sister." She fixed him with a stern eye. "She isn't like so many of the girls. She hasn't been around a lot—I don't care how she acts. I don't want you takin' advantage of her. Do you hear me?"

Lonnie said, "Okay." That seemed to be the safest thing to say, considering her stern eye.

Georgia gave a little shake of her head, pivoted and walked back into the store.

Lonnie pressed on the gas pedal and sent the truck flying up on the blacktop, headed home. He didn't want to go home. He was feeling much more restless now than he had before he'd gotten all worked up with Crystal. But he couldn't think of anywhere else to go.

ᤡ 12

RUBY DEE AWOKE so early, the eastern sky wasn't even hinting at light. She smelled coffee, though. When she got to the kitchen, she found Will Starr peering into the mirror hung inside a cabinet door, poking at the wound on his face. He winced and let out a curse.

"Oh, mercy sakes, why don't you just let me tend that?" She gave this off as she went across the room to let Sally out the door.

She came back and pushed close, watching in the mirror as Will dabbed at the cut on his face with a swab.

"It is festerin'," she said. "You need to clean it out."

He cut his eyes to hers in the mirror. "It's not festering. It just has a little bit of pus."

"Wouldn't you wash a wound like that on a horse? Here, sit on this stool and let me take care of it. Then you can forget about it."

She dragged over the kitchen stool. Then she stood there, hand on her hip, and looked at him, waiting. She let her eyes tell him that she could wait all day.

With a resigned expression, he handed her the swab and sat.

While Ruby Dee ran the water warm from the tap, she studied the wound and took in his whole face. He was freshly shaved, his hair combed. It was shaggy, though, above his ears. She liked the way his thick mustache curved downward at the corners of his lips.

She wet a cloth and pressed it against the wound. "Here, hold that, while I go get my kit." She took his hand and put it where she wanted it.

She hurried upstairs and brought back her medicine kit. Using surgical soap, she went to work to soften the wound and wash it out. Will Starr didn't say anything, but he squinted, and his eyes watered.

Talking to draw his attention from the pain, she said, "Why is it that men have to endure a certain amount of suffering before they have their hurts attended to? It's like a man thinks he is more of one by suffering. Every man I've ever known has been that way."

"How many men have you known?"

"Don't cock your eyebrow." She took hold of his chin and tilted his head downward. "Lots. Patients, you know."

"Oh," he said, and Ruby Dee had the idea he had been thinking along the lines of lovers.

"I've had one lover," she said.

His eyes came up and met hers. "And did he turn you off men?"

She looked back at his wound. "Pretty much. This is gonna leave a scar. If you would have let me stitch it in the first place, it wouldn't have, but it will now."

"I'll be lucky you don't kill me," he said thinly.

"Lockjaw can sure kill you. Have you had a tetanus shot?"

"Sometime."

"Is that how you treat your horses? You give them tetanus vaccines, don't you?"

"I'll see the vet soon as I can."

Ruby Dee blotted the wound with a soft, dry cloth and leaned close to peer at it, looking for any lingering pus or foreign substances.

Then she was looking into his eyes, only inches from her own. Slashes of brilliant blue, with silvery flecks and long lashes set in a sun-toughened face.

She looked at him, and he looked at her. Heat swirled between them. Enough heat to make her quit breathing.

Ruby Dee stood up straight, her back stiff, and turned to her kit. "I think you still need a couple of little tucky stitches."

She dabbed antiseptic on the wound and took two small stitches. She had to make her hands not tremble. Will Starr winced and his eyelashes flickered, but his hands remained palms down on his knees, and he didn't say a word. He was smart enough, and disciplined enough, to keep his facial muscles totally relaxed.

The silence between them seemed strangely loud. Ruby Dee thought Will Starr surely had beautiful hair, the way it swept back from his temples. And she thought about how here she was, touching him all over the face, and how her thigh was brushing his, and how her belly touched his arm, and how she wished he would put his arm around her and kiss her, and do a whole lot of other things, too.

Then she put a firm stop to those thoughts.

She said, "I'm gonna put some castor oil on this, and maybe that will help keep the scarring down."

His steely blue eyes flashed over at her, but she only glanced at him. His eyes made her nervous. She was afraid he could read exactly what she was thinking.

The scent of coffee awakened Hardy. He was somewhat annoyed at smelling it, because he figured if he could smell it, he was still alive. He had counted on being dead.

He was further annoyed when he came out of the bathroom, looked through the dining room and saw Will and the gal in the kitchen, illuminated by the light over sink, their heads just about touching.

The two were so intent on each other that they hadn't heard him clattering around on his crutches. Dillydallying, just like he had expected all along, by God! Furious, he was just about to go in there and put a stop to it, when the gal turned Will's head, and Hardy realized she was working over the cut on his cheek.

The cut had looked pretty bad last night, Hardy thought, and guilt stabbed him. He'd done that.

But he hadn't done it on purpose. It had just happened. The guilt faded as he balanced there, watching them. There was something about the two of them that struck him, as if he had seen such a scene before.

Then it came to him that he had better get back to his room before they heard him or saw him. He did not want them, or anyone else, to know that he could get around as well as he could. No, sir. He wanted them to think of him as an invalid.

Using the crutches and tiptoeing on the foot with the sprained ankle, he headed as quietly and quickly as possible to his bedroom. He caught the door frame with one of the crutches and almost went sprawling. He bit back a string of curses and got himself over to the bed. He set aside the crutches and positioned himself, reclining on the pillows, his ankle again resting on the rolled up towel.

Through the window he saw the sky getting lighter. That he had lived to see another day depressed him.

The whole day and night before, Hardy had tried his best to die. He had thought that if he told his heart long and hard enough to quit beating, it would. Sort of like throwing a leg over the fence, and the rest of the body followed. He'd kept throwing his mind into heaven. thinking his body would follow.

He considered keeping at it, but he felt like he might be fighting a losing battle.

He could, of course, take more drastic action. The option of blowing his brains out was gone, since he couldn't get his hands on a gun, but there remained his pocket knife or drinking the drain cleaner in the bathroom.

Drain cleaner took a little while. His cousin Mason had drunk it to kill himself. The theory was that Mason had counted on his wife finding him in time to save him, but his wife had gone off to the hairdresser. Mason never had been very smart.

However, Hardy considered thinking himself dead an entirely different thing than using more violent means. Thinking was honorable and within the realm of God. The other—guns and knives and drain cleaner—Hardy considered dishonorable and weak, which was why Mason had done it. Mason had been a weasely, weak man, and Hardy didn't want to put himself in the same category.

He considered the honorableness of starving himself. Just quit eating, passively protesting against his life. But if he did that, they would surely take him to the hospital and hook him up to tubes. He might eventually die, but not until he had undergone untold discomfort and indignities. It wouldn't be worth it.

He heard the back door open and close, then some movement from the kitchen. Hardy found it poor on their part that neither the gal nor Will had come in to check on him. He could be dead and start stinking for all the attention they paid him.

"Hey! Gal!" he called.

He reached for a glass left on his nightstand and his pocket knife. He clanged the knife against the glass.

"Hey, gal!"

He kept up the clanging until the gal appeared in the doorway.

"Well, good mornin', Mr. Starr . . . and my name is Ruby Dee, not gal." As she came forward, her dress outlined her legs and fluttered down just above her ankles.

It suddenly came to Hardy why seeing her and Will together earlier had seemed so familiar. He had a similar image in his memory—of him and Jooney, when Jooney had cut his hair.

"How's your ankle this mornin'?" she asked, bending over it.

"It hurts," Hardy said. "Go get me some coffee, with sugar and cream."

"You aren't supposed to have sugar."

"Yeah, and what's gonna happen—I might die?"

She laughed aloud at that, and then she did a really fool thing. She bent and kissed his cheek.

"Get the hell away from me!" Hardy stammered.

The gal laughed again. "I guess if you didn't die from me doin' that, you ain't gonna. I'll get your coffee."

And she flounced out of the room, leaving Hardy staring after her. A second later, he realized he had been watching her swaying hips.

You're still a man, she had told him, and he supposed he was, after all. The thought confused him terribly.

～13

WITH A QUICK glance, Will could see that the swelling in the old man's ankle had gone down quite a bit, but he said he couldn't use it.

"I ought to know if I can use the dang ankle or not," he insisted. "I'm the one grittin' my teeth with it."

Will brought up the idea of going down to the doctor, but the old man flatly refused.

"I ain't goin'," he said, and that was that. It was clear from the set of his face that he intended to make his bed the last stand at the Alamo.

Will wasn't going to argue with him. He had better things to do. Also, he didn't like the way the veins stood out on the old man's neck every time the word *doctor* was mentioned.

Taking him to the doctor was postponed, but Ruby Dee said she needed groceries, or she wasn't going to be making any more biscuits, and there was enough coffee for only one more pot. Lonnie took on about the prospect of no biscuits. Lonnie could evermore act the fool.

Will said Reeves's Quick Stop over in Harney would have coffee and flour in small containers, and eggs and bacon, too. Ruby Dee decided to go right away, before the heat of the day.

Before she left, she instructed Will to make certain he took his daddy the snack she had prepared and left in the refrigerator. Then she handed him a sheet of paper.

"Here's a report on Hardy's day yesterday. I do this for all my patients. It comes in handy when we need to track down causes of symptoms and things."

Surprised, Will took the paper. "You typed it?" It was done in columns, with events, observations and times noted.

"I have terrible handwriting. You wouldn't be able to read it."

Will walked her out to the car. He found himself doing it, even opening the back door for her, telling her to charge whatever she needed to the ranch account. He began to wish he didn't have to stay with the old man. It crossed his mind to holler for Lonnie to come stay with him, so he could go with Ruby Dee.

It turned out that Lonnie was two steps ahead of him. He had brought the Galaxie over into the shade of the elm, had even put the top down. His arms folded, he leaned his hip against the driver's door and grinned at Ruby Dee. Lonnie said, "I'll take you in to Reeves's, Ruby Dee. I need some Skoal, and a burrito sounds pretty good, too."

"You just ate," Will said. He should have known Lonnie would do this.

"Hey, that was way over an hour ago." Lonnie opened the driver's door for Ruby Dee.

She told him he could drive and circled the front

of the car. Lonnie stepped around to get the passenger door for her, but Will was quicker.

Ruby Dee slid into the seat and called for Sally, who came bounding up onto her lap and over into the back seat. Will shut the door. Ruby Dee stuck her hat on her head and lifted her face, her eyes coming up to Will's.

"Thanks," she said. "We won't be long."

Will stepped back, shoving his hands into his rear pockets. "Watch my little brother." He nodded at Lonnie. "He thinks he's at the Indy half the time."

Lonnie smirked at him and dropped the shift arm.

The car shot ahead, leaving Will standing there, the dust spiraling around his legs.

The yellow hood of the convertible gleamed in the bright sunlight as the car sped over the narrow two-lane blacktop highway. The road broke through hills and dipped down into flat river-bottom land. Here they could see the broken rust-colored earth, canyons cut eons ago by the river. Grassland, no trees, except for a rare, scraggly, bent nub. The river was a flat, winding trickle now at summer.

Ruby Dee liked this land the best, liked the wildness of it.

Lonnie had the same type of wildness, she thought, looking at him. He sat relaxed, high, wide and handsome. He had tossed his hat in the back seat, and the sun glimmered on his dark hair.

What she liked about Lonnie was that he liked her, and he surely didn't hide it. His hazel eyes told her she looked good, and that he thought she was just wonderful. That he probably looked at all women that way didn't change the way it made her feel.

"This is one great machine!" he said, raising his voice above the roar of the wind.

"Yep." Ruby Dee smacked her hand on the top of her hat, holding it on. She was suddenly glad to be away from the ranch, riding beside a man who thought she was pretty.

Her mind went back to Will. He had looked so forlorn she'd wished he could come with them. She knew it would help Will Starr a lot to get out and have fun.

She thought then that the land was like Will, too—tough and enduring.

Ruby Dee savored these thoughts. She found them profound. It had been her experience that profound thoughts might not be any more truthful than those that are not profound, such as thinking that white toilet paper was more pristine than the colored variety, but she believed profound thoughts were a lot prettier. She really enjoyed profound thinking, and she kept it up all the way to Harney.

In fact, she was thinking so hard that it was almost a surprise to pull into the gravel lot of Reeves's Quick Stop. Blinking, Ruby Dee threw her hat in the back seat and ran her fingers through her hair, fluffing it on top. "Come on, Sally, get up here in the shade." She motioned for Sally to lie next to the brick building.

"She can come inside," Lonnie said. "You aren't in the city, Ruby Dee." He cast her that easy grin and held open the door.

Well, the first person Ruby Dee saw was Georgia Reeves behind the cash register. Ruby Dee felt really silly, because only in that moment did the name of the store and the name of the woman come together in her mind.

Georgia had on a white blouse with silver button covers. Small silver earrings dotted her lobes, and every hair was in place. She looked more ready to host a luncheon for the Friends of the Library than to clerk in a convenience store.

Ruby Dee admired Georgia's attention to her person, but she felt no more liking for the woman than she had the day before. And she was really glad she had put on lipstick—Summer Coral, which looked much more natural than Georgia's fiery crimson. Probably, though, Georgia was more concerned with appearing striking than appearing natural. And she succeeded.

"Hello, Georgia . . . this is Ruby Dee," Lonnie said. "I think you two met yesterday, out at our place."

Georgia nodded. "Hi." Speculation ripe as a juicy peach shone in her eyes, which moved from Ruby Dee to Lonnie and back again.

Ruby Dee said, "Hello," and offered a perfectly friendly smile, to be polite, and to be one up.

Georgia just looked at her. Ruby Dee suspected no one ever got to be one up on Georgia.

"Is the grill open, Georgia?" Lonnie asked, turning Ruby Dee toward the back of the store. "I'd sure like one of your burritos, and Ruby Dee will have . . ." He looked at her.

"I'll just have a Coke."

"I'll get your burrito, Lon," Georgia said, following on her side of the counter.

His hand on her elbow, Lonnie guided Ruby Dee to a booth. Sally padded along beside them, tail and shoulders down, totally uncertain.

Two elderly men in overalls and ball caps sat in one of the booths. They were playing dominoes. Lonnie exchanged greetings with them, but didn't introduce Ruby Dee. She cast them a friendly smile, and they gave her a quick, curious nod before returning to their game. They appeared intensely involved in it.

Ruby Dee slid into the booth, and Sally went under the table. Lonnie went to get the soft drinks.

When he came back, he leaned across the table and whispered, "They don't play for pennies." He inclined his head toward the men in the other booth. "Most of those games involve upwards of five hundred dollars. Sin City, right here in Harney." He winked.

Ruby Dee looked at them again. Men in clean but worn overalls and thin, long-sleeve plaid shirts. Their hands were veined and weathered. She wondered if Lonnie was pulling her leg.

She cast quick glances at them while Lonnie ate his burrito and she sucked on the straw of her Coke. Once she saw the skinny one pull a wad of bills from the pocket of his overalls, peel off what she thought was a hundred-dollar bill and hand it to his opponent.

After she finished her Coke, she excused herself and went back to the rest room, where she could reapply her lipstick. Ruby Dee never applied her lipstick in public. It seemed tawdry, like adjusting a bra strap. And the whole point of wearing lipstick was to give the illusion that your lips really were that colorful and moist. If everyone saw you put it on, what was the point?

When she came out of the rest room, she almost bumped into Georgia, who was getting a roll of paper towels from one of the big cardboard boxes stored against the wall.

"How's old Hardy doin'?" Georgia asked.

"He's pretty depressed about hurtin' his ankle. He can only get around with crutches." Ruby Dee wondered why Georgia didn't discuss this with Will. She also wondered if Georgia's eyelashes were real.

"Will ought to put him in a home. It'd be a lot better all the way around."

Well, that turned Ruby Dee to ice. "Oh?" she said. "A lot better for who?"

Georgia gave a little laugh. "I guess it wouldn't be better for you. The Starrs wouldn't need your . . . ah, services then . . . would they?" She arched her eyebrow like a question mark, then turned and walked off before Ruby Dee could press her about what she meant.

Ruby Dee could say one thing for Georgia: the woman said what she thought.

Lonnie had already started to get the groceries he wanted: Oreos, corn chips and mixed nuts. He followed Ruby Dee while she gathered the supplies she needed. Actually, she got more than she needed, going on to canned pineapple slices and peaches in natural juices. Seeing the price on the peaches, she put them back on the shelf, but Lonnie then snatched them up. They carried all the groceries to the front, so Georgia could tally up the bill.

A pretty young woman had joined Georgia. She had silky brown hair to her shoulders, tender green eyes and the kind of figure to turn men's heads. She cast Ruby Dee a curious but friendly grin and nod and then poured those tender green eyes all over Lonnie.

"Hi, Lonnie . . . how's it goin'?" The girl eyed Lonnie as if he were a great big chocolate sundae and she had been on a starvation diet.

Oh, dear, Ruby Dee thought. She happened to

glance at Georgia, to see that woman read it all, too, and was none too pleased.

"Hey, Crystal," Lonnie said, giving her the same charming grin he gave Ruby Dee and even Georgia.

He proceeded to make introductions, then explained that Crystal was Georgia's sister. Ruby Dee noticed the resemblance, although Georgia was hard-ass wise and Crystal tender-reed green.

Crystal's tender eyes clouded when she observed Ruby Dee, but Ruby Dee smiled at her, and the younger woman smiled back and said, "I hope you can help Hardy." She meant it, because it wasn't in the young woman to put on a face.

As Ruby Dee and Lonnie left, Georgia said, "Tell Will I said hello, Lonnie." But while she spoke to him, her eyes were aimed like bullets at Ruby Dee.

There were two sisters who were crazy for the Starr brothers, Ruby Dee thought as, half blinded by the sudden bright sunshine, she made her way around to the passenger side of the Galaxie. She and Lonnie set their bags in the back seat. He opened the door and waved her inside, as if he was a prince and she a princess. She felt self-conscious, because she caught sight of Crystal standing at the glass door and looking at them.

Lonnie slammed the door securely and flashed her one of his grins. Ruby Dee's heart got heavy. The Lord had sure pulled a joke when he made people so they hankered after other people, she thought, jamming her hat on her head.

She wondered how serious things were between Will and Georgia. Lonnie might know, but she knew no way to ask him and not appear to be asking. Besides, it was none of her business, and she didn't want it to be, either. It was hard enough to live her life, without trying to know about everybody else's.

Lonnie didn't head straight for home but showed Ruby Dee the sights. The town consisted of the building at each corner of the crossroads and a number of small houses and mobile homes fanning out down the roads. To the west about a mile was the school, a combination of brick and steel buildings, elementary through high school housed in separate wings beneath the same roof.

The brick Baptist church boasted a small belltower and had a brick archway above its cemetery entry. Lonnie said the Methodist church was about four miles to the east. It was simple white clapboard and still possessed the original separate outhouses for men and women.

"Out in this part of the country, people are either Baptists or Methodists," Lonnie said. "Any other persuasions are suspect, and to some Baptists even Methodists are suspect."

"Are the Starrs suspect?"

He frowned thoughtfully. "Well, now, Daddy walked out of the Baptist church when he married Mama, whose family were nonpracticing Catholics from way back. He tried the Methodist church, but quit them, too, when they wanted money for indoor toilets. My Aunt Roe was a Methodist, and she made me and Will come along with her to church, but then she brought home her second husband from a missionary trip to Africa, and he was a Presbyterian lay minister, who started having services at their house, so we all quit the Methodist Church, too. My cousin J-Jean went away and came back a minister in the Church of Divine Love; she's a circuit preacher down in Elk City and Clinton. My second cousin, Rollie, and his whole family were converted to some church on the television, and they ended up going to Chicago where the television church came from.

"You are all suspect, aren't you?"

"Yes, ma'am, we are."

A grin played at the corners of his mouth. He was just made to laugh and to make people laugh with him. And, boy howdy, he knew how to make a woman feel like a woman.

The rodeo grounds sat out in the middle of nowhere. There was already a sign up for the annual fall rodeo, in September. Someone had hand-lettered a big sign next to it that said, "Y'all Come!"

"Are you and Will gonna ride in the rodeo?" Ruby Dee asked.

Lonnie shrugged. "We did, a few years back." His gaze came around to hers, and he reached out and took her hand and pulled it to the middle of the seat. "Maybe we will this year . . . if you'll be there."

She didn't know what to say, and mercy, his hand was warm over hers. "I don't know if I'll still be here. Your daddy will probably fire me when he gets on his feet again."

Looking forward again, Lonnie lifted his hand from hers and returned it to the steering wheel, carefully directing the car to avoid the roughest ruts of the road that circled the rodeo grounds.

"Broke my arm the first time at this arena," he said. "High school rodeo, ridin' a bronc. I was sixteen." His hazel eyes cut to her. "I won, though. I went to nationals for the first time that year."

She could see him, high and wild on a horse. "And you've been ridin' broncs ever since."

"I did for a long time, until I discovered calf roping. I broke my arm once and my leg twice in bronc ridin'. I've only broken my finger in calf ropin', and

I have two cow ponies that generally make more money than I do, 'cause so many of the guys are willin' to pay to use 'em. It's a lot less work to rent out a horse than it is to ride him.''

Oh, my, how she liked it—riding around with Lonnie, listening to him, the way his eyes felt all over her.

What she could not have admitted to a living soul—didn't even care to admit to Miss Edna and God—was the fantasy that flitted through her mind: the image of Lonnie pulling her across the seat of the Galaxie into his arms and kissing her face off.

The fantasy wanted to return, but she refused it, because it was stupid. It shocked her somewhat. She couldn't look at it closely at the moment, since she was so distracted by Lonnie and all, but in instinctive defense of herself, she thought that she was a woman, one born with the normal weaknesses that threatened good sense.

And it would be difficult not to flirt with Lonnie, because doing it seemed to please him so much.

So they drove around and flirted as the sun grew hotter and little Sally drooled over the side of the car, while Lonnie showed her places and talked about them and ran his eyes all over Ruby Dee.

Over and above all the flirting, however, Ruby Dee suspected that another reason Lonnie kept driving around, thinking up places to show her, was that he wasn't in a hurry to get back to the ranch. He didn't turn toward home until Ruby Dee told him she needed to return, and then he drove a lot slower going back home than he had coming out.

When he turned the car beneath the Starr Ranch sign, Lonnie became downright quiet. Of course, it had gotten awfully hot. When she got out of the car, she found her dress sticking to the back of her thighs. Spreading her legs, she lifted her dress in the back and waved it, encouraging the air to circulate up her bare skin and over the nylon lace panties clinging to her rear. Whew! That felt good.

Then her gaze came up, and she saw Will striding toward her from the house. His eyes were straight on her.

For an instant she felt buck naked.

She dropped her dress in place and brought her legs together. She felt silly as could be. Silly and naked.

And then the brothers crowded around her, getting the groceries out of the back of the car. Ruby Dee would have moved, but they seemed to trap her.

Will was in front of her, snatching a bag right out of her hands. "I'll get it." He pulled another up from the seat, his forearm tanned and hard and straining below his brown denim shirt sleeve.

"I'll get these, Ruby Dee." Lonnie bent in front of her. His shirt stretched tight over his lean back.

Scents of fresh perspiration and warm after shave . . . and male virility. Lordy. It was unnerving. And exciting.

When she got to the kitchen, she grabbed the things she had brought Hardy from the bags and hurriedly left the room. She couldn't really explain why, because she had no time to sort it all out, and besides, she didn't really want to.

She didn't want to think about it at all; she just wanted to be away from Will and Lonnie and the confused feelings that churned inside her. By golly, her thoughts were too embarrassing to be allowed to do more than flit through her mind, and she wouldn't have let them do that if she could have stopped them.

She went to Hardy, thinking: Lordy, Ruby Dee, get a hold of yourself.

Miss Edna's voice came to her: *"Straighten up!"*

"Thank you, Miss Edna," Ruby Dee whispered, breathing deeply, as calm returned.

Hardy Starr himself did wonders for taking Ruby Dee's mind off its carnal bent. There he was—just lying in that bed, just as he had been when she left, staring out the window, all rumpled and with tobacco stains on his shirt. He looked so pitiful he probably would have made even Georgia Reeves cry.

Ruby Dee stopped in the doorway when she saw him. For a second she wanted to throw herself across his bed and wail, and at the same time she wanted to jerk him up by his shirt front and give him a good shaking.

"Mr. Starr, you are tryin' me. You surely are," she said, marching into the room. "I brought you some things to read."

He looked at her, his pale eyes hard behind his glasses. "I never asked you to."

"I know that. I was being kind. You have heard of it before, haven't you—kindness? Here. I have today's paper from Oklahoma City and the *Western Horseman* and the *Louis L'Amour Western Magazine*— it has lots of western stories in it—and the *Farm and Ranch Trader*."

She had hoped especially to delight him with the last one, which had lots of pictures of items for sale.

"It doesn't matter if you can read any of them, because I'll read them to you, and you're gonna learn."

But he didn't so much as glance at any of them. He said, "Did you happen to get me some Skoal?" Of course he didn't think she had.

With great pleasure, Ruby Dee pulled the small tin from her dress pocket and waved it in his face. "Lonnie said you liked spearmint. Ha!"

Thankfully that got a reaction. He stared at her in surprise, with his mouth hanging open. Ruby Dee dumped the newspaper and magazines in his lap and dropped the tin of chewing tobacco on top of them.

"You are gonna have to change that shirt, Mr. Starr." She went to his closet, flipped through the few that hung there and chose a pale green plaid.

On a second thought, she took all the shirts out of his closet, tossed him the plaid one and left with the others over her arm, saying, "I'll have your lunch in half an hour."

With relief, she found Lonnie and Will gone, and she was left alone to load the washer, put the groceries away and ponder ways to make Hardy Starr want to be alive. Considering all that didn't leave her time to think about the stirrings inside herself.

14

BY THE FOLLOWING day, Hardy gave up completely on trying to die, although he wasn't really trying to live, either. He just lay there because he didn't know what else to do and didn't feel like doing anything else.

He did feel like getting a drink. He felt it powerfully, but the opportunity to go into the kitchen and get the bottle of Jack Daniel's in the cabinet beneath the sink never presented itself. His need for the whiskey was outweighed by his need to keep all of them thinking he couldn't get around. It depressed the hell out of him.

And the gal kept pestering him. He thought that no man, even one who was reaching for Saint Peter, would have been allowed to die with that gal around.

She came popping into his room, her steamy brown eyes falling all over him, her smoky voice nagging him—change his shirt, eat his lunch, read, watch television. She read to him for thirty minutes at a time, and she pestered him to read for her, which he wouldn't do.

Not being able to read very much at all embarrassed him, but he didn't like to think about that, and he didn't appreciate the gal making him think about it.

And she kept asking him questions. What did he think of her Mexican omelets? . . . What did he think of the President? . . . How did he like the drink she had made him in her juicer?

He told her he didn't want to read and he didn't want to watch television. He liked eggs fried, period; he'd never liked any of the Presidents; and he wasn't gonna drink anything that was the color of snot.

He told her that unless she wanted to bring him a bottle of whiskey, to leave him the hell alone. He threw the magazines on the floor and turned off the television. She picked up the magazines and turned the television back on.

She moved around him, slinging her womanliness so that it seemed like it scattered all over the room and hovered even after she'd taken her little body sashaying out of there. Her movements stayed in his memory, and he realized she moved like Jooney, graceful and fluid.

It startled Hardy when he realized he was watching her move, mostly watching her breasts bobbing as she adjusted the roll underneath his ankle. The idea that he could be his age and looking at a woman's breasts with even a whisper of lust confused him. Hardy had not looked at a woman with lust since Lila had walked out on him. He had taken lust and all other passions out to the trash barrel and burned them right along with his and Lila's marriage certificate and a nightgown she had left behind.

He was thinking about all this, when he suddenly

heard Woody Guthrie singing through the house: "... dust storm comin' ... from Oklahoma City ... to the Rio Grande ... "

It took him a few minutes to realize it was Woody Guthrie singing. He hadn't heard Woody Guthrie for ... well, he couldn't remember when he had last heard Woody Guthrie.

When it came down to it, Woody Guthrie's voice wasn't something Hardy figured anyone would miss. Woody's voice was similar to the sound of a saw biting through wood and sending sawdust flying, at least in Hardy's opinion.

But Woody's music was real music, yes, sir, guitar to be understood as a guitar and harmonica to be understood as a harmonica. And words that could be understood, that told how it was to live when people had to work for a living.

The gal came swaying into his room. "I brought you some tomato juice, Mr. Starr. It's red, not green."

"Where'd you get that ... those songs of Guthrie's?" he demanded. "What in the hell do you know about Woody Guthrie?" It did not seem right for her, young and fresh like she was, to be playing Woody Guthrie.

"Why, I imagine every Oklahoman knows somethin' about Woody Guthrie," she said. "A friend of mine, Miss Edna, told me all about him. She knew him."

"Huh ... probably half the old farts in the state say they knew Woody Guthrie."

"Did you?" she asked, her eyes fully on him.

"Yeah, I did. Weren't so many people around back then. Folks knew folks."

She went swaying back out of the room and then

she reappeared, bringing a black portable stereo. Without asking him, she left Woody Guthrie singing beside the bed.

Hardy lay there listening to the craggy voice sing about the land blowing away and people blowing with it. "Dust Pneumonia Blues." "Dust Storm Disaster." "Vigilante Man." "Blowing Down This Road." The sawdusty voice singing about desperate, dusty days to tunes picked on a plain old guitar and blown on a plain old harmonica.

Woody Guthrie sang about how it was for them, and he made a name and a living for himself doing it, too. He did it mostly out in California, while the rest of them were still blowing away back in Kansas and Oklahoma and Texas. But they had his songs to sing, and that helped.

It was hearing all those old songs from his virile youth, when he still had hopes and dreams, that started something cracking inside Hardy, the same as hard, dry ground yielded to the power of moist green sprouts.

"Mr. Starr, would you like me to give you a shave?"

The gal stood leaning against the doorjamb, a hand on one of her slim hips, her left leg forward just enough for her dress to outline her thighs.

Hardy said, "I reckon you won't be satisfied until you get your hands on me." His voice was thick.

A grin swept her full lips and lit her entire face like a sunbeam. "I've been after you all the time," she said in her smoky voice.

In that moment, she was Jooney. And he accepted it.

* * *

When Will saw the old man stretched out in the old green Lazy-boy and Ruby Dee hovering over him, his heart went into his throat. He thought maybe the old man was dying. It did occur to him, though, to wonder about the recliner being in the old man's room, crowded up against the bed. It belonged in the living room, in the corner.

Then Ruby Dee laughed. "Oh, Hardy Starr, who was the Queen of Sheba, anyway?"

She straightened and Will saw the razor—a straight razor, no less—in her hand. His heart jumped. He saw shaving cream coating the old man's face.

Ruby Dee was shaving the old man.

The old man growled, "Ain't you ever read your Bible, gal?"

Will took it all in, his gaze moving from the old man, back to the razor, and then to the bowl of water in which Ruby Dee rinsed the blade.

The two of them saw Will. The old man slowly looked away.

Ruby Dee said, "I'll be a little late with dinner, 'cause I'm givin' your daddy a shave."

Will nodded. "Okay."

He watched her bend over the old man again. Her earrings dangled against her cheek, and the neckline of her dress hung low.

He turned and walked away. Halfway through the dining room, he stopped, hesitated, then went back, walking softly. He peered furtively around the door, not wanting them to see him. Ruby Dee was again bending over the old man, talking softly to him. Too softly for Will to hear.

Will went back to the kitchen.

"What's Ruby Dee makin' for lunch?" Lonnie

asked. He had his head in the refrigerator. "She hasn't started anything yet." He came out of the refrigerator, bottle of Red Dog in his hand and a puzzled look on his face.

"I don't know," Will said and slipped in and got himself a beer.

"What's she doin'?" Lonnie craned his neck, looking toward the back hall.

"Givin' the old man a shave." Will gave the bottle cap a hard twist. He threw it across the room into the sink, strode to his office and shut the door behind him.

Three days after he'd put his foot through the rotten flooring, the swelling on Hardy's Starr's ankle was completely gone. By the fourth day, he was eating heartily, bathing without a fight and had given up his overalls in favor of jeans or slacks and a shirt. But by the end of the week, he still wasn't on his feet. Ruby Dee figured he would get up when he got more tired of lying around than of annoying his sons, but Hardy thought of something better. On Saturday, he had Lonnie bring the wheelchair in from the shop.

Well, that didn't do Will Starr any good at all. He already felt like his daddy's injury was his fault, and when he came in at noon and saw his daddy sitting there in the kitchen in that chair, he demanded, "What in the hell is this?"

"It oughta make you happy. You been tryin' to get me into this chair for a year."

"I ain't never tried to get you into that chair." When Will Starr got mad, his tone and speech became very rustic.

"Then why'd you buy it . . . and nag me 'bout usin' it?"

"Aw, geez, Dad." Will Starr got all red in the face, then pointed his finger at his daddy. "If your leg is all that bad, by God, you're goin' down to the doctor on Monday." Then he turned around and stormed out.

Ruby Dee was drying a bowl as she peered out the window, watching him walk down the drive. She dried the bowl so hard, she polished it. Setting it aside with a clunk and not saying even an excuse me to Hardy or Lonnie, she went out the back door.

She knew Will went straight to that roan mustang any time he and his daddy got into it, which was at least once a day. He would get a cigarette from his pickup truck if he didn't have one in his shirt pocket, and go down and smoke it in the shade of a dying cottonwood at the corner of the tall fence corral.

When she reached him, she didn't bother to make small talk. It was too hot to strain herself. She did pet the colt, who stuck his nose over the fence at her. "There is not a thing wrong with your daddy's legs," she said. "He could walk if he wanted to."

"What makes you so certain of that?" He took the cigarette out of his mouth and raked a hand through his hair.

"How do you know when this colt is feeling co-operative or is wantin' to run off?" Ruby Dee rubbed the colt's forehead. "You just know; you feel it. Well, I just know there is nothin' wrong with your daddy's leg. Oh, he has aches and pains in it, just like he has for years. But the reason he doesn't walk is that he doesn't want to."

His steely eyes studied her for a long second, then

doubt flickered across his face. "I've been thinkin' the same thing. But he's had that wheelchair for a year and refused to use it. He was too dang proud to use it. Now he suddenly gives in?" He shook his head and threw the cigarette butt in the dirt.

"You and your daddy are cut from the same cloth, Will Starr." Exasperation rose up and took hold of her. "You told him you were leavin' when he got on his feet again. He's not gonna get on his feet, because he doesn't want you to leave, but he sure doesn't want to have to ask you to stay, either. I don't think this is anything it takes an Einstein to figure out. Now, if you want to get your daddy out of that chair, you just go in there and tell him you are not leavin'."

Will stared at her, his steely-blue eyes brilliant and his jaw tight as petrified stone. "I can't do that."

"You can't or you won't?"

He gazed off into the distance and said, "I guess it doesn't make much difference which one it is."

"No, I don't suppose it does," Ruby Dee said after a few seconds.

In the past few days she had come to learn that Will Starr was not one to spare himself. He wasn't one to place blame on anyone besides himself, or spend a lot of time with "if-onlys." He tried to see things as they were and go with them. She had come to admire that about him.

The colt got tired of being ignored and began to nibble the grass. Ruby Dee gazed off in the same direction as Will, seeing the white pipe fencing, the sunburned grass, grazing horses.

"You know, I never had a place to call home, not like you have here, a place where you grew up with your family and everything. I always wanted a place like this."

"This is Dad's place," he said. "I want a place of my own."

Ruby Dee could understand it, a little.

He propped his boot on the bottom rail and leaned his forearms on the top one, intertwining his fingers. "Here I'm always standing in the old man's shadow, having to do things his way or answer for it. Here I'm just a hired hand—a foreman, but a hired one all the same. Dad thinks I want to take it away from him, but I don't." He turned to Ruby Dee. "It isn't about takin' from him. It's about what I need. I need my own place."

Ruby Dee turned and leaned her back against the fence rails. She thought about how Will's leaving would affect Hardy, but she didn't speak of it. Instead she said, "What about this place? Hardy can't run it on his own, even when he's back on his feet again."

"He can get a foreman to do the same things I do, and I'll still look in," Will said, looking down at his folded hands. "I don't mean I won't check in and be here to help out."

It crossed Ruby Dee's mind that neither of them had mentioned Lonnie. Lonnie kept himself unattached.

His brilliant gaze came up to her. "I never thought you'd be here a week. I sure appreciate you stickin' it out."

She chuckled. "I told you I would stay, Will Starr." She liked to say his name.

"Yeah . . . you did, Ruby Dee."

He said her name hesitantly, like a boy stealing a feel. And a hint of a smile touched his lips and lit his eyes. His eyes searched hers, and she felt the heat deep inside. She had the urge to put her hand on his cheek, to touch the lingering scab on the wound, to soothe him. And to know him, inch by inch.

It was there between them, a knowing and wanting, but neither of them spoke of it. What was there to say?

"It can't be easy, bein' a woman in our household. I want you to know I appreciate all you've done for the old man . . . and for me and Lonnie, too." He shifted and shoved a hand into his jeans pocket, looking embarrassed.

"Well, I'd like to pretend it's all been terribly hard," she said. Turning, she fingered the peeling paint on the top rail. "But it hasn't been so much. Oh, Hardy gave me a tussle, but he's come around. And I'll tell you, Will Starr, this job is easy compared to those when I have to be at a deathbed, helping the patient over and trying to keep the family from losin' their minds to heartbreak, or bein' called on to tend not only the sick but all the puny, selfish relatives.

"Here I get to have a lot of time to myself and to nap, while I'm gettin' paid, and believe me—I need the rest and the money."

There was an awkward pause, then Ruby Dee said, "I've had a hard time over losin' Miss Edna. She was my mama and my best friend in one. And goin' through those last weeks with her were hard enough, without all the strain of the bills pilin' up. Miss Edna had cancer off and on for six years, and it didn't only eat her up, but it ate up what little savings she had, insurance, everything. Her medicine bills alone rivaled the national debt. Oh, yes, there was Medicare, only Medicare forgets that people have to eat, if they manage to stay alive. I make good money—as you know—but there just never seemed enough, and I didn't work at all the last month, except for caring for Miss Edna. Medicare owes me for that."

She looked at him then. "We all like to pretend that the consideration of money comes second, after the life of a person, but it doesn't and it can't, because you've got to have money to keep a roof over your head and food on the table, plain and simple. Right now, I'm so glad that it's you havin' to think of that and not me."

He gazed down at her. "It makes me feel better," he said, his voice low and heavy, "to know we could offer you somethin' more than headaches."

His steely-blue eyes were on her, straight and strong. And Ruby Dee felt something shift deep inside and set her off balance.

Suddenly nervous, she pushed away from the fence. "I'd better get back, or you're gonna be havin' your dinner at suppertime. I'll set it out in fifteen minutes."

She walked quickly, only vaguely realizing she was doing so, keeping her face straight ahead, while all the time her mind was back there beneath the cottonwood tree with Will Starr and looking up into his intense, brilliant eyes. And wanting to touch him, too.

Entering the kitchen, she found Lonnie gone and Hardy, still in his wheelchair, slamming cabinet doors and cursing. He glared up at her.

She went to the top shelf of the corner cabinet and pulled out the amber pint bottle. "Is this what you are lookin' for?" She gave it to him.

He looked at her in surprise, but she just went

about getting the meal on the table. He swiveled his wheelchair and went off to his bedroom. The wheelchair was electric and took some getting used to. He bumped into the door frame going through, and she heard him hit the one into the hallway, too.

Ruby Dee squeezed her eyes closed and prayed to God that she had done the right thing, that Hardy Starr wouldn't end up drinking himself into an early grave. How would she explain her actions, should that happen? Could Will Starr possibly understand that she felt Hardy's pride and dignity were far more important than her own or anyone else's judgment about how he should live his life?

Thankfully, though she smelled whiskey on Hardy's breath on occasion, he did not get drunk. She told him a few days later, "It's a good thing you aren't gettin' drunk, because you can't drive that wheelchair even when you're sober."

And one quiet evening after Will Starr had eaten a big supper topped off by two pieces of apple pie, she explained what she'd done. He didn't say anything, only nodded.

They took Hardy to the doctor in Cheyenne on Wednesday, which was the earliest appointment Will could get. Ruby Dee knew Will was worried about his daddy and that he saw taking him to the doctor as his responsibility to do all he could for Hardy's well-being.

But she thought he was also trying to force his daddy into capitulating. He was gambling that Hardy would hate the idea of going to the doctor so much that he would get out of the wheelchair.

Hardy was made of stern stuff, though. He hung in there and went to the doctor.

Ruby Dee did not hold a very favorable opinion of doctors in general. She had seen too many doctors who considered themselves as very near holy and who treated elderly people as if they were either children or stupid and either way were of little use, except to keep handing out money. She also abhorred the practice of prescribing a pill for every ill, when so many problems could be controlled by proper diet, exercise and soul searching. Of course, doctors weren't all to blame for the pill-popping; most people wanted to take a pill to cure them, since it required the least amount of effort on their part.

Dr. Maybrey, however, treated Hardy with respect and care. After a thorough exam, he pronounced him in very good overall health. After speaking with Ruby Dee, he even decided to reduce his blood pressure medicine. The doctor could find no reason why Hardy shouldn't be able to use his ankle. Arthritis showed up in all of Hardy's joints, severely in his crippled knee, but it was no worse than it had been the previous year. The doctor proceeded, since he was thorough and respectful of Hardy's mental faculties, to bring up a host of theories, from nerve damage to bone cancer. He suggested Hardy see a neurologist in Oklahoma City.

Poor Will, he had expected either something to be found or for the doctor to say absolutely nothing was wrong with him. He wasn't prepared to have to face a standoff, which was what Hardy gave him by staying in the wheelchair and insisting he couldn't use that ankle, and the only way he was going to see a specialist was to be dragged feet first.

✲15

"COME ON, RUBY Dee . . . come down to Harney with me. I'll treat you to a hot fudge sundae down in Cheyenne." Lonnie parked himself in her way as she came up the stairs and gave her his best grin. "Have mercy on a poor boy."

She didn't smile—Ruby Dee didn't smile much with her lips—but there was a spicy gleam in her eye, and she put her hand on her hip in that way she had that was sexy as all get-out. If Lonnie had dared, he would have laid his hand over hers right there. But Ruby Dee drew a line, and he wouldn't doubt she'd smack him right down the stairs if he crossed it. He liked that about her. He liked seeing how close he could get to that line.

Her right eyebrow curved upward. "All right, cowboy—your Justins are shined, your Wranglers starched, and you smell good enough to eat. Is that all for me, or for some other girl?"

"You, sweetheart," he said smartly.

She eyed him, and he experienced a nervous flutter inside.

"What will you do someday, Lonnie Starr, if I take you up on your flirtin'?"

"Is that a promise?" For the space of a heartbeat, the nervous flutter flew high.

The next instant he saw the spice fade from her eyes, and she shook her head. "I was on my way up to tell you that Crystal just called and said she won't be ready until near six. She's been held up in Cheyenne."

Lonnie, feeling easy again, said, "Then I guess I'm all yours," and opened his arms wide.

Ruby Dee swished at him with her hands. "Oh, Lonnie, get out of my way—go on and make the women of the county happy."

"Somebody's gotta do it," he said, sounding serious. He moved aside, but as she started past him, he boldly caught her and kissed her neck.

She pushed him away. "Lonnie! I'll call your daddy, and he'll come run you down with his wheelchair."

Lonnie's sparkling eyes tugged at Ruby Dee's heart. "Go on," she said again, gazing down at him now, "but I want to tell you somethin' that Miss Edna used to say: 'Passion can carry a person down river but not bring them back.'"

"On a river such as that, who wants to come back?"

He gave her a wink and sauntered away.

Poised there, her hands on the banister, Ruby Dee watched him go and said a small prayer for him. Lonnie Starr had a great need inside of him for feminine attention, needed it as strongly as a person bleeding to death needed a transfusion of blood.

Ruby Dee guessed that her need was to give him attention, so the arrangement was satisfactory, although she sometimes had the fearful feeling that he might suck her dry.

Just then, she lifted her head and saw Will Starr, standing at the top rail, gazing at her.

She felt his tug, the fluttering in her belly.

He had just come from the shower. His hair was wet and shiny, and he was slipping on a shirt and straightening its collar. He quickly covered his bare chest, hard muscled from wrangling calves and hay bales and feed sacks. Will never came around her without his shirt, and he always made Lonnie put his on around her, too.

Her steps slowed. What did he think about her and Lonnie and their teasing? His expression revealed nothing.

Over the past weeks, Ruby Dee had come to feel that Will Starr could hear her with his eyes, without her saying a word. She often found his gaze on her, but she never could read his expression. He kept his emotions bound and gagged, except for his anger, which often broke loose.

"Are you still plannin' to drive up to Woodward later?" he asked, buttoning his shirt.

"Yes." Ruby Dee nodded. "Do you want me to pick up anything for you?" Her gaze remained on his thick shoulders.

He shook his head. "No. I told you I'd change the oil in your car. It'll take about fifteen minutes."

"I won't be ready for nearly an hour."

"Okay." He nodded a good-bye and went on down the stairs in his socks. His work boots would be at the back door.

Ruby Dee's gaze followed Will's back until he disappeared into the dining room. She went into her room, closed the door and leaned against it.

How odd it seemed now that she had never realized what it would be like in this household of men. She had believed this job would be no different than any private care she had done, except she had counted on it not being quite as intense and draining, since Hardy was not on his deathbed. She had often lived in and taken care of a single man. Often the household would have other perfectly healthy men living there, too. Ruby Dee did her job, and that was all.

But this situation was proving quite different. These men were so very healthy and so very available. And she was so very vulnerable.

Crossing to the window, she lifted her arms, straining to unbutton her dress in the back. She had the playful thought that she could have asked Will to unbutton it for her. He would have blushed blood-red.

That was his charm and attraction, she thought. His reserve about sexual feelings made them all the hotter, same as filching a fresh-baked cookie made it all the sweeter.

She paused at the window, looked down and saw Lonnie in his pickup stop to speak to Will. Then Lonnie went racing away, which was the only way he could drive. Or move, for that matter. Lonnie was always moving in a hurry.

Will walked on toward the tractor barn, and Sally joined him, her silky tail swishing. Sally had taken a shine to Will Starr. That said something about the man, because Sally was a shy dog. Will walked slowly, as was his fashion. He wasn't a man to hurry. He had a lazy, sexy way of walking, and Ruby Dee liked to watch him. She watched until he disappeared inside the barn.

Still she stood at the window, holding her dress now, waiting to see him come out, get in the Galaxie and drive it into the shade of the tractor barn.

It was Will who took care of Lonnie and Hardy, and of Ruby Dee, too.

Will made certain she had cash in the drawer for groceries or anything else she might want. He never questioned her. Sometimes she found Sally's food bowl full, and she knew it was Will who'd filled it. He wouldn't let her take out the trash, said it was too heavy for her to lug. According to Will, the iron Dutch oven was too heavy for her to bring out of the oven. He made certain the gas tank of her car was full, and he had gotten so concerned over the state of her tires that he had exchanged them for some he had in the barn.

He had contacted a friend at a bank in Elk City about getting a loan to buy land. Ruby Dee had overheard the telephone conversation. He had never said anything to Hardy about it, though. He worked hard, rode the roan mustang a lot and kept to himself. It was as if a No Trespassing sign hung around his neck. He did bring his daddy a new bottle of Jack Daniel's, though, when his daddy ran out.

Now, watching him out at the tractor barn, bending over the car engine, Ruby Dee pressed her hand to the window pane. Oh, sometimes she ached to touch Will Starr!

The thought startled her, and, clutching her dress to her chest, she whirled from the window and the sight of him, as if she could whirl away from the thought.

She showered, lotioned and powdered her body and slipped into a black chemise and over that a thin rayon peach-and-black-flowered dress. Leaning toward the mirror, she carefully applied Ripe Apricot lipstick, which exactly matched the flowers in the dress. Her boots were taupe, with black stitching. Standing in the middle of the room, she checked herself in the full-length mirror she had propped against the wall.

She knew good and well she had dressed to catch Will Starr's eye.

"He looks at me, Miss Edna," she whispered. "He looks at me, and I like it."

Not wanting to hear anything Miss Edna might tell her, she grabbed her purse and headed downstairs.

Hardy was in the kitchen, still in his wheelchair. Oh, what a stubborn man!

He had pulled his wheelchair up to the table, and had his leather and tools spread out on it. He had taken to braiding, weaving and carving leather pieces, since he could easily do that from the wheelchair. He was supremely talented, a real artist, although he only grunted when she told him that. Hardy Starr was a prideful man but not a boastful one. He could carve leather and weave it into bridles and reins and even bracelets. She wore a bracelet he had woven for her.

Of course, he hadn't wanted to appear to give it to her. What he had said was, "Here . . . go on an' take it. I'm tired of lookin' at it." As if he hadn't been making it for her the whole time.

Any hint of tenderness set Hardy on edge. It seemed to Ruby Dee that Hardy Starr was not afraid of anything on earth—except warm feelings, his own especially. She tried not to press in on him too much, because she sensed that somehow he hurt when she did, the same way getting too close to a flaming wood stove hurt.

Now his eyebrows went up when he saw her, and he stared.

"Well, thank you, sir," she said and did a pirouette, making the dress swirl around her legs.

"Where you goin'? Got a hot date?" he said. His voice betrayed emotion, even though he went back to splitting leather on a board across the arms of the wheelchair.

"I know you'll miss me terribly, but I'm goin' out for a drive. If there's a fire you're gonna have to save yourself."

He eyed her and then said very sourly, "Then you'd better bring me a bucket of water."

She got a little plastic bucket from the back porch, filled it with water and set it on the table. That made his eyebrows shoot up again.

Chuckling, she couldn't resist kissing his cheek. "Oh, Hardy, you sure know how to look at a gal and make her feel lovely."

"Yah . . . get off me."

But she knew his pleasure. Her heart squeezed. She was becoming much too fond of him.

The fading heat of a summer day hit her when she stepped out the back door. The sun was far to the west, and the sky above forever clear. To Ruby Dee, Oklahoma had the most beautiful evenings in the world. Of course, she had never been anywhere else. She didn't much care to go.

Will had brought the Galaxie up into the shade of the elm and put the top down for her. Turning, she saw him over at the training pen, saddling the mustang. Every morning or evening, Will worked that horse for at least an hour. Sally was there, too, lying in shade. She wagged her tail as Ruby Dee came but didn't bother to get up.

Carefully, Ruby Dee climbed up on the tall fence. Will gave her a small nod and swung into the saddle. She thought she detected a spark of male admiration when he looked at her, but she couldn't be certain. Not being certain was disappointing.

"He's sure gettin' quiet," she said, and nodded at the horse.

"He'll do," Will said.

His steely-blue eyes met hers, and then his gaze slid over her. She thought she saw a flicker of male interest . . . but only a flicker, and it was quickly gone, hidden behind indifference.

"Thank you for seeing to the Galaxie. Thank you for takin' care of me, Will Starr."

His gaze met hers. "No problem," he said.

"Your daddy's in the kitchen, watchin' television and workin' with his leather."

A few seconds went by before he said, "I'll check on him."

"You might want to just holler at him from the door. I don't want to come home and find one of you killed the other. Could be you that's dead—Hardy's laid up, but he's strong."

He grinned in the way that had become familiar— a twitching of his lips and a flicker in his eyes—and tipped his hat. "Yes, ma'am. I'll be good."

She climbed off the fence and headed away, then stopped and came back. He watched her the whole time, quietly, sitting there on the horse. "Do you suppose I could ride sometime? I haven't ridden in a long time, but I do know how."

"Okay. Let me have time to tune a horse up for you."

"I can ride pretty good. You don't have to worry."

He didn't say anything to that.

She headed to her car, feeling his gaze on her every step of the way. When she casually looked back, he was still sitting there, atop the horse, watching her.

Sally came running and jumped over into the seat. Ruby Dee slapped her brown hat on her head and headed the car down the drive, waving at Will as she passed. Dust billowed up behind, and she ignored it and flew over the ruts of the drive and the washboard of the dirt road all the way to the state blacktop. She turned north, away from Harney and toward Woodward, an hour's drive through rolling grassland.

It was a wonderful evening for riding in a convertible, but Ruby Dee wished she weren't alone. She talked to Miss Edna some: "Isn't this beautiful country? Why didn't we ever come out this way on our drives? It's higher up here, isn't it? I think I'll get some house plants at the Wal-mart. You know I gave all of yours to Mrs. Gleason, all except the philodendron in the little boot. I kept it. The Starr house could sure use some plants."

At the Wal-mart, she bought a new Revlon lipstick and fingernail polish to match. From the book section, she chose a Louis L'Amour western and a big splashy one by an author named Johnny Quarles, because it took place in Oklahoma. She thought Hardy might especially enjoy that one. For herself she got a new western romance by Genell Dellin. Maybe she'd even read it to Hardy. It might do him good.

Over in the garden shop, she picked up a big green peace plant, a deep blue African Violet and a lovely cactus garden made up in a painted terra-cotta dish. On her way out, she went by the lingerie section and happened upon a good sale. She bought three sets of panties and matching bras. She had a real weakness for colorful lingerie. Near the check-out there was a display of packaged socks, and she bought some for Will and Lonnie. Theirs were get-ting awfully ragged.

Afterward she stopped at the IGA and picked up some canned staples and packages of chicken, chips and Coca-Cola on sale. She kept a little cooler in the car, in which she put the chicken to keep it from spoiling in the heat.

Over at the Sonic drive-in, she got a corn dog and cherry-limeade. Whoever made her cherry-limeade put six real cherries in it. She sat there, fishing them out and plucking them off the stems, while young teens drove by, admiring her Galaxie. That was fun, but it made her feel lonely.

She and Sally drove home, with the starry sky above and country music playing from the radio. It was terribly beautiful and romantic, and was a pointed reminder to Ruby Dee that she was living in a house with three men yet was alone, except for a dog. She told herself that Sally was a very special dog.

When she reached the house, the lights were blaz-ing from the kitchen and back porch. Surprisingly, Lonnie's truck was back in its place. And then she saw a figure coming out across the yard . . . Lonnie. Her heart leaped in her throat, and her first thought was of Hardy.

But then Lonnie was asking if she was all right.

"Well, yes. Why?"

He looked uncomfortable. "You've just never been

out so late. It's after eleven. Here, let me help you with your bags."

And then they were entering the kitchen, and there were Hardy and Will. Both of them in the room together, and not fighting!

She saw the relief on their faces. They each looked quickly at her, as if ascertaining that she was real, and then they looked away.

Hardy said, "It's about time, woman," and gathered up his leather pieces from the table. Will turned his back to pour a cup of coffee.

Well. They had been worried about her.

She went racing up to her room, threw herself across her bed and cried and cried. She didn't want them to worry about her. She didn't want to care for them. She wasn't staying here. She was saving her money and buying her farm house and having her babies in overalls. Oh, Lordy, she knew they were just going to complicate everything.

A hesitant knock sounded at her door. "Ruby Dee . . . are you all right? Are you sick?"

It was Will's voice, uncertain and worried.

"I'm fine," she said after a long minute, and she spoke sharply, without knowing why.

She heard footsteps in the hallway, and Lonnie saying, "Women just cry like that at certain times of the month."

~ 16

WHILE WORKING TO repair fence, Wildcat sliced his palm open on the barbed wire. Depending on the chore at hand, Wildcat had to either slice or rip or pound or burn his hand at least once.

Will tossed his fence pliers into the battered wooden tool box. "Lon, you finish up here while I take Wildcat up to the house so's Ruby Dee can doctor his hand."

"Why in the hell do you get to take him, and I have to finish the work?" Lonnie pushed back his hat and assumed a belligerent stance.

"Because once you get in the house with Ruby Dee, drinkin' ice tea and eatin' cookies, you won't ever come out."

As he walked away, he heard Lonnie cursing under his breath. Will opened the pickup door, then turned. "When you finish up here, get on over to the spring creek and check that section of fence. I'll meet you over there."

Lonnie threw down his hammer, clearly wishing to have thrown it at Will.

"You're aggravatin' that boy," Wildcat said, when Will slipped into the seat.

"I know. I don't have a lot of pleasures, since I started tryin' to give up cigarettes."

"Me and Charlene saw a thing about cigarettes on the news the other night. Do you know, there is some research to indicate that smokers have less cavities? And also, there's research that conflicts about smoking being bad for the heart. . . ."

Wildcat went on about cigarette research all the way back to the house. Will drifted off. He had been short-tempered lately, more so than normal.

He missed Georgia.

No, he missed getting laid. And it was somewhat amazing to him to find his body could exhibit so much control over him in that area. That it did annoyed him.

He didn't actually miss Georgia so much, which surprised him. After all their years together, on and off, he should miss her more. He had certainly had regrets when she married Frank. He could see now that what he'd felt was regret over their relationship. He had wasted a lot of years with Georgia. Now, though, what he felt mostly was relief. He didn't have to wonder if he really loved her and if they might have made it, given another chance, because they'd had chances and it was finally over for good. The relief should have made him feel better than he did, though.

The relief did not override his missing something. He missed holding a woman and snuggling with her softness. He also missed being able to hang out at Georgia's. He had no good place to go now to get away from the ranch.

He had nowhere to go to get away from seeing

the old man in that damn wheelchair, and his desire to get away didn't have anything to do with worrying about the old man's leg, because there was nothing wrong with that leg that hadn't been wrong with it twenty years ago. Will was sure of that now. It had to do with thinking the old man would squander his remaining years in that chair, when he didn't have to, just to annoy Will. Just to control him and Lonnie, and even Ruby Dee.

Ruby Dee. He tried really hard not to think a lot about Ruby Dee, and to stay away from her, too, because being around her just set him into hot, horny confusion. Ruby Dee was the main cause of his short temper.

When they reached the house, they found Ruby Dee's car gone. Will remembered then that she had said something about taking the old man into Reeves's Quick Stop. She was trying to interest him in playing dominoes with T. Boone and Jenks Larson. She wanted to get the old man out of the house, but he kept refusing to go anywhere in particular, although he had allowed her to drive him around Harney, where everyone could see him in a flashy convertible driven by a pretty young woman.

That the old man would do that was a good surprise, but not compared to all the other things he had started doing. The old man did a lot of things with Ruby Dee that he never had with anyone else.

Every day now, he got himself spiffed up in jeans or khaki trousers and one of the new shirts Ruby Dee had gotten for him down in Cheyenne. He shaved every day, too, and he let Ruby Dee do it for him half the time, while he lay back in the old green recliner. He'd even let her give him a haircut, shorter on top and longer in the back. Will had been startled by how much younger the old man looked with his hair cut that way. These days the old man had begun to look more like the man Will remembered, the one who used to wheel and deal at the stockyards, trading cattle and stories and making money out of both.

Almost every evening Ruby Dee and the old man would go into his bedroom and read to each other. At first Ruby Dee had read to the old man, whether he wanted her to or not. But gradually she had gotten him to start reading to her.

Just last evening, when Will had been coming through the dining room, he had caught the sound of the old man's voice, reading. He'd stopped right there in the middle of the room, surprised.

"Now, when the queen of Sheba heard of the fame of Solomon con . . . con-cerning the name of the Lord, she came to test him with hard ques-tions . . ."

Ruby Dee interrupted. "Oh, so Sheba wasn't her name, it was a place. I never knew that. We'll have to look it up. . . . I'll make a note."

"Are you done? Can I pro-ceed?"

The old man seemed to be learning bigger words from Ruby Dee, too.

His stubbornness aside, the old man was crafty, and Will was of the opinion that the reason he let Ruby Dee read to him and he read to her was to keep her occupied with him every evening.

Will had come to the amazing conclusion that the old man was struck on Ruby Dee. Further, Will had been shocked to catch a hint of sexuality in the way the old man looked at her, too.

Since Ruby Dee wasn't there, Wildcat proposed going on home, but Will figured he had better doctor Wildcat's hand. "At least let's clean it up and put a bandage on it."

They were walking toward the house, Wildcat with quite a bit of reluctance, when the Galaxie came flying up the drive. Ruby Dee tooted and waved, then stopped with a loud crunch of gravel. The back end of the car swayed, because she'd stomped on the brakes.

Wildcat was greatly relieved. "No offense, boss, but Ruby Dee is a nurse."

"Hardy and I bought dominoes!" Ruby Dee cried, swinging up a bag as she got out of the car. "He's gonna teach me to play. Then we're gonna go down and sit at Reeves's and rake in the money. Aren't we, Hardy?"

"You'll probably annoy me into it eventually," Hardy said. "Get my chair," he ordered Will, who was already on his way to do just that.

After the old man settled into his chair, Will told Ruby Dee about Wildcat's hand, which had the effect of diverting her attention from the old man and gave Will a small slice of satisfaction. He understood the sentiment as a petty one, but he wasn't sorry for it.

In the kitchen, Wildcat laid his hand on the table, content to let Ruby Dee work him over. Wildcat had come to believe Ruby Dee was some kind of shaman. He and Charlene tended toward hypochondria, anyway, and they had taken to consulting Ruby Dee on everything from headaches to ingrown toenails.

No living thing escaped Ruby Dee's tending, and castor oil appeared the remedy of choice—not through the mouth, but applied to the body. For a week, Ruby Dee had made Will rub it on the wound on his cheek every morning and night, supposedly to reduce the scarring. Lonnie got it put on his hands to soften his callouses, and Wildcat got castor-oil-soaked patches to soothe his eyes, strained from too much television watching, a remedy he took home to Charlene. The cat got his ears doused with it for mites, the roan colt got it rubbed on his hocks when Will overworked him, and several mama cows got their fly bites doctored with it.

Will had to admit that in each case, Ruby Dee and her castor oil hadn't hurt anything and did appear to help. Wildcat claimed his eyes didn't burn like they had, and Charlene was so impressed that she took to using it for her house cat's ear mites. If the wound on Will's cheek left a scar, it would be small, and the colt's hocks were back to normal overnight.

The castor oil's one failure seemed to be with the old man. He'd consented to have Ruby Dee rub it on his ankle and knee and bind them up each morning for the first two weeks after his accident. But now almost a month had gone by, and he remained in the wheelchair.

Will figured that in this case the power of castor oil was outmatched by the old man's stubbornness.

Then he realized that he was staring at the feminine curve of Ruby Dee's backside, where she bent over Wildcat's hand. He glanced over and saw the old man looking at him, his eyes sharp and knowing.

Turning, Will reached into the refrigerator and pulled out a can of Dr. Pepper. "I'm gonna check the water in the pickup radiator, Wildcat. I'll be out there when Ruby Dee's finished with you."

He almost burned his hand on the radiator cap before he found a rag to use. Steam poured out. The old pickup needed a lot of work.

He threw the rag on the ground. Letting the radiator cool, he sat in the seat, with the door open, and smoked his third cigarette of the day. The snapping of sheets like sails in the wind caught his attention. The sheets were bright white on Ruby Dee's clothesline, and next to them fluttered several sets of bras and panties, like colorful signal flags around a car lot.

Ruby Dee was still here. Hardy's grouchiness hadn't run her off; nor had the considerable lack of privacy, the repetitive work, the isolation, the blowing dust.

Yes, she'd stayed, and the sheets hanging there alongside the bras and panties were proof of her existence and the changes she had made in their lives.

With Ruby Dee in the house, boots and spurs were left at the back door, and spitting and cursing and farting stopped there, too. Ruby Dee was so much a woman that a man felt called on to be a gentleman. He and Lonnie said please and thank you and took their hats off. And now they had to take their clothes into the bathroom with them when they showered, because they couldn't go running around in their birthday suits, and they had to remember to close the door, too.

Will kept forgetting that door. It was fortunate that there was a shower curtain, because once, he'd been buck naked, about to step into the shower, when Ruby Dee came waltzing through the open door with an armload of towels. He'd grabbed the shower curtain faster than a gunslinger going for his guns. It had embarrassed the hell out of him, but Ruby Dee had said blandly, "I've seen a lot of naked bodies, Will Starr, doin' what I do."

She'd been amused by his embarrassment. In his opinion Ruby Dee had little respect for private personal things. Maybe she had seen a lot of naked bodies, but his wasn't among them, and especially his with a hard-on.

With Ruby Dee in the house, every morning there was an enormous breakfast on the table, every noon a light meal, and every evening another enormous meal. There was ice tea and fresh-squeezed orange juice in the refrigerator and fresh baked cookies in the cookie jar.

With Ruby Dee, there was prayer before meals, lingering afterward over the best coffee Will had ever tasted, and watching while Ruby Dee hummed her way through clearing the dishes. There were clean towels on the rods, clean socks and underwear in their drawers and clean sheets on their beds each Wednesday. Sheets that smelled like summer air, because she strung the clothesline from her aluminum trailer to the corner of the tractor barn.

Will had propped a two-by-four in the middle of it to keep it from sagging when it was loaded with sheets or her endless array of underthings.

With Ruby Dee in the house, Will saw more bras and panties in a month than he had seen in his entire lifetime—hanging all over the shower rod, fallen on the floor, lying on the washer. In Will's opinion, the woman was a little careless with clothes that were not meant to be seen.

One afternoon, he found a bra lying on the stairway. It was startling pink against the worn brown wood. As far as Will could tell, Ruby Dee didn't have a stitch of white underwear.

He hesitated, then picked up the delicate article, held it gingerly with his fingers. It struck him that, aside from undoing clasps when these things were on a female, he had never touched one.

He could hear her singing in her bedroom. He

went on up and stopped in the open doorway of her room. She was peering into the mirror above the dresser and swaying to the sound of her own singing. Will imagined quite clearly what the pink bra and matching panties would look like on her beneath the dress she wore.

Seeing him in the mirror, she whirled around. "Will, you scared the daylights out of me! I guess I was thinkin' hard." ·

"The door was open," he said. "Ah . . . you dropped this on the stairs." He held out the bra.

She didn't so much as blush. "Oh, gosh, thank you so much. I just carried a load down to the washer. I want to hang them out in the moonlight tonight." She said it as if the moonlight were something very important.

She turned back to the mirror, and Will's gaze roamed the room. It had become the most colorful place in the house. Scarves draped here and there, old movie and circus posters, books and magazines, that urn on the dresser.

"Will, I've got somethin' in my eye. . . . I can't see anything, and I've blinked and blinked. Can you see anything?"

She came over to him, just like that, and lifted her face to him. There was that about Ruby Dee—she didn't keep distance with anyone. She touched people with her hands and her eyes and her voice.

He looked closely. "I think . . . yeah, there's a piece of fuzz. Don't blink." His fingers felt big and clumsy, but he managed to pick away the fine, crinkled filament caught in her lashes. "There."

"Thanks . . . oh, that's better." She blinked rapidly. And then her eyes were on his, and he knew she was feeling the same heat he was, because those brown eyes began to steam.

That she would feel what he did came as a distinct surprise. Later he wondered if he had imagined it. Maybe it had been some other emotion.

With Ruby Dee in the house, there was so much emotion, like her underwear, cast all over the place. Her coffee-brown eyes shimmered and simmered with feelings, the same as a neon sign, and she didn't try to hide them any more than she did her underwear.

She didn't laugh a lot, but she had a way of smiling quietly, and she could sure snap like summer lightning if she was mad. She turned to liquid when she was sad. The woman could cry . . . at a sad movie, a song on the radio, a dead bird left by the cat, and over nothing in particular at all.

Ruby Dee's frank display of emotions unnerved Will. Aside from anger, which he tried to keep under wraps, he wasn't used to emotions being on open display. Giving way to feelings just wasn't done in his world. The fight he and the old man had had was a prime example of what could happen when they weren't contained.

As for crying, he had seen his father cry one time in his life, and that had been the day his mother left. He remembered his daddy calling Lonnie a sissy for crying. Aunt Roe had held that an emotional display was so unseemly that at her own husband's funeral she had gotten up and served cake, dry-eyed and grand with grace, and when his cousin BettyJo started crying, Aunt Roe had cuffed her good and sent her from the room. After that, anyone in the room even thinking about crying had dried up.

Ruby Dee's emotions swirling all around made

Will pointedly aware of emotions inside himself that he didn't understand and didn't want to understand, by God.

They also made him powerfully aware of living the life of a monk, a life he had not chosen at all.

Tossing his cigarette butt into the dirt, Will went to see if he could find a can of stop-leak for the radiator. As far as he could tell, deep thinking got a man nowhere but confused.

Wildcat went home after Ruby Dee bandaged his hand, and Will went back to fixing fence with Lonnie. Apparently Lonnie felt the need to cover the older man's absence by talking.

"I heard on the weather channel this mornin' that rain isn't in sight for another two weeks. We're gonna burn up. . . . Wildcat says he hasn't seen a summer like this one since 1980. I don't recall how it was that year. I didn't pay much attention to the weather in high school. . . . Wildcat, he eats and sleeps weather and movies."

"Hand me a couple of clips," Will broke in, wiping sweat from his eyes with his shirt sleeve.

"I really hate workin' with these things. Staples in wood posts are easier. 'Course, wood posts rot. I don't know how such stupid creatures as these cattle can always manage to find the one place they can get through. Seems like—"

"Lonnie, can you shut up for five minutes?"

Lonnie grinned. He had been intent on annoying Will, and he had succeeded. Lonnie did know his brother well. "If you'd like to be rid of me, I'll just knock off for the day."

Will straightened. "Okay, you win. You'll talk me to death if I don't give in."

Will was still trying to get his stiff legs to work by the time Lonnie had the tools and supplies stowed in the back of the truck. As far as Lonnie was concerned, cows would always be getting out and fences would always need fixing, and there was no need to get overworked about it.

Soaked with sweat and irritated at leaving a job half done, Will headed the truck toward home on the red sandy road. A quarter of a mile from the drive, they saw Ruby Dee and Sally at the mailbox, getting the mail. Lonnie reached over and tooted the horn. Shielding her eyes with her hand, Ruby Dee stood there and watched them come, her legs apart, clearly outlined by her dress.

Will had come to the conclusion that Ruby Dee never was going to put on a pair of pants. He had never seen that she had any.

"You two ladies are an awful pretty sight," Lonnie called and went sailing out the door before Will got the truck stopped.

"You want a ride back to the house?" Will asked, but Ruby Dee shook her head.

"We're a lot cooler out here than squashed in that truck, and the whole purpose of walkin' down for the mail is for me and Sally to get some exercise." She held the mail out to him. "You want to look now?"

He shook his head. "Lonnie might." Then he drove on, careful to go slowly so as not to stir up dust.

He watched them in the rearview mirror. Lonnie took her hand once, briefly. Will didn't know if Lonnie had let go of her hand or if Ruby Dee had drawn away. She laughed and ran a few feet, and Lonnie chased her . . . playing like kids. Both of them were like that, with the dog yipping around them in circles.

Then Will looked straight ahead. He felt old and shut out. He had the urge to put his hand through the dusty windshield.

From his bedroom window, Hardy watched his younger son and Ruby Dee. Lonnie was showing off, and for the space of half a minute Hardy felt a deep kinship with his son. It was painful, watching his son, who was a reminder of the man Hardy had once been . . . a man long dead.

Hardy swiveled the wheelchair and bumped into the bedpost. "Damn!" It seemed the wheelchair was out to kill him. Finally he got it over to the nightstand. Bending, he lifted a colorful tin. It had contained Whitman's candies about twenty years ago.

He lifted its lid and pulled out a small black folder. He opened it and stared at the portrait inside. Jooney. She wore a coat with fur up around the neck. It had belonged to the photographer. She looked like a lady in it, despite she had only been fifteen at the time.

"Dad?"

Will's voice startled him. He twisted around to see Will poking his head in the door.

"What'd ya want?"

"I was just checkin' to see if you needed anything."

"Privacy. I need privacy. Somebody's always pokin' their head in my room."

"Not because it gives us a lot of pleasure," Will said sharply.

He went upstairs to beat Lonnie to the shower. More and more he was feeling the need to beat his brother out on a few things. He was getting pretty darn tired of having Lonnie's charms with women played out right in front of his face. Lonnie wasn't the only one who could make Ruby Dee light up. Will could, too, and he had an idea about how to make her glow, and all for him.

~ 17

TWO EVENINGS LATER, after supper, Will said, "I got a horse for you, Ruby Dee, if you're still wantin' to ride."

Her face lit up like that of a child seeing a Christmas tree. "Oh, you do? Oh, yes, I'd like that a lot. Now?" Then she was up and eagerly clearing the table. "I'll just stack the dishes and wash them up later." And she smiled at him, a really bright smile.

Lonnie stared at Will with curiosity—and annoyance, too. He didn't like having Ruby Dee's attention stolen from him. Lighting up Ruby Dee and putting a damper on his brother at the same time made Will quite satisfied all the way around.

He felt so satisfied that for a few foolish minutes he harbored the idea that he might have Ruby Dee all to himself. But of course Lonnie and the old man had to go out and take part. Lonnie went and saddled up his paint pony, while Ruby Dee and Will got the old man into the Galaxie and drove him over to the training pen, where Will wanted to start. He was going to make darn certain Ruby Dee really could ride before she struck out into wide open spaces.

The old man's and Lonnie's eyebrows went up when they saw the horse Will had for Ruby Dee. It was a twelve-year-old dappled gray Will had sold two years ago to the Millers, who had wanted an older horse for their son to learn on. None of the ranch horses would have been suitable for Ruby Dee to ride, at least not without Will worrying himself to death. They didn't pay particular attention to getting a ranch horse well-broke. Even the ten-year-olds they had could be wild, and Will didn't keep horses much past that age.

The dappled gray was naturally quiet and had been well trained in during its two years with the Millers.

"Oh, she's lovely," Ruby Dee said. "What's her name?"

Will shrugged. "I don't recall. Lonnie, do you recall this horse's name?"

"Oh, somethin' Smokey. She's one of those Doc horses."

"Well, she has to have a name," Ruby Dee said, as if Will had better produce one.

Will felt he had let her down, but he just couldn't think of a name. "I guess you could name her whatever you want." He thought that was saving the day, but she didn't seem any happier about it. "Are you ready?" he asked, eager to change the subject.

Her expression brightened again, and she nodded, reaching up to grab hold on the saddle.

"Are you gonna ride like that?" the old man demanded, shouting from the front seat of the convertible.

"Like what?" She looked downward. "I'm wearin' boots."

"In that dress, dang it. You can't ride in that dress."

"Why not? It's loose, see." She lifted out the skirt to show it was wide and roomy.

"'Cause you're gonna show all the way to yer fanny, that's why not."

She gave a little laugh. "Oh, Hardy, you know I don't ever wear pants . . . and you've seen a girl's fanny before."

On occasion Ruby Dee did say embarrassing things like that, but it was a little startling to hear her say it to the old man. Will's eyes met Lonnie's, and he saw his brother was also taken aback.

"You hold that horse, Will, until she's sittin' good," the old man called, even while Will had hold of the horse's bridle. Ruby Dee swung up into the saddle with only a flash of bare thighs. Will had to adjust the stirrup leathers for her, and he made certain the reins were straight before he let her go. Lonnie, sitting on his paint pony outside the fence, was fairly fuming, which added to Will's enjoyment.

"All set?" he asked.

Her dark eyes eager and just a little nervous, she nodded. He stepped back to watch from the middle of the round pen, to be there in case she should have some trouble. The gray mare was calm and quiet but not unspirited. And any horse was a wild animal and not totally predictable.

She could ride, just as she had said she could. She was nervous and stiff at first, but she had a good seat, and she was firm enough so that the horse didn't act up. Within minutes she was galloping around the pen, her hair flying back, delight beaming from her face. Standing there and watching her, pleasure spilled all over Will. She was awfully pretty, riding in the golden glow of a western sun.

Of course the confines of the training pen weren't going to contain her for long. Will didn't wait for her to ask but went over and opened the gates that led into the arena. She shot over in there, and Will flung himself on top of the mustang to join her, leaving Lonnie to answer the old man's demand to be driven over to a better watching spot.

Ruby Dee acted the same on the mare as she did in the convertible—she wanted to run.

After getting the car parked to the old man's specifications, Lonnie joined them on his paint pony. He and Will fell to mirroring each other, back and forth on their horses, like football players trying to block each other, each trying to outturn the other. Showing off for Ruby Dee, of course. Will didn't cut Lonnie any slack at all. Lonnie was younger, but Will never felt his years on the back of a horse. In the saddle, he knew who he was.

Lonnie thought he was the better rider, but Will came off better in this game, Lonnie guessed, because his own horse was trained for calf roping, not turning. He was surprised at how well the scrub mustang could turn, and the way Will was acting annoyed him. He wasn't used to Will acting so flashy. He let Will be the one to break off to rest.

"What's wrong, gettin' old?" Lonnie knew Will's weakest point.

But Will just said, "Years bring experience, boy."

The three of them rode until the sun started down behind the hills. They would ride a bit, then sit a bit and talk, letting the horses breathe. Every now and again, Ruby Dee would ride over to the rail and talk with the old man sitting in the car. He'd give her instruction, and she'd practice whatever he said.

Lonnie felt a stab of envy. The old man never had given him riding instruction, not like that, anyway. What the old man gave him was criticism, whenever he bothered to act like Lonnie was alive at all.

Perspiration stuck Ruby Dee's dress to her skin, but she was having a wonderful time, and could have ridden all night. However, she felt a little guilty that Hardy was getting tired of sitting and watching something he could no longer do. And Lonnie and Will seemed on the verge of wearing themselves out, vying for her attention. She felt a little like a pulley bone from Sunday's roast chicken, everyone tugging on her at once.

"I've really had enough," she said. "I'm ready to go get a glass of ice tea." Giving the mare a final caress, Ruby Dee left her in Will's care and slipped behind the wheel of the Galaxie.

"You know, you were right about this dress not being a good idea," she told Hardy as she shifted into gear. "Sweat and saddle leather have just about taken the hide off the inside of my thighs."

Hardy looked as surprised as if she had flashed those bare thighs at him, and then a very rare grin split his face. He actually laughed, a deep, resonant belly laugh, the first she had ever heard out of him. Then he actually lifted his hand to the back of the seat, patted her shoulder, and left his hand there.

Sitting there on the back of the mustang, Will heard the old man's laugh. It hit him hard. He watched them drive off, Ruby Dee and the old man, and got a sick, sinking feeling. Later, Ruby Dee would be taken up with reading to the old man or playing dominoes.

Here he and Lonnie had been vying for her attention like two cowboys set on proving their manhood, and still the old man was getting Ruby Dee in the end. And there wasn't a single damn thing Will could do about it.

It all made him so aggravated that soon after Lonnie left for Harney, Will went, too . . . as if he could drive away from the gnawing inside of him.

He hadn't really intended to go down to Reeves's Quick Stop, since that was probably where Georgia would be and where he shouldn't be at all. But he felt the restlessness churning and bubbling inside him, taking hold of him and edging out good sense. He embraced the restlessness. It was as if he were standing off and watching himself, knowing he was going to get into trouble and knowing that was the entire point of the mood. He could understand trouble.

At Reeves's, Georgia was behind the check-out counter. She was sure surprised to see him, but Georgia never did stay surprised long.

She said, "Well, hello, Will. Haven't seen you around in a while," and with those words and her expression she practically invited Will to come into her bedroom.

"Hello, Georgia." He stood there for a second, looking at her. "Where's Frank?"

"Somewhere between here and Fort Worth with a load of cattle." Something like memories lit her eyes, and he had to smile at her.

Then he walked to the back, got a bottle of Red Dog from the cooler and went over to the pool tables, where Lonnie was already playing with Cletus

Unsell. Lonnie was so surprised to see him that he missed his shot. Crystal sat on a stool against the wall, Lonnie's hat on her head.

Lonnie and Will paired up against Cletus and Roman Torres and played for beers. Will was rusty, but Cletus was half drunk, so Lonnie and Roman being pretty good evened things out. Will and Lonnie would win a game and Cletus and Roman would win a game, and either way the beers kept coming.

It seemed like the more beer Will drank, the better his pool playing got. The beer loosened him up, gave him the feeling he was ready for the world.

Georgia came over and shot a few balls with them. "You've gotten good," Will said, standing aside with her while Lonnie made his play.

She leaned against his arm. "Frank's gone a lot," she murmured, and then she reached up, took his beer and had a drink, then gave it back to him.

Realizing that Georgia was unhappy with Frank suddenly made Will feel very low. He felt guilty that he hadn't missed her, and that she seemed like she missed him.

He walked away from Georgia and over to the table where they were setting their empty beer bottles. The table was loaded with long-neck bottles and aluminum cans, twice as many cans, because Cletus was drinking from them. Cletus never had been known for having good taste. Will felt called on to point this out to him, as he got another round of beers from the cooler.

Cletus said, "And I guess you know all about taste, don't you, Will? You got a taste of little chicky ass out at your place, don't ya?"

"You have a nasty mouth, Cletus," Will said,

twisting the cap off his beer and tossing it on the table. "You can shut it now."

"What'd I say?" Cletus cast Will a lopsided grin, his eyes going like a snake's between Will and Georgia. "I'm not makin' anything up. . . . I'm just repeatin' what everybody's sayin'. And we all know how it is. It's envy talkin', that's what. The only thing we're all wonderin' is, what do you fellas do—draw straws for turns for a piece of pussy?"

"There's ladies present, Cletus. Am I gonna have to teach you what your mama didn't?" Will gripped his pool stick. It would have been easy to whip across and catch Cletus upside the head.

"Oh, sure, Will. Okay. All the little chicky does is cook and clean and take care of daddy." Then he laughed and said something to Roman that Will couldn't hear but knew was not something he would like.

What it amounted to was that Cletus had a low mind and was envious, and Will had a low mood and wanted to fight. He was all worked up, restless as a stud kept too long next to a mare in heat.

"Aw, Will, it's not like anyone ever listens to Cletus," Lonnie said, trying to divert him. "Come on, I'll bet a ten I can sink these three balls with one shot."

Lonnie didn't want to fight. Cletus Unsell wasn't worth fighting with, and everyone knew it. He was one of those people who plain hated baths and work of any sort. He had never in his life held a job for more than six months, even during the oil boom, when everybody and their half-brain cousin had a job. Even the army had sent him home. In Lonnie's opinion, Cletus was about as sorry as a man could get and still show his face in public.

Lonnie figured a better way to get Cletus to shut his mouth would be to get him drunk enough to pass out or to get him all involved in the game, either way leaving Lonnie free to keep paying attention to Crystal, rather than getting in a stupid fight and having his lips all busted up. When Lonnie got a few beers inside him, he would rather make love than fight. He considered the trait the high point of his character.

Cletus and Will continued to toss insults at each other, and Lonnie got dragged into the dang argument because he was Will's brother and had to back him up when Roman stood up for Cletus. Roman had do that because he was staying at Cletus's house.

"You boys go outside to play," Georgia ordered, shoving them all outside.

"Oh, Will ain't got the balls to come outside with me," Cletus said.

"I'm breathin' down your neck, Cletus, so don't look behind you."

The few other customers in the Quick Stop came out to watch.

As fights went, this one was a medium. Cletus was a real blowhard and got into fights with some regularity. He got Will pinned against a pickup pretty quickly and got a couple of good punches to his face. But Cletus had put away more beers than Will, and he gave out sooner, so Will managed a good blow to his midsection, which doubled him over. Will knocked him to his knees, and then all the way down and sat on him.

Lonnie and Roman really only pretended to fight, and when Will looked up from sitting on Cletus, he saw they were both sitting back watching. Crystal went over, knelt down and took Lonnie in her arms to comfort him.

"You've done well, my brother, in defending the honor of women everywhere," Lonnie said.

Will breathed hard. The burning was gone from inside him, and now all he felt was tired and depressed. And old.

Cletus started hacking and choking, like he was going to vomit. "Get off me, Will."

Will struggled up. He looked around for his hat. He felt as if he were moving in slow motion. He wasn't drunk now, not too much anyway. He was just beat numb and depressed as hell.

At least he wasn't throwing up, which Cletus was doing pretty good.

Then Georgia was there, saying, "Come on back to the house with me, Will, and get cleaned up."

"No . . . I don't think so." His head felt as if ocean waves were washing through it—clear and smooth one second and foamy the next. "I haven't sunk that low yet."

He wasn't aware of how that sounded, until he noticed Georgia turning in a huff. He called after her, but she kept on going back inside. Lonnie came up as Will was slipping into his pickup. "You okay, buddy?"

"I'm not so old that I can't live through half a fight," Will said. He touched his fingers to his lip; they came away bloody.

He dug some napkins out of the console while Lonnie said, "I didn't say you were. You're closin' in on being stupid, though, fightin' the stupidest man in Harney."

Will closed the truck door in Lonnie's face.

"Where in the hell are you goin', Will?"

"Shit, I don't know. You want to come with me? Maybe we'll just drive over to Amarillo and get us a steak."

He really wanted Lonnie to go with him, just to ride with him. But then Crystal was at Lonnie's side and Lonnie was walking off with her. Will never had stood a chance with Lonnie against some pretty girl.

As he turned the pickup and headed it for the highway, he began to be aware of aching all over. He might have come out on top of Cletus, but he didn't feel like the winner.

It made him sick to think about Georgia coming on to him the way she had. He was glad he hadn't married her—although he didn't think his life could be much worse off than it was at that moment. How much worse could being married to a woman with a wandering eye be than being forty-two, single and living a life of a monk in the same house with a sexy-as-hell woman and his own daddy, who still called him boy?

He went home, of course, though he didn't realize where he was going until he got there. The light was on above the kitchen sink. Ruby Dee's bedroom window was dark. He looked at her window for long seconds, and then he slowly slid out of the seat of the pickup and headed for the house, his hands stuffed in his pockets, his gaze on the ground.

Suddenly Sally came wiggling out of the darkness beneath the elm tree, pressing her nose against his leg for her pat. Knowing sliced through Will, and he looked up, peering across the dark yard. In the patches of light filtering through the tree from the pole lamp at the corner of the yard, he saw Ruby Dee sitting on the back steps.

"Hello, Will," she said softly, her voice sultry as a gulf breeze.

"Hi."

He slowly walked toward her. She was wearing her pink robe, though it didn't look pink in the dim, silvery light. He could see no color, only shades of gray. She was a small figure. Her eyes looked very large, and her hair fell in waves around her face. She had her arms draped over her bent knees. The ruffle of her nightgown and her bare toes poked out from the edge of her robe.

He stopped a few feet away. "It's a nice night for sittin'." With the light behind him and his hat on, he knew he was in deep shadow.

"Yes, it is.... You want to sit down?" She scooted over to make room for him.

Easing his pants legs, Will lowered himself beside her. He looked down, keeping his face shadowed by his hat. He caught her scent, sweet, like roses. Roses in the hot sunshine. Sometimes he smelled that scent in the bathroom after she'd had a bath.

"Listen," she said in a bare whisper.

He sat very still. "Coyotes," he said. He'd heard them all his life and rarely noticed them anymore. "They're down in the spring canyon, I imagine."

He sensed her continuing to listen, while the sound moved further and further away. They sat within an inch of each other, though not touching. Will was so aware of her, he could practically hear her heartbeat.

He knew he should get up and go inside, just get

up and go away. But he couldn't. He wouldn't. The wondering about how it would be to kiss her had been a long time in the back of his mind. Now would be a perfect time to find out.

⚘ 18

RUBY DEE HAD been sitting there for over half an hour, hoping that Will would come. She'd imagined sitting with him in the warm summer night, with night birds calling and the cicadas chirping.

But now that Will was actually sitting right there beside her, she felt suddenly shy and a little fearful, too. Without touching him, without really even looking at him, she was aware of his virility.

He shifted, removing his hat and plopping it on a nearby bush. He dug into his pocket and came up with a cigarette. He held it up to the light. It was bent.

Ruby Dee chuckled, and then she saw his face in the silvery light. It didn't look right—the corner of his mouth was cut, and there was a black streak along his jawline.

"Oh, Will!"

He cast her crooked grin. "It's nothin' . . . just had a little altercation."

Meanwhile her gaze was moving downward, and

she saw that his shirt pocket was half ripped off and the placket was torn.

"Well, come on inside where I can see the extent of the damage and get you tended."

She started to rise, but he reached out and grabbed her wrist.

"No. It's just a broken lip. The rest is only dirt and bruises."

She gazed down at him, at his hand holding her. It was the first time he had ever truly touched her.

"Right now the nurse is off-duty," he said. "Sit back down with me for a bit."

Slowly, her heartbeat skittering, she lowered herself once more beside him. He let go of her wrist then.

"What does the other guy look like?" She pulled her legs back up and tucked her gown and robe tight around them. Suddenly she was very aware of wearing only her thin gown and robe.

"A lot better than me," he said, striking a match on the cement step. "But I did leave him throwin' up."

"Well, that's a bonus," she said. "What were you fightin' about?"

He breathed deeply, saying after long seconds, "Manners. And honor, of course. Mostly because both of us felt like fightin'."

"Both of you felt like gettin' beat up?"

He chuckled around the cigarette between his lips. "No one ever looks at it like that. Both of us felt like givin' punches, not gettin' them."

She stared at him for a second, then said, "I can't stand fightin' with anybody. I just hate to argue or have cross words. I hate to hurt somebody, and I sure hate to be hurt. Usually the body can heal pretty well, but it's a lot harder for the heart."

"I don't think this fella's heart was involved."

"Well, that's good. And I guess yours wasn't, either."

"Not a bit."

They shared a smile and then fell into silence. Will's cigarette smoke curled up into the silver light and disappeared into the shadows. Ruby Dee wondered if he was as aware of her as she was of him. She didn't see how he *couldn't* be.

Then Will said, "Tell me somethin'," and his voice came low and husky.

"Okay . . . if I can." Anticipating an intimate question, a small shiver went down her spine.

But what he came out with was, "Why don't you ever wear jeans or trousers?"

Well. She saw he was frowning seriously.

"I just don't like to," she said, pulling her robe tightly around her bent legs. "I like dresses a lot better, long ones. I can move easily in a dress. Dresses are cooler in the summer, and in winter I wear leggin's or long johns, and that's real comfortable. And, well, I just don't like to have my legs hangin' out. It makes me feel funny, naked. I guess that sounds awfully odd."

"Not from you," Will said, and for an instant Ruby Dee wondered if he was making fun of her. But he didn't sound like he was.

They fell silent for a few more minutes, and then Ruby Dee pointed out a firefly. And then another. They were like stars flying around, she told him. He said there was a place up in Iowa, some medical research place, that paid for fireflies in the summer. Then they turned their attention to the stars, and Ruby Dee commented that they could have seen the stars a lot better, were it not for the pole lamp at the edge of the yard.

"I'll fix that." Will got to his feet so suddenly that he startled her. Then he was striding across the yard.

She jumped to her feet, too, clutching the fold of her robe, and called to him in a loud whisper, "What are you gonna do?"

He didn't answer. She thought at first that maybe he could turn the light off at the pole, but he kept on going to his pickup. And he came back with a rifle!

"Oh, Lordy, are you gonna shoot it? Don't do that!"

"Just one shot," he said, stopping in the edge of the yard, lifting the rifle and taking aim.

"Oh, Will Starr—don't break that lamp! You'll wake your daddy!"

He slowly let the rifle down and came toward her down the walk. When he stood in front of her, he said, "You don't want me to wake up Dad?"

She felt caught. Her cheeks burned, but she shook her head. "I don't see the need to disturb him."

He nodded. "I guess you're right. So maybe we'd better do this. . . ."

He slipped up beside her and snaked his arm inside the screen door; the pole lamp went out, plunging them into darkness.

"Oh, Will . . . you tease." She laughed. It was the first time he had ever teased her. The very first time! And her heart swelled with that special, warm joy.

He slipped back down past her, brushing against her as he moved. Setting the rifle aside, he reached for her hand and pulled her out to see the sky. She wouldn't step off the cement walk, though, because of her bare feet.

"Oh, look, Will, the Milky Way! It's like a trail. There must be thousands and thousands of stars. It doesn't look like that in winter, does it?"

"No. The stars move with the seasons."

"We move," she said.

"The universe moves."

"Yes."

And then they were just standing there in the thin moonlight, looking at each other. Ruby Dee suddenly felt an enormous, overwhelming fear, as if some cloud was about to overtake her.

"I'd better go in," she said and turned toward the house, while all along she wanted him to call her back. She had reached the first step, when Will called softly to her.

"Ruby Dee." His voice stopped her, held her.

She turned, gazed at him. He came toward her, and she could not take her eyes from him. She couldn't see his expression clearly, but she could feel the strength of his emotion. It held her there. Desire swirled up from her belly and went humming through her veins.

With his face directly in front of hers, he slipped his hands up to cup her face. He didn't have to pull her to him, because she was already falling. She saw his lips part just before they met hers.

His kiss was gentle, seeking, exploring. Erotic. She caught a taste of blood and remembered his cut lip, but that faded as desire turned the kiss long and deep and hard. His muscles were full beneath her hands, and the scent of him, all manly sweat and after-shave, filled her.

Out of breath, they broke apart. He looked at her, his eyes holding hers. He rubbed his thumb over her lips. Wanting thrummed through her. She slipped her arms around his neck and pulled his face back to hers, and then they were going at each other again, clutching and tugging, and Ruby Dee was thinking, *"Oh, Lord . . . oh, Lord . . . oohh, Lord."*

She had gotten swept down the river of passion before she even realized it. The two of them probably would have gone right on down that river and on to the ground, except that suddenly Will broke away. She saw him gasp for breath, his chest heaving.

Ruby Dee laid her forehead against the base of his neck. Oh, he was warm, and she felt his pulse, his arms strong around her, his scent and virility all over her. It was beautiful. She wanted to stay there forever.

Will thought of his bed, above the old man's; of Ruby Dee's bed, up the stairs from the old man's; of the jumbled bed in Lonnie's horse trailer; and even of the old mattress down in the cottage Wildcat used to use. Then he drew himself up, took hold of her arms and set her from him.

She gazed at him, her face all warm and wanting and questioning, and with her right shoulder bare where her gown and robe had fallen loose. She didn't have a thing on under those two thin layers of fabric, either. Will had felt her warm flesh right through them, as if they hadn't even been there.

Tightly, he said, "I think you'd better go in now."

She nodded. "Okay." Her voice was a hoarse whisper. And she didn't say yes, but okay, as if she would do whatever he said.

She turned, took the two steps and opened the screen door. Then she stopped and looked back at him for a second, before going quickly inside.

He listened to the faint sound of her bare feet going across the kitchen floor. The next instant there was Sally, up on the steps, looking at the screen door and wagging her tail expectantly. Will opened the door and let the dog inside.

There was no way he could go in, though.

Snatching up his hat and rifle, he went back to his truck, started it up and headed back down the drive, then turned west, without the slightest idea of where he was going. He only knew that he had to go somewhere other than his room, right down the hall from Ruby Dee's.

He felt all confused. One part of him felt awfully happy. He'd made Ruby Dee smile and he'd kissed her, and she'd kissed him back, and it had been everything he had imagined.

On the other hand, now he was more frustrated than ever, and fearful, too, about where he might be headed with her.

He drove west a bit and then north, finally heading over to the old James place. He hadn't been certain about buying the place from Ambrose . . . but the minute he pulled up the drive, he began to think of it as his.

At least he wouldn't have to share this place with his dad and his brother, the way he had to share Ruby Dee.

He drove up the lane to the empty cottage and dilapidated barns. It all looked eerie in the thin moonlight. Will sat smoking a cigarette and gazing at the house. He had the somewhat startling thought that maybe he had at last fallen in love. He figured that could be the only reason he was feeling so happy and sad at the same time.

* * *

Crystal's voice woke him. "Lonnie... Lonnie, wake up. We fell asleep." She was shaking him.

He opened his eyes to see her looming over him, her face all flushed and her hair curled all around it. He smiled and reached for her.

"No, Lonnie. Get off my jeans. Oh... we went and fell asleep, and it's almost mornin'. What if someone comes? I'll just die if someone comes."

They were still on a blanket in the grass, in the Methodist cemetery, to be exact, where they had come last night. Lonnie, blinking, saw that first light had come. He could easily make out the grave markers stretching out around them.

He and Crystal had put the blanket in an empty place between his cousin Son-Jack and the grave of Leonard Houston's three wives. Son-Jack's real name had been Jackson; he'd been one of Lonnie's childhood friends, despite the old man had hated him since he was from Mama's side of the family. He had been killed in the Navy, in a freak accident on an aircraft carrier, when a plane had crashed on the deck. What was buried in the grave was the duffel bag of effects the Navy had sent home, because they had never found enough of Son-Jack to call a body.

Leonard Houston's three wives were all buried in the same grave, one on top of the other. They had been sisters. The first had had to be lifted out and the hole dug deeper for the second, and then again for the third. There was only one marker, with all their names on it.

Crystal tugged at her jeans, which Lonnie was lying on. He teased her by refusing to move. She had on his shirt, little, itty-bitty pink panties and nothing else.

She said, "You have got to get me home, Lonnie. Georgia is gonna raise the roof. She'll probably come after you with a gun."

"Sister Georgia has her own sins." He sat up slowly, feeling happy and totally satisfied, even though he hated mornings. His back itched from mosquito bites, and he went to scratching.

"Come on, Lonnie. What if somebody comes? It's *Sunday*."

He hurried then, to please her. He never cared much what people said of him, but he didn't want Crystal embarrassed. Hopping from foot to foot, he put on his boots and told her to keep his shirt. She gave him his hat—he felt funny putting it on without a shirt—and snatched up her bra and blouse and the quilt. He grabbed the empty soft-drink and beer bottles and threw them in the bed of the pickup. When he slipped behind the wheel, he scratched his mosquito bites against the seat.

Crystal snuggled up against him during the short drive to Georgia's. Crystal was staying at her sister's, behind the Quick Stop, which was why they had been at the cemetery in the first place. It was that or a motel, and Lonnie counted the cemetery as a much more romantic place. Instead of a tawdry room they'd had the magic of the stars and moonlight and fragrant night breeze.

He liked the feel of Crystal snuggled against him, liked the scent and feel of her, which served to make him recall pleasurably what they had shared in the night.

"Don't go around back," Crystal said when he drove into the gravel lot of the store. "Maybe Georgia'll be asleep. When Frank's off drivin' the truck, she sleeps in."

"What's Frank bein' away have to do with it? Doesn't he let her sleep in?"

Crystal shook her head. "She says he snores, and she can't hardly sleep at all. Half the time she sleeps on the couch."

Lonnie didn't think he needed to comment on that. She wrapped her arms around his neck, and he kissed her, running his hand up beneath his shirt for one last caress of her silky, soft breasts. She shuddered and moved against his hand, and he squeezed gently.

Then she clutched him around the neck and whispered fiercely, "I love you, Lonnie."

Lonnie tightened inside. He hugged her to him and whispered, "Oh, Crystal . . . Crystal." Then he kissed her again, before she could say anything else.

"I got to go, Lon." She gave him a tender smile, then slipped out of the truck and raced away, her brown hair and the tails of his shirt flying.

He listened but didn't hear the door, and he guessed he wouldn't, since she was trying to be quiet. As quietly as he could, he turned the pickup toward the road. The morning wind blew in the window, and on his right the sky glowed golden.

What Crystal had said, that she loved him, whispered across his thoughts. Her words struck something inside him, some secret, tender place that quivered and shook. And hurt.

A lot of women had said they loved him. Some of them had meant it, but he supposed none more than Crystal. He was glad, but it made him feel like he was about to get caught in the saddle rigging.

He had never told a girl that he loved her. He wasn't certain he believed in love, not as a lasting emotion, anyway. From what Lonnie had seen, a

person could say he loved someone one day and
didn't the next. It wasn't that people lied, but that
hearts were unreliable. He himself had experienced
what could be called in-love a hundred times, but
eventually the feeling passed. It seemed to Lonnie
that love wasn't all it was cracked up to be. It surely
didn't keep people together until death do them
part.

He did care for Crystal, a lot. What he felt for
Crystal was an aching to hold her and kiss her and
screw her. He simply liked to touch her and to see
her, and he liked to talk to her, too. He liked to flirt
with her and watch her grin. And he would admit
that he felt all of that more strongly for Crystal than
he could recall feeling for a woman in quite some
time. But he still wasn't prepared to call it love ev-
erlasting.

When he pulled into the ranch drive and looked
up at the house, he got as nervous as Crystal had
been. The sun was rising, which meant Will and
Ruby Dee would be up. He anticipated Will's cutting
remarks. Worse, he imagined Ruby Dee's face.

What would she think of him coming in at this
time of the morning?

Oh, she knew he was seeing Crystal, but not how
close things were between them. When a man came
in at dawn, however, it was pretty plain what he
had been up to the night before. Ninety-nine percent
of the time the man had either been drinking, coon
hunting or spending the night with a woman. In
Lonnie's case, it was well known he was averse to
too much drinking and to coon hunting at all.

He didn't want Ruby Dee to know about him and
Crystal. He was afraid if she knew, it would change
things between them.

Lonnie had come to think of Ruby Dee as a part of his days and Crystal as a part of his nights. Two women in two separate areas of his life. He felt about Ruby Dee the same way he felt about Crystal. He wanted the same things from her, and when it came down to it, he got them all, except one. Sometimes he held hopes of getting that one thing. But no matter; he didn't want to risk losing everything she already gave him. He wasn't certain what place he had found in Ruby Dee's life, but he did know he had found a place, and he didn't want to lose it.

Lying was the only safe course, and while he searched for a shirt in the pile of things in the back seat of his truck, his mind raced with plausible excuses. He found a shirt, wrinkled but near in color to the one he had worn the night before, and as he slipped into it, he looked over and realized Will's pickup was gone. He didn't see it parked anywhere.

The back door stood open, but the kitchen was empty. There was no aroma of coffee and no sausage sizzling. Not a sound, either.

His mind reeled with horror stories of people being killed in their beds. But what had happened was that Lonnie had lucked out.

When he found the old man still in bed and snoring, Lonnie right then took off his boots and tiptoed up the stairs. Ruby Dee's bedroom door was closed, and Will's bed was plumb empty. It hadn't ever been slept in, by the look of it.

Lonnie paused and looked once more at Ruby Dee's closed door. But then he remembered that Will's pickup was not outside.

He tiptoed down the hall to his room and closed the door, stripped down to his underwear and stretched out. He wondered where Will had gone.

Then he was struck by a disturbing thought: maybe Ruby Dee wasn't actually in her bedroom. Perhaps she was off with Will somewhere.

Of course that wasn't likely, because neither of them was likely to leave the old man alone. Nevertheless, the thought niggled at him and caused him to get up, crack his door open, and peer across to Ruby Dee's door. He didn't figure he could peek in on her, without her door creaking and waking her up. Every door in this dang house creaked with the age of Moses.

There was nothing he could do but wait. Leaving his door open, he went back to bed. He dozed lightly, until Ruby Dee came out of her room. Then he fell asleep.

He awoke an hour later to the aromas of coffee and sizzling meat and sun-warmed walls. Quickly he showered and went downstairs. The old man was in the bathroom, with the shower running, and Ruby Dee was at the kitchen sink, still in her pink bathrobe and barefooted. There was no sign of Will.

"Good mornin', beautiful." Lonnie dared to kiss her cheek but not to pat her behind.

She gave him a bit of a smile along with a mug of coffee, but the way her gaze passed over him made Lonnie wonder if she knew about last night. Ruby Dee had a way of seeing right into a person, and she could have heard him come in.

He shook off the notion and filled his plate with fried turkey, baked apples and slices of pan-toasted bread.

"Where's Will this mornin'?" he asked as sank into a chair.

"I don't know."

That brought his eyes up, but something kept him

from asking anything further. The next instant Ruby Dee dropped the coffeepot, and it shattered all over the floor, and she went to crying. Right after that the old man came rolling into the room, so Lonnie didn't get any good time alone with Ruby Dee.

Before the old man knew the facts, he jumped all over Lonnie for making Ruby Dee cry. Even when he was told the facts of it, he still considered Ruby Dee's dropping the coffeepot all Lonnie's fault.

☙ 19

IN THE CLEAR light of day, the wonderful, warm, fuzzy feeling of desire and the romantic fantasies that had been wrapped around Ruby Dee faded right away.

Goodness, she had gotten so carried away, kissing Will, it embarrassed her. She had so *revealed* herself.

And wasn't she being silly to make a mountain out of the molehill of a few romantic minutes and a few hot kisses? She wasn't a naïve ninny; she had shared romantic moments and kisses before. People had their needs. Sometimes loneliness just welled up in a person.

Once, when she'd been twenty-one, or maybe just twenty, she had been on a Greyhound bus going from Muskogee to Oklahoma City. It was January, just after the Christmas holidays, which she had spent working at a nursing home, filling in for several people who'd wanted off to spend the holidays with their families. She didn't have a family. A young man about her age sat next to her. All she could recall about him now was that he had been attractive and polite, though shabby. Pretty soon they had started talking, and then, when the bus took a few good slides on the icy road, they had started holding hands. The winter storm had set in before they left, and halfway to Oklahoma City, the bus had had to pull off and wait in the parking lot of a Love's Country Store.

It had been sort of like a party, with everyone buying Coca-Colas and hotdogs and popcorn at the Love's. She and the young man had kept holding hands, and a couple of times they kissed during the night. In the early hours of the morning, when they finally got to Oklahoma City, they said good-bye.

She had certainly been lonely last night, and she knew Will had, too.

But this time she wasn't going somewhere on a bus, and the kisses she had shared with Will Starr were not the sort easily forgotten. She could never before remember experiencing what she had last night . . . such longing and urgency and quenching all wrapped up in one. No, she hadn't. Not even with Beauford, whom she had loved.

She could love Will Starr, she thought. Maybe she already did. And maybe she had started loving him that first day, when she had come out of the bathroom and into the kitchen and seen him standing there, sort of like a wild mustang, all hemmed in in the kitchen and needing care.

She was thinking about that as she served breakfast to Hardy and Lonnie, and just then, when she looked from one to the other, she saw, clearly and concisely, in big capital letters in her mind: HARDY AND LONNIE and HELL TO PAY.

Well. There it was.

Never had she thought to be in this position. She loved them all, each in a special way. She did not want to see any one of them hurt, and she surely didn't want to be the cause of their pain. She couldn't, wouldn't, come between these men. She told herself this over and over. She told herself to push the thought of Will giving her babies right out of her mind. She could not wish that Will cared for her. She prayed to God to take the longing for Will from her heart and to make her behave.

She worried a lot about how she would act when she saw Will. How he would act when he saw her. Few times in her life had Ruby Dee felt called upon to hide her emotions. Generally she considered hiding emotions unhealthy and dishonest, and besides, her feelings just seemed to pop out of her.

But this time one of her strongest emotions was the sense to hide. She was considering going off for a day of shopping, perhaps all the way to Amarillo, or maybe back to OKC, where she could see if her cottage had been sold, when Will's pickup came up the drive. She thought urgently that she could go to her room.

But she didn't. She stood right there at the sink.

Behind her, at the table, Lonnie and Hardy sat with their coffee, watching *Outdoor Oklahoma* on the tiny television. The screen door creaked, and Will's boots scraped on the porch. A rush of gladness touched her, and then Ruby Dee turned and looked right at him as he came in the door.

When her eyes met his, for just that instant, she felt like the ruby stone for which she was named, touched by the sun.

Grabbing a towel and wiping her hands, she said, "I saved you a plate."

He tossed his hat on top of the refrigerator. "Thanks. I'll just go wash up."

Again their eyes held, and then they looked away at the same instant.

She turned to the oven. Behind her, at the table, Hardy and Lonnie didn't say anything more than, "Mornin'." No one said a word about the scrapes on Will's face or his torn shirt.

Will came back and sat at the table with Lonnie and Hardy and ate his breakfast. Lonnie asked where Will had been, and Will just said, "Campin'."

He sat there and had his coffee. He didn't say a word, not one word, but Ruby Dee could feel his eyes on her. Sometimes she looked at him.

Lonnie got tired, went into the living room and stretched out on the couch for a nap. Will kept sitting at the table, and so did Hardy, the entire time Ruby Dee finished cleaning the kitchen and making fresh ice tea. When there was absolutely nothing left to be done, Ruby Dee said she was going upstairs to lie down.

She needed to sort out her emotions. It was certainly wearing her out, trying to hide them.

Late that afternoon, Will came in from feeding the stock and said, "Go get yourself ready, Ruby Dee. I'm takin' everybody down to Cheyenne for a Mexican dinner."

His lips said everyone, but his eyes said *her*.

Ruby Dee went flying to her room to put on her black dress with the apricot flowers and apply Ripe Apricot lipstick. When she came downstairs, she heard Hardy complaining that he didn't feel like going all the way down to Cheyenne. She paused, thinking that she just couldn't leave him behind. He was perfectly capable of staying alone, but it seemed too cruel to go off to a wonderful supper without him.

"We'll be glad to bring somethin' back for you, Dad," Will told him.

Hardy said, "Ain't no good with grease all gone cold. I guess I'll go."

Lonnie met them down at the restaurant, because he wanted to drive his own truck. He thought he might stay down and visit friends afterward.

The restaurant was friendly and colorful, filled with the rich aroma of spicy meats. It was not too crowded. Lonnie and Will were both greeted by name. Lonnie maneuvered himself to sit beside Ruby Dee, and he looked pleased with himself. Will cast her a resigned grin. He sat across from her, and they put Hardy at the end, in his wheelchair. Hardy was plainly ill at ease in it, and after a few minutes he told Will to help him move to a regular chair—specifically Lonnie's chair, beside Ruby Dee. Lonnie had to go around and sit next to Will.

Ruby Dee began to feel a little like the chicken pulley bone again. She saw Will's eyes on her, repeatedly, and found her eyes drawn to him. She fluctuated between enjoyment and tenseness. In one of her favorite dresses and with her hair up in a ribbon, she felt bright as a shiny new penny. She wished very much to be alone with Will, yet she was very happy to be with all three men. The men, however, didn't appear to be nearly as pleased to be together.

There they sat: Will, looking pleasant enough, played with the sweat beads on his bottle of Mexican beer; Lonnie, smiling at Ruby Dee, peeled the label off his; and Hardy, scowling, said his tasted like piss and for Will to go over and get him a Budweiser.

Just after Will returned with his father's beer, a couple passed by from the rear of the restaurant.

"Well, good gravy, if it isn't Hardy Starr!" The woman stopped beside him.

She was tall and buxom, with snow-white hair braided and twisted around her head. It had so many twists that it would be quite long when let down. She wore wonderful Indian jewelry—it dangled from her ears, neck and wrists. Her dress was a simple cotton shirtwaist, yet she wore it with style. She was a handsome woman, and her smile was bright and lively. She beamed at Hardy.

"I don't think I've seen you in at least a year. I heard you had a stroke—but I knew you weren't dead, because I read the obituaries every day . . . to make certain I'm still alive," she said, laughing. "Will and Lonnie . . . I have not seen you-all in a decade, if it's been a day. Well, I see you sometimes, Will, at the bank . . . but Lonnie, I haven't seen you since my Rosasharon's wedding, and you were kissin' all the girls."

"Hello, Miz Vinson. How are you?" Will said with a slow grin. Lonnie smiled at her and nodded.

It would have been hard to look at this lady and not smile; Ruby Dee just sat there grinning. Hardy, though, did not look at her.

"Fair to middlin'." Her lively eyes fell on Ruby Dee, and they seemed to jump with curiosity. Will made the introductions. The woman's name was Cora Jean Vinson, an old friend of the family.

Cora Jean said, "Nice to meet you, Ruby Dee. That sure is a pretty name." Her intense gaze made Ruby Dee wonder if she had a smear of salsa on her face.

Then Cora Jean drew back, as if remembering her companion. "Oh, and this is Eugene Wheeler. He's my restaurant companion. I love to eat in restaurants, but not alone, so Eugene is kind enough to take me."

Mr. Wheeler was a small, shy man, who was far too skinny for his polyester sport coat and at least half a foot shorter than Cora Jean. He bobbed his head in a hello, then averted his eyes.

"Well, how are you, Hardy?" Cora Jean looked at him until he replied. The woman was not put off by Hardy one bit.

"I'm old but I'm still breathin'," he said tersely.

"Well, goodness, we're all old. Half the time I don't recognize myself in the mirror. I pass by and think: who is that old woman?" She laughed that lovely laugh. "You're lookin' well, Hardy, and here with your sons and all."

With a great sigh, Cora Jean ran her gaze over the men again. "Yes, I'm an old friend of these fellas, honey," she said to Ruby Dee. "Hardy and I are among the dwindling number of folks whose parents came out here to make farms and ranches out of land stolen from the Indians and Mother Nature. I've known Hardy all of my life, and these two since they were born. I taught each one in school."

She gazed at Will. "Why, I was there the night Will was born at Dr. Anderson's clinic." Then she explained to Ruby Dee, "I was helping out my sister-in-law, who was Dr. Anderson's nurse. We did such things in those days; weren't so many laws like today.

"I got to hand Will to his daddy," she said, putting a hand on Will's shoulder, "and little Will promptly did his business right in Hardy's hand. Hardy wouldn't let go of him, though. He was so proud. He said he'd cleaned up after cattle, he guessed he could clean up after his own son.

Will's eyes went to his daddy, who was staring at his plate.

Miz Vinson went on without missing a beat. Inclining her head toward Lonnie, she said, "When Lonnie was born, I was right down the hall, where I'd delivered Camellia. Me and Johnny, God rest his soul, only had girls—five of them. It's hard to believe now, but Lonnie was the puniest, ugliest baby. He could hardly suck, and formula made him sick. I remember three nights after Camellia and Lonnie were born, I got up and there was Hardy rocking Lonnie right in the hall and feeding him goat's milk from a bottle. Hardy kept two goats tied up back of the hospital until Lonnie could be taken home."

"You always could talk a blue streak, Cora Jean," Hardy said.

Lonnie was staring at the table, a curious expression on his face.

"And you used to tell me that often enough. One time he gave me a whole dime to go talk somewhere else." Her eyes danced. "He was sparkin' my sister." There came that musical laugh. "Oh, Law, I didn't mean to go on so. Y'all have just brought back the memories. Remember that time you threatened to beat up Mr. Irwin?" She tapped Hardy's shoulder. "I won't forget that, because I had to work at liking that man, and I never did it very well. He even made the teachers call him Mr. Irwin. Oh, gosh, I'm started again. Well, that's enough."

She squeezed Hardy's shoulder in a familiar way. "It is good to see you, Hardy. Y'all enjoy your supper. They have the best guacamole here." Then she leaned over behind Hardy, toward Ruby Dee, and spoke in a loud whisper. "That time Will pooped in

his hand, Hardy said he could never again eat guacamole and not think of it. No . . . I really am going
now. Here comes the girl with your food, and Eugene needs to get home to watch 'Murder, She
Wrote.' I got a little fruit stand west of Harney. Y'all
come see me sometime. I know you won't, Hardy,
but maybe the rest of you will." She left them with
a smile and a wave.

"She's quite something," Ruby Dee said, feeling
as if they had been visited by a whirling dervish.

Then the waitress was setting their food in front
of them. Everyone except Hardy agreed their meals
were delicious. When Ruby Dee asked Hardy what
he thought of his food, he said it was okay. Then he
asked if anyone wanted his helping of guacamole,
which made them all chuckle.

After a few minutes, Ruby Dee asked, "Who was
Mr. Irwin and why were you gonna beat him up?"

Hardy glanced at her, then looked at his plate and
forked his food. Will said he didn't remember, and
then Lonnie said that Mr. Irwin had been the school
principal in Harney for a couple of years.

"He gave me licks one time." He looked at Hardy.
"Fifth grade. I could hardly sit down that night.
Dad, you went up to school and got into it with
him."

Hardy cleared his throat. "Huh . . . I guess I did."
He nodded slightly, and acted as if that were all he
was going to say, but then he added thoughtfully,
"He was a mealy sort of fella, from up north, too. I
didn't threaten him, though. I just told him that if
he felt the need to use that board again on my son,
I was gonna come up there and stuff it down his
throat."

Will cracked a smile. "Dad gave us whippins, but

he didn't want somebody outside the family doin' it." Then Lonnie was chuckling, and even Hardy smiled, almost.

Reaching for his beer, Hardy said, "How were you gonna do your chores, if that fool kept takin' a board to ya? 'Sides, the whole thing was over a gal sayin' you said somethin' dirty to her. There's two things I know about this boy: he wouldn't ever say somethin' ugly to a gal, even then, and if he says he didn't do somethin', he didn't do it."

Well. Hardy saying that mouthful surprised them all.

He said hardly another word during the rest of the meal, but still Ruby Dee felt that this evening the men had made a connection they had not felt for some time. A connection that had been beat down and covered over by years of hurt and resentment.

When they came out of the restaurant, Will put his hand on Ruby Dee's back. Oh, how she felt that casual touch. He guided her to the front seat of the pickup, then helped his dad get into the back seat. Lonnie stopped at her window to say good-bye, explaining that he would be home a little later, but it was Ruby Dee he looked at the whole time. When he walked away, Ruby Dee looked over to see Will's intense gaze upon her.

It was dark when they got home. Will suggested sitting on the front porch, and Ruby Dee got them ice tea. She was always thirsty after Mexican food. Hardy sat in his wheelchair, Ruby Dee got the only porch chair, an old rocker, and Will sat at the edge of the porch floor, his back against the post, with Sally's head lying on his thigh.

It was nice and quiet, and for once the sense of anger wasn't vibrating between Will and Hardy.

Ruby Dee suspected that Will was recalling some of the memories from supper. Cora Jean had been like an angel coming to them, she thought.

"What happened to the swing?" she asked Hardy, looking up at the ceiling, where she could just make out the hooks in the dim light coming through the window.

He shrugged. "Darned if I remember. I don't rightly recall there ever bein' one. That Cora Jean would probably know. She has one of those photo memories, I guess."

Not a half hour later, Lonnie was home, and he came to sit out on the porch, too.

For the next hour, while the moon rose in the sky, they all sat there. Every once in a while someone would say something, about the weather, about fireflies, about the coyotes—which each of the men called ki-oats, in the old way—and how they were getting awfully thick again.

Will explained to Ruby Dee that when the coyotes started attacking the calves, the men had to get together to hunt them or call in hunters. As a warning to other coyotes, they would hang a coyote carcass on the fence.

"That works?" Ruby Dee asked, surprised.

Will nodded. "Coyotes are smart." He stroked Sally's head. "They know enough not to challenge men or dogs straight on, but they'll tease and lure a dog out from his own yard and then kill him. Not hounds, though. Coyotes won't mess with hounds, at least that's what I've always heard."

And Hardy said, "No, coyotes won't mess with hounds. Coyotes don't like a hound's foghorn bark. Don't need to worry about this little collie, either.

Coyotes only get the stupid dogs." Then he added, "I always did like coyotes, though."

Ruby Dee, rocking in the creaky chair, talked about Miss Edna's porch swing and how sometimes when a person swung in it, the hooks would start making this god-awful squeal, and the best thing she'd ever used to quiet it was Crisco shortening. "I guess Crisco wouldn't work on this chair, though." She didn't realize she'd said something funny until Will and Lonnie laughed.

Lonnie brought up the subject of Cora Jean's daughter, Camellia, and how he had heard she was down in Fort Worth, making a fortune shining shoes. She owned several chairs and had people working under her, too, down at Billy Bob's and the hotels and the rodeos and horse shows.

"Camellia bought Cora Jean that champagne Cadillac she drives, from shining shoes." After a minute he added, "All Cora Jean's girls were named after flowers."

They sat on the porch until nearly eleven, when Ruby Dee rose to go upstairs. She felt that if she wasn't the first to get up, they might all just sit there until morning.

Lying in her bed with the sheet spread over her, she listened to the men as they each settled in for the night. She heard Lonnie's boot steps come along the landing first. He had a jaunty way of walking, even when he was being quiet. Then she heard Will's footsteps, in his sock feet, but heavy. Slow.

She heard them stop outside her door! She closed her eyes and hardly breathed and tried not to think about how much she wished he would come in and make love to her.

His steps went on to the bathroom, and the door

closed. After several quiet seconds, Ruby Dee rose
and turned on the bedside lamp. She reached for her
dream paper, and looked at it for a long time. Re-
folding it, she tucked it beneath the lamp, turned out
the lamp and settled back down.

She knew she could not put Will's face to the picture on the dream paper. She just kept thinking:
HELL TO PAY.

She clutched one of her feather pillows, because
she ached so badly to have Will make love to her.

Fully clothed except for his boots, Will lay
stretched out in his bed, watching cigarette smoke
twirl upward in the moonlight and thinking about
Ruby Dee, only five strides down the hall. Not a
sound came from her room.

He thought, too, about what had been said at supper. He'd heard the story about Hardy holding him
as a newborn, of course, but not in at least twenty
years ... not in twenty-five years since his mother
had left. His dad had let his mother take away a lot
more than just herself and their marriage. For a minute he felt angry, but then he felt sad, and then he
felt a sort of wonder, because it seemed like now that
Ruby Dee had come, his dad was returning to what
he'd once been.

He sat up and raked his hand through his hair,
the sense of wonder turning to a cold, knowing chill.
He wanted Ruby Dee for his own. But how could he
take her from the old man now?

He slept little and fitfully, was up early the next
morning and went out to take a walk. Right after
breakfast, he told Lonnie to take Wildcat and start
baling the alfalfa they had cut the week before.
"Anything that comes up, Lon, you handle it. Like

as not, I won't be back until afternoon. Don't set a lunch for me, Ruby Dee." Not wanting to give Lonnie time to go asking questions, he was already heading toward the door.

His gaze touched Ruby Dee's, though, for just a second. Her quick look was enough to make him feel excited.

Will met Ambrose Bell over at the old James place, and together they walked for two hours around the surrounding land, until they struck an agreement. Will would buy the house and surrounding quarter section, because he just had to own some land of his own, and would lease six sections of range. He would also work for Ambrose part-time in exchange for a small salary and the use of Ambrose's equipment.

"I guess we have a deal, Ambrose." Will stuck out his hand, and the older man took it in a firm grip.

Hefting up his pants, which sagged beneath his paunch, Ambrose said, "It's more than I started with at your age."

"Things are a lot different now," Will said.

Ambrose nodded. "You got that right. A man can't hardly start a place these days. But I guess it was always a chancy thing." He cast Will a curious look, but he didn't ask why Will was leaving the Starr. "That's why I sent J.R. to chiropractor school. I never wanted him to be a rancher . . . and I have a bad back," he added with a grin.

Ambrose was making plans for selling out his operation in another couple of years, getting ready for retirement. His only son was a chiropractor down in Clinton. Will thought a man was lucky when he felt he could do any number of things. For himself, he only wanted to ranch. He was like so many men these days, trying to make a bygone way of life fit into a computer-driven century.

Ambrose said, "Might be easier to just move a mobile home up here and forget about the house. The only good thing about it is that it's brick. That's why it's stood here so long. Me and my Rosie used to talk about fixing it up ourselves, but we just never got to it. Seemed like one thing after another came first. And once we moved in with Rosie's mama, I couldn't get her loose."

Will nodded in understanding.

Together, they headed for their vehicles. Will said, "I'll go on to the bank and get this deal goin', Ambrose. It shouldn't take more than a couple of weeks, three at the most, for the appraisal and legalities."

Ambrose nodded. "I'm glad it's you gettin' this place. And like I said, I have three more sections you're welcome to lease, if you come to need it."

"Thanks. I'm hoping I will eventually." Will stuffed his hands in his pockets. "Ah, Ambrose, I'd appreciate it if you'd keep our deal to yourself. I'd rather not have a lot of people know just yet."

Ambrose said, without raising an eyebrow, "I'll sure do that, Will. People around here are nosy as hell, aren't they? Gets on my nerves. I don't like a lot of people knowin' my business all the time. Good luck to you, son," the older man added, waving as he opened the door to his black Lincoln, a big boat from twenty years ago that was still going strong.

Will stayed there, looking out over the rolling hills for a few minutes after Ambrose left. A quarter section wasn't much, not in this part of the country, but he had bought it outright just because he had to have land to call his own. It had a good tank on it, too, that held water at least half the summer.

He walked on to the house, up the two steps and in through the back porch door that hung crooked, through the kitchen and on through the other rooms, with their peeling wallpaper and cracked plaster. The house was forty-five years old, and had sat empty for the past eighteen years.

But it was his now, and he'd fix it.

Outside again, looking over the rolling hills that stretched away to the high plain of Texas, he felt a rush of excitement, and then a great disappointment that there was no one to share it with. He would have liked to show Ruby Dee . . . and Lonnie . . . and the old man, crazy as that was, because he could just hear the old man ragging him about the how poor the house was and how he wouldn't do much with a quarter section.

Slowly Will went to his pickup and climbed in. Pulling a cigarette from his pocket, he lit it and then headed home, with the windows down and the hot summer air blowing away the cigarette smoke. The air had grown heavy, and white cottony clouds were coming from the west. He anticipated rain, if not tonight, then soon. Finally. Out in this country, rain always came like that . . . just when a person was certain it was never going to rain again. It seemed a lot like his life.

He was making a beginning, he thought. When the bank loan went through, he would have a house—almost one, anyway—a well, a cement storm cellar, a couple of barns, and in spring, stands of purple irises. He would also have a mortgage, which he would be hard-pressed at first to make by ranching on his own.

Few new ranchers made it. That was a fact. The ranching operations that remained today were those that had been started by the previous generation, like his family's. And for many of those, like the Starrs, oil leases had brought them to where they were, as much as any of them hated to admit it. A lot of the younger men today had a regular job with a regular paycheck and ranched on the side. Will would have to do that once he left the old man's employ.

Leaving the old man was another big step that weighed heavily on him. It appeared the old man was settled into that wheelchair. Will didn't like that, but he wasn't going to let the old man use it to stop him. He still worried, though, about him and the old man getting into a fight that ended up with the old man having a big stroke. This fear was one of the things holding him back.

Ruby Dee. He thought of her brown eyes, which could hold such sadness one minute and the next light with sunshine . . . and that could make Will feel things he had not known he could.

But he wasn't the only one to get pleasure from Ruby Dee's eyes. After all these lonely years, the old man had finally found a woman to bring him some joy. And Lonnie had finally found a woman who made a real home for him. Will just couldn't get past any of that. Things were rocky enough between all three of them, without Will upsetting the goodness that had come into their lives. Without Will going after a woman they all claimed.

It would be like the old man, he thought, to have a stroke on purpose, just to get back at him.

Will drove right to the bank in Elk City, to speak with Garland Snyder about a loan. He could have phoned Garland, told him a deal had been struck, but Will wanted to tell him in person and talk a little about his plans with someone. He wasn't quite ready to tell them back home. Garland took him to lunch as a sort of celebration.

It was late afternoon before Will got back to the house. He saw the old ranch pickup parked near the barn, and Lonnie's pickup was there, too. Wildcat's truck was gone.

Will knew Lonnie would be inside, with Ruby Dee.

Jumping out of his own truck, Will slammed the door, hard, and strode into the house. And there the three of them were—Lonnie, just as Will had known he would be, slouched in a chair at the kitchen table, a glass of ice tea in hand, Hardy across from him, in his wheelchair, and Ruby Dee near the counter, gazing happily at an object in the middle of the kitchen floor.

It was a porch swing.

Lonnie had bought it down in Harney at the Lumber and Feed, and he was quite pleased with himself.

"What about the alfalfa?" Will asked, breathing fire.

"Oh . . . baler broke down," Lonnie said, acting unconcerned, knowing full well he was provoking Will. "Wildcat had to go all the way to Woodward for a part, so I told him just to knock off after he got it. It's too dang hot to be balin' or anything else out there, anyway. And you know, Wildcat's gettin' on," he added piously.

"*You* aren't gettin' on, Lonnie," Will said, pointedly.

Lonnie just gave him a bland look.

Will said, "You'll wish you'd sweated a little bit, when winter comes and you don't have anythin' to feed your fancy horses."

Will always liked to have the last word.

☙ 20

AUGUST WAS TURNING into September, the time of final haying and equipment overheating and breakdowns, fences needing to be repaired, plans made for returning the bulls to the lots, and the weaning of cows and calves, and the selling of steers.

During these weeks, Will took what time he could away from the ranch to start fixing up his new old house and the corrals for his horses and bull. Ambrose had said to consider the place his right from their handshake, so Will wasn't wasting time waiting for papers to be signed.

Many nights he worked himself into exhaustion, which kept him from lying in his bed and thinking about all the confusion inside himself. And about Ruby Dee, just five strides down the hall.

He ached to tell them all about the place. He felt like a child, wanting to say: see what I've done. He doubted he'd receive approval from the old man.

The best thing was not to say anything until he was ready to move in, which he figured would be as soon as he got hot and cold water running. All the renovation could be made while he lived in it. It only then occurred to him that he had no furniture to call his own, no dishes, sheets or towels. He was going to have to buy all of it.

Once, while he was making plans for the house, he realized he was measuring everything by questions: what would Ruby Dee think? Would she like the place? Would she want to live there with him? Did he even want to carry it that far with her?

He guessed he still had that to find out.

He snatched what time alone he could with Ruby Dee. Each morning, he made a point of being the first to the kitchen, where he waited for her, instead of going outside to do chores. Usually he had twenty or thirty minutes alone with her, before Lonnie and the old man came in.

During this time, they sat together out on the back step, with their coffee, and watched the land wake up. Will felt shy, and he could tell Ruby Dee did, too, but he could also tell she welcomed having him around.

Their talk was just about everyday things, what she planned for supper, the condition of baseball, that Will kept the old ranch truck because the newer ones were all electronic and harder to repair. But from these things he learned that she loved garden tomatoes and would only eat them during the season, and that she knew nothing about baseball but enjoyed rodeo and performance horse events and that she knew a lot about the workings of an engine.

And from comments she made he learned that she wanted children and a house of her own in the country.

"What about a husband?" he found himself asking.

She said seriously, "I don't know if I want one of those."

Will decided he didn't want to pursue the reasons behind that. And he figured whether they talked about tomatoes or life plans didn't matter, because the whole time he was sitting there, talking or listening, his mind wasn't on any of it. What he was thinking about was how just looking at her made him feel, and even more, how her looking at him made him feel. How her skin would feel against his palm and beneath his lips, and how she would move and moan beneath him when he went into her.

And instinct told him she would be willing.

But he wasn't ready to go down that road yet. No, sir. Will had the distinct sense that if he made love to Ruby Dee, he'd be completely lost, that there would be no going back, because he would belong to her body and soul. So he didn't dare so much as touch her, because he figured he wouldn't be able to stop.

By the end of the week, though, the old man started getting up earlier, coming into the kitchen on Ruby Dee's heels. And he told Will with just one look that he was doing it on purpose.

Ruby Dee herself proved a big problem, too, when it came to getting her away from the old man. She always wanted to make certain he didn't feel left out of anything. She was as protective of him as a she-bear, and many times Will had to remind himself that he had hired her to see to the old man. He himself had directed that her prime responsibility was to see to the old man's welfare.

About the only time Will could be certain to get Ruby Dee away from the old man was in the evenings, for horseback riding. Since Ruby Dee's mare had proved calm and reliable, they went riding further afield, which left the old man behind, although Ruby Dee never would stay out and leave him alone for too long. Also, Lonnie was always along. Lonnie was sort of like the proverbial bad penny that wouldn't go away.

One night, while Will saddled Ruby Dee's horse, he said to Lonnie, "Why don't you go on down to Harney?"

Lonnie just laughed. "The old man himself told me to get my mess out here and ride with you."

That was the old man's way of making certain neither of them was alone with Ruby Dee.

One evening the three of them rode along the ridge above the spring creek—Lonnie on his favorite black-and-white paint, Ruby Dee on Lady Gray, as she had named her, and Will on the mustang, which Ruby Dee had christened Taco. They let the horses pick their way down the side of the ridge to the soft ground of the creek bed. It felt as if it were air-conditioned, and it smelled of damp earth and sweet green growing things.

Ruby Dee took off her boots and socks and rolled up the silk long underwear she'd taken to wearing under her dress when she rode. She only rolled the underwear legs to her knees, though, and she didn't lift her dress any higher than that, either, while she went wading.

Will and Lonnie, holding the horses' reins, sat on a rock and watched. She grinned at them and tried to splash them, but there wasn't enough water in the creek, and they were sitting too far away. Then she spied a butterfly on the limb of a buckthorn bush. "Look!" Excited as if she had found gold, she went after that butterfly, chasing it all over.

"It's a monarch," Will told her, "probably goin' south for the winter, and you're gonna wear it out before it gets there." He couldn't take his eyes off her shiny swinging hair and her pale arms and legs dancing through the air.

Just then Lonnie said, "You know, she's just like wonder wrapped in a body," and his eyes were rapt upon her.

Watching her slip her hand carefully up beside the butterfly on a limb, Will had to agree. Then he cut his eyes to Lonnie, and they looked at each other for a second.

"There's only two things to do with a woman like that," Lonnie drawled in a low voice. "Either join in and be just as crazy . . . or else make love to her." A hint of a challenge twinkled in his eyes.

Will jumped to his feet, and in long strides, tugging along his horse and Ruby Dee's too, with Lonnie shouting after him, he reached Ruby Dee, looped his arm around her waist and hauled her clear off the ground. With her kicking and laughing, he held her against him for the space of three heartbeats, and then he swung her up into her saddle, easy as slinging a light sack of grain and feeling the sweet surge of recklessness while doing it.

Lonnie came running with her socks and boots, and together, Lon on one side and Will on the other and Ruby Dee laughing atop the nervous horse that was wondering what in the world was going on, they jammed socks and boots on her feet.

When Will swung himself into the saddle, he saw Lonnie looking at him, grinning with great enjoyment.

With Will leading, they rode through the trees and up again onto the ridge, where they dismounted and let the horses drag rein and graze, while the three of them sat side by side on the edge of the ridge and watched the red sun slip down behind the Texas plain.

Will looked over at Ruby Dee, sitting between himself and Lonnie. The breeze tugged at the stray, damp hairs around her face. She smiled at him and then turned her face to the coral sun.

Will's gaze slid over and met Lonnie's, and the connection between them burned away the rivalry. In that moment, he and Lonnie shared their caring for this one special woman.

The instant the red sun disappeared, Lonnie jumped up and went after his horse. Ruby Dee and Will were right behind him. All three of them were laughing and yelling like wild young things and trying to get on the backs of their startled horses. Lonnie went galloping toward home, and Ruby Dee raced off right after him. Will followed, giving his horse his head even while he was swinging into the saddle and riding hell-bent with an abandonment he'd long forgotten.

About halfway home, Will overtook Ruby Dee, and in unspoken agreement they hung back, walking their horses. They didn't talk, but Will thought it said a lot that she chose to stay back with him. Lonnie was frowning when they finally rode into the horse barn. He got back at Will by reaching up and helping Ruby Dee out of the saddle. Rather than set her to the ground, he held her by the waist and whirled around, making her laugh. She had to hold on to him when he finally did set her down.

Standing there, holding her, Lonnie shot Will a satisfied look.

When they got back to the house, they found out

that the old man had spent his time alone painting the porch swing for Ruby Dee. He had gotten several cans of partially used paint from the cupboards on the back porch and mixed them to a dusky blue, the color Ruby Dee had mentioned she wanted for the swing.

"Now, just how did you get your wheelchair around on the porch to get into that cupboard, Dad?" Will asked him.

"I roll down on that porch every time I have to go outside," Hardy said.

"And what about the front doorjamb. You didn't have any trouble gettin' over that?"

"Son, this is a top-of-the-line wheelchair you boys bought me. I can go anywhere in it."

Ruby Dee said, "Oh, Hardy, the color is just perfect. I can hardly wait to sit in it."

She was so pleased that Will wasn't about to push an argument with the old man. One thing Ruby Dee had done was bring happiness to the house, and none of them wanted to ruin that.

One afternoon Lonnie observed, "She's talkin' to herself again. You know, Ruby Dee may be a little crazy."

Standing at the opening of the tractor barn, where he and Will were working on the swather, he watched her hanging her colorful bras and panties on the clothesline. Will, wiping his hands on a rag, walked up to look, too. He saw her dress flattened against her legs by the breeze and heard snatches of her voice.

"Nah," he said. "She's not talkin' to herself. . . . She's talkin' to that friend of hers—Miss Edna."

Lonnie was so surprised at his straight-arrow

brother saying something that absurd that his eyebrows shot up, and for once he didn't have a comeback. A few minutes later, though, he said, "You know, Will, I don't know how we'd ever go back to bein' without her."

Will met his brother's gaze, then sighed. "Me, either, Lon. Me, either."

And then one afternoon Will got a pretty big surprise, which made him realize Ruby Dee wasn't just wrapped up in them and content to take what they gave her. Ruby Dee had plans.

He came into the kitchen and heard her on the phone, talking to someone about a mortgage. He heard that clearly—*mortgage*—and then something about fixed rates and a down payment. He didn't have to hear much to know she was speaking about the price of a house. He saw the real estate section of the county newspaper open on the table, marked up with red ink, and lying there, too, was that peculiar paper, the one he had seen in her bedroom with the pictures pasted on it.

After she hung up, she looked at him. He said, "Are you lookin' for a house to buy?"

She nodded. "I'm gettin' a lot closer to havin' the down payment." Her eyes were fully on his.

Will swallowed. "The old man has come around. I imagine you'll have a place here as long as you want it." Then he added, "Dad probably couldn't get along without you now." He almost said *we*, but he didn't.

She looked back down to the newspaper. "I was checking on a place down in Cheyenne. That way I'd still be able to take care of Hardy."

Will didn't know what to say to that, he was so surprised, even though he began to realize he shouldn't have been. All this time he'd been thinking of his plans, and not taking hers into account at all. He was angry that she would have plans separate from theirs.

She lifted her coffee-brown eyes to his and said, "I can't live with other people forever. I want my own house and my own babies to tend."

"But not necessarily a man, right?" He hadn't forgotten she'd said that.

And she answered smartly, "Not necessarily, I guess."

Will turned and walked out the back door. He probably should have spoken up right then, but he figured she already knew how he felt about her. She had to know, and she had to know how the old man and Lonnie felt, too. They certainly did everything but cartwheels to make her feel welcome. If she didn't see that, it was because she didn't want to.

Ruby Dee went to the back door, to the screen door of the porch and watched Will stalk off up the hill. She didn't think she should have to explain herself. Did he expect her not to have any future at all—to just go on caring for the three Starr men until she couldn't do it anymore? To not want anything for herself? Will Starr of all people ought to know what it was to want something for oneself!

She was mad at him for not doing anything since their one kiss to show her that he wanted her. Oh, he was friendly, even affectionate. He sat with her in the mornings and talked, and he'd gotten the horse for her and he rode with her, but Lonnie did things like that, too, and so did Hardy. They all were sweet as they could be to her. All three of them!

That was the whole problem, and there was no use being angry at Will about it, she thought, depression falling over her like water, clean washing the anger away. All three of them wanted her.

She wasn't certain what Lonnie might do if she chose Will, but she knew Hardy would have a fit. He'd have a fit and then he'd slip right back to the way he'd been before she'd come, one foot sliding into the grave, while the other one miserably kicked at everyone. Will and his daddy would be split apart again and Lonnie would be left dangling on the fringe. HELL TO PAY, that's what would happen, and it would be all her fault.

She started to cry. Hardy came in and asked her what in the hell she was crying about now. She didn't answer him, but grabbed her papers and went upstairs. He hollered after her to not cry so long that she couldn't start supper. He was just trying to josh her out of crying, and that sweetness made her cry all the harder.

She sat on her bed and looked at her dream paper and the few listings in the county newspaper. She couldn't bring herself to call about the cottage all the way down in Oklahoma City, so far away from Hardy, who did need her. But she had to get her own place. She could rent something until she could buy. She could still stay on with Hardy, but she'd have her own place and could get started on those babies. Lord, she wanted babies.

Days passed, though, and she didn't go look at anything. She didn't do a blessed thing. She just kept thinking how upset the men would be if she moved out, and how she would miss them so much.

Miss Edna said to her, *"Ruby Dee, you have to stick to your plan."* And Ruby Dee answered, "Miss Edna, don't bother me. I'm doin' the best I can."

Will seemed to keep his distance after their little

snit that afternoon, but Ruby Dee sensed that his deep inner pockets were ripping wider and wider and everything was getting ready to spill out. She felt her own inner ripping and tearing. There was a tug-of-war going on inside her between her desire for her own home and babies, and her desire to care for the Starr men. She couldn't have stopped loving the three of them, and she couldn't have stopped wanting Will most of all, any more than she could have stopped breathing.

Then the rain came at last and by heavy storms. Hardy said it was always that way at the end of summer. The wind and thunder and lightning bore down on them in the early hours of the morning and brought them all out of their beds. Will and Lonnie jerked on their jeans and boots, while Ruby Dee, wrapping her robe around her, ran around unplugging everything electric, and Hardy monitored the reports on their weather radio and the television. Ruby Dee wanted to unplug the radio and television, but Hardy insisted they remain on.

Having expected the storms, Will had the generator ready in case of power outage, and he and Lonnie had already stowed or tied down anything that could blow away, so they all just sat around the kitchen while Ruby Dee made breakfast. She used water sparingly, frightened of turning on the faucet and perhaps drawing lightning. All of Will's assurances wouldn't change her way of thinking.

Will didn't respect storms enough to suit Ruby Dee. He loved them and went out on the front porch to watch.

Ruby Dee called, "Don't be out there. Lightnin' could get you. You could be sucked up!"

He came back in, to keep her calm.

Lightning flashed like camera bulbs—the blinding bright ones used for television—and the thunder rolled like cannon fire. It scared Ruby Dee so bad that she dropped the bowl she was mixing pancakes in and broke it. "It was my favorite bowl. . . . Oh, Hardy, was it your Mama's? It was so old."

"Hell, it was Lila's, so it's nothin' but good riddance."

Hardy tried to get her to go down to the storm shelter, even said he was going to take her down, but Ruby Dee was more afraid of holes in the ground than she was of storms. A storm made her think of a hole in the ground. She tried to hold herself together, because panicking sure wasn't going to help anything. She'd do pretty good one minute, and then here'd come the thunder again.

Will asked her to fix him a double helping of pancakes, and she whipped up more batter. As she was doing that, lightning came like shell fire over the house, and she whirled from the stove and right into his arms, clutching him, hiding her head on his chest, and she didn't think one iota about Lonnie and Hardy being there, either. She couldn't. She was ashamed of herself, but fear had her by the throat. Anyone would have such a fear after they had been through a storm that blew away the house around them, taking a handful of people with it. With each crack of lightning, she kept seeing the woman who had been her foster mother, knocked up against a tree, dead, with a stick of wood right through her eyeball.

Will held her tightly, whispering that it would be all right. Then he told Lonnie to slide the doors between the dining room and living room together and shut the dining room drapes. "We'll just move everything in to the big table, Ruby Dee." He said it like he was planning a party.

The dining room was at the center of the house, and it did feel a lot more sheltered. Hardy started telling storm stories, funny ones, like how a tornado had chased him to the house once, and had picked up his bucket of nails and set it down over at the Cottons' place, five miles away, without losing a nail. He swore it was so, and that Cora Jean would know. Lonnie said he once saw a big oak tree picked up, turned around, and set back down in exactly the same spot. Ruby Dee thought that may have been made up, but Lonnie swore it wasn't. After breakfast, Hardy had Ruby Dee rub castor oil on the joints of both legs and bind them. She knew the men were doing all these things to keep her from thinking about the storm, and their tender regard made her want to cry.

As it turned out, none of the tornados sighted came anywhere near the ranch. The winds had been severe, however, and as soon as the rain quit, Will and Lonnie went out to look around. They reported that shingles had been blown off the house, one of the windows in the old man's shop had been rattled out, and a piece of tin had been peeled up atop the old tractor barn, but everything else looked fine. The telephone in the house was out, and Lonnie tried using Will's cellular phone to reach the Reeves's store, but he couldn't get through, so he drove down to find out how they had fared.

Ruby Dee let Sally out the screen door and then slowly stepped out behind her. As frightened as she was of storms, she loved the time afterward. The heat and dust were washed away, leaving the sweetest earthy smell, and the sun, like the mighty power of the Lord, came breaking through the purple clouds, shining down on everything so still that it was as if the world had stopped turning.

Looking around, savoring the freshness, Ruby Dee walked across the yard and up the sloping drive toward the horse barn, where she had seen Will go. When she reached the big entry of the barn, she peered down the wide alley and saw Will's form at the far end, silhouetted against the brighter light outside.

He heard her and turned, then called her to come see the rainbow. She hurried to his side, and he pointed. "There."

"Why, it's a double!"

The barn sat higher than the miles and miles of rolling hills to the southeast, and the ribbons of the rainbows arched from one hill to another. Captivated, Ruby Dee stood rooted to the spot, watching the colors deepen and then pale, fade and move to another spot.

"Look! It's moved. . . . Oh, goodness, there's another one!"

Then Will's hand took her arm, and he turned her to him. His brilliant, steel-gray eyes danced with heat. She averted her eyes, suddenly embarrassed, knowing she had come looking for him because of the longing inside herself. It was as if the storm had stirred her as it had the tree limbs and grasses.

"I'm sorry about how I behaved during the storm—"she began, but she never got to explain, because he bent his head and kissed her.

When he lifted his head, she backed up, thinking that she should return to the house . . . yes, she most certainly should . . . and not be here with him, and not be having the desires she was having.

He came toward her, and she back up, until she found herself against the wall of a horse stall. And then Will was kissing her again, and she was kissing him, her heart pounding and blood thrumming. She tried to keep her hands flattened against the wall behind her, but the next instant she had wrapped them around his neck, and he had his around her head and pulled her against him, and sweet, hot passion pooled deep in her intimate parts, bubbled up and flowed all over her.

She kissed his mouth and his neck, tasted his salty skin and inhaled the heady scent of him, felt his warm, silky hair and his large, strong muscles. He kissed her eyes and her neck and as far down on her breasts as the neckline of her dress would allow, and she wished he would tear her dress right off and get to all of her.

Then he was holding her against his hard body, her head pressed to his chest, hearing the thudding of his heart, while her own heart beat with longing and her pelvis pressed against his, all of its own accord.

He drew back, and she lifted her head to look into his intense, stormy eyes. He let go of her, stepped back and raked a hand through his hair. Ruby Dee wrapped her arms around herself and choked back tears.

He looked at her almost angrily. "I'm twelve years older than you are," he said.

Well. She hadn't known that bothered him. Instinctively she went to him, put her hand up to his neck.

"I'm the one who listens to Elvis," she said, and a bit of a grin twitched his lips beneath his mustache.

Gazing at that mustache, she put her finger to it

and stroked the coarse auburn hairs. And she knew exactly what she was doing.

Then she was looking again into his eyes and he was looking heavily at her. They kissed, quickly. Drew apart and looked at each other, saying silently with their eyes the things words couldn't express: caring and fear and doubt . . . and longing. Mostly the longing that wanted to get past all the rest.

"Oh, Will, I don't want to come between you and your daddy and Lonnie."

"I know."

Will didn't know what else to say to that. He didn't want to hurt his father or brother, either.

But he wanted Ruby Dee.

He reached out and brought her to him again, slowly but deliberately. He kissed her, brief and hard, and then again, seductively, wanting to give her something to remember, before finally letting her go, when she drew away. She went slowly, and he let his hand caress her neck at the very last.

Then she hurried away from him, back to the house, and to the old man waiting there.

In that instant, stabbed with jealousy, Will had a sudden understanding of his father and what had happened with his mother, her just nineteen and the old man forty-three, his time running out and his manhood running hot.

But the old man had had his chance, Will thought angrily.

Hardy knew when Ruby Dee came in that she had been with Will. Passion was all over her face, and her lips were moist and swollen. There were tears in her eyes, too.

He pretended not to notice any of this, pretended

to work intently on the bridle he was making, all the while wanting to reach over and draw her to him. His gaze stopped on his hands.

They were old hands, spotted with age . . . hands he hardly recognized anymore. It was like he was two men. The one inside, the Hardy he knew, was strong. And if some might call him coarse and hard, he was an honest man and a powerful one, too. Then there was the other man, the one in the wheelchair, who was bent when he walked, whose face resembled Father Time and who sometimes had to struggle to not piss on himself.

He clenched his fist, damning the putrid body that trapped him, because that was what it was, a trap from which the only escape was death. People never realized this when they were young, never thought about it, but the truth of the matter was that everyone was trapped in a mortal, aging body, and there wasn't one damn thing on God's green earth that anyone, much less Hardy and his sinful ways, could do about it. The most he could hope for was to have what little pleasures he could enjoy, like working with his leather and drinking his whiskey and annoying everyone else in the Goddamn universe. And being able to see and smell and touch this gal here from time to time.

His mind sped back and lighted on himself and Jooney, running among the cemetery markers. He was chasing her, and then he was kissing her, and she was sweet as candy. Her skin was soft and warm beneath his hand, her eyes begging him to fill her.

He blinked, and the image was gone.

Then, not really knowing he was going to do it, he said, "Let's go for a drive."

Ruby Dee whirled and looked at him in surprise.

"I don't know, Hardy. My car may not make it down the muddy road."

"We'll take my pickup. It needs to be driven, 'fore it dies."

"But—"

He had already pushed himself out of the wheelchair and was reaching for his cane. "Come on. I like to look at things after a storm."

He went out to the truck on his own. He was more stiff than usual—always was after rain. But he got out to his pickup easily enough, and managed to get behind the steering wheel. Ruby Dee opened the door on the passenger side and said she thought she should go tell Will.

"Get in, gal. Will's smart enough to figure it out."

They rolled down the windows, and the sweet, rain-fresh air blew through, because now the wind was coming up again. Just as Hardy turned down the drive, Will came out of the barn. Hardy didn't so much as turn his head or slow down, although Ruby Dee waved and called that they were going for a ride.

Hardy drove out the lane and turned west. The road was river-bottom sand, and the rain drained away quickly, except for puddles here and there, and through those he pressed the accelerator and sent mud spraying. Each time they came up on a rise, they could see all the way to Texas, where the sun already shone on the high plains, making it like a glistening jewel.

On the highest rise, Hardy stopped and gestured. "Either side of the road here, far as you can see clearly, is Starr land."

Ruby Dee didn't say anything, just looked at him

in a curious way, with her dark, quiet, coffee-black eyes. Jooney's eyes.

Coming to a rough oiled road, Hardy turned north for a mile, until he turned into the old gravel road beneath the wrought-iron entry that proclaimed, White Rose Cemetery.

It was a sparse acre set on rugged earth, sand and rock and sparse clumps of grass, not the planted Bermuda of fancy church cemeteries. Along the edge of the cemetery grew a line of hedge-apple trees.

The ground was soft from the recent rain, and Hardy's cane sank into it. Some of the markers were worn, so the names were all but gone. The place was tended. The last Hardy knew, Lindy Penny had taken on the job. Hardy had not come here in a long time, not since Lila had left him.

He pointed out the names on the markers. "This here cemetery was started by the four families to begin homesteadin' this land . . . Starr, Penny, Cotton, Gattenby."

There was his grandpappy's grave, and his mother's and father's, their three babies', who hadn't lived over a day, his brother, Wild, who one day had been pounding in a fence post and just dropped dead.

Hardy propped himself on Pappy's large marker, where he could look straight across at Jooney's. He watched Ruby Dee walk around, reading the names. Names like Delight Penny and Honey Bee Gattenby. Hardy's mother had been named Arta Bellah.

When Ruby Dee came to Jooney's gravestone, Hardy watched her carefully. "Jooney Moon Cotton," she read aloud and looked over her shoulder at him. "That's so pretty. . . . That's your friend, isn't it? The healer?"

Hardy nodded, and she looked again at the

marker. She looked at it a long time, ran her hand over it. Hardy stared at her slim back, and for an instant he was young again, and here on a Sunday afternoon with Jooney.

21

THROUGH THE FILMY, dusty windshield, Will saw the swather at the far end of the field, speeding over the grass as if in a race.

"Lonnie looks like he wants to be done," Wildcat commented.

"Shit." Will shifted gears and sent the big old truck bouncing across the field. They were halfway across the field from the swather, when they saw the reels stop. The swather gave up a couple puffs of smoke and seemed to settle down on the grass like a dead elephant.

Will barreled up and braked, threw himself out of the cab. "Damn it all to hell, Lonnie!"

Lonnie came stepping down from the swather. "I guess it got plugged up," he said, same as he would have said hello. "Geez, it's hot. Did y'all get the beer?"

Will jerked off his hat and flapped it. "You aren't drivin' on the interstate, damnit! You're cuttin' grass. I know it's askin' a lot of you to pay attention and do the job decently, but it does pay the bills."

"You don't like the way I do the job, you do it

yourself," Lonnie said, swept off his Western Plains
Co-op ballcap and sat on the swather step.

"That's your answer for everything, isn't it?"

Will stood for a second, feeling the frustration roll
inside him like a tornado trying to get out of a plastic bag. And then the bag burst, and he leaped over,
grabbed hold of Lonnie, jerked him up and slammed
him back against the swather.

"I'm tired of havin' to do your work and mine,
too, by God."

"Nobody asked you to!"

They went at it then, letting loose the pent-up heat
and sweat and frustration. It was so hot that both of
them lost their burst of fighting energy after a few
good punches, and they went to rolling and scraping
on the ground. They ended up on the grass that had
been cut, and the prickly stalks poked and stung
their faces and necks. Seeds and dust choked Will's
nose, and his lungs began to burn. Lonnie's face was
smeared with blood from his nose.

"You ain't so pretty now," Will huffed.

"And you never were." Lonnie lunged at him.
"Had enough, old man?"

Will bent his head and tackled Lonnie again, taking him down. Grunting and gasping for breath,
they pounded each other's bodies. With each punch
he took and each one he gave, Will felt the pressure
release.

Suddenly they were being sprayed.

"That's enough, boys. We can't get this grass cut
with you two wastin' energy like this."

It was Wildcat. He had two bottles of beer, one in
each hand, and was using them like a fire hose.

Lonnie stumbled backward. "Damn, Wildcat,
you're blindin' me."

"You're wastin' good beer," Will cried out and jumped toward the older man.

Then Lonnie was beside him, and the chase was on, Will reveling in the recklessness that had taken hold of him.

He and Lonnie, stumbling more than running, chased Wildcat, who was high-stepping through the uncut grass and calling, "Snake . . . get away, snake . . . I'm comin'!" while he held the foaming bottles of beer out in front of him.

Will made a flying tackle for Wildcat's legs and missed but succeeded in knocking him down. Lonnie landed on top of them, and they were all half-laughing, half-groaning. It was at least five minutes before any of them could say a good word. Lonnie spoke first, when he jumped up and went to smacking at the air.

"Shit! That damn thing thinks I'm a flower." He swatted again and ran off.

"I don't think you can outrun a yellow jacket, Lon," Will said, dragging himself to his feet.

The sticky mixture of sweat, beer and traces of blood drew the buzzing critters like nectar. Will smacked a fly on his neck and scratched gnats out of his ears.

"I guess we'd better get back to the house and get showered before we get carried off to Oz."

They found the two bottles of beer Wildcat had thrown when he fell. Lonnie gratefully finished what was left, and each of them each quickly drank one of the remaining cold beers from the six-pack Will and Wildcat had brought.

The plan had been to trade off on the swather and keep it going into full dark, trying to make short work of the grass cutting. No rain was in the forecast, but it always seemed like when they went to haying, rain came in.

"You want to come up to the house, too, Wildcat—take a break for supper before we start in again?"

"Naw . . . I'll get the header dug out and see if the sickles are okay. You could bring me out somethin'. . . . Ruby Dee, she sure does make some great biscuits. I don't say anythin' to Charlene, 'cause it wouldn't set well, but she just can't seem to get 'em as light as Ruby Dee does. Oh, and you better bring them extra sickles you bought the other day. And maybe some ice tea."

"Would you like to make out a list, Wildcat?" Lonnie asked, as he slid into the old dually pickup.

"No, I don't reckon . . . unless you think you need one."

Slowly Will made a circle in the field, avoiding the windrows of cut hay this time, and headed back to the road. The wind felt good blowing in the windows, but the flies and gnats came in, too. Lonnie swatted at the flies that landed on him, and said something that Will didn't quite catch.

"What?"

"My hat . . . I forgot it back there. Wish I hadn't."

"You want to go back for it?"

"Naw. Plenty more ball caps at the house."

"Yeah."

Will wanted to explain to Lonnie what had happened to him back at the swather, but he couldn't find the words. How was he going to explain that he was on edge because he needed to do something that was going to make everyone mad at him and because he was wanting to screw Ruby Dee so bad it hurt?

Lonnie said, "How many ball caps you reckon we have? You think we have as many as fifty?"

"I think the old man has fifty of his own."

"I have at least ten in my room, and I'll bet there's ten or better in the tack room." He paused, then asked, "Are you gonna take half of them with you when you leave?"

Will glanced at him. "I'm not concerned with ball caps, Lonnie." A feeling of dread crept up his back.

Lonnie was looking out his side window. "No . . . I didn't think you were." After a minute, he said, "So when are you gonna move out to Ambrose Bell's old place?"

Will looked over at him, hit a rut and had to look back at the road. "How do you know about Ambrose's place?"

"Same way I know that George Jensen is foolin' around behind Jenny's back with a man from Elk City, and that Margie Waggoner lost all of hers and Rob's savings over at Remington Park. I hear things. And it sure wasn't gonna stay secret too long, with you buyin' all that stuff down at Harney Lumber. Then one night, I just followed you."

Will drove on, keeping his eyes on the rutted dirt road. Suddenly Lonnie mumbled something and then was swinging out the door, even as Will drove along at forty miles an hour.

"Damnit, Lonnie!"

Will braked. The passenger door fluttered like a bent wing, creaking like it was about to break off. Lonnie was back in the road, just standing there. Will shoved the shift arm into reverse and roared backward, causing Lonnie to jump out of the way. Then Will got out and slammed the door.

The two of them glared at each other over the hood of the truck.

Then Lonnie let loose and banged his fist on the hood. "Damn you, Will! I can understand you not tellin' the old man, but why didn't you tell me? I'm your brother! We . . . Damnit, didn't you even think about how what you're doin' might affect me?"

The raw hurt on Lonnie's face shot straight through Will's heart, but his brother's words also made him mad. That was Lonnie—always thinking of himself!

"You heard very well what I told the old man that day and the next morning. And as for me thinkin' about how this might affect you, let me just say that every fuckin' decision of my life has been made by thinkin' how it would affect you and the old man. This one time I couldn't afford to do that. This one time I'm doin' this for me." And he jabbed his finger at his chest.

Lonnie glared at him a second, and then he turned away, walked a few steps and stopped.

Already guilt was settling on Will shoulders. He tried to find the middle ground, to explain his feelings.

"Lon—you're my brother. I . . ." Will broke off, and then tried again. "When you've gone off to the rodeo, leavin' me behind, or gone foolin' around with women, leavin' me to carry the load of the ranch, you know good and well you didn't spend a lot of time thinkin' about how any of that would affect me. But still—did any of those times mean that you thought any less of me as your brother? Did it have anything much to do with me at all—or was it more what you needed for yourself?"

Will paused, waiting, refusing to go on until Lonnie looked at him. Slowly, Lonnie turned.

"It's the same with me, Lon. My doin' this doesn't change how I feel about you. You're my brother, and you always will be. I'll always be there for you as much as I can . . . as much as I've ever been. Nothin's gonna change that.

"I'd cut my arm off for you, Lon, if you needed it, and I'd stay at the ranch, if I thought you absolutely had to have it that way, but I can't see that, not anymore."

Will gazed at Lonnie with a dogged, hopeful look. Lonnie felt a flicker of relief. Will was trying to explain, was trying to keep the connection between them. Lonnie wished he could explain the fears tearing at him, but he couldn't. He barely understood them himself, and he couldn't ever speak of them.

"How in the hell are you just gonna leave the ranch?" he asked. "The old man sure can't run it, Will. And *why* are you leavin'? I know the old man ties your hands a lot, and that you want a place to run on your own. I guess I get that, but Will, the Starr's gonna be yours in the not-too-distant future, when the old man's gone. After all these years, why do this now? Why not just wait the old man out?"

"You think Dad will leave the ranch to me and not to the both of us?"

"I don't think he'll leave me a red cent."

Will breathed deeply, looked downward and then back at Lonnie. "The old man, bein' who he is, might be inclined not to leave either of us a red cent, although I happen to believe he'll leave at least a major part of the ranch to both of us, because we are the continuation of the Starrs. No matter how you may think Dad feels about you, Lonnie, you are a male Starr, and he won't cut you out.

"But inheriting the Starr won't give me what I'm wanting now, Lonnie. I want to experiment with crossbreeding, just to see what I can do. And I don't want to wait until the old man's gone. I want to show him, I guess."

Lonnie thought he could understand.

Then Will said, "I'm not plannin' on just leavin', Lon. Oh, that's what I thought back when I was so mad, but now I figure I'll be around. It's not like I'm movin' to another country, you know." He ran a hand through his hair. "I could handle the Starr and my own operation, with some more help, but I guess how much I'm around will depend on the old man. He may just want to get another manager. I'll still keep lookin' in, though. That ranch is a part of me, Lon, and I'm not turnin' my back on it. I'm just lookin' for somethin' more."

For a long moment, he and Lonnie gazed at each other.

Then Will raised an eyebrow at his brother. "You know, the best thing would be for you to take over managing the Starr right now."

Lonnie looked surprised and then shook his head. "Aw, Will, I can't handle the ranch. Shit, I'd have us in the poorhouse in six months."

"Now, why do you say that?" Will's temper flared. "You know as much about the operation as I do."

"I know about the operation. Keepin' it runnin' is another thing. I don't have a head for that sort of thing."

"I'd be right there, helpin' you, whenever you wanted me to."

Lonnie shook his head. "I'm not cut out for it, Will. The old man rides me hard enough as it is. I'm not gonna take on handling the ranch and give him somethin' more to hound me about. I don't even know if I can stay there without you, Will."

That made Will feel caught like a rat in a trap. He pushed the guilt away. "Suit yourself, Lon. That's your decision." He headed for the driver's door, saying, "Are you comin'?"

It was too long and hot a walk home, so Lonnie got back in the truck.

When Will turned the pickup up the drive, Lonnie said, "How much of your choosin' to go over to Ambrose Bell's place has to do with Ruby Dee?"

Will sighed heavily. "I'd go anyway . . . but now I'm considering her. I want a wife and family, Lon. I have for a long time."

"Shit, Will. We just get things good here, and you've got to go screw it up." He let that sit there, then he added, "The old man's gonna fight you for Ruby Dee."

Will gave a faint grunt. Then he said, "And what about you? Are you gonna get in the way, too?"

Lonnie didn't know what to say, didn't know if he would get in his brother's way or not. He said, "I sure don't like the idea of you maybe takin' her off."

When they pulled around the back of the house, Ruby Dee was just coming out the back door. At the sight of her, Lonnie's heart gave a small jump. He said, "I sure never did feel about another woman the way I feel about Ruby Dee."

~ 22

FOR THE FOLLOWING two nights and days, Will dealt with getting the hay cut, doctoring calves and beginning the preliminary selection of the steers, bred cows and cow-calf pairs the ranch would take to market in October. They would let go a few select bull calves, too. All told, the cattle sale would be small, as their major sale was always held in the spring, right on the ranch.

The whole time Will was doing these tasks, though, he was imagining how he was going to tell the old man he had a place and was moving out. He dreaded another confrontation.

It turned out, however, that Ruby Dee had more to say on the subject than the old man did.

Will told her early one morning, when he had a few minutes with her before the old man got up. He was excited to finally be telling her. He wanted her to see that he had a house for her.

But Ruby Dee said sharply, "I think you should have told your daddy about this place when you bought it."

"I didn't see any need to cause problems until my

plans were certain." Will wondered why she was so mad with him, because she clearly was.

"Problems? Is it a problem to let your own father into your life?"

"It has proved to be at times in the past," Will said honestly, which only made her cheeks get more flushed.

"So now you're just gonna tell him one minute and then fly right on out of here the next?" Her expression accused him of all types of wrongdoing.

"I'm not flyin' anywhere. I'm only going about five miles northwest. I'm not plannin' on deserting Dad," he added, because he was beginning to get an inkling of why she was angry.

She frowned. "Well, I don't know what his reaction will be, but don't worry about his health. He's stronger than when I first came by a long shot. Your daddy is not an invalid. He rolls around in that wheelchair because it suits him. He's doing it because he chooses to, and one of the reasons he chooses to is to annoy you, which is a sign that he is in full possession of his mental faculties. If at times he might seem to think slower than you do, it is only because he has eighty-five years stuffed into his brain. He's going to be disappointed, I know, that his son has shut him out of his life."

Then she stalked away, leaving Will thoroughly disappointed and confused. He didn't know what he had done to infuriate her. She had somehow managed to make the fact of the old man rolling around in a wheelchair when he didn't have to sound as if it made sense, and to make Will feel like a neglectful son.

The thought of Will moving out of the house upset Ruby Dee considerably. For her to move to her own home was one thing; for Will to move out was another. It didn't matter that he was not moving far, or that no doubt he would still be coming to the ranch every day. He would no longer be a part of them, just down the hall from her at night, or making coffee in the early morning. Or out working his mustang, or simply walking around outside. And without him doing those things, nothing was going to be the same.

What she thought was: by heaven, I haven't moved out, and you have no business doing it, either!

Ruby Dee liked things as they had been these long summer weeks. She did not want Will to move off and change things. She was afraid of losing what she had found with these men. She was afraid of losing Will. Though she doubted it quite accurate to say she even had him.

That evening, over the after-supper coffee, Will told the old man about the house he had bought and the land he had leased.

The old man looked at him a long second. Will looked back. The old man had absolutely no expression. Then he asked, "When do you want to quit here?"

It took Will a second to answer. "I thought I could move over to the house tonight. I figure we can move my stock in the coming week. But I can continue to work here as long as I'm needed."

The old man nodded thoughtfully. His eyes fell to his coffee cup.

Will glanced at Lonnie. Lonnie looked equally puzzled.

"You know as well as I do that it could take

awhile to find someone to replace you. I'll count on you until we do." The old man's tone was cold and distant.

"I'd planned on that," Will said, with equal distance. And then he wasn't looking at the old man but at the gray formica tabletop and wondering why he felt so let down. Felt like he was going to fall through the chair and keep on going.

Ruby Dee, sitting on the stairway, listening, knotted her hands into tight fists. "Just listen to them, Miss Edna," she whispered. "They are so stubborn—hurting each other out of their stupid pride."

Hardy asked Will if he knew any men who might be interested in the manager's job, and Will mentioned a couple of names. Lonnie suggested someone, too.

Then Will said, "Lonnie could handle things. He knows as much as I do about the ranch."

"That would keep Lonnie tied more than he's able," Hardy said. "I'd 'preciate it if you'd contact those you've mentioned and see if they'd be interested. I'll talk to any who are. And you'd better see to placin' some ads for the job, too."

Ruby Dee listened to Will volunteer to stay on until the sale of the fall cattle, even should they find a manager in the coming weeks. But Hardy said that he wouldn't want to hold Will up.

"I ain't never cared much for the fall sellin' anyway. Spring's always better."

Hardy spoke in a grating tone. Ruby Dee imagined Will choking back a retort, no doubt afraid of provoking Hardy into a stroke.

Will said he would need to go over the records with Hardy and make certain the cattle were split correctly.

"I trust you to divide 'em up as you see fit," Hardy said. Those words, flatly spoken, were the only trace of emotion that Hardy gave.

Then Ruby Dee heard the chair legs scrape and boots thump heavily on the floor; the back door opened and closed. A few minutes later, she heard Hardy's footsteps and the thump of his cane as he came through the dining room.

Then he was looking at her. Out of his wheelchair, standing.

"You could have stayed in the kitchen to hear better," he said.

"Why did you do that?" she asked, holding on to her fury.

"What'd I do?" he said, eyebrows raised, as if he didn't know.

Ruby Dee pressed her fists against her lap. "Why didn't you ask him to keep on managing the ranch? He wanted you to give him that, at least."

His eyes got hard as quartz. "He wants to leave. Let him go."

"No, he doesn't want to leave. So he wants something of his own! That doesn't mean he wants to leave behind what he has with you." She stood and grasped the stair rail. "He wants you to ask him to stay. He wants you to give him that small thing."

But Hardy's face was set. "I never asked him to leave—he decided that for hisself. He can decide to stay for hisself, if he wants."

Suddenly something struck Ruby Dee. "Are you doin' this because of me?" She knew it suddenly, even as she watched his eyes give a little jump. He knew what was happening between her and Will, and he wanted to stop it.

Hardy said, "I ain't doin' nothin'. The boy has

said he wants to go. Let him go give it a try."

"He's not a boy, Hardy. He's a man, and he's your son. They both are." She shut her mouth tight for an instant, and then erupted again, leaning toward him and shaking with emotion. "Will wants you to acknowledge that he has done a good job here, that you are proud of him. One little sign that he has proven himself to you. And Lonnie . . . would it have hurt you to ask him to manage the place? Maybe he wouldn't want to, but he would like you to acknowledge that he could do it—that you think he could do it. They need your approval, Hardy. They need you to show them you are proud of the men they have become."

Of course, even as she said all this, she knew no one ever got anywhere by criticizing Hardy Starr. He got all tight, shuttering his eyes and ears and heart, so that the words just bounced off him.

"If they're men, they don't need any of that," he said.

"Oh, Hardy, is that what you really think?" She gazed at him, pressed her fist across her stomach. "People need to know they are valued, Hardy. Sons need that. Need isn't a weakness. It's the necessary ingredient to understanding. It's the shining tie that binds, Hardy."

"Are you finished?" he asked, his face still hard as stone.

"I guess I'll add one more thing, which is that you owe Will a lot. One of the things you owe him for is bringing me here in the first place."

Hardy's eyes glittered for a silent moment. "I'm not so certain of that right this minute," he said, and stalked into his bedroom.

Whirling, Ruby Dee raced up to her bedroom,

slammed the door and threw herself across the bed, crying out her anger and her sorrow. At one point, in Miss Edna's voice, the question came, *"What are you crying about, Ruby Dee?"*

Well. That gave her pause, because she wasn't certain. She only knew that her heart hurt, that she felt she was losing something precious. Some bright, shining tie of need that was now stretched near to breaking.

She never should have gotten so involved. She knew that. She had begun to feel like these men were her family, that she had a place here, but that was foolish. She was a care-giver, paid for her services. This house was not hers and these people were not hers, no matter how much she cared for them.

From the shade of the tractor barn, where he was smoking a cigarette, Will saw the old man come out the back door and go to his shop.

Walking to the edge of the barn, Lonnie spit a stream of tobacco and then said, "It looks like the old man has finally decided to get out of that chair."

"Yep," Will said.

The old man doing that was like one more stab at him. One more little joke, he thought. And for some reason he experienced a strange twinge of pride— that man was his father, and there really wasn't another man on God's green earth like Hardy Starr.

"You'll be stayin' around for a bit, won't you, Lonnie?"

"Yeah, I guess so. Unless the old man fires me . . . or fires Ruby Dee. I doubt there's much chance of that, though."

"No, I don't imagine there is," Will agreed, and

he was thinking of the irony in the situation, when Lonnie spoke about it.

You know, it's pretty funny, when you think about it. You got into the fit of leavin' by making the old man accept Ruby Dee, and now he's lettin' you go and keepin' her."

"I'd been thinkin' about my own place for a while before Ruby Dee. I spoke to Ambrose Bell back before Dad had his stroke." After the old man's stroke, he'd let the idea of leaving pass . . . or he thought he had.

Will threw down his cigarette and crushed it with his boot. "I don't want to crowd you, Lon, but I could sure use your help, while we try to get things straight. And there's Ruby Dee. She might need help. I know she likes havin' you around, too."

"You're just goin' down the road, Will. Are you plannin' never to come over here?"

"No . . ." Will shook his head, feeling sheepish. "It's just gonna be different."

"Yeah, well, I thought that was the point."

Lonnie shot Will a questioning look. Lonnie could sure surprise Will on occasion.

"You're right," he said, punching his brother in the shoulder. "You aren't very often, but when you are, you are."

Lonnie said virtuously, "My wisdom comes from hangin' around women so much. You learn a lot about stuff like that from women."

Lonnie went off to find a sleeping bag and other things Will might need, and Will went up to his room, threw clothes into a duffel bag and grabbed a handful of shirts and jeans on hangers.

As he came along the upstairs landing he paused at Ruby Dee's door. Then he knocked. When she opened the door, he could tell she'd been crying.

He fumbled inside himself for the words, and finally came up with, "I want you to stay, for a while longer. Please."

She nodded, and then her tears welled up. "He loves you, Will. He really does."

Will didn't know what to say to that. He leaned over and kissed her quickly, then went down the stairs. He ended up driving off and not even speaking to the old man. He didn't have anything particular to say to him.

Ruby Dee slept restlessly and lightly. When she awoke, she lay there a few seconds, listening, trying to place the sound she'd barely heard. It was first light, she saw. The nights were cooler now, and she had left her window open, and the fresh morning air drifted through. So did the scent of coffee. And the sound of footsteps on gravel.

She slipped out of bed and went over to the window. She could just make out Will's figure, standing in the driveway and looking up at her window.

Pushing the window wide, she leaned near the screen. He saw her. "I'll be right down," she called softly.

She threw on her robe and, with Sally right at her heels, flew down the stairs in bare feet, staying near the wall, so as not to make the stairs creak. Through the kitchen, where the light was on over the sink, just like always, and the coffee maker was steaming, just like always. And then she and Sally were outside on the concrete step, and Will was right in front of them.

Grinning, he said, "Good mornin'."

Her heart hammered. "Good morning."

He lifted his steaming cup. "I don't have a coffee-pot over at my house."

She gazed into his steely-blue eyes. "You have one here," she said.

With surprise, she saw the flame of desire in his eyes an instant before he reached up, slipped his hand behind her neck and drew her to him. He kissed her full and hard, taking her breath and senses, before breaking off and stepping backward.

Well. She could only stand there, breathing hard, staring at him. Wanting him, there on the concrete steps in the first light of morning. And she thought how quick and easy it would have been, too, primed and ready as they both were.

Amazed and embarrassed by her thoughts, she broke the gaze, looked down at the grass.

Will, his voice husky, said, "Sit with me on the steps for a few minutes, and I'll share my coffee with you."

If she shared his coffee, she wouldn't make noise getting her own. They sat side by side on the steps. A blue jay swooped and chattered at Sally, and in the far distance coyotes yipped.

Ruby Dee asked Will how he had liked his first night in his house, and he said it had been uncomfortable, because not only didn't he have a coffeepot, but he didn't have a bed, either. Then he gave her specific directions to his place, which was just over five miles away. "You'll know you're close when you see the old cattle loading pens on the right."

His eyes rested on hers for long seconds. He was giving her an invitation, and Ruby Dee felt a warm excitement wash over her.

He started talking about the land then. Only a hundred and sixty acres would be his, but he would have access to two thousand more. That was small by comparison to the Starr ranch, or almost any of the other ranches around, but it was plenty for him to begin a breeding program. What he wanted to do, he said, was try for a new cross, which would combine the Starr-registered Herefords and the best qualities of Red Angus and Brahmans.

There was something different about Will today, she thought, watching his earnest expression. There was a certainty about him, as if he had crossed a bridge in his mind and was heading resolutely down the road, face forward.

It made Ruby Dee feel at once excited for him and uneasy, too, because she didn't want him to go down that road and leave her behind. Yet she wasn't certain she wanted to go with him, either. She was even less certain that he wanted her to go with him.

Minutes later they heard the sound of Hardy's cane on the kitchen floor. Will cast her a reluctant grin and rose. "Guess our day is startin'."

He handed her the coffee cup and rose.

"Will . . ." He turned. "You are havin' breakfast with us, aren't you?" She didn't know what to expect anymore.

He nodded and gave that slight, slow grin. "Yes, ma'am. I don't have any food at my place, either."

"Well, there's food here," she said.

And he said, "Even better, there's you." And then he walked away in that easy saunter he had.

For the following week it was almost as if Will had never moved away. He came for coffee each morning and took most of his meals with them. He spent the days working with Lonnie and Wildcat, when he wasn't in his office. But every evening after supper, he left to go to work on his own place, so Ruby Dee saw little of him.

Several times she brought up the subject of going to see Will's house, but Hardy said, "I've seen it."

Hardy had taken up what Ruby Dee considered passive resistance. Once more he spent long hours out in his shop, and when he was around either Will or Lonnie, he had very little to say to either of them. Of course, Hardy never had been much of a talker. His resistance now came in the form of attitude. He barely even acknowledged his sons with so much as a nod.

One afternoon Ruby Dee drove up to Woodward for shopping, and to simply have time alone to drive around and have a hot dog and cherry limeade at the Sonic. She left Sally with Hardy, since she didn't want to leave him alone. Deep inside she felt guilty because she fully intended to drive by Will's house on the way home. She didn't know why she should feel guilty about that, but she did.

She took Will a coffee maker as a housewarming present. Having a gift made going by easier to do.

It turned out that Georgia Reeves had picked the same evening to pay Will a visit.

Ruby Dee didn't see Georgia's red Suburban. She was carrying the carrying the big box containing the Braun coffee maker, and she had her eyes fastened on the side door, which she figured led into the kitchen. She kept thinking he would have heard her car and come out, but as she neared the screen door, she heard voices and figured he was busy talking to someone and hadn't heard her come up. Not until she was standing right smack in front of the screen door did Ruby Dee recognize Georgia's voice.

Georgia said, "Frank is off in Fort Worth. He's

been gone four days, and he's called once. That's about the way it is."

Through the screen, peering over the top of the box, Ruby Dee saw Will and Georgia facing each other in the glaring light of the kitchen.

Will said, "Well, I'm sorry, Georgia."

Right then Ruby Dee figured she had better sneak away or bust in, because she didn't want to get caught just standing there. She said, "Hello, in there."

Will's head jerked up, and then he was hurrying forward to open the door for her and welcoming her in. Ruby Dee thought he did seem glad to see her. She said hello to Georgia, and if looks could kill, Georgia's would have buried Ruby Dee.

"This is a housewarming present." Ruby Dee handed Will the box.

He thanked her profusely. Georgia said he would probably need to get bottled water, or the coffee maker would be clogged up in a few days. "The way Will drinks coffee, you know," she said, as if she were intimately aware of Will's habits.

Ruby Dee said, "He does love his coffee, doesn't he?" in the same manner, showing Georgia right off that she could match that game.

Georgia pressed her lips into a tight line. Will looked from Ruby Dee to Georgia as if he wished to be somewhere else.

"You sure are doin' a lot of work, aren't you?" Ruby Dee said and started to look around.

Will hurried to show her all he had done in the house and what he planned to do. Georgia went right along with them. It was a small house with almost everything gutted but the bathroom, so it didn't take long to see it. Back in the kitchen, Will offered cold drinks, and suddenly, with Georgia and Will both drinking Red Dog beer and Ruby Dee drinking Dr. Pepper, Ruby Dee felt distinctly out of place.

She set her half-empty glass on the counter, saying, "I guess I'd better get back. I don't want to worry Hardy . . . he's waitin' on me to play dominoes." She made that up as she went to the door.

Will followed her out to her car. Ruby Dee saw Georgia's Suburban then, parked over to the side, between two big cedars. As if she had tried to hide it.

"Thanks for the coffee maker," Will said, as Ruby Dee slipped behind the wheel.

"You're welcome."

His hands were on the door, his eyes hard on her. "I'm glad you came over. If you'll wait a minute, I'll drive on home with you."

But Ruby Dee said, "No need. I know the way." She sent the Galaxie speeding back down the drive. When she turned onto the road, she almost hit the ditch, because she had trouble seeing through her tears.

Georgia waited back in the kitchen. Will snatched his Red Dog off the counter and downed the contents in three long swallows.

Georgia said, "All those years I waited for you to move off from your daddy, and now you finally do it. Why, Will? For her?"

Will shook his head. "I don't have to leave the old man for Ruby Dee." Then he added ruefully, "I might be fightin' him for her, though."

Georgia's eyes went wide with questions, but Will wasn't about to explain it to her. He knew she would never understand. He barely did himself.

Setting her empty bottle on the counter, she said, "Well, we could ease each other," and her eyes were heavy with invitation.

But Will said he had somewhere to go, and opened the screen door.

When she left, Georgia said, "I wish you luck with Ruby Dee, Will. . . . One of us should find somethin' with someone." She shifted into gear, and then she looked at him again, her face shadowed now in dim light. "But I'll be around, should you change your mind."

Will said, "Georgia, don't do that to yourself. We were done a long time ago. It just took us awhile to find it out."

He thought he heard her swear at him before she drove off.

Will turned out the lights in his house, then drove over to the ranch. Light streamed out the back door. Ruby Dee and the old man were at the table, playing dominoes. Ruby Dee looked at him with surprise, and then with doubt. But he caught a hint of pleasure, too. Ruby Dee never had been able to hide anything.

Will poured himself a cup of Ruby Dee's coffee and sat and watched the game, offering occasional suggestions to both sides. Hardy told him to shut up, but Will just said, "I figure after all those weeks you spent in the wheelchair, it's my turn to annoy you."

Hardy's eyebrows rose, and then, imperceptibly, a grin played at the corners of his mouth.

During the following days, the old man met with Billy Stumblingbear and Mike Tilley, the two men Will had recommended for the manager's job. The old man was polite enough, but he told each one to send him a written résumé.

"I want to wait for answers to our ads and take a look at every possible prospect," he told Will. "I can handle things, if you're in a hurry to be off."

His tone made Will want to dump it all in his lap, but Will was too busy to spend much time being annoyed. After the haying and cattle work, he spent every available minute working on his house. He put Lonnie and Wildcat to work there, too, and both helped long after the workday was done. Will wanted the house to be ready, so he would have a place to bring Ruby Dee when he asked her to marry him.

✒ 23

THE FIRST SATURDAY of September brought the Harney rodeo, which included a barbecue supper before the rodeo and a dance afterward. Will had asked Ruby Dee to go with him to the rodeo and dance. He had asked her right in front of the old man, because he thought it best for the old man to see. He had not expected the old man to up and say he thought he would go, too.

"I asked Ruby Dee, Dad," Will said. "It's a date."

To which the old man said, "That's fine, but I don't see that I have to miss out."

There was no sense in Will saying he wouldn't take the old man. Ruby Dee wouldn't have had that.

At about three o'clock the house began to buzz with activity, showers going in both bathrooms, Elvis singing out from Ruby Dee's room, Lonnie hollering for polish for his belt buckle.

Will dressed in his good Larry Mahan turquoise shirt and starched Wranglers, although he had to forgo his dress snakeskin boots in favor of his bullhide Noconas, because he was competing in the steer wrestling. He'd been practicing all week. He hadn't competed in a rodeo for at least six years, but he hadn't lost his ability to steer-wrestle. After all, he did wrestle cattle all the time.

He had no illusions about winning—well, maybe he had a few fantasies—but he figured he wouldn't embarrass himself in front of Ruby Dee. She was the reason he entered. Lonnie was entered in the calf roping, to show off for Ruby Dee and Crystal, and Will didn't want to be left out. If that was childish, it sure felt good.

Lonnie turned out in a flashy roping shirt and sporting one of his winning silver belt buckles. He looked handsome as a cowboy calendar model, although Will didn't tell him so. Lonnie knew too well how good-looking he was.

Will loaded his dogging horse last into Lonnie's trailer. Pete sometimes liked to kick, so he went in last, away from Lonnie's horses. Lonnie's horses were worth twice as much as any Will had these days. Lonnie closed the doors securely, and Will told him that he and Ruby Dee and the old man would be coming behind him.

"You'll let Ruby Dee dance some with me, too, won't you?" Lonnie said, rapping his knuckles on Will's chest. "There's no need for you to hog her."

"Hog her? I'm already sharin' her with the old man."

"Hey, then one more won't hurt. You bring a walletful of money to bet on me, hear?" With a happy wave, Lonnie was off.

Will stood there and watched the dust spiral behind the trailer as it disappeared down the drive. In the past few days he'd sensed Lonnie backing off about Ruby Dee. He didn't think his brother had actually planned to give up his claim on her, but it did seem to be what was happening. Will no longer felt the heavy worry of hurting his brother because of her.

But he still had the old man to consider.

"You ready, Dad?" Will called as he entered the house.

The old man came thumping through the dining room. Will stared—from the fine gray Stetson on the old man's head to the starched white shirt, silver-and-turquoise clasp on his string tie, tweed sport coat, brown slacks and gleaming brown boots.

Here was the Hardy Starr whom Will remembered.

For a long minute Will just looked at his father, and then Hardy said, "What are you starin' at? Did you remember to get the lawn chairs? I cain't be sittin' up in those stands. Come on . . . let's get outside. I'd like to sneak a chew 'afore Ruby Dee comes."

Ruby Dee checked her image in the mirror, smiling as she saw the movement of her dress. It was new, bought for her date with Will—and it was a date, never mind that Hardy was along. She wore her best silver earrings, in the shape of hearts, and a silver cuff bracelet.

"I guess I have a date with both of them, Miss Edna," she whispered, feeling a twinge of guilt for her gladness.

"You may have to make a decision, Ruby Dee."

"Well, there's no need in thinkin' about it now and spoilin' today."

Leaning close to the mirror, Ruby Dee applied Summer Sunset to her lips. It perfectly matched her fingernails, the tiny dots of red flowers in the brown dress and her red Noconas, too. When she and Sally came walking across the yard toward Will and

Hardy, the way both men looked at her was enough to send her heart skipping over her ribs.

And then she was looking at them, and my goodness, they were so handsome . . . so commanding. Hardy looked splendid. His gaze touched hers, and she went to him and straightened his tie, just to touch him. He smiled at her, a smile only she ever saw. She was proud of him.

Then she turned to Will, brushed imaginary specks from his shirt front and told him not to put cigarettes in his pocket. His eyes were on her . . . his turquoise shirt brought them out, shimmering and brilliant in his tanned face. They stirred a warmth deep inside Ruby Dee. She almost touched his face, then drew her hand back, conscious of Hardy looking on.

Hardy held the door for her to get into the front seat. Will was there to help Hardy into the back seat, but he said, "Three can ride in front," and, with Will's help, he got up into the tall pickup and sat beside Ruby Dee.

Will said, "I don't think we can go without Sally," and let the dog hop into the back seat.

Hardy's arm rested along the back of the seat, and as they turned onto the blacktop, heading for Harney, his hand came to rest on Ruby Dee's shoulder. Will noticed it when he went to put his own arm behind her on the back of the seat.

There was a festive air about Harney. Vehicles streamed through the crossroads, all headed toward the rodeo grounds. It was early enough, however, that Hardy could choose the place he wanted beside the arena to set up the lawn chairs. Lonnie joined them, bestowing a charming grin on Ruby Dee, and even planting a kiss on her cheek. He was so handsome that he turned heads, both male and female, and he knew it, reveled in it.

Will and Lonnie went off and brought back the barbecue dinners and drinks. The crowd continued to grow, kids raced around chasing one another, and riders began working their horses in the arena.

People called greetings to the Starrs and stopped to talk. Will and Lonnie gave up their lawn chairs so many times that they ended up eating in a squatting position. Ruby Dee was amazed by how comfortable they seemed.

Hardy was something of a revelation. He took on the role of grand patriarch, seeming to grow taller each time someone greeted him. A lot of people were plainly surprised to see him.

"Hardy Starr! I thought you'd passed on."

"Well, I ain't."

"Hardy Starr . . . you haven't changed a bit."

"Who in hell was that, Will?"

"Moser Huggins."

"Good God, that's Moser Huggins? He got old, didn't he?" And then, "Who's that young fella just waved at us? He looks familiar."

"B.J. Coley, Jr."

Hardy's eyebrows shot up. "Oh." He looked thoughtful. "How's his daddy?"

Will said, "Last I heard Buck was down at Graceful Manor," and drank deeply from his soft-drink cup.

Hardy looked startled, then said, "That's too bad."

"Who's Buck?" Ruby Dee asked, curious about their manner.

Hardy kept his gaze averted from hers, like he

always did when he didn't intend to answer.

Will said, "Buck Coley—he was an old enemy of Dad's." He glanced at his father, and his lips twitched. "He caught Dad with his wife once."

Well. Ruby Dee looked at Hardy in some amazement.

"A long time ago, 'afore any of you were born," Hardy said. Lonnie was staring at his father. He plainly hadn't known of this episode, either.

Among the people saying hello and visiting, there were certainly a lot of young women who stopped to flirt with Lonnie. At one point Hardy said, "Is there a pretty gal in this county you don't know?"

"If there is, I don't know who she is," Lonnie answered with high satisfaction.

Crystal came along with another young woman named Shauna, who giggled when spoken to. Crystal greeted Ruby Dee with a friendly smile, Will with a soft hello, and looked at Hardy as if he might yell at her any minute. He ignored her. Ruby Dee thought Crystal looked awfully pretty in a shimmering soft blue silk blouse and slim-fitting jeans. She looked pretty beside Lonnie. She gazed at him like he was a god, and after a minute hooked her finger in Lonnie's back pocket and took bites of his sandwich.

Wildcat came by with Charlene, and Ruby Dee finally got to meet her. Charlene was small and plump, with gray, poodle-cut hair, and she wore a polyester pants suit that made her resemble a round cluster of lilac flowers. But there was a certain passion in her eyes, especially when she turned those eyes on Wildcat. Ruby Dee was almost startled by the depth of her passion. It just went to show that people were like books and shouldn't be judged by their covers.

Ruby Dee caught sight of Georgia and a man she assumed was Frank Reeves making their way up into the stands. Georgia gave Ruby Dee that dead-and-buried look. Then she looked at Will, and Will saw her, too. Ruby Dee thought he was going to wave, but Georgia turned her head.

And then along came Cora Jean Vinson, in a long, full denim dress with a big concho belt and flashing Indian jewelry. With a hearty hello to them all, she bent down and kissed Hardy on the cheek. He turned red, but he liked it, Ruby Dee could tell, no matter that he spoke gruffly. He was enjoying all the attention.

Ruby Dee was very pleased that Cora Jean remembered her. Cora Jean was one of those people you couldn't help but like. Once again, though, her close scrutiny made Ruby Dee wonder if there was a smudge on her face.

With Cora Jean was a husky young man, her grandson, who was going to be a contestant in the calf roping. Will and Lonnie knew him, and immediately started talking about roping. In the space of a few minutes, a number of men joined them: young men, with low-crowned, wide-brimmed hats and wearing chaps and spurs or carrying ropes over their shoulders, and older men, with the tall-crown, curved-brimmed hats and work-worn faces.

Talking low, the men moved off toward the cattle pens and chutes. Even Hardy rose to go. Will leaned down to tell Ruby Dee he'd be back. Lonnie kissed Crystal and sent her to the stands, while he followed his brother.

"Time for men stuff," Cora Jean said, sitting heavily in the chair Hardy had vacated. "They have to go over there and check out the buckin' bulls and broncs and ropin' stock. It's sort of like how they go around and kick the tires of a car they might buy. Doesn't have a bit of meaning, but they need to do it." She was laughing and fanning herself.

"Whew . . . I'll sit here a bit with you, if you don't mind. I just have to have a rest from those grandkids of mine. After awhile they wear me out."

"I'd enjoy your company," Ruby Dee said. It occurred to her then that she was hungry to talk to another woman. She hadn't chatted with a woman since she had come to the Starrs, over two months ago.

Sally nosed Cora Jean's knee for a pat, and the older woman stroked her head. "Goodness, when did Hardy get a dog . . . or is this one of the boys'? I've never known Hardy to have a dog."

"She's mine. Her name is Sally."

"You have certainly trained her well. Look at her—she got her little pettin' from me and then lay down. Most dogs just have to pester and jump up and slobber."

"I didn't train her. I found her at a 7-Eleven, and she's always been like that. She knows just what anyone tells her."

"Hum . . . I believe that. Animals understand a lot more than people think they do. I have cats myself, but I've always liked dogs." Her gaze sharpened. "You and Hardy appear to be gettin' on well."

"We are now. I had an awful time with him at first. He made up his mind he wanted to die, and just laid in that bed, waitin'. But I kept after him, and now he even likes me, even if he wouldn't say it."

"No, he wouldn't say it," Cora Jean agreed, smiling ruefully. "Well, he's lookin' real good"—a mischievous grin twitched her lips—"so it must be true what they say."

"And what's that?" Ruby Dee asked.

"That you've pepped him up."

"Is that how 'they' are puttin' it?"

"When they're bein' polite." Cora Jean laughed. She had a wonderful laugh. Her gaze turned curious. "I heard that he had hurt his bad leg and was in a wheelchair. Seems like he's come along out of that."

Ruby Dee nodded. "He hurt his ankle, but it never was anything serious."

"Oh, Hardy's a tough one. He's had to be, or else he'd have been crippled long before now. He hurt that bad leg when he wasn't but fifteen—when he was ridin' with my sister Jooney one time, and his horse fell on it. Jooney had to set it right there beside the river, and Hardy was so proud that he bit off the tip of his tongue rather than cry out." She chuckled softly.

Ruby Dee's curiosity jumped sky-high. "He's spoken of Jooney," she said quickly. "You were her sister?"

Cora Jean nodded thoughtfully. "Jooney was the eldest. They used to say she was the prettiest girl in the county."

"Hardy said Jooney was the one who did the doctoring around here when he was young."

"She did." Cora Jean turned her gaze toward the distant setting sun. "Jooney took care of everybody—she delivered babies, doctored sick and laid out the dead. I guess she delivered our mama's last three babies, and I was one of them. She was only about thirteen when she did that. Real doctors were up in Woodward or down in Cheyenne, but either place was far and cost dearly, considering how poor we were." Her eyes cut back to Ruby Dee. "She and Hardy were supposed to be married, but Jooney died."

"I thought maybe she was special to him. How did she die?"

Cora Jean breathed deeply. "Law, it was a bad day when that happened. It was nearly sixty-five years ago, but I recall it—a person doesn't forget watchin' someone catch on fire."

"Jooney caught on fire? How?"

There was commotion all around them, people riding by on horses, two little boys wrestling only a yard away, but all that faded as Ruby Dee listened to Cora Jean.

"Daddy was gone, like he always was. Daddy wasn't worth much, and Mama was dead a year. Hardy was out beside the barn, splittin' wood. Him and Jooney had been sweethearts since they were small, and he was always lendin' a hand. Jooney, she took care of all five of us. I was the fourth one, five years old then, and Lyle was still crawlin'.

"That day Jooney was treatin' our heads for coo-ties—sounds terrible, but kids get lice no matter how clean they are, and Jooney kept us clean. But in those days we didn't have fancy preparations to get rid of the lice, like today. It could be a battle once you got them. We used kerosene to douse our heads with, and that's what Jooney was doin', when the next thing, her and Tommy, our middle brother, went up in flames. Too close to the lantern or somethin', I never did know, really.

"Well, Jooney went to beatin' Tommy's hair out,

but her hands and arms were flaming. Everything happened so fast, it really was a blur. Jooney threw herself outside to keep the house from goin' up. We were all screamin', but I'll never forget the sound of Jooney's scream."

"Oh, my God," Ruby Dee whispered, feeling as if she couldn't breathe.

The story kept on flowing out of Cora Jean. "There is no worse sight than a burned-up person. Hardy came runnin' and threw himself on Jooney, but it was too late. She was burned black in so many places. You know, though, she was still alive, and she said to him, 'Help Peter take care of the rest.' "

Cora Jean stopped speaking, and despite the sounds of talking and yelling and laughter all around her, a dead silence rang in Ruby Dee's ears.

Cora Jean pulled a tissue from her dress pocket and blew her nose. "I haven't talked about it in a long time."

Ruby Dee wiped the tears from her cheeks with one of Miss Edna's hankies and struggled to breathe. She just couldn't seem to get her breath.

"Oh, goodness, honey. I'm sorry to upset you . . . are you all right?" Cora Jean asked, putting a hand on Ruby Dee's knee.

"Yes . . ." Ruby Dee breathed deeply. "I could just see it so clearly." Sally pressed up against her leg.

"Are you sure you're okay?"

Ruby Dee nodded. "I just cry a lot. And, well, I was burned once, a long time ago. I caught my nightgown on fire on the flame of an open gas heater. I only have a few scars, really hardly anything, considerin'. But I can imagine how it was for Jooney." Her own memory threatened to engulf her, and Ruby Dee pushed it away, stroking Sally's sleek head. More clearly, she asked, "Did Hardy help Peter take care of the rest of you?"

"Yes, he did." Cora Jean bobbed her head. "Oh, none of us had much out here—it was the dry years, you know. But Hardy was always lookin' in and makin' certain we had food and firewood. When Peter wanted to go to Amarillo for a job, Hardy lent him the money."

Hesitantly, Ruby Dee asked, "From a few things Lonnie's said, I take it Lila left Hardy and her sons for some other man." She was prying, but she figured she should take advantage to learn all she could.

"Oh, Lila! Hardy was silly to marry her in the first place. . . . He was twice her age." She snorted. "Hardy Starr never could feel for Lila what he'd felt for Jooney, and put that together with Lila being as shallow as the day is long, and it wasn't ever gonna work. I never could for the life of me figure out why he took her leavin' so hard. Lila wasn't much. She was pretty but so puny."

"He must have loved her, if he took it hard."

She shrugged. "Maybe so, but I imagine it was more his pride that took the beating. Hardy is a man made of pride."

"Yes, he is," Ruby Dee agreed.

Music was coming out of the loudspeakers now, and the arena had filled with riders, all going around the outer edge in a circle, some slow, some fast. Cora Jean pointed to one of her grandsons, a tiny boy in a big red cowboy hat, riding a fat pinto pony. He bounced atop that pony like a little rubber ball.

Cora Jean said Hardy had given her her first horse, a little bay pony, when she was about nine.

"Oh, he got wild after Jooney died, chasin' women and drinkin', but he wasn't a bad man. He just had a hair-trigger temper. That and his drinkin' landed him in jail on more than one occasion. One time, and he was near thirty by then, he had to take off, when Buck Coley come after him with a shotgun for foolin' with his wife. He wasn't afraid of Buck, but he did have sense enough to know he might've ended up killin' him. Hardy's temper was that bad."

"He still drinks some," Ruby Dee said, "and he sure has a temper. But he doesn't seem to like women at all." She had trouble imagining him running wild with women.

"Well, that's Lila's doin'." Cora Jean flattened her lips. "Lila's leavin' made him go to hatin' just about everything and everyone, especially women. I think watchin' Hardy and Lila caused Will not to trust people much at all, and Lonnie, he missed having a mama so much that he just hankers after all women. You know, he really takes after his daddy as he was at that age."

"Lonnie would be amazed at that statement, and I don't imagine he would appreciate it, either. He doesn't like to have anything at all to do with Hardy." As soon as the words were out of her mouth, Ruby Dee wished she hadn't said it. She felt she had betrayed a private family matter.

"Hardy simply quit being a dad to Lonnie when Lila left. He let Will do it."

Ruby Dee thought she would change the direction of the conversation. "You said you taught Will in school. Did you have him when he was small?" She wondered what Will had been like as a boy.

Cora Jean eyed her knowingly, and Ruby Dee felt a blush sweep her cheeks. "Yes," Cora Jean said, "I was Will's first-grade teacher and later his fifth-grade teacher, and then I had him again in high school, when I went to teaching history and government. Will wasn't a rebel. He was one of the quiet ones, very respectful. Hardy made certain of that. But every once in awhile Will would up and do something outrageous—like the time he rode his horse through the school lunch room. In and out, and left us all wonderin' if we had really seen it. I used to think that Will kept himself hemmed in, until he just had to break loose."

Ruby Dee agreed with that, but she kept it to herself. Hugged it to herself.

The rodeo announcer's voice interrupted the music from the loudspeaker and caused both Ruby Dee and Cora Jean to jump. "Lord'a Mercy, I wish they wouldn't turn that thing so high," Cora Jean said. Ruby Dee noticed then that sunlight was fading and the pole lamps surrounding the arena had come on.

As the riders cleared the arena to make way for the grand entry, Cora Jean rose, saying she ought to get back to her brood. "And your menfolk are headin' back this way."

Standing beside her, Ruby Dee saw Hardy and Will and Lonnie walking toward them. In that instant, seeing the three men together, she was struck by how alike they were. She had seen it before, of course, but now the similarity stood out so boldly. Perhaps that was the root of their animosity, as well as the attraction each held for her, for they were like younger and older mirrors of the same man.

Cora Jean said, "I was partial to Hardy for a long time. He never saw me, though."

Her gaze was on Hardy, and her voice echoed with long-ago sadness. Then she was looking at

Ruby Dee, a curious expression on her face. "Ruby Dee, I want to tell you somethin'." She paused, her eyes searching Ruby Dee's face. "I don't have a picture of Jooney—the only one we had got lost back in the sixties, when a tornado blew Peter's mobile home up to Kansas. But in my memory, you are a spittin' image of her."

Looking into the older woman's intense eyes, Ruby Dee felt a shiver go down her spine. "Really?"

"Oh, yes. And I imagine why Hardy's so taken with you, after all this time, is that he's seen the same thing I have."

Cora Jean patted Ruby Dee's arm and walked away.

₰ 24

THE HARNEY RODEO was a small, hometown event. Only a couple of the contestants, like Lonnie, had professional experience. Most were everyday or weekend cowboys riding for a dab of hometown glory, or young teens getting their first taste of the sport and the two minutes of glory.

The second bareback bronc rider, a young man who was no bigger than a minute, got thrown, and landed right in front of Ruby Dee's eyes with so hard a plop it could be clearly heard. Will's hand tugging at her kept Ruby Dee from dashing out to see to the boy, even as the medics came running. As the ambulance bore him away, the announcer reported that the young man had a broken shoulder, which was Ruby Dee's guess from where she stood.

During the rodeo-queen coronation, the queen's horse got spooked by waving flowers and took off running and bounced the girl in her silvery shirt into the dirt. The frantic horse almost trampled a man who tried to catch it. Lonnie rode out on his paint horse and caught the runaway animal, then waved to the cheering crowd. He was a real showman.

Ruby Dee got so excited for Will in the steer wrestling that she ran right up to the fence, urging him on with her own energy. She was thrilled by the look on his face when he got up from twisting the big-horned steer to the ground. He was beaming, and people were cheering. He came in second out of twelve contestants. He acted modest, dusting himself off as he sauntered back over to his horse, but Ruby Dee could see the pride in that saunter. There was such a presence about Will Starr.

Lonnie won his event—calf roping—by catching and tying a calf in ten seconds, which Hardy said was not Lonnie's best time by far. He took his time letting the calf loose and catching his horse, so he was still out there when his time was called, and he lifted his hands in victory.

Ruby Dee's heart beat so proudly for both men, and pride was evident on Hardy's face, too. Hardy was a different person that night—the man he truly was, Ruby Dee thought.

The ladies' barrel racing had Ruby Dee yelling, and by the time of the final event, bull riding, she was worn out from all the excitement. Considered the most dangerous event, bull riding was always saved for last. The huge bulls, mostly Brahmans, were impressive even in the chutes. One tried to jump clear over his chute while a rider was getting settled on top of him.

Lonnie was helping the rider. He'd stayed over at the chutes after his event, but Will had come right back. With the opening of each bull's chute, Ruby Dee would glimpse the man waving like a bundle of rags tied atop the giant animal, then she'd hold tight to Will's hand, close her eyes and hide her face against his starched sleeve. Therefore she missed seeing one rider knocked into the fence by his bull and seeing another bull chase men back up into the chutes, Lonnie being one of them. She had to ask what had happened each time, and Hardy and Will teased that they wouldn't tell her.

Will did tell her, but it wasn't the same as seeing the eye-popping happenings, and she wished she could keep her eyes open.

And then it was over, the blaring loudspeaker silent and people's voices coming in moderate tones, as they streamed away from the arena. It seemed a sense of excitement lingered, a sense of euphoria from having seen up close the line between life and death.

Ruby Dee held tight to Will's hand. His eyes met hers, and he smiled.

All evening, even while he had been chatting with friends or watching the rodeo, his eyes had returned repeatedly to Ruby Dee, looking at her intently, sometimes with a question, sometimes with desire.

He said to Hardy now, "I'll be glad to take you home, Dad. You must be tired."

"Well, I'm not. I've been sittin' for the better part of four hours. I'd like to go on over and hear the music."

Will frowned, but Ruby Dee tugged on his hand, and he smiled at her. As they walked toward the dance, his hand held hers tightly, and he rubbed his thumb over her fingers.

The dance was held in a big metal building. The country band was at one end and at the other were refreshments and tables and chairs, which were given over to older people and a few children. Hardy sat down at a table at the edge of the dance area, and Sally skittered beneath it and lay down, her ears erect.

Hardy told Will to go get him a beer before he took Ruby Dee off to dance. No sooner had Will left than Hardy stood, swept off his hat and said, "Give me this first dance, gal." His eyes sparkled with mischief, and she couldn't help but laugh.

Leaving his cane propped against the table, he swept her into his arms and moved out onto the dance floor to a slow ballad.

Ruby Dee had never been in Hardy's arms before, but it did not seem strange at all. He held her lightly, very properly. He acted courtly. People smiled at them, and Ruby Dee felt like a princess.

Why, he could dance! He was stiff on his bad leg, but he had a sense of grace as he waltzed her around. His face was that of an old man, but for the minutes that he moved with her to the music, his eyes were young again. For an instant, gazing into his eyes, she thought about what Cora Jean had told her—that she reminded him of Jooney.

Was he looking at her and seeing Jooney? There was something about the supposition that struck a chord inside of her. She was afraid of it, but she didn't want to spoil the moment by thinking about it. At that moment nothing mattered but the music and the pleasure vibrating between herself and Hardy.

The song ended. They gazed at each other, and then Hardy, his rough hand holding hers, led her back to the table. Will was standing there, waiting. Ruby Dee couldn't read his expression, but she sensed a fire leap between him and Hardy.

Then Will swept her away into his arms. The music was a lively two-step. Will held her loosely with his arms but tightly with his brilliant eyes. His look was like a passionate, intimate touch, bringing heat to the intimate places inside Ruby Dee. The sensual scent of him—of musky cologne and warm skin and night air—assailed her senses.

The music played, fast and lively, and Will guided her far from Hardy. Briefly Ruby Dee saw familiar faces: Wildcat dancing with Charlene, one of the old domino players with a young woman, Georgia with the tall, gray-haired man, Lonnie with Crystal, Cora Jean with her grandson. . . .

The music ended and then started again, and suddenly Lonnie was there, taking Ruby Dee's hand and placing Crystal's into Will's. Will shot his brother a look and then smiled at Crystal, as Lonnie swung Ruby Dee away.

Lonnie startled Ruby Dee by pulling her close against him and putting his cheek against hers.

"Let me have this little bit, Ruby Dee," he whispered into her ear, and she didn't push him away. She looked at his cheek and saw it was almost boyishly smooth. He smelled of manly cologne and male sweat and sweet earth. And of a woman's perfume.

Around they went to the music. There was Will with Crystal . . . a flaming-haired woman with the old domino player . . . and Hardy with Cora Jean.

Hardy was waiting to take her from Lonnie. He danced slowly, no matter how fast the beat of the music. And then Will claimed her again. And whether she was dancing with Hardy or Lonnie, or even, once, with Wildcat, and another time with a young man she didn't even know, she was aware of Will's eyes upon her. Watching her, drawing her eyes and her body and her desire toward him.

* * *

Lonnie led Crystal outside and over into the dark shadows. He swore as he stumbled on something. He stopped and pulled Crystal into his arms, finding her by feel. Her lips were warm and pliable, moist and willing. Every part of him that was male rose up to demand more.

"Georgia and Frank are here," he whispered. "Let's go over to your place."

But Crystal shook her head. "Georgia's angry about Will—she won't stay long." She kissed him. "Oh, Lonnie, let's go to the cemetery. Nobody'll be around there."

He kept his arm around her as they went over to his pickup, which he suddenly remembered was hooked to the horse trailer. They had left one horse tied to it and the other two inside. Lonnie didn't want to unhook the pickup, so he and Crystal slipped into the seat. It was dark, private.

As he kissed her, he pulled her blouse clear of her jeans and ran his hands up beneath it, over her skin that was at once warm and cool and smelled like flowers. Suddenly his need was pounding in him, a need that had started with so many dances with Crystal . . . and Ruby Dee.

As his hands released Crystal's bra and found her silky breasts, he lost track of exactly which woman he was making love to. For a moment, Crystal's breasts became Ruby Dee's . . . the hands pulling at his head Ruby Dee's hands . . . the warm skin beneath his lips, Ruby Dee's skin.

But it was Crystal's voice saying, "Lonnie . . . we shouldn't."

"It's okay. No one can see." He eased her down in the seat.

"No . . . it's—"

But he stopped her words with his mouth and slipped his hand into her jeans, and she spread her legs for him.

Afterward, Crystal started to cry in his arms. This surprised him, because Crystal had never cried before.

"Hey, darlin', what is it?"

That just made her cry harder. The next instant she shoved herself away from him and went to furiously putting on her clothes. Lonnie didn't have to do much more than get his pants zipped up and his shirt buttoned. Then they sat there, Crystal giving a sniff now and again.

Lonnie felt bad. He knew he had offended her in some way, but he didn't know how. If she had not wanted him to make love to her, he had sure missed the signal.

All of a sudden she said, "You love her, don't you?"

"Who?" he asked, startled and confused, though deep inside he had an idea of who she meant. He thought wildly of what he should say.

"Ruby Dee."

After long seconds, he said quietly, "I like Ruby Dee a lot. I care for her, and I can't deny it. But I care for you, too, Crystal. And it's you I'm with."

More long seconds passed, and then Crystal came flying at him. "Oh, Lonnie, I love you!" She buried her face in his chest.

Slowly he brought his arms around her. He held her and kissed her hair. It was so soft and silky. She was a tender thing, the most tender woman he had ever known.

And then she pulled back and looked up at him, her face so shadowed that he couldn't see her expression. She said, "Lonnie, I'm pregnant."

If there was anything he less expected her to say right then, that was it. Good Lord, he had just . . .

He went cold, because he wasn't certain he should have been doing with a pregnant woman what he had just been doing.

He swallowed. "Are you sure? I've used a condom—" He broke off, remembering.

She shook her head. "We didn't. Not that first time."

"But only that one time." A desperation was clutching him.

"It only takes that, Lon," she said, tears in her voice, and panic, too. "I've done two of those tests, and they both were positive. Mama won't let me come home. She says she has enough with the little ones still there. And Georgia . . . she isn't gonna want me and a baby, not one that isn't hers."

Lonnie sat there, feeling roped, tied and branded. He knew he was supposed to say something about marrying her, but he just couldn't say it.

He didn't think he *could* marry her.

"Do you think I should get an abortion?" she asked in a ragged whisper.

The idea made him sick. "Do you want to?"

"No."

"I don't want you to, either." He breathed deeply, and then, hardly realizing what he was doing, he reached for her. "I'll help you, Crystal, just don't get rid of it."

"It's not an it. It's a he or she."

Lonnie recognized his feeling then. He felt responsible for her. Protective of her, and of what was inside her. Never before had he felt responsible for anyone, and it confused the hell out of him.

But he still couldn't say he would marry her.

On the way home, Will followed the taillights of Lonnie's horse trailer. It was after midnight. The old man had made it through the entire dance. He'd danced his share, too.

The glow of the dash lights shone on Ruby Dee, sitting beside Will. But not alone, because there was the old man, again, on the other side of her, his arm stretched out and his hand resting on her shoulder.

When they reached the ranch, Lonnie pulled up to the horse barn. "I'll get 'em put away," he hollered to Will, who drove on to the back walk of the house.

"I'm okay," Hardy said, when Will came around to help him out of the pickup. And then the old man turned, extending a hand to Ruby Dee.

After Will had let the dog out, he followed them into the house. In the kitchen, the old man turned and looked at Will for a moment, almost challengingly.

Will said, "Ruby Dee, are you too tired to make a cup of your great coffee?" and he plopped himself down in a chair and took off his hat.

"Oh . . . that sounds good—it'll take the chill off."

The old man stood there for a few more seconds, and then he walked through the dining room. Will heard the bathroom door close.

Slowly he rose, crossed the kitchen to Ruby Dee and stopped right behind her. With her hair just below his face, he inhaled the sweet, womanly scent of her. She continued to scoop coffee. When she was finished, she stood very still, and he stayed right where he was . . . close enough to feel her body move as she breathed. Then she turned and looked up at him.

She wet her lips. "I had so much fun tonight, Will. Thank you for taking me."

He stared at her lips. "Thank you for goin' with me."

Then they were gazing into each other's eyes, and her eyes were saying she wanted him, and he was saying the same thing back to her with his.

"Thank you for bein' so generous with Hardy," she said, in a breathless whisper. Her eyes were like liquid heat.

"He's my father."

Her lips parted, and her palm came up to rest on his chest, in invitation.

Will gazed at her, waiting and listening for a sound from the rooms beyond. He detected movement then, in the hallway. He cupped Ruby Dee's face in both hands and kissed her. Her lips parted for him, drew him to her. Urgent and pleading. Will broke away, looked down and saw the desire glazing her liquid black eyes. Her hands moved to his waist, clutching him. He kissed her again, hot and hard and branding her as his own.

He didn't let her mouth go until he had her gasping for breath. Until he had shown the old man what he intended, because when they broke away, there was the old man, standing in the kitchen doorway.

With a firm grip on Ruby Dee, Will looked at his father, and his father looked back, until he lowered his gaze and walked away, heavily, to his room.

Ruby Dee dropped her forehead against Will's chest, and he felt her tremble. Questions swirled around them. She clutched his waist with her fists.

He stroked her hair and gazed into the darkness where the old man had stood.

He had shown the old man: there was something he could give Ruby Dee that his dad never would be able to. And the old man had seen what Ruby Dee felt for Will.

At last Will swallowed and managed to speak, quietly, reluctantly. "It's late."

"Yes," she whispered. She raised shimmering eyes to him.

He kissed her quickly before leaving her there, staring after him.

As he went busting out the back door, he thought that this was not the time, was not the place. But he was getting damned tired of waiting for the right time and place.

Ruby Dee watched Will's pickup pass the kitchen window. Then she turned off the coffee maker and hurried upstairs, furtively passing Hardy's room. Thank heaven his door was closed.

She couldn't face him, couldn't stand to see his hurt. Couldn't bear for him to see her caught in the swells of the river of passion . . . with his son.

✧ 25

RUBY DEE DRIFTED up out of an erotic dream. The sensations lingered, taunting her and making her face burn. Making her damp and her body ache.

The dream had been of Will, that he had made love to her . . . in ways she had certainly never imagined in her waking hours.

Will would give her a home and her precious babies. Lonnie would cope with that—he had Crystal. But there was Hardy to consider. Hardy, whom she couldn't bear to hurt . . . even for her home and precious babies.

Suddenly she realized that it was nearly eight o'clock. Goodness! She couldn't recall the last time she had stayed in bed so late. And she smelled coffee. . . .

Thinking eagerly of Will, she jumped up and grabbed her robe. But then she thought of Hardy, and slowed. Tentatively, on tiptoe, with Sally quietly walking behind her, she went downstairs.

But it was Lonnie in the kitchen, leaning back

against the counter, his shirttail hanging out, his feet bare, coffee cup in hand.

Ruby Dee stopped in surprise when she saw him.

"I made coffee," he said. "I'm not very good at it, though." He looked apologetic. And tired. Lonnie never got up this early on a Sunday morning.

"It's black and hot. That's good enough this mornin'," Ruby Dee told him and went to get a cup. She tightened the sash of her robe, her gaze going out the window, her heart farther still . . . all the way to Will.

His kiss still lingered on her lips and in her soul. He had kissed her like that on purpose, she thought suddenly. So why wasn't he here?

Lonnie was getting the milk from the refrigerator for his coffee as Ruby Dee turned away from the window. They almost collided. "I'm sorry," they said in unison.

And then they were looking at each other. Ruby Dee trembled deep inside. The reaction of her feverish body startled her, and so did the need that she saw reflected in Lonnie's eyes. Eyes so much like Will's.

But he wasn't Will.

They dropped their gazes at the same time and moved to sit across from each other at the table.

Ruby Dee talked about making breakfast, but she continued to sit there. Lonnie said he needed to feed the horses, but he didn't move.

Ruby Dee was struck by the notion that Lonnie was different that morning. He never rose so early on a Sunday morning. And he looked as if something was troubling him. She thought perhaps he wanted to talk about it, but then they heard Hardy getting up, so Lonnie rose to feed the horses.

"I'll make pancakes," Ruby Dee called to him as he left. Pancakes were his favorite. He turned and gave her a wan smile.

Lonnie stayed out a long time, feeding the horses and walking around. He thought a lot about loading up his horses and heading over to Oklahoma City. The State Fair was going on, lots of buddies over there at the rodeo and horse shows. The idea grew in his mind as exactly the thing to do.

On his way, he could stop off and give Crystal everything in his savings account. That would get her her own place for awhile. He'd promise to send more when he could. He started cleaning out his trailer for the trip, but then Ruby Dee called him for breakfast.

After breakfast, he thought about driving over to talk to Will, but he figured Will would yell at him and tell him he had better marry Crystal.

He wanted to talk to Ruby Dee, but he knew that once he did, she would be lost to him forever.

Lonnie wished things didn't have to change from how they had been for the past months, ever since the first day Ruby Dee had come.

But their lives were changing. Will had moved out—and he wanted to take Ruby Dee with him . . . and Crystal was pregnant. Summer was turning into fall, and Lonnie himself was going on thirty-one years old. He wasn't a boy anymore, and he had to face that. It scared him, because he didn't know how to be any other way.

That afternoon, when the old man was out in his shop and Ruby Dee was sitting on the front porch in her blue swing, reading, Lonnie went to her. She was sure pretty, in a blue dress almost the same color as the swing. He told her so, and she looked pleased. He loved to see her like that, with her Mona Lisa smile and the dreamy look in her eyes.

He leaned against the porch post and gazed out across the sweeping pasture that stretched a quarter of a mile to the road. Behind him, although he couldn't see her, he knew Ruby Dee had closed her book and laid it in her lap.

He turned around, folded his arms and tucked his hands up beneath his arms. Ruby Dee's eyes were on him.

He said, "Crystal's pregnant."

She inhaled sharply, then said, "All babies are blessings, Lonnie." Her look questioned him.

He sighed. "I don't know what to do." He shook his head.

"Well, what do you *want* to do?"

"If I knew that, I'd be ahead." He cast her a sheepish grin.

"And you want me to tell you what to do," she said, her eyes knowing.

He shrugged. Ruby Dee knew about living; of that Lonnie was certain.

She gave a little shake of her head. "Well, I can't tell you what to do. You're the only one who can decide that. But I guess, since you asked, that I'll give you my opinion. Which is to marry Crystal and be a daddy to the baby."

He hadn't expected her to say exactly that, and it annoyed him. "You're saying I should own up to the responsibility and all that stuff, right?"

"You asked me, Lonnie," she pointed out, which didn't ease his irritation. Then she added, "But what I'm really sayin' is, don't throw away the wonderful opportunity being handed to you to be a husband and a father."

"A father? I don't know anything about bein' a father, and I sure don't think I can be a husband." He paced, rubbing the back of his neck. "I don't know if I can give Crystal what she's expectin' from me. I don't even know if I love her."

He looked at Ruby Dee, and he almost asked, "How can I love her, when I feel what I do for you?" But he stopped short of that. Some things had to remain unsaid, although that didn't mean they weren't understood. He could tell by the way Ruby Dee was looking at him that she knew how he felt about her. And he thought she felt a lot for him, too.

"Lonnie, when you go to join your life with someone else's, it matters a lot less how you feel about them than deciding to be devoted to them."

He looked at her closely. Her eyes were dark and earnest.

"You don't have to feel an undying love for Crystal," she said intently. "Not right now. All you have to do is devote yourself to being a husband to her. That is the action of love. You started somethin' with her. You made a baby with her. If you devote yourself to her and the baby, the feelings of love will follow."

"And what if they don't? What if I just plain screw up?"

"Oh, Lonnie, do you think like that before enterin' a rodeo? Your success is not always guaranteed there, but you try anyway, and even if you lose, you learn from each time. You gain something. You have everything to gain here, too." She leaned forward. "Do you want to throw away what you can have with Crystal and your own child, simply because you're afraid of failing? Lonnie, no matter how you feel about Crystal, that child is a part of you. Your child." She smiled slowly and softly. "And how many men have a woman who looks at him the way Crystal looks at you? She has enough love for the both of you, Lonnie, if you just give her a chance." Then she said, "I know you—you will make a wonderful husband and father, because you have it in you."

He wanted to believe her. And he thought that he might be able to let Crystal go . . . but not the baby. His own child.

His gaze drifted to the long driveway, and he remembered his mother driving away that day, leaving behind a five-year-old boy of her own flesh. And how just about ever since, his father had ignored him. The old man had left him the same as his mother had.

Lonnie did not want his kid to ever feel as he had—thrown away.

"Well, I guess I'd better go see her," he said, and something jumped inside of him. He'd hardly ever been able to turn away from a challenge.

Ruby Dee got up and put her arms around him. He held her to him for a long minute.

Feeling tears threaten, Ruby Dee broke the embrace. "Call and tell her you're comin', so she has time to fix herself up for you."

He opened the door, then paused. "Ruby Dee, don't ever go away." And he went into the house.

Ruby Dee sat back down in the swing and pushed it gently into motion. She put her hand to her belly. A child . . . Crystal was carrying Lonnie's baby.

The longing came sudden and hard, a longing for Will to fill her with himself . . . and with a child.

But right on the heels of that thought came: HELL TO PAY.

Hardy wasn't one to give over. Oh, it would hurt him! He would accept her moving off to her own place much more easily than he would accept her going with Will.

She was really caught, she thought. She could have everything on her dream paper, if she was willing to hurt Hardy.

But she didn't think she could stand to do that. She loved him, too.

Lonnie and Crystal went off that very afternoon to Oklahoma City, where they planned to be married the following day and enjoy a short three-day honeymoon at the Waterford, which was Will's wedding gift.

Will came while Lonnie was packing and Crystal was bathing upstairs. She hadn't been able to bathe at Georgia's, because Georgia was throwing a hissy fit about her being pregnant and marrying Lonnie. "She shoved Crystal down the hall, and she threatened to geld me with a kitchen knife," Lonnie told them, clearly confounded.

Crystal defended her sister. "Georgia wanted me to get a college degree before marriage. She's been upset that I didn't go back this year. And last week Mama had to go and say that Georgia was headed for an early change and needed hormones. Georgia's been real upset since then."

Ruby Dee made a present to Crystal of a red nightgown, still in tissue in a Dillard's box. She had bought it the second time she and Beauford were going to be married. "I've never worn it. I was saving it for a special time."

Crystal was delighted. "It's real silk, isn't it? I've never had a real silk nightgown."

When they were alone in Ruby Dee's room, she said, "I know Lonnie loves you, Ruby Dee. And it's easy to see why."

Ruby Dee sat on the bed beside her and took her hands. "Lonnie and I are close friends, but don't be worried about that. You are who he is marrying, who is giving him a child. And you are who he needs, Crystal. No one can give him what you can."

Crystal surprised Ruby Dee by saying, "I think so, too. I just wanted you to know that I know, and I understand."

Ruby Dee thought that most people probably vastly underestimated Crystal.

And then the two lovers were getting ready to leave. Beside Lonnie's truck, Will shook his brother's hand, and then he hauled off and took Lonnie in a back-slapping hug, his face reddening at the rare show of emotion. Lonnie was clearly surprised, but also pleased.

Tears running down her face, Ruby Dee hugged Crystal and then Lonnie, saying, "God bless . . . and have a wonderful time. We'll have a party for you when you come home, won't we, Hardy?"

Hardy so far had not said a word. Ruby Dee prodded him with a look.

Hardy frowned back at her, but then he drew himself up and stuck out his hand to Lonnie, saying, "Good luck, boy. You're gonna need it. You'll have a job here, and you're gonna need that, too." He nodded at Crystal.

Just then Georgia's red Suburban came flying up the drive. For one horrifying instant Ruby Dee thought it was going to ram Lonnie's truck, and they all scattered. The Suburban veered into the yard, and even before it stopped, Will was shoving Lonnie and

Crystal ahead of him toward Lonnie's pickup. "Get in!"

Georgia jumped out of the Suburban, and she had a shotgun! "Damn you! You Starrs think you can just use a woman however you want." She had been drinking, was wobbling but bringing that shotgun up nevertheless. "I'm not gonna let you do that to my sister."

The shotgun went off, and Georgia seemed momentarily as shocked as the rest of them. The shot went far to their left, and Ruby Dee had the odd thought that it might have hit one of the cows out in the pasture.

Then Georgia was aiming at Will, who stood beside the driver's door, with Lonnie right in line with him inside. "I'm not lettin' him take Crystal and ruin her life."

Well. Ruby Dee was tempted to go over there and slap Georgia's face, but she was rooted to the spot.

The next instant Hardy stepped forward . . . right in front of Will.

"That's enough, Georgia."

"Get outta my way, Hardy, 'cause I'd just as soon shoot you, too. You're the whole cause of it, anyway." Her finger was on the trigger.

Hardy started forward, thumping his cane on the gravel.

Oh, Lord, Ruby Dee thought, if the shotgun went off, it would cut him in two. *Lord, protect him.*

And then Hardy's arm snaked out, his hand clamped on the barrel, and he ripped the gun out of Georgia's hands. "Any shootin' done on my place, I do it," he said. With a powerful swing, he threw the shotgun over the pasture fence.

Georgia crumpled against the Suburban like a broken doll and went to sobbing. Will hurried toward her, Ruby Dee coming right behind him, followed by Lonnie and Crystal. Crystal was crying, and Lonnie was holding on to her. Georgia screamed and pummeled Will.

"Frank isn't home," Crystal said, when Will asked. "I think he's over to Amarillo, but I'm not sure."

Georgia said she didn't need Frank, that she didn't need any Goddamn man in this universe. She tried to slap Will, and anyone else within arm's length.

After a few minutes Hardy told Lonnie and Crystal to go on. "You ain't helpin' her right now. Just go on, and we'll see to her."

Crystal hung back. "What will you do? You won't call the sheriff, will you?" Her pleading eyes moved from Will to Hardy.

"Nah, we won't call the sheriff," Hardy told her. But after they had driven away, he said, "Well, I guess we maybe should call the sheriff."

Will had gotten Georgia into the passenger side of the Suburban, and he stood there listening to her cry and scream at him. Ruby Dee felt helpless. Every time she approached, Georgia seemed to get wilder.

"No, don't call the sheriff." Will breathed heavily. "I can handle her. I'll take her home, try to locate Frank and stay with her until he gets there."

"That could take a day or two," Hardy pointed out.

"If I can't get Frank, her brother Pate'll come over."

He got Georgia out of the Suburban and into his pickup. She was beginning to be wrung out now from alcohol and emotion, yet every hair was still in place, and her clothes still looked perfect. It was a little eerie.

Ruby Dee thought to get Georgia's purse from the Suburban and hand it to Will to tuck beside her. A woman always needed her purse, especially in a crisis.

As he left, Will said, "I'll let you know somethin' as soon as I can."

Ruby Dee and Hardy fed the horses that evening. Afterward, Ruby Dee made sandwiches for supper, and she let Hardy have extra cheese on his. The house was certainly quiet, after all the commotion of the afternoon.

Hardy commented, "I always thought that Georgia had a screw or two loose."

"Most of us have a screw or two loose," Ruby Dee said. "We just usually keep it hidden."

Hardy chewed thoughtfully, then said, "I think you're right."

"Hardy, you could have been killed, steppin' in front of that shotgun like that." Ruby Dee stretched out her hand and covered Hardy's, squeezing it, as if to confirm that he was there and safe.

"Nah . . . she'd already scared herself too much to pull the other trigger."

"She could have done it accidentally, like she did the first time."

He just shrugged.

A few minutes later, she said, "Oh, Hardy, do you think Will is all right? She was awfully crazy."

"He's fine. Will ain't no fool."

Then Ruby Dee suddenly thought about how the shot might have hit one of the cattle. Hardy told her it wasn't likely any were close enough to get hit.

"Shotgun like that's for close range. We were all dang lucky not to catch any of it." Fortunately Georgia had been pointing away from where the horses were, and Sally had been cowering beneath Will's pickup. "It's too dark to go look at any cattle now, anyway," he said.

Georgia lay on her bed, sobbing and sobbing. "It'snot fairWill." That was how her words sounded, all run together. "Crystal's soyoung. Shehasyears aheadof her tohavea baby. I want a baby . . . I'm forty, andIwantababy."

She had been crying like this ever since she had woke up, after passing out. Will figured this was the heart of the matter.

"Georgia, you can adopt a baby."

"No . . . I want my own. You should have given me a baby, Will."

"I didn't know you wanted one, Georgia." Which was true, not that he had ever thought much about it. They had never discussed it. Georgia had never even seemed that fond of children. She'd always said she'd had enough taking care of her mother's babies. Georgia's mother had had six other children, all much younger than Georgia. Ten years ago her mother had remarried, and since that time had had little to do with her grown children.

"You wouldn't have done it anyway," Georgia accused. "And Frank's goneallthe time. I'm alone, Will. It'snotfair!" and she went to sobbing again.

Will kept placating her and trying to locate Frank. He felt like he was drowning in tears. He'd found tranquilizers in the bathroom cabinet, but he wouldn't let her have one. He kind of figured she had taken some before, and then she had started drinking, and the combination was what had set her off so crazy.

Georgia rarely drank, because she and liquor didn't get along; it generally made her erratic as hell. The one thing that kept Will from taking her to the hospital was that he had twice before been through similar episodes with her—once right after her divorce, and again after her father had died.

At last she fell into what seemed a true sleep, and Will was free to call all over and locate Frank. When he finally found him, Will told him it wouldn't hurt for him to bring home a baby.

"Nothin', Frank," he said hurriedly to Frank's surprised question. "Just get home, and I'll explain everything."

"Was that Will?" Ruby Dee asked, hurrying down the stairs. She had just come out of the shower and heard the phone ring.

Hardy nodded. "He's okay."

That was all he was going to say, and Ruby Dee pressed him to find out that Georgia was asleep, Frank was on his way from Amarillo, and Lonnie and Crystal had called from the hotel in Oklahoma City.

Ruby Dee experienced an empty feeling, the kind that comes after running on high for hours. It was all over, the danger had passed, she didn't quite know what to do with herself.

She and Hardy sat out on the front porch, and the evening seemed strangely peaceful after the commotion of the day. The nights were getting cooler, and Ruby Dee wore her heavy velour robe and slippers.

She began to talk about having a party for Lonnie

and Crystal. She wanted to make them a three-tier cake. "I once took care of a baker, and he taught me how to do decorative icing." The weather forecaster had predicted a warm, sunny week, perfect for an outdoor afternoon party. Ruby Dee thought she could manage simple sandwiches for fifty people.

Suddenly she realized Hardy hadn't said anything. "I'm sorry, Hardy. It's not my place to be designing a party."

"Stop that," he said gruffly. "Right here is most certainly your place. You want to give them a party, we'll give them a party."

Ruby Dee didn't know what to say to that. She pushed the swing faster. Tears threatened, and her heart filled to overflowing.

"I don't think you need to be doin' all the work, though," Hardy said. "We can get ribs and things brought it."

"I think a party would be fun, Hardy." And then she ventured to add, "But mostly it would mean so much to Lonnie to have one . . . to know that you would give him one."

Hardy didn't say anything.

They sat in silence, except for the gentle creak of the swing's chains. Lonnie and Crystal were in Oklahoma City now, Ruby Dee thought. She was envious, thinking of Lonnie and Crystal together . . . of the baby Crystal carried.

She said, "You're gonna have a grandchild, Hardy."

He just gave a little grunt.

Lonnie's having a youngun made Hardy think about how poor a daddy he had been to Lonnie. He had always managed to shrug off the regret of this, but this night he had trouble doing so.

Hardy thought about what it had been like when he married Lila. Her crazy daddy had come after him with a shotgun, because he hadn't wanted Hardy to marry her. One thing no one ever knew was that Hardy had gotten Lila pregnant, which was why he'd married her in the first place. Back in those days, when a man got a woman pregnant, he did one of two things: married her or ran off to the city. Hardy hadn't wanted to run off.

Lila had miscarried, though, just two weeks after they were married. That was what she'd told him, anyway. Hardy had always wondered if she hadn't lied the whole time, just to get him to marry her.

Ruby Dee awoke when she heard Will's truck on the gravel drive just after one in the morning. She had been waiting for word from him. Slipping from bed, she padded quickly to the open window.

She glimpsed the sparkling stars, then the tail end of Will's truck. The rest of it was hidden by the elm tree. In the glow of the pole lamp she could see Will coming along the walk. Her heart thudded. There was a sense of knowing inside her. Will had come instead of calling, because he wanted to see her, talk with her. She was about to race down to meet him, when she caught a glimpse of the kitchen light coming on and shining out across the grass.

So Hardy was awake!

Ruby Dee stilled. She heard the back door open and Hardy's step on the porch. Will stopped, stood looking in but not entering. And Hardy didn't invite him.

Hardy said, "I guess you got Georgia taken care of."

"Yeah . . . I waited for Frank to get there. I didn't

see any need of advertisin' Georgia's trouble by callin' in anyone else."

Georgia's trouble? Ruby Dee figured it had been trouble for all of them. But she guessed she was proud of Will for wanting to shield Georgia. Ruby Dee would have wanted the same for herself.

Hardy said, "Well, you were thinkin' right there. . . . People'd chew on this for a month of Sundays, and wouldn't none of us be left out. What's Frank gonna do with her?"

Will sighed. "I don't know. He's with her, for a start. He said he'll get ahold of a doctor tomorrow. She's sorry, Dad. She . . . well, sometimes when she drinks she gets crazy like that."

"That wasn't just no drunk prank on her part," Hardy said. "She was out to shoot the balls off you boys. That woman's mad, and I sure don't want her comin' back here, possibly after Ruby Dee."

"She won't do anything to Ruby Dee. Ruby Dee has nothin' to do with what set her off." Then, after a second, "Dad . . . I'm grateful to you for steppin' in."

Hardy gave his little snort, and Ruby Dee imagined his shrug. He asked, "What about her Suburban?"

"Frank's gonna send a couple of boys for it tomorrow."

Another snort from Hardy.

Then there was a long silence. The two of them just looked at each other, from what Ruby Dee could see of Will, which was mostly from his hat down to his boots, but not his face at all.

"Ruby Dee's gone to bed," Hardy said, his voice dropping, so that she just barely caught the next words. "There's no use gettin' her up now. I'll tell her what you've told me."

"Dad . . . I'm goin' to ask Ruby Dee to marry me."

Will's voice was low, but it carried up to her. Ruby Dee put a fist to her wildly beating heart and held her breath, straining to hear Hardy's reply.

But his voice was too low. She heard him speak, but couldn't catch his words.

Whatever they were, Will had nothing to say in response. He turned and walked away. Her hand on the windowsill, Ruby Dee watched his pickup disappear around the corner of the house.

≈ 26

WILL WALKED INTO a dark, empty house. He flipped on the light and stood there staring at his kitchen, which was almost finished; cabinet doors stacked against the wall, awaiting varnish; new refrigerator and stove; Spanish-tile floor. The counter was strewn with empty soft-drink cans and beer bottles, washed paint brushes, a can of wallpaper paste, and a four-day-old box of fried chicken.

He threw his hat on the refrigerator and went through the dining room and down the narrow hallway. He stopped in the doorway of the bedroom. There, taking up a good deal of the small, newly wallpapered bedroom, was the queen-sized cherry-wood-and-iron bed he had bought that day. It had cost a small fortune. He had driven all the way to Oklahoma City for it. He wanted it for when he brought Ruby Dee here.

He stood staring at the bed for a long time, thinking nothing, yet feeling his mind racing. Pictures passed through his mind: Ruby Dee's eyes, Lonnie and Crystal driving away, Georgia sobbing about wanting a baby.

And then he was seeing the old man step in front of him, in front of the barrel of that shotgun. That picture went through his mind again and again, as if someone kept rewinding the tape. And last, he heard again what the old man had said, when Will told him he intended to ask Ruby Dee to marry him.

"Don't take her away from me, just because you can."

That plea, along with everything else, kept going around and around inside of Will.

Worn, Will sat on the cherry-wood bed, removed his boots, lay back and fell deeply asleep. He slept far past sunup the following morning. He showered and dressed but didn't take time to make coffee. He hurried to the ranch, anticipating Ruby Dee's coffee. Anticipating Ruby Dee.

But Ruby Dee and the old man were were in the Galaxie, about to leave, with Ruby Dee behind the wheel. Despite the coolness of the morning, the convertible top was down. Instead of a hat, Ruby Dee had her hair pulled back in a ribbon. She wore a soft brown sweater. The old man was dressed sharply, in a starched white shirt and his tweed sport coat and his winter felt hat. He looked far younger than his eighty-five years.

"We're goin' down to Elk City to see about a caterer for Lonnie's party," Ruby Dee said. She removed her sunglasses, looked at him intently with her dark eyes. There were smudges beneath them, making them look more exotic than usual. "I left you some ham and biscuits in the oven."

He thanked her, and she said she was glad he had

been able to get Frank home to Georgia. "I hope she'll be all right," she said.

The old man asked Will about getting the cows and calves separated, and Will said he would see to it.

"Well, we can't wait until your brother comes home," the old man said. "You call Jeb Koss and his boys to come over and start today." Will didn't argue.

For a long minute he watched the Galaxie go down the drive, stirring up a wake of dust.

Will knew that the old man had thought up a reason to take Ruby Dee to town. The old man was determined to keep Ruby Dee away from him for as long as possible. Permanently, if he could.

Will tried to be angry with the old man, but the memory of so many things, not the least of which was the old man stepping in front of that shotgun in order to protect him and Lonnie, kept getting in the way.

"Don't take her away from me, just because you can."

The only time Will had ever heard that particular tone in his father's voice was when he had asked their mother not to leave.

The air blew cool around the windshield as they headed south on the blacktop highway. Hardy really enjoyed the convertible, but the air did chill him. Damned old body, he thought. He was glad Ruby Dee turned on the heat, but he wouldn't have told her so. He remembered when he would ride a horse all through the winter and not bother with much more than a light coat. He remembered a lot of things, he told himself, but they were all gone.

When they reached Elk City, he directed Ruby Dee to the downtown area.

"Just pull over here," he said, pointing to the bank. "I need to go in there and do some bankin', and Dave Secrest in there'll tell us where to find a caterer for your party."

"I wish you wouldn't keep callin' it my party," she grumbled when she came around to his side of the car and held the door.

He said, "I wish you wouldn't keep actin' like you have to help me out of the car."

On the sidewalk, he extended his arm to her, and she took it. It felt good to walk with her. Inside, he withdrew some cash and then went over to Secrest's big office. The man seemed truly glad to see Hardy, but Hardy only shook his hand and asked for the name of a good caterer. "One that makes good barbecue. I figure a man in your position probably has a lot of parties and ought to know somebody good."

Secrest mentioned a couple of people, then had his secretary write down their names and addresses. "I didn't know a banker had to be a social secretary," he joked.

And Hardy said, "I guess my banker holdin' all my money can be whatever I need him to be."

Secrest got red at that, but Hardy didn't care.

Outside the bank, Hardy told Ruby Dee to go look up the caterer and make the arrangements. He pulled out his money clip, peeled off five one-hundred-dollar bills and handed them to her. "This ought to be enough for a down payment. Order enough food for about seventy people—I don't want no more people than that at my place, and if it turns out that not that many come, we'll have lots of leftovers."

Ruby Dee looked startled. "You want me to just leave you here?"

"I don't need you to hold my hand every minute, do I?"

"Well, no, you don't."

"Then you go on. Well, I might as well tell you. I'm goin' to see my lawyer, right down the street, here—Harold Thelen, Attorney at Law. And don't be tellin' nobody. I don't like people to know my bizness. I'll be a little while, so you go fix things with one of them caterers and then come pick me up down there."

She stared at him, her eyes wide. He turned and headed down the sidewalk. He felt the best he had in many a year. There was nothing like perplexing people to make an old man feel young.

Harold Thelen was some annoyed with Hardy for coming in without an appointment, but he got over it. Especially when his curiosity rose about the changes Hardy wanted made in the set up of the ranch and in his will. Hardy told him, "I don't pay you to understand my reasonin', Thelen, just to make what I want legal."

Ruby Dee was waiting outside in the Galaxie when Hardy came out of Thelen's office. When Thelen saw Ruby Dee, he almost dropped his teeth, which Hardy knew were false. Hardy had always been proud to have all of his own teeth.

Thelen got this look in his eye, one-fourth like he thought Hardy a fool and three-fourths like pure-D envy.

As Ruby Dee drove away, Hardy said, "You know, gal, I couldn't feel grander if you was the queen of Sheba. Let's go find a steak for lunch. I promise I'll eat vegetables, too, and no sugar in my coffee," he added.

After lunch, they went shopping, and Hardy went so far as to buy a new coat and a pair of boots for the party, and picked out four more shirts, too. Ruby Dee bought a new dress, which looked beautiful on her. As she modeled it for Hardy, he remembered Jooney. He wanted to pay for the dress, but she wouldn't let him. So while she changed, Hardy went over to the jewelry counter. He had a pair of Indian silver earrings boxed and in his pocket by the time Ruby Dee joined him.

It was late afternoon before they started home. Only a few minutes after they hit the open road, Hardy put his head back and fell asleep. Ruby Dee worried he would get a crick in his neck, but he always had been good at sleeping sitting up.

Ruby Dee drove along in the sunshine, the wind tugging at her hair. It had been a wonderful day. She'd had such a good time with Hardy. She glanced at him and thought how different he was now from that first day she had come. It really was amazing what a balanced diet and simple care could do for a person, she thought.

Ruby Dee knew deep inside that she had brought Hardy life again. That he cared for her . . . that he thought of her as the Jooney he had lost, and it made no difference whether or not she really was. And she cared for him, too, in a way she could never explain to anyone. In a way she didn't exactly understand herself. The feelings were powerful, and real, and not what she'd have felt for a father.

Then her thoughts turned to Will. Excitement fluttered in her chest as she recalled, for the hundredth time, that he had said he was going to ask her to marry him. Every time she thought of it, her mind went into a tailspin, like a horse that rears up to throw off its rider's weight and then runs wildly away.

Miss Edna's insistent voice came: *"What will your answer be, Ruby Dee?"*

"Oh, Miss Edna, if I say yes, what will happen to Hardy?"

She heard only silence. "You shouldn't pick now to quit tellin' me what to do, Miss Edna."

Ruby Dee had already turned off the highway when Hardy roused himself. "Where are we? Dang, we're here already. Slow up, gal."

"What is it, Hardy?"

"I want to show you somethin' . . . up here, on the next hill."

They were still a mile from the ranch house when he directed her to pull into a narrow graveled road that led across a cattle guard, past the sign that read: Starr Number One. The sun was far to the west now, slanting golden across the land. The road lead to a gently pumping rocker arm. Ruby Dee stopped the car in front of it, looked at it and then glanced curiously at Hardy.

It was the first well to be sunk on his ranch, Hardy told her. There were eight oil and gas wells bearing the Starr name now, and he still got royalties from them, even in today's depressed market. He told her, too, that until those wells, he'd always had to carry a mortgage on the ranch, but the oil and gas money paid that mortgage, and he'd never again taken another.

"I own this land, free and clear," he said, gazing out beyond the well to the hills and pastures rolling east, south and west. "Look that way . . . and that way. That's all Starr land. Bought it up, piece by piece, over the years. 'Course, I didn't make it—the Almighty did that. But I like to think I've taken good care of it for him." The pride vibrated in his voice and struck Ruby Dee clear through.

"It's beautiful, Hardy."

"Not everyone can appreciate this part of the country. It's dry a lot, and the wind sometimes blows like hell. I guess there's some that hate it. My own mama did."

He looked at Ruby Dee. She was still staring off at the land.

He said, "If you'll pledge to stay with me until they carry me off to the White Rose cemetery, I'll deed a third of all this over to you." Her head swung around, and she gazed at him with shock. "I can't give you what a younger man can . . . but I can give you what most can't, and that's a sizable fortune, in this land and all my assets. We can get married, if you want, but we don't have to. I'll settle for your pledge."

She stared at him a moment longer, and then turned her gaze out the windshield.

Well.

He was offering her a fortune. A white clapboard house and barns and pastures, and with a fortune, she could buy her babies, so she would be assured of having them. And she could still have Hardy . . . although probably not Will.

There just wasn't anything Hardy wouldn't do to have his way.

She faced him, looked at him with blurred vision.

A pained expression on his face, he said, "Now, don't go cryin' on me, gal. Just say your piece."

"Damn your hide, Hardy Starr. How can you

think that you can buy me—chain me to you with money? I'm paid a salary, and just like everyone else, I need that salary, but that's not why I'm here. I could work anywhere. If I hadn't wanted to stay and be around you, I'd have left months ago. I have my own plans, Hardy! I would have left after that first day, because you can be real ornery.''

Her brown eyes were dark as gun barrels. "I'm your friend, for as long as you want. I love you, Hardy, in my way. That's my pledge, and either it will do or it won't. I can offer you no more . . . and I can't be chained. Chains just choke hearts, Hardy.''

Then she flounced back in the seat.

Hardy was angry himself. He had made her what he considered a sizeable offer, and she had thrown it back in his face. And then she had lectured him, when he had expected her to be grateful, and at the least impressed.

He had wanted to secure her for himself. To assure himself that she would never leave him, not even for his son. He wasn't particularly proud of cutting Will out, but he wasn't particularly sorry, either. Will was young and had years ahead of him, but Hardy did not.

He said then, "I changed my will today. I've already deeded you one third of everything upon my death. You don't need to marry me or anyone else to get it.''

Ruby Dee had known Hardy could be a hard man, but she hadn't known he could be downright mean.

"Well, I won't take it, Hardy.''

Then she started the car and drove them home.

~ 27

WHEN WILL GOT to the ranch house, it was nearly dark. He had taken time to shower and dress in a good shirt and jeans. As he came up the walk, he looked up and saw Ruby Dee standing at the screen door, waiting.

"Supper is just now ready," she said, as he came through the door. "It's only sandwiches, but I made potato salad, and we have those late tomatoes Wildcat brought from Charlene's garden."

Her eyes were on him, warm as velvet in sunshine, and he almost grabbed her and asked her right there, but a movement caught his eye, and as he looked over her head, he saw the old man gazing at him.

She went about putting things on the table, and he helped her. Will took his seat across from the old man, who was still wearing the starched shirt and creased slacks.

Will asked if they had gotten everything they needed in town. The old man nodded, but it was Ruby Dee who told about hiring the caterer and

347

what they had bought. It apppeared the old man was turning loose some money.

Her eyes sparkling with excitement, Ruby Dee talked about their plans for the party. Will looked at his dad in surprise. He had never known the old man to have such a hoopty-do at the ranch. Each spring they hosted the stock sale, but all they had was Jimmy Mack come in with his concession wagon and supply cheese nachos, hamburgers and cold drinks. And the old man grumbled about that, said he didn't like buying food for a bunch of people, most who weren't gonna buy squat and who he didn't want on his ranch in the first place. And now he was agreeing to a party, with awnings and rugs and waiters. And all for Lonnie.

No, Will thought, understanding slicing through him. It was all for Ruby Dee.

"I thought Saturday afternoon would be the best," Ruby Dee was saying, "but I can change that, if I call tomorrow."

"Saturday afternoon is fine," Will told her.

"You can help me make a list of people to invite. You and Hardy both, maybe right after we eat." Her gaze moved between him and the old man. The old man grunted, and Will said he'd be glad to.

Will told about getting the bulls up to the lots that day, and that he had arranged for help to separate the cows and calves. He had decided to wait until Lonnie returned to do that. The old man argued against waiting, saying that the calves were of weaning weight and some beyond. And if rain set in, there could be further delays.

Will answered that he would separate them in the rain, if necessary.

Then Hardy said, "I guess I can hire me a crew to

move my cows." He said it mean and cold as January ice.

And Will replied, "Go right ahead. I can give you phone numbers of people to call." Anger almost pushed him to his feet, but he refused it. The old man was goading him, seeking to push him away from Ruby Dee again. With his eyes Will told the old man he wasn't going anywhere, and when Ruby Dee rose to clear the table, Will rose to help her.

She thanked him, and her eyes were on him and it was between them, heavy and warm.

Will left the kitchen and went out to feed the stock. He worked automatically, passing out hay and grain and filling water troughs, all the while thinking of the old man inside with Ruby Dee. She was the reason for the change in the old man—the reason he was suddenly buying thirty-dollar shirts and five-hundred-dollar boots and looking ten years younger and more alive than he had in twenty-five years.

What would happen to him, if Will took her away from here?

She would just be a few miles down the road, Will argued with himself. It wouldn't be like he was really taking her away. No doubt she would be down here with Hardy half the time anyway.

And she had said she wanted her own house. Like as not she wasn't going to stay here forever. The old man wouldn't see it that way, though. Her leaving for a place of her own or leaving with Will were two entirely different things.

When Will got back to the house, Ruby Dee and the old man were working on the list of people to invite to the party. There wouldn't be time to send out invitations; everyone would have to be contacted personally. It was the old man who suggested having Cora Jean do some of the inviting. "The woman's better than the radio," he said.

Ruby Dee got up right then and called Cora Jean, and while the women chatted on the telephone, Will and the old man sat and looked at each other across the table. Then Will went into his office and began opening the two days' worth of mail stacked in the middle of his desk, most of it junk.

He was surprised when the old man came in.

The old man said, "Once we have the calves weaned, I'm gonna let Wildcat handle things on the ranch for the winter, so you can go ahead and cut yourself loose whenever you want."

Will's temper flared. He managed to hold on to himself as he said, "Wildcat's a good man, and he knows ranchin', but he doesn't know how to keep records. And I got them all on computer now."

"Won't be so much durin' the winter. Besides, this ranch survived eighty-plus years without a computer." The old man's eyes got hard. "I'm shuttin' the ranchin' operation down. I'll have Thelen see to it, and no doubt he'll have accountants addin' things up."

That announcement took anything Will might have said right out of him.

"When?" he managed to ask after a full minute.

"Over the winter. I figure dispersing the stock at the usual sale time will work out best."

Will felt as if he had been hit in the gut. "It's taken forty years to get the breeding stock we've got."

"Ought to get some good money from it," the old man said and walked out, smacking his cane on the floor.

Will sank into the oak chair. He couldn't imagine

the Starr shut down, the cattle dispersed . . . years of work gone.

And the old man hadn't even spoken to him about the decision, Will thought, fire in his chest. The old man would sooner shut down the ranch, sell off everything, than hand it over to his sons. The old man would cut off their heritage.

Why? Was it one more effort to push Will from Ruby Dee? Did the old man think that in getting rid of the ranch, he would get rid of Will? Or was it simply to show that he could do it, that he remained in power? Or was he trying to punish Will because he'd dared to seek something of his own . . . and Ruby Dee, too?

How could the man who had stepped in front of a wild woman with a loaded shotgun in order to protect his sons do this to them?

If Will had known how to cry, he might have. After a minute, he walked outside and drove away.

Still in her clothes, Ruby Dee lay on her side, propped up on several pillows, with a light cotton blanket thrown over her legs. Through the open window came the faint sound of an engine, then of tires crunching on gravel. The sound roused her, and she sat up, wondering if she'd been dreaming. She heard the squeak of the truck door opening, the clunk of it closing.

Throwing aside the blanket, she went to the window. Will's pickup was parked near the horse barn. Straining to see in the dimness, she caught sight of a shadowy figure walking into the wide entry of the barn in the first light of morning. The light of her digital clock glowed red. He was nearly an hour earlier than usual.

Picking up her boots, she padded quietly down the stairs in sock feet, with Sally following. The stairs creaked softly, and Sally's nails clicked on the floor, but Hardy snored on.

On the back step, Ruby Dee tugged on her boots and then half-ran up the slope to the barn. The gravel crunching beneath her steps sounded loud in the silence. The sweet, early morning air caressed her face and chilled her arms. Already it grew lighter, and she felt the sense of urgency, of time running out.

She peered down the long barn aisle. There came the scents of damp earth and animals. Two lights were on at the far end. Will was there—the light shown on his pale hat and denim-clad shoulders. Several horses snorted anxiously as he poured grain into their feeders.

Suddenly Ruby Dee felt shy, fearful. He hadn't waited to speak to her last night, and this morning he'd come so quietly, almost like a thief not wanting to be caught.

As if he sensed her presence, he looked up and saw her.

"Will?" Hesitantly, she stepped forward. He tossed aside his bucket and came striding forcefully toward her.

There was something about him . . . an intensity. She saw the shadow of a beard on his face and dark circles beneath his eyes. Her heart fluttered as he gazed down at her.

She asked, "Where did you go last night? What's wrong?"

But then he cupped her face and kissed her, stopping her questions and taking away her breath. *Oh, my goodness . . . oh!* He kissed her again and yet again. Her head spun. *He did want her!*

Then he looked into her eyes and said, "I love you, Ruby Dee. I want to marry you."

"Oh, Will," was all she could say and that only a whisper. She went against his chest, buried herself there, feeling his strong arms close around her, hearing the rapid thudding of his heart and inhaling the male scent of him. She held onto him while he rubbed his hands up and down her back and his cheek against her hair.

"I'm forty-two, Ruby Dee, and I don't know if I can give you children, but I'll try, and I can give you a good house, and you can keep nursing, or whatever you want to do."

"Oh, Will."

The next instant he pulled away, and she wanted to protest, but then he had her by the hand and was leading her to the far end of the barn. She knew then that he was going to make love to her. And that she wanted him to beyond all reason.

He brought a canvas duster from inside the tack room, spread it on the soft mounds of hay strewn about and turned out the lights. The early morning brought a soft, ethereal glow to the corner of the barn.

Ruby Dee tossed her dress aside, and when he raised himself up from removing his boots, she was standing there before him in only her bra and panties. His eyes fastened on her, and she shivered. With his gaze hot upon her, he jerked off his shirt and spread it with the duster, then drew her down with him. The canvas duster crackled and the hay whispered as they lay upon it. The hay was so fragrant . . . so soft! And Will was so hard, all over.

For a moment, Will stopped to gaze at her, to run his hand slowly over her breasts and down her belly. His eyes darkened and caressed her, just as his touch did. Slowly, oh, so slowly his head came down, and he traced a line across the tops of her breasts with his lips. And then he was touching her all over. Touching her with his strong, calloused hands, bringing desire trembling and pounding through her.

Then nothing was slow or gentle, because the passion, so long lying just beneath the surface, so long held there and denied, flashed over them like fire across the prairie. Urgently they sought each other with their lips and their hands, their arms and their legs. Nothing at all leisurely, only greedily, all hot and fiery and crazy wild. Ruby Dee, aching and throbbing, pleaded with him with her hands. She couldn't stop herself. She wanted him, had to have him.

Will slipped between her legs and pressed himself against her. There he paused for an agonizing instant, brought his lips to hers and kissed her deeply, as he thrust inside her. The pain surprised Ruby Dee, but then she was rising, higher and higher, like a kite caught in the hot summer wind.

Will had not meant for it to happen, at least not then. He hadn't meant even to see her this morning, because he needed to think things through. But when he'd seen her, there had been no way he could stop himself.

He had known Ruby Dee would be hot. He had suspected, from what she'd said, that she would be nearly virginal. She had been both of these things, and so much more. He was struck with a sense of amazement at what had happened with her, and with himself. The force of his emotions startled him.

Ruby Dee shivered, and Will tightened his arm around her as he brought the edge of the duster up around her hips, which nestled against him. Her tears wet his shoulder and trailed down his neck. He kissed her silky hair and inhaled its sweet scent. She was softer all over than he had imagined. Her shoulder glowed in the morning light falling through the barn door. "You're beautiful," he whispered, and she stirred against him, burying her face deeper into his neck. The delicious sense of arousal stirred again in his groin.

Lifting up on her elbow, she kissed his shoulder and moved downward to his breast. She raised her face and looked at him, her eyes all full of heat, her hair falling all around her pale cheeks. "Will . . . well, my goodness."

"Yeah," he said and kissed her, long and lingering.

But the sense of time growing short crept back over him. He rolled her to her back and looked into her face. He picked hay from her hair, caressed her cheek.

"I take it you are gonna marry me," he said, with a crooked grin, though inside he quivered with uncertainty.

"I want to," she said, her eyes warm upon him.

That she didn't say yes bothered him.

Hardly speaking, they got dressed, and then Ruby Dee sat on a bale of hay with Will's denim jacket around her shoulders, while he stood three feet away, smoking a cigarette at the edge of the door. The sun, not yet up, was turning the eastern sky golden, but the sky to the west was dark with clouds.

Ruby Dee was the first to say it. "What about Hardy?"

Will blew out a stream of smoke. "We'll get someone else to stay with him. You'll be able to come as much as you want. It won't be like you're leavin' him."

She stared at the pattern the morning glow had begun to make on the barn floor. Will heard again his father's plea: don't take her, just because you can. He thought he understood, now that he had made love to her. This was something Will could give Ruby Dee that the old man never could.

"You tried other people before me."

"We found you. We'll find someone else."

Her dark eyes rose to look into his. "He won't take anyone else. Look how he's changed since I came. He's a man again."

He tossed his cigarette outside in the dirt and pressed his boot on it. Then he came and crouched in front of her, taking her hands in his.

"Ruby Dee, I don't want to hurt him. I see how he's changed, and I know why he's changed. I know it's you that's brought him back to life. But I don't want to let go of what we could have. . . . I can't let him take this away from us. We have a right to our own life."

"I know," she said, simply . . . but as if it made no difference. Her brown eyes searched his. "I love you, Will." Her lips trembled, while his heart thudded, waiting for what would come next. "I want . . . we may have already made a baby," and she gave a trembling smile, then it faded, and her eyes filled with pain. "But I love Hardy, too. Can you understand?" Her eyes begged him to.

And he did, in a way. "I know. It's okay."

"Oh, Will, I'm so caught. And I can't stand knowin' that I've come between you and your daddy." The words came out so painfully, and then she was sobbing.

Will straightened, bringing her up with him. He lifted her face to look into it. "Honey, it isn't you. It's between me and Dad. And there's nothin' you or anybody can do to change it."

"Maybe you could talk to him. Maybe you could tell him you would come back to live here, with him." She regarded him hopefully. "You could still keep the other place for your own cattle."

Will shook his head. "No. Dad's closin' the Starr. There won't be a job here for me anymore." There wouldn't be a reason for him to be there at all, he thought.

She looked shocked, disbelieving. Then she squeezed her eyes closed and dropped her forehead against his chest. He held her, and he knew he wasn't going to let her go, no matter the price he had to pay.

She raised her head. "Hardy may close the ranch, but he will still be here, alone."

They looked at each other her for a long moment.

Will breathed deeply. "I'll wait, give him time, for awhile." And then he kissed her. A kiss to make her remember.

When she left him, he thought how crazy it was that her love for the old man was exactly what he himself loved about her so much.

* * *

Hardy knew, of course. He knew it the minute he looked at her, when she came into the kitchen. He was just entering the room, as if he had been listening for her footsteps.

Ruby Dee met his gaze, felt her face burn and throbbing start low in her belly, as what she and Will had shared filled her mind. She saw Hardy's anger, and then his hurt. She didn't know what to say to him, so she turned away to begin breakfast.

Will came in and ate breakfast with them. The meal was silent.

28

THERE WAS SO much to be done for the party. Phone calls to be made and answered, cleaning and polishing, the grass to be trimmed, presents and flowers and extra food to be bought.

For the better part of two days, Will and Wildcat worked to ready his house for the newlyweds, where they would stay, using his second bedroom, until they could find a place of their own. Ruby Dee thought it was sad that Lonnie wouldn't be living at the ranch, but she supposed it was for the best. Crystal seemed quite frightened of Hardy, who didn't care to have anyone new around him.

Hardy withdrew to his shop, where he spent long hours. After lunch on Tuesday, Ruby Dee plunked the telephone and the guest list in front of him on the table. "I can't call everyone, Hardy."

He grunted, but after a minute, he picked up the receiver and began to dial. Ruby Dee brought him a cup of coffee, with a bit of sugar. As soon as Hardy had finished his calls, he got up and went out the back door, without a word to Ruby Dee, leaving his coffee untouched.

In the afternoon she brought him peanut butter crackers and tomato juice. "With you spendin' so much time out here, you're probably hungry," she said, squeezing past Hardy to set the plate and glass on the workbench.

Hardy didn't take his gaze off the leather he carved. He didn't even speak to her.

"That's a new saddle, isn't it?"

"Yep," he said, after a minute. He continued to work, making a diamond pattern.

"It's really beautiful."

Nothing, not even a grunt.

"I think we've called everyone about the party. I only asked sixty, because I figure we might get some people just droppin' by or comin' along with others. I know you don't want any more than about seventy people."

He didn't say a word.

"Hardy, are you gonna talk to me?" She waited, staring at him. She would stand there and stare at him all afternoon, if he wanted it that way, she thought.

He raised his eyes at last. "Just what is it you want me to say?" His voice was hard.

"Not a thing, Hardy Starr, not one blessed thing." She stalked out of the shop, only to turn around and come back and ask if it would be okay to lend Lonnie and Crystal bed sheets and blankets. She thought she certainly had better ask, or Hardy might suggest they were stealing from him.

"Aw'ight," was all Hardy said.

Ruby Dee had the feeling she could have put her hand out and touched the glass wall Hardy had put around himself. She didn't know how she could have expected anything else; Hardy was hurt, and Hardy hurt could be vicious.

Again and again she questioned herself about why she felt what she did for him. She had come here to take care of him, and he had become her charge. She never took that lightly. Now on top of that she had come to truly care for him, to love him in a way she couldn't explain. She was like that, and Will understood it. He didn't press her, and as guilty as she felt about hurting Hardy, she felt the same way for putting Will off.

A hundred times she thought to tell Will about his daddy and Jooney, and how Cora Jean had said that Ruby Dee looked like Jooney, enough to be her twin. She wanted to explain that and so many other things, so he would understand what she meant to his daddy. But somehow she couldn't do it. Somehow, even though she and Hardy had never spoken of it, it was their private secret. Surely Jooney was Hardy's secret, kept safe within him all these years. Ruby Dee did not want to violate it . . . and maybe, too, she wanted to hold onto that tie with Hardy.

Only once did she almost tell Will about Hardy's offer of a third of the ranch if she stayed with him. But she decided she would never tell anyone about it. She would not add to the hurt Hardy was already inflicting by dissolving the Starr Ranch, instead of giving it to his flesh and blood, his sons.

If ever she came close to hating Hardy, it was over this. Her anger about it was so intense that one day she blurted out, "How can you offer to will me, a stranger, one-third of the ranch and then go and shut it down and take away your sons' heritage?"

Hardy looked at her. "My daddy didn't give me

this ranch. I bought it from him. It's mine, and I can do with it as I see fit."

"Did it ever occur to you, Hardy Starr, that your daddy was wrong? You're hurtin' Will terrible by this, Hardy. If you doubt that, you're not at all the man I thought you were."

He said nothing. Hardy never had been one to explain himself.

At least now Ruby Dee understood where Hardy got his hardness. She explained it to Will, late Wednesday afternoon, while they were loading linens and other household items into his pickup.

"Hardy had to buy this ranch from his daddy. Did you know that?"

"No. No, I didn't know." He was obviously surprised. "I always knew Dad had to work hard for everything he ever had, but I never knew my grandfather, except by rumor. Most said Dad was like Grandpa, just like they always said I was like Hardy. I've spent a good deal of time tryin' not to be," he added, and there was sadness in his voice.

"Will, you are like Hardy," Ruby Dee said, and he frowned at her. "You're all the good parts, the strong and honorable parts. The part that lives as you wish and makes no apology to anyone, and doesn't place blame, either. It's why I love you." Her voice grew faint. Quite suddenly she trembled, had the urge to run and hide.

Then Will kissed her, and the fearful urge vanished. She touched his cheek.

He said, "We could get married tomorrow."

She didn't answer, but what she thought was: who would be with Hardy?

After a long minute, Will said, "I'm not stayin' for

supper. I promised to help Ambrose Bell finish haulin' his hay in from the field.''

He was stiff and cold. She'd hurt him.

She had a sense of being pressed on both sides, as if she were trapped in an envelope.

Feeling depressed, Ruby Dee took a long hot bath, in bath oil, and did the entire work up: skin, hair, nails, hands and feet. She was combing out her wet hair when the telephone on her dresser rang.

''Lonnie?'' She was glad to hear his voice! Suddenly, as odd as it seemed, she felt she could tell Lonnie her feelings. Of all people, Lonnie would understand, and she almost blurted it out, but then his voice sounded so happy, that she just couldn't burden him.

Holding her robe around her, she sat on the bed to listen as he described how much Crystal liked the State Fair and how she was scared to death on the ferris wheel but kept wanting to ride on it again and again. He sounded like Crystal's hero. He seemed truly happy.

Ruby Dee told him about the party on Saturday. Will had told him about it, but with none of the details. ''Your daddy has hired a caterer to put on a big spread,'' Ruby Dee said, ''and there'll be music, too.''

''Dad's springin' for all this?''

''Yes, Lonnie. He's even bought new clothes for the party.''

Lonnie reported that Frank and Georgia were flying down to Cozumel for a week's vacation, so they wouldn't be coming. Ruby Dee had been wondering whether to invite them. She told him Will had invited Crystal's mother, and Lonnie gave her a few more names of people to contact. Crystal wanted her cousin up in Dalhart, Texas, to come, and it took her a few minutes to find the telephone number for Ruby Dee.

Just before they hung up, Ruby Dee said, "Do you want to speak to your daddy? I'll take him the cordless phone."

"No," Lonnie said. "We've got to get back over to the fairgrounds. Toby Keith is entertainin' at the rodeo tonight, and Crystal sure doesn't want to miss him. We'll see y'all tomorrow afternoon," and then he was gone.

Ruby Dee hung up and felt foolishly let down, tossed aside. Well, for goodness' sake, she scolded herself, she wanted Lonnie to be happy! Besides, happiness was so fleeting, she thought pensively.

She stared at the pink glow the scarf-covered lamp cast on the wall. She guessed Will hadn't told Lonnie about Hardy closing down the ranch. She didn't think it would affect Lonnie the way it did Will, though.

Tying her robe, she slipped on moccasins and went downstairs. The house was quiet and dim, with the day's light fading. Hardy's room was empty. Letting Sally out the back door, Ruby Dee looked across and saw a light burning in Hardy's shop.

Will had not come for supper, and Hardy was staying away.

Almost before she realized what she was doing, she was out the screen door and striding toward the shop. Hand upon the cool ceramic knob, the door creaking.

Hardy glanced at her. His glasses were partway down the bridge of his nose, his shoulders hunched, his hands dark with the stain he applied to the skirt of a saddle.

"It's really coming along," she said, nodding at the saddle.

Hardy kept on rubbing on the leather.

"How long have you been makin' this saddle, Hardy?"

He shrugged. "I don't keep track." Rub, rub went his hand.

Ruby Dee stood there several more minutes. "I thought you might want to play a game of dominoes."

"No."

"I'll wait for you to finish here."

"I'll be awhile." His hands were still working.

Ruby Dee put her hand to her hip. "Well, I can wait awhile. I don't suppose you're gonna be all night."

"I might." Rub, rub.

Still she stood there in the doorway, while words got all clogged up in her throat.

He said, "Shut the door. You're lettin' in moths."

She went out and shut the door, hard. He wanted to be cold and close her out, so be it!

But then her mind whispered: *You've dealt with this before. He shut you out when you first came, and you wouldn't let him. You are simply being as stubborn as he is.*

The whisper sounded suspiciously like Miss Edna's voice.

"Miss Edna, you never could learn not to criticize. What are you doin' up in heaven—tellin' God all his faults?"

But Ruby Dee knew the whisper was true. Hardy was simply being the same way he had been all along—stubborn, angry at not getting his way. Still trying to manipulate everyone.

And he was doing a darn good job of it, too.

Halfway across the drive to the house, she veered, walking beneath the big elm and over to the west pasture fence. She put her hands upon the pipe rail, cool and smooth from a fresh coat of paint. Wildcat had done it yesterday, for the party.

How beautiful the earth was at this time of evening, she thought. Any hardness and ugliness of the earth faded into shadows, leaving only the beauty. The fall night air held its own special freshness. There was a bull in the pasture, far away, munching hay. A night bird called: chuck-will's-widow . . . chuck-will's-widow. Only a few weeks ago that call had come through the night. Tonight the call was sparse, because fall was slipping up on them.

"Miss Edna," Ruby Dee said, "I'm devoted to two people, and that just doesn't work."

"You are putting Hardy before Will," Miss Edna said.

"I know . . . that's what I was talkin' about." She breathed heavily. "How can I leave Hardy? He's so alone."

"Aloneness is his own choice . . . not yours."

Yes, that was true, Ruby Dee thought with great sadness. He pushed everyone away.

Her gaze drifted downward, and something caught her eye, lying just a few feet on the other side of the fence. Why, it was the shotgun Georgia had used, trying to blow them all away!

Bending, she carefully slipped through the fence and retrieved the gun. Everyone had forgotten it, and Wildcat only saw what he was looking straight at, which would have been the fence. She slipped back through the fence, then stood there holding the gun.

She had held few guns in her life. She remembered reading somewhere that you should always point the barrel upward. What if one accidentally killed a flying bird, or shot a plane?

The moment when the gun had gone off in Georgia's hands flashed through her mind, and then she saw Georgia pointing it at Will and Lonnie ... and then Hardy stepping in front of it.

And suddenly the thought came: If Hardy had been killed, I could go on. I would have been hurt, would have had a hole in my life, missed him forever, but my life would not have changed. But if Will had been killed, my life would never, ever have been the same. Will is half my life. He is my future.

It was a startling revelation.

The next instant, she turned and hurried toward the shop. Sally came bounding beside her, as if caught up in the vigor.

Hand upon the cool ceramic knob again, and Ruby Dee opened the shop door and stepped inside. Hardy's head came up in surprise; his hands stilled on the saddle. He looked at her, and then at the gun in her hand.

Ruby Dee said, "It's Georgia's shotgun." She looked at it, too, then carried it with her as she crossed the small room. She crouched beside him, set the gun on the floor and leaned it against the saddle, then looked up at him.

"Hardy, you pride yourself on being a realist, on seeing things as they are. Isn't that what you yourself would tell me to do—see things as they are? Oh, Hardy, I love you, and I always will need you in my life, but I love Will, too. And Will is my future. Will wants to marry me and give me children. Will wants to grow old with me, Hardy. He'll be there for me, in sickness and health and no matter what. If you love me, as you seem to, if you love Will, you will want this for us."

Her voice broke. She looked for signs that Hardy understood, but his face was as if carved in stone.

"Hardy, Will and I need your blessing." She waited, holding her breath, searching his face.

He said, "You two know what you want. You don't need nothin' from me."

Slowly she straightened. She had the strong urge to slap his face. Tears blurred her vision. She whirled and ran out.

Hardy sat there staring at the night outside the door she had left open. Letting in the moths.

He was mad. At Will and Ruby Dee, at himself, at the trick God had played on them and called it life. That's all it was, he thought. Some being up there playing with all of them.

He felt as if he were losing his Jooney all over again, and the pain went deep.

Ruby Dee went straight to her room, grabbed underwear from a drawer and ripped a blue print knit dress from its hanger. Quickly she dressed, brushed her hair, almost dry now, and hurriedly applied lipstick. Her hand was shaking. Her eyes were large in the mirror, lit only by the scarf-covered lamp.

Pausing, she looked at the objects on the dresser, Miss Edna's urn and her mother and father's picture and Miss Edna's Bible. And her dream paper on the nightstand.

She decided to leave them. She'd be coming back, at least by morning.

Grabbing her purse, she hurried down the stairs and out to her car. With her hand on the door handle, she looked over at the shop. The light still burned there, and she saw Hardy clearly through the wavy window glass, still on the stool, in front of the saddle.

No, she told herself. Hardy would not shoot himself. He had too much pride for something like that, although he might get drunk. She really did think he could weather it, though, as his health was so much better.

He isn't an invalid, she told herself. She could call later. She'd come back early in the morning.

Maybe she should go speak to him now, she thought, hesitating, her hand still on the handle. But what would she say? Oh, Lord, it was hard to leave him.

Finally, she called Sally, got into the Galaxie and drove away. She knew the lane well and didn't really need to see to go down it, but she almost hit the mailbox, because her vision was blurred by tears.

She had stopped crying, though, by the time she turned onto Will's road. Her heartbeat raced, as she anticipated seeing him, anticipated the look on his face. Her heart ached. She certainly hoped he still wanted her.

But then she turned into his driveway and saw the house was dark. Will wasn't there.

After a moment, Ruby Dee said, ''Come on, Sally . . . we can be a surprise for him.'' She and Sally got out of the car and went in the side door. As expected, it was unlocked.

✒ 29

WILL WAS SO tired and depressed that when he came pulling into his driveway, he almost ran right into Ruby Dee's Galaxie.

Jerking to a stop, he stared at the Galaxie's rear end, illuminated in his truck headlights. He looked at the house. It was dark, except for the back-door light. Still, Ruby Dee had to be inside.

Will jumped out of the pickup and strode to the house. Opened the back door. All was quiet. A faint light shone down the hallway from his bedroom. In the bedroom doorway, he stopped.

The bedside lamp cast a shadowy glow over Ruby Dee, who was on the bed, head on the pillows and the quilt partially pulled over her. She was fully dressed, except for her boots that sat near the nightstand. Sally lay at her feet; she wagged the tip of her silky tail.

Quietly, Will went over to the bed and crouched down, gazing at Ruby Dee's face. It was amazingly young and soft in sleep. Her womanly scent came to him—soap and powder and perfume. Something, maybe his staring at her, caused her to stir and open her eyes.

She smiled sleepily. "Oh, Will, I've been waitin' for you." The next instant she looked straight at him.

"Do you like the bed?" he asked.

"Oh, yes. It's beautiful."

She was here. . . . She liked the bed. Her eyes were warm and wanting.

"I told Hardy that we were going to be married," she said. "He was in his shop when I left, workin' on a saddle."

They gazed at each other for a long moment, making silent assurances and promises.

Will leaned forward and kissed her.

When he broke away, Ruby Dee tried to pull him back, but he said, "I need a shower." He peeled off his shirt as he strode toward the bathroom.

Ten minutes later, a towel wrapped around his hips and his hair still damp, Will returned. From the doorway, he saw Sally curled on the floor . . . Ruby Dee's flowered dress and pink bra draped over the footboard of the bed . . . Ruby Dee beneath the covers . . . her tousled hair dark against the white pillow . . . her brown eyes, dark and steaming, gazing at him.

This time, Will thought, he intended to take his time. He slipped in beside her, and she opened her arms to him.

The scent of her filled him . . . the scent of her hair, like flowers, of her skin, like musk. He caressed her and savored the way she moved beneath his touch, as he had imagined she would. He savored the taste of her lips, moist and sweet and tender . . . and the taste of her skin, warm and salty and soft. He kissed her and he touched her, and she kissed him and touched him. Their passion flowed like a rich, full-flowing river, surging and pulsing at the banks and pounding onward with force, sucking everything along in its path.

Her breath was warm and wet upon his neck, her hands urgent and hot upon his back. His heart pounded, and she trembled and moaned and called out his name. He rolled her to her back and slipped between her legs. She lifted her hips toward him. When they came together, it was the best it had ever been.

Dust motes and Will's cigarette smoke mingled in the early morning sunbeams that stole between the slats of the wooden blinds. They lay there, not saying much, looking at each other, caressing each other. Will felt satisfied, happy. The feeling was strange, wonderful and a little frightening.

Ruby Dee lay facing him, a sensual dreaminess in her dark eyes. The sheet stretched carelessly across her curved hip, her hair spread back revealing her burnished pewter earring stark against her ivory neck. She rubbed her palm across his chest and down his abdomen. "Oh, Will Starr," she said. There was satisfaction and wonderment in her voice.

He put out his cigarette, then turned to kiss her. As he caressed her breast with the back of his knuckles, he watched the heat simmer in her dreamy eyes. Watched her lips part, her breathing get shallow. He kissed her again.

She said so suddenly it startled him, "You know what?"

"What?"

"I don't know your middle name."

"Do you think that's important?"

"Well, Miss Edna always did. She said you could tell a lot about a person by their name."

"What does it say about me that I don't have a middle name?" She blinked, then looked skeptical. "You're teasin' me, Will."

"I don't have a middle name. I'm Will Starr, period. Not even William. And Lonnie is Lonnie Starr, period."

"Well, my goodness."

"So, would I pass Miss Edna's test?" She looked thoughtful.

"I think she would say you are stable and reliable, yes."

"Well, the people at the selective service found my lack of a middle name suspicious."

She laughed at that. Yawning, she rolled onto her back and stretched, lazy and uninhibited. He saw the scars then. Vaguely he recalled feeling them before, but they were slight and hadn't made much of an impression.

"What happened?" he asked, tracing them with his finger.

"I was burned when I was young—my nightgown caught on fire. I have these on my side, and some more here, on my legs." She showed him the inside of her thighs.

He bent and kissed the small marks, and she lay back, trembling, as he caressed her. She was his to caress, to have and to hold.

He raised up on his elbow and looked into her eyes. "Until death do us part, Ruby Dee."

She smiled a tremulous, teary smile and snaked

her arms around his neck. "Yes . . . until death do us part, Will Starr."

They kissed and loved and lay there, making plans—silly plans, like how they would breakfast on toast and peanut butter—and hang Western art on the walls, and have at least two children, and possibly four, God willing, and yes, Ruby Dee could name a girl Zoe. Will said he would give her anything she desired.

They were still lying in bed, savoring each other, when they heard a vehicle pulling into the drive.

"Who could that be so early?" Ruby Dee sat up, pulling the sheet over her breasts.

Will reached for his jeans. "I don't know."

"I hope it's not someone about Hardy." Her voice and eyes were anxious. It was the first time she had mentioned the old man.

"He's fine. It's only been one night." The vehicle's door slammed. Will tugged on his boots, then bent and kissed her quickly. "Don't go anywhere," he shot over his shoulder as he strode down the short hallway, slipping on a shirt. Will figured it was Wildcat, or maybe Ambrose Bell. Then, through the dining room window, he glimpsed the old man on the narrow cement walk, leaning on his cane, sunlight bright upon his battered straw Resistol. Will's steps slowed. The old man looked bent and gray.

Will opened the door and stepped outside, softly closing the door behind him.

The old man looked at him, and Will looked back.

Will said, "If you've come for breakfast, you're a mite early. We haven't even made coffee yet."

The old man said, "I imagine you've had better

things to do than make coffee." He was looking at Will's chest, where he hadn't buttoned his shirt.

"Yes, sir," Will said.

That sat there a few seconds. Then the old man said, "I didn't come for breakfast. I came to give Ruby Dee somethin' she asked for." He paused, and his eyes were sharp. "She seemed to think it important that I give my blessin' to you both. I came to give you that—you and her. You both have my blessing."

"I'll tell her," Will said. He wanted to go forward, to touch his father, but he sensed no invitation from the old man. Layers—years—of hurt separated them.

The next instant the screen door behind him creaked, and Ruby Dee, wrapped in Will's big blue robe, came to stand beside him. She laid her hand upon his arm. Her gaze moved from him to the old man.

"Oh, Hardy!" She ran forward, the folds of the robe rippling out behind her, and the old man opened his arms.

Will watched them embrace, and it somewhat startled him. He had never seen the old man embrace anyone. And here he was embracing the woman Will loved.

He knew in that moment that there would be a part of this woman, his woman, that would forever belong to the old man. And that suddenly didn't seem too unfair. He could not begrudge the old man, for Will knew he himself had the best part of her. He had her devotion . . . and her tender comfort on dark nights for years to come. It was enough. He did not need to own her body and soul, because then he would surely lose her.

Above Ruby Dee's head, the old man raised his eyes to Will, and his look seemed to echo Will's thoughts.

They parted, and Ruby Dee stepped back, casting a worried glance at Will. Her hand was still on Hardy's arm.

"I'll make coffee. You two can talk while I do," she said, and, clutching the robe closed, she went back into the house.

Will and the old man glanced at each other, both saying silently: *you know she's at the window, watching and listening.* In an unspoken accord, they walked a few feet away, to the pump house and leaned against it. The old man stuck a pinch of Skoal in his lip. Will wished mightily for a cigarette, but settled for picking a blade of dry grass and playing it between his fingers.

The old man said, "You two gonna get married tomorrow at the ranch? You might as well take advantage of the party—no use in havin' another one."

"We haven't discussed it, but it seems like a good time."

"Well, I want you to know that you're welcome to do it," the old man said, with effort, and then with even more effort, and not looking at Will, he added, "I'd like you to be married at the place, with the party and all."

"Thanks, Dad. I'd really like that, too." Will's throat got tight. He thought a minute, then he asked, "Will you stand up and give Ruby Dee away?" He had to ask that, had to have the understanding between them.

The old man stared at the grass. He nodded. "I'll do it." His voice was husky.

They stood there. Will tore the dried piece of grass into pieces, and the old man spit a stream of Skoal to the side.

"It's a good place here," the old man said. "Got a good view, and yer blocked from the north wind. Land's good . . . never been over-grazed, this grass."

Will prodded the ground with the toe of his boot. "I've been thinkin' that we could let Lonnie and Crystal come live here, and Ruby Dee and I could come back to the house and live with you . . . if you'd have us."

He hadn't really known he was going to say that, but once he got started, the words came easy enough. He glanced up, and the old man's look of surprise made Will feel good. Maybe he'd topped his dad at last.

The old man didn't look at him. "It's an idea," he said. He cleared his throat. "And maybe you ought to keep on managin' the Starr, too."

"I thought you were gonna close down and disperse."

"A man can change his mind," Hardy said righteously. "Besides, you boys both need jobs, now that yer takin' on families."

"I got this place here," Will said, "and Ambrose Bell can give both me and Lonnie jobs." A stubbornness had taken hold of him.

Hardy frowned and thumped his cane a couple of times. He and Ambrose Bell had always been competitors.

Will said, "I got a quarter section here that the house sets on. It's not much, but I've also leased six sections of Ambrose's land." The old man's sharp gaze was fixed on him. "All that would be a good addition to the Starr."

The old man's eyes narrowed. "And what does the Starr need with more land? We got enough, don't need to lease."

"If the Starr's gonna support two growin' families, it's gonna have to expand. We got to have at least this house, and we'll need the land."

Hardy looked off in the distance for a minute, and then he said, "All right. You boys are Starrs. You both come back to the Starr, and we'll work out a partnership. Does that suit you?"

Will figured that was a lot for the old man to say . . . a hell of a lot more than Will had ever in his life expected him to say.

Standing at the screen door, Ruby Dee saw Will and Hardy shake hands. Well, that was something. She called, "Coffee's ready!" and ducked back inside. She didn't want them to think she'd been spying. She had been trying to listen, but they'd been too far away for her to hear.

Hardy came in first, and in one quick look she noticed that he looked fine. She had smelled a bit of whiskey when she'd hugged him, but he obviously hadn't gotten drunk. He sat at the table in one of the two chairs, Ruby Dee took the other chair, and Will leaned against the counter. She had made pan-fried toast and spread it with a little jam—that was about all the food Will had in the house—for she was certain Hardy hadn't eaten a thing that morning.

"Dad thinks it would be a good idea for us to get married at the party on Saturday." Will raised an eyebrow at her.

"Oh, thank you, Hardy! I was hopin' we could

do that. We can be married under the elm there, Will."

Hardy, in typical fashion, pointed out there might be birds in the trees. Will said he would shoot a shotgun in the air right before the ceremony, and his eyes sparkled at her.

It was going to be all right, she thought.

Hardy never was one to linger and as soon as he'd had one cup of coffee, he was ready to leave. Will and Ruby Dee walked out to his truck with him, and Ruby Dee said she would be right over to fix him a decent breakfast.

"It's goin' on lunch time, gal," Hardy said, and then he was driving away.

Will kept his arm around her as they walked back into the house. "You're comin' over with me, aren't you, Will?" she asked. "We can have breakfast, and I'll have to see about Hardy's medicine. And there's so much left to do for the party, and now, with us gettin' married ... Oh, Will!"

Chuckling, he reached out and pulled her back against him, kissing her neck. She turned in his arms, eager to see him and to hold him. He gazed down at her and said, "Dad and I have worked out a deal. He isn't gonna shut down the Starr. And we'll live over there, Ruby Dee ... in the house with Dad, if you want to."

Well. She stared up at him, searching his face for a clue as to how he felt about it. Suddenly she didn't know how she felt anymore.

She slipped from his arms and went down the hallway to the bedroom, to the cherry-wood bed. She began to make it up.

Will came to the doorway. "Have you changed your mind about living back there with him? I thought you wanted to," he said with a confused frown.

Ruby Dee snapped the sheet and smoothed it. "I did . . . but you wanted this place. You've worked so hard on this house, and you got us this bed." She straightened, looking at him. "You said you wanted something of your own, Will. I don't want you to give that up for me, or for Hardy, either."

"A man can change his mind," he said, his lips twitching in a grin.

She didn't find that amusing. "Have you changed your mind?" She didn't see how he could do that.

He said, "I guess I've had somethin' of my own all along. I've had me . . . and I've had Dad and Lonnie. And now I have you." He came forward, took hold of her arms, and gazed down at her, and his eyes were full of emotion.

"All I really wanted, I guess, was for Dad to acknowledge that he needs me. He's done that now. And you know, all these years Dad has held so tight to havin' something of his own that he's almost lost what really matters in this life. I don't want to do that, Ruby Dee."

"My goodness, Will Starr . . . you are somethin'." She pressed her face against his chest and cried. Then she said, "Will, I want to take the bed. It's our marriage bed. Could you get it over there tonight?"

Ruby Dee and Will were married beneath the elm tree in the backyard. Ruby Dee wore the dress she had bought on Monday—she thought it was perfect, even though it was an untraditional flower print of dusky rose and blue. She never had

looked her best in white or pastels, and her red
Noconas went perfectly with the dress. So did the
silver earrings from Hardy.

He gave them to her right before the ceremony,
as she was freshening her lipstick—Dusky Si-
enna—at the mirror in the kitchen.

"I have a wedding present for you," he said
awkwardly, and held out a small white box.

"Oh!" she said when she opened the box. Then
she dashed to the mirror to put them on. "Aren't
they wonderful?" she asked, turning her head to
him.

He grunted and nodded. Hardy did not know
how to give a compliment.

Then Crystal was hollering from the porch.
"Y'all, everyone's ready!"

Hardy went on ahead, and Ruby Dee picked up
the bouquet of tiger lilies Lonnie had gotten for
her—she had forgotten all about flowers. She
couldn't imagine where Lonnie had found lilies at
this time of year. But that he had chosen this
flower went to show how well he knew her.

With her arm through Hardy's, she walked toward Will. All the guests stood, because they
didn't have enough chairs. Out of the sea of
strange faces, Ruby Dee recognized some. There
was one of the domino players, and Crystal near
the back, because her stomach was unsteady and
she might have to duck out. There was Cora Jean,
with her long white braid, and a younger woman
who must be her daughter. And Wildcat in a sport
coat. She almost didn't recognize him.

Lonnie and Will wore their best hats for the occasion . . . and my goodness, they looked handsome
in their suits. Lonnie grinned at her.

Once she looked into Will's brilliant eyes, she didn't notice anything else.

The rest of the afternoon passed in a blur of cake cutting—Lonnie and Crystal, Will and Ruby Dee together—and eating and dancing. Hardy seemed to get into the swing of being the land-baron host. He stayed on his feet, moving among the guests, and he danced a number of times with Cora Jean.

Sally went quietly beneath all the tables, where she happily feasted on dropped food. Crystal fainted. That scared Lonnie to pieces, but Ruby Dee reassured him that Crystal had simply had too much excitement. They took her inside to rest, Ruby Dee brewed her a cup of saffron tea and Lonnie sat with her.

Finally it was time for them to leave for their honeymoon—a week of camping down along the Red River. Will could hardly believe Ruby Dee wanted to do this, but she really did.

"It will be so romantic in my camper—just the two of us."

Will liked that idea. And he was amazed when he looked inside her trailer. All these months, and he had never seen inside it. It was like a tiny cottage, all done in royal blue—curtains, slipcovers and pillows.

Ruby Dee went upstairs for a last-minute check. She stuffed her hair dryer and makeup kit into one of the two bags on the cherry-wood bed. A pair of Will's jeans lay over the back of the flowered chair, and one of his ball caps hung on the closet door-knob.

Gazing in the mirror, Ruby Dee brushed her hair and tied it back in a ribbon. She freshened her lipstick, and then paused, looking down at Miss Edna's urn.

"Miss Edna . . . I've finally done it. I'm a married woman, got a home and am workin' on my babies."

"It's not going to be at all what you think," Miss Edna said.

"Nothing is ever what we think, is it?"

"At least you've learned that much."

Ruby Dee touched the urn. "I'm not alone anymore, Miss Edna. I have a family."

And then Will was calling to her from the stairs. "Are you about ready?"

She ran her gaze over her dresser—Miss Edna's urn and her Bible, her mother and father's picture, her dictionary and the stack of Elvis CDs.

Will came in and took up the bags. "Got everything you want to take?"

Ruby Dee glanced back at the dresser, and then she kissed him lightly. "I have everything for now. Everything else will be waitin' here when we get back."

Then they were driving away down the lane, the top down and the aluminum camper jolting behind, Will at the wheel and Sally with her nose stuck out in the wind. Ruby Dee twisted around and looked back. Hardy and Lonnie stood side by side. She waved at them, and they waved back.

Ruby Dee sat back down, and Will put his arm around her and drew her close. His shirt was crisp against her cheek, and he smelled of sensual aftershave and tobacco, scents that were now sweetly familiar. The sky above was azure-blue and clear, as it had been that first day she had come to the Starr ranch.

It struck Ruby Dee that she had come up this road the same way, bouncing over the ruts, pulling her trailer and all her hopes and dreams. But then she had been all alone. Now she was with Will. Together they were pulling all their hopes and dreams.

After two miles, Will stopped, just to kiss her.

"Promise me to still do that when I'm seventy-five," Ruby Dee said.

"I'll do it as long as I live," Will promised her.

✥ 30

Nine years later.

RUBY DEE AND WILL's fourth child was born one
week before Hardy died, in February.

Ruby Dee had had three children in seven
years, and had decided that was enough. But they'd
gotten a surprise in their ninth year. Crystal also had
three children in the same amount of time, and Lonnie had had himself fixed so there would be no sur-
prises for them.

Hardy died peacefully, sat down to take off his
boots and fell over dead on the bed. Cora Jean told
Ruby Dee that Jooney had died on the same day, so
many years before. They buried him in the White
Rose Cemetery. Since there were no official plots, and
no official grave diggers, either, Ruby Dee asked Will
and Lonnie to dig the plot next to Jooney's. Of course
they were curious. She just said that Jooney had been
a special friend, and that Hardy would like it.

"He won't like being squashed up there next to
his parents. You know he hated to be crowded."

385

The afternoon of the funeral was clear and crisp but windless. The sun beat down and warmed the ground. With the fine weather, Ruby Dee didn't worry about bringing the baby—little Zoe, finally after three boys.

The funeral was small. Those who had come were loyal friends. Hardy had changed a lot in those last years. He'd taken to playing dominoes twice a week down at Reeves's Quick Stop; either Ruby Dee or Will would take him. Each Sunday they had a family dinner at the Starr Ranch, and Hardy enjoyed everyone being there, most especially the babies. It was discovered that babies liked him. Whenever one of them got colic or plain fussy, it was Hardy who rocked them. Crystal's second baby spent a number of nights in Hardy's arms.

"I trust Hardy with my baby like I don't trust anyone else," Crystal once confided to Ruby Dee. Crystal generally whispered around Hardy.

That evening, after everyone had finally left and all but the two oldest children, Crystal and Lonnie's daughter Kendra and Ruby Dee and Will's son J.W., were asleep, the family gathered around the kitchen table. The table was big, as was the entire house. Will had built on a two-story addition, because he said he needed room.

On the table was the colorful Whitman's chocolate tin Hardy had kept in his room. He had left instructions that the box be opened after his funeral. Everyone wondered what was in it, but no one had peeked.

Lonnie took his finger and scooted the box over in front of Will. He still deferred to his brother.

Hesitantly, as if a snake might pop out, Will lifted the lid.

Inside were three envelopes, one addressed simply: *To all of you*, another with Will's name on it, and a third with Lonnie's. Will opened the envelope addressed to them all. As he unfolded the paper, he cast a glance at Ruby Dee, and she laid her hand on his thigh.

Will scanned the words before he cleared his throat and read aloud. Ruby Dee was already smiling. She could hear Hardy's voice in every word.

> *You all know by now that you have inhairited a lot more money than you thought I had. Ha! on you. If you boys have a problem with me leavin your wives equal shares, too bad. They cooked for me.*
>
> *I didn't put a note in here for Crystal, cause she and I never did talk much anyway. Just so she don't feel left out, tho, I want her to know I have apresiated her trusting me with her babies.*
>
> *I didn't put a note in here for Ruby Dee, cause she and I most generally said anything we needed to while I was alive.*
>
> *Hello, I'm gone.*
>
> —*Hardy W. Starr*

They all had to chuckle. And to point out all the misspellings. Crystal said that even if he'd made her nervous, she had liked him, at least after the first couple of years.

Will and Lonnie set their letters aside, and then, their spirits lighter, they delved into the tin.

"I can't see, Mama," Kendra said as she and J.W. battled for space.

There was a clean Skoal can containing a lot of baby teeth, surely Will's and Lonnie's. There was a pearl-handled pocket knife, and a spoon with the image of a cowboy on the handle. Crystal said it was

Tom Mix; she was into collectibles. There was a pair of dice, very old, and a wedding ring, whose no one knew. There were pictures of Hardy's mother and father—and one of Lila, too. He had scratched an X across her face.

"She was beautiful," Ruby Dee said.

"I can't believe Dad kept her picture." Bitterness laced Lonnie's voice.

"I can," Will said, thoughtfully. His eyes met Ruby Dee's, and understanding passed between them.

Last, Will picked up a tattered folio and opened it. He looked astonished, glanced from the folio to Ruby Dee. J.W. wormed up beneath his father's arm.

"It's a picture of Mama," J.W. said, unimpressed. He liked the pocket knife.

"What?" Ruby Dee craned to see.

The face in the photograph did resemble her. Somewhat. The resemblance startled her. It was an old photograph, from the twenties or thirties, Ruby Dee guessed from the style of the woman's hair and the picture itself. On the inside of the folio was written: "For my dearest H. S., with love, Jooney."

"Good Lord, she looks just like Ruby Dee," Crystal said.

"Her hair's different," Kendra said, practically.

Will and Lonnie and Crystal stared at Ruby Dee, as if she had better explain. Ruby Dee sat back in her chair.

She said, "Hardy and Jooney were lovers when they were young. She died before they got married."

Understanding came into each set of eyes, like the dawning of the sun. Ruby Dee kept looking at Will. She couldn't read his expression. Even after these years, he could hide from her.

J.W. said, "You mean this isn't Mama?" He glanced from one adult to another.

Kendra told him, "No, pea brain. It's just someone who looked like her."

Later the envelopes for Will and Lonnie disappeared. Ruby Dee guessed that Lonnie had taken his with him. She saw Will in their big chair, reading his, when she came into the bedroom after settling J.W. and checking on the two other boys.

She went over to look down at Zoe in the bassinet. She looked like Ruby Dee, but seemed to have Will's eyes. She wondered whether they would darken. Each of the boys had her eyes.

"I sure have more babies than I bargained for, Miss Edna," she whispered.

"Don't put this one in overalls, Ruby Dee. It'll encourage her to be a tomboy."

Fine, Ruby Dee thought.

Glancing over at Will, she saw him drop his hands in his lap, then lay his head back. She went to him, moved the letter and settled gingerly in his lap. There were tears at the outer corners of his eyes. She pressed her cheek next to his.

"What did he say?" she asked hoarsely.

Without opening his eyes, he handed her the letter. It was brief, as Hardy always had been.

> *"I weren't much of a daddy, but you've always been a good son. I did love you and I'm proud of you. Take care of Ruby Dee. Guess you saw the pictur. If I get to heaven and Jooney ain't there, I'll know the truth.*
>
> *—Hardy*
> *(Guess I won't know if I go to the other place.)*

After he was gone and no one could call him to account for it, he'd expressed what he had never been able to say aloud. Ruby Dee knew this was the gift Hardy had given to Lonnie, too. Or tried to give. It was up to Lonnie to accept.

Later, Ruby Dee and Will lay in the cherry-wood bed in their big bedroom, with its picture window and view of the high plains. So many lights sparkled in the distance nowadays. Ruby Dee lay in Will's arm and looked at them.

"Are you okay?" Will asked.

"Uh-huh. I'm not real sad. I guess that sounds strange, but I'm so relieved that Hardy lived right up until he died. I wouldn't have wanted less for him." She could not have stood seeing him suffer.

Will patted her arm.

They lay there quietly for long minutes. Ruby Dee listened to Will's heart beating. She never tired of that. Will drew circles with his thumb on her arm through the sleeve of her gown. She didn't often sleep bare these days, in case she had to jump up and see to the children.

Will said, "You knew about Jooney . . . that Dad thought you were her, right?"

"Cora Jean told me. I don't know if he thought I was her, or just that I reminded him of her. Hardy and I never spoke of it. I considered it something private for him. None of anyone's business."

"How did she die?" Will asked. "You know, don't you?"

"She got burned up."

He didn't say anything to that.

"Have you been sorry, Will, that we came back here to live?" She hadn't thought he was, but she worried sometimes.

"I've never been sorry, and I've never been jealous of Dad. Don't you know what you are, Ruby Dee? You're our hub . . . for all of us. Good God, I'm so glad to have you."

The emotion, the fervency, in his voice startled her. For an instant she didn't even dare breathe. And then she threw herself at him. "Oh, Will Starr."

He kissed her and held her until he slipped off to sleep.

Ruby Dee lay there safe and secure in Will's arms and listened to the baby nearby in the bassinet, squirming because soon she would awake. Sally got up from beneath the bassinet and hopped up on the bed, sniffing at Ruby Dee to make certain she was awake to take care of the baby.

Ruby Dee stroked Sally's silky fur and recalled the day she had come driving up that dusty dirt road with Miss Edna's urn in the front seat and the dream paper in her pocket.